... the
... ery Series

... rouble

"McCoy is as adept at creating colorful, compelling characters, two-legged and four-legged, and writing sharply humorous prose as she is at crafting a cleverly constructed plot." —*Booklist*

"Primo dog walker Ellie has more than a gift for talking to her four-legged charges. She's also got a talent for getting caught up in her boyfriend's murder investigations. McCoy puts her in the action with flair and an easy humor." —*Romantic Times*

"Charming and funny."
—*New York Times* bestselling author
MaryJanice Davidson

Death in Show

"Elli... ...way of
comm... ...r laugh
out l... ...*Times*

"Mc... ...ing up
with ... ...ystery
and then perfectly seasoning the plot with just the right dash of romance." —*Booklist*

Heir of the Dog

"McCoy brings back professional dog walker Ellie Engleman and her reincarnated pooch with a witty and fast-paced mystery set in New York's fashionable Upper East Side. McCoy has a simmering plan of vengeance, peppered with humor that readers will love."
—*Romantic Times*

continued ...

Hounding the Pavement

"McCoy fills this delightful story with humor, quirky characters, and delicious hints of romance."
—*Publishers Weekly* (starred review)

"The crisp writing, humorous dialogue, and delightful characters, both human and canine, all make this book a winner."
—*Romantic Times*

"Judi McCoy writes with heart and humor. Anyone who loves dogs or books will have a howling good time."
—Lois Greiman

"A delightful dog's-eye-view romp through the streets of New York. If you've ever talked to your dog and wished that he would answer back, this is the book for you. Four paws up!"
—Laurien Berenson, author of *Doggie Day Care Murder*

"Engaging characters and a cute premise kick off this delightful series. This canine caper will have you begging for more!"
—Nancy J. Cohen, author of the Bad Hair Day Mystery series

"A treat for everyone, whether a dog lover or not.... Ms. McCoy has written a cozy mystery sure to please."
—Fresh Fiction

Also in the Dog Walker Mystery Series

Fashion Faux Paw

A DOG WALKER MYSTERY

JUDI MCCOY

AN OBSIDIAN MYSTERY

OBSIDIAN

Published by New American Library, a division of
Penguin Group (USA) Inc., 375 Hudson Street,
New York, New York 10014, USA

Penguin Group (Canada), 90 Eglinton Avenue East, Suite 700, Toronto,
Ontario M4P 2Y3, Canada (a division of Pearson Penguin Canada Inc.)

Penguin Books Ltd., 80 Strand, London WC2R 0RL, England

Penguin Ireland, 25 St. Stephen's Green, Dublin 2,
Ireland (a division of Penguin Books Ltd.)

Penguin Group (Australia), 250 Camberwell Road, Camberwell, Victoria 3124,
Australia (a division of Pearson Australia Group Pty. Ltd.)

Penguin Books India Pvt. Ltd., 11 Community Centre, Panchsheel Park,
New Delhi - 110 017, India

Penguin Group (NZ), 67 Apollo Drive, Rosedale, Auckland 0632,
New Zealand (a division of Pearson New Zealand Ltd.)

Penguin Books (South Africa) (Pty.) Ltd., 24 Sturdee Avenue,
Rosebank, Johannesburg 2196, South Africa

Penguin Books Ltd., Registered Offices:
80 Strand, London WC2R 0RL, England

First published by Obsidian, an imprint of New American Library,
a division of Penguin Group (USA) Inc.

First Printing, March 2012
10 9 8 7 6 5 4 3 2 1

So many people helped in the writing of my Dog Walker series, but this particular story, *Fashion Faux Paw*, was a tough one. A huge thank-you to my editor, Kerry Donovan, who did so much to help me get this book into shape.

To my agent, Helen Breitwieser, for always being on my side, especially during life-threatening moments. Thank you, Helen, for New York and for other things too numerous to mention.

For Karen Hood, hairstylist extraordinaire. Thanks so much for all your insights into the fashion world.

And I cannot forget the Miniature Schnauzer Rescue of Houston, run by Karen Coleman. They do a wonderful job with one of the most adorable of small breeds. If you're interested in adopting one of these bright, energetic, and happy little guys, please contact Karen at rescue@msrh.org.

Acknowledgments

Congratulations to the following, who each won a different organization's raffle to be a character in my next Dog Walker mystery:

Cassandra McQuagge, National Greyhound Adoption Program, Virginia Beach Affiliate

Claire Smith, Hampton Roads Writers

Beatriz Alfonso, Miniature Schnauzer Rescue of Houston

Chapter 1

Ellie Engleman hoisted her packed tote bag over her shoulder, kept Rudy's leash in her left hand, and balanced a Caramel Bliss coffee in the other. Then she stepped into one of the cavernous rooms that had been prepared to ready the participants for New York City's most glamorous event. Fashion Week, a yearly celebration, was being held for the first time in the industry's newly remodeled building near Penn Station.

She still couldn't believe that she got to be on the sidelines. The winner of the grand finale competition of the show would capture a one-hundred-thousand-dollar prize and a two-year contract with Nola Morgan Design, known in the trade as NMD, a manufacturer of women's high-end ready-to-wear. The line would be available in Bloomingdale's, Bergdorf's, Saks, and other upscale mall department stores around the country by the end of next year.

Ellie knew the competition was garnering a lot of attention in the fashion industry. Thirty-five hopefuls had submitted designs based on their idea of what a typical modern woman might wear while at work or out on the town. Four finalists were chosen to compete by the CFDA, the Council of Fashion Designers of America, and they and this contest were the culmination of Fashion Week.

She had first heard about it from Patti Fallgrave, one of her clients. As one of the models asked to strut the catwalk, Patti had an in with the committee, and she'd finagled a great job for her dog-walker friend once she learned canines were involved in one of the fashion shows. Ellie was now in charge of the models' dogs, and would watch over them while their owners were fitted, accessorized, dressed, and had their hair and makeup done.

And for the final day, it was her responsibility to see to it that the dogs in her care were outfitted from head to tail in creations made by each designer to match their owners' outfit. Whichever pair wowed the committee and Nola Morgan Design would win the prize.

As she entered the room, she scanned the mass of drinking straws with heads and noted that most of the women appeared to walk, talk, and act untouchable as they went about their business for opening day. Those who were the tallest had to be the models, especially since they were the ones who looked as if they hadn't eaten in a decade.

And the rest? She'd bet her last dime that most of the hairstylists, makeup artists, designers, and runners participating in the show were on the same lettuce leaf and one cracker a day diet.

"Geez. Ya think anybody in this crowd knows how to swallow more than a single piece of kibble at a sitting?" Rudy asked.

She smiled down at him, her voice low. "We'll talk about it later. For now, let's just find our spot and stay out of trouble."

"Hey, trouble is our middle name. We live for trouble. In fact, we're trouble experts. We—"

She ignored his rambling and jerked on his lead for good measure. The security guard they'd passed on the way in had told her he had no idea where the canines were being kept, but she was welcome to find the area herself. From the amount of activity taking place in this room, she doubted anyone could help her locate the dog pens, which meant she and her boy had to check it out on their own.

After studying the mob of serious fashionistas, Ellie glanced at her work clothes. Her job for the next few days was all dog, so she'd dressed in preparation for poop stains, pee stains, food stains, puke stains, and anything else a furry, four-legged friend might have a paw in creating.

She wore a peach-colored sweater in a washable fabric, with no designer label, and Skechers Kinetix Response shoes, perfect for walking her usual ten-mile-per-day route. Her special touch for the event was her Calvin Klein Ultimate Skinny jeans, which she'd found on a half-price markdown rack. Her best friend, Viv, had insisted it was the least she should wear to work the world's biggest fashion event, and she'd grudgingly agreed.

"'Scuse me," a voice said as someone pushed past her with an overloaded clothing rack.

She darted out of the way and bumped into a girl carrying a stack of shoe boxes. The top box hit the ground and Ellie bent to pick it up. Repacking the four-inch, snakeskin Ferragamo heels, she took note of the size and gave herself a mental high five. The model who owned this shoe wore a ten, a full size larger than her. If she got really depressed about her size-twelve Calvins, she'd go barefoot and show off one of her best features: her shapely feet and their freshly pedicured toes.

She set the shoe box on top of the pile, and the person behind the cardboard mountain mumbled a thank-you and stumbled on through the crowd.

"Ellie! Hey, Ellie! I'm over here."

Raising her head, she eventually spotted Patti Fall-grave waving at her from across the room. At six feet tall, the supermodel was easy to find in a normal crowd, but it wasn't so simple locating her in this group of towering pencil figures.

Ellie edged through the bustling room, dodging worker-bees and half-naked women standing on podiums, waiting to be clothed. "I'm exhausted just watching all that's going on," she said when she reached her dog-walking client. "Is it always like this?"

Patti cradled Cheech—one of two Chihuahua brothers Ellie serviced—in her left arm and clasped Ellie's elbow in her free hand. "This?" She laughed. "It's nothing compared to showtime. Just get in sync with the vibes. And be careful of Rudy. Most of the people working this scene love animals, but they're not used to having them underfoot. That's why they hired you."

They dodged another clothes trolley, sidled behind a group of mirrored tables and chairs where two models sat while hairstylists teased and sprayed, and stopped at an open area where a stretchy metal gate formed an eight-foot-diameter pen. "This is the best I could set up for you," the supermodel said.

Sitting down on one of three chairs wedged between a water cooler and a long table filled with fruit, veggies, protein bars, and high-energy drinks, Patti pointed to a corner. "This is just one of several snack tables set up throughout the show. And around that corner is a patch of fake grass, where the dogs can do their business if there's an emergency. After that is a door to the outside, so you can come and go with your charges as needed."

Ellie took a seat and heaved a breath. Resting her tote bag on a knee, she peered at the shelf under the table, half-filled with more food and drinks. "And I guess I can store my stuff down there?"

"Absolutely. In fact, you should probably keep an eye on all of it, because there's no security guard at this end. I'd make sure my cash and credit cards were tucked in my pocket instead of in the bag, in case someone stopped by and started digging. If you ask, they'll tell you they're looking through their bag, but it could be yours."

Ellie shook her head. "They can look in my bag all they want, but the only thing they'll find is canine gear. I brought gourmet biscuits, extra leashes, folding water bowls, a couple of old throws, and anything else I thought the dogs might need that their owners would forget."

"Perfect. And guess what?" Patti raised an expertly arched brow. "I got you a runner. Kitty's around here somewhere and she can't wait to be your assistant."

Ellie smothered a smile. She had an assistant named Kitty and they were herding a group of dogs? There had to be a joke in there somewhere.

"And the models and their babies?"

"They'll be here soon. The designers are already on-site, of course, but they have yet to see the dogs in person. All they know is the breed."

"Do you have that list I asked for? With the names of the designers, and the models and their dogs?"

Patti pulled a small spiral pad from her alligator bag and Ellie had to grin. It looked just like the kind her boyfriend, Sam, carried when he was on a case. In fact, it was exactly what she'd used in July, when she and Viv had run into a murder in the Hamptons.

"Here you go," she said, passing her the tablet. "Janice wrote down the details. I hope it's what you were looking for."

"Your sister did a great job. It's exactly what I wanted," said Ellie, flipping through the pages. "So, what should I do now?"

Patti handed her Cheech, checked her watch, and tucked her own bag under the table. "Since there are usually three or four shows going on at the same time, most of the girls are modeling for other designers until it's time for the NMD walk. For instance, I have a fitting for a Vena Cava evening gown; then I'm scheduled to show three outfits for another up-and-comer, so I have to run."

Patti stood. "I guess your first job would be to keep my baby happy and wait for the mob to arrive. His travel bed is in my bag. Just get ready to meet some huge personalities while you wait for the models to drop off their dogs, and the designers to show up. If you're into people-watching, this is the place to be."

When she sauntered away with her shiny dark brown hair swinging down her slender back, there was no doubt in Ellie's mind that her client was a supermodel. Patti commanded attention, even when she wore a tank top, faded jeans, and red leather ankle boots.

"Too bad a doll like Patti's wastin' her time on that hairball," Rudy groused, giving the Chihuahua the fish eye. *"I still say somebody should report him and his brother to INS."*

"Oh, stop." Ellie kissed Cheech's tiny nose, then placed him gently in the pen and dug his doggie bed out of Patti's bag. "Cheech and Chong are not illegal immigrants. They're bona fide residents of this country, and even if they weren't, it's none of your business."

"I'm just sayin'—"

"Too much. Now let's people-watch, like Patti suggested."

"How about you let me sit up there with you? The less time I gotta spend down here with the hairless wonder, the better."

She patted the chair next to her and trained her eyes on the passersby, while Rudy bolted into position and sat at attention. Her heart skipped a beat when she saw two famous faces. "Look, there's Christian Siriano walking with Michael Kors." She watched the men as they raced past, talking quietly. "Viv will die when I tell her who was here."

Just then, a tall, attractive man arrived on the scene, along with a beautifully dressed older woman. Behind them strode two assistants, each carrying a huge box. "I'm Jeffery King," the man said, grabbing Ellie's hand. "And this is Nola McKay." He nodded toward his companion. "We have gifts for the models and designers from Nola Morgan Design." He flashed a bright smile. "And you, too, if you're Ellie Engleman."

"That's me," she said, matching his grin. She then shook the woman's hand. "Ms. McKay, it's so nice to meet you. Thank you for giving me the opportunity to work your show."

"We're happy to have you. Now if you don't mind, I have a ton of things to take care of." She nodded at the assistants, who were unloading and lining up baskets covered in colored plastic wrap onto the table. "I'll let Jeffery tell you what this is all about."

Giving a wave, she left the scene, and Jeffery took over.

"These are gift baskets, or swag bags, as we call them. You're in charge of them until my sister gets here, so watch over them carefully. The swag in each basket adds up to about five thousand retail, and every one is tagged for its owner because the items inside were targeted directly for them." He searched the line and picked up a basket wrapped in pale green plastic. "Patti Fallgrave handpicked the items in yours, so speak to her if you're not happy with your loot."

Ellie held the basket to her chest. "Thanks, and I'll be sure to take care of these. Will you be around or—"

A tiny woman with blond spiky hair and a huge smile rushed over, clasped Ellie's hand, and said, "Hi, I'm Kitty King, and I'm so sorry I'm late." She gasped for breath. "I'm your assistant for the next four days."

Two hours later, Ellie finally had the time to study her runner, who was no more than five feet tall and looked to be just out of high school. So far, the diminutive girl had worked her butt off, welcoming models, collecting their dogs, kowtowing to designers, and running errands for whoever needed her. She'd even held a one-sided conversation with Rudy, who had found an out-of-the-way spot under the table and made it his own.

In short, she'd been a breath of fresh air in the middle of high fashion chaos.

Because it was near noon, things had quieted down, so Ellie asked Kitty to sit with her next to the water cooler. "You seem to know everyone," she said. "Have you worked in this industry long?"

"I've been an assistant for the past three years while I studied at Parsons School for Design. My brother—"

"The man who delivered the baskets?"

"Right. When he finally got his big break with NMD, the company sponsoring this event, I got a break, too. He's their new Director of Promotions, so he's my boss."

The information had Ellie recalculating Kitty's age. "Do you mind if I ask you another personal question?"

"You want to know how old I am, right?"

Pleased to see that Kitty was smiling, she said, "Sorry. You must get that a lot."

"At least once a week, and I don't mind." When Rudy crawled out from under the table and jumped in her lap, Kitty ruffled his ears. "I mean, I'll probably be happy that I have this baby face in another twenty years or so." She ran a hand through her blond hair. "I'll be twenty-five on my next birthday."

"Wow, that's amazing. And Rudy seems to like you, too, which is a good sign, considering he doesn't cuddle up to just anyone."

Her yorkiepoo gave a groan of contentment under Kitty's gentle hand. *This chick is too much.*

Unaware of Rudy's positive comment, Kitty said, "Your boy's a cutie, but I'm into all dogs. What about you?" Then she giggled. "Oh, gosh, that was a totally dumb thing to say. Of course you are. I mean, you make your living working with dogs, so you must love them, right?"

"Dogs are the center of my life," Ellie answered, hoping her sincerity showed. "When I rescued Rudy, he rescued me, and he's become my best four-legged friend. I also walk some of the greatest canines in this city. It's a treat being here with little guys, because they're my favorite size."

"Mine, too," Kitty said, scratching Rudy under his chin. "But my building is a no-go on pets. As soon as my designs make money, I'm going to move to a place that will let me have a dog." She heaved a sigh, leaned back in her chair, and surveyed the people still rushing past. "We may be here all night, even though the designers are supposed to be finished with their first piece by four. The initial runway walk is scheduled to close the day at five, but with everyone jockeying for Karen Hood to do their hair and Eduardo to do their makeup, it'll be a miracle if they make it on time."

Ellie'd been hoping to meet someone besides Patti who had an inside track on the fashion business—someone who could fill her in on industry gossip and secrets—and it sounded as if Kitty would be able to do just that. "I guess you know quite a bit about this contest? What it took for the designers to get here and all?"

Kitty glanced at the industry professionals walking around the pen, stopping at the water cooler, grazing the snack table, and interacting with the dogs. Sizing up the bodies covered in tattoos, alienlike hairdos, and strange clothing combinations, she said, "This business is crazy. You'll meet folks from every walk of life here, all hoping for their big break. Each day is different, and I love it that way."

She lowered her chin, and Ellie moved closer. "But not everyone in the industry is pleasant. There's backbiting and smack talk, plus a lot of design theft." Her eyes filled with tears. "Believe me, I know that firsthand."

Before Ellie could comment, a dark-haired woman appeared before them. Dressed in red spandex pants, a red tunic, and red strappy heels, she parted the crowd with her presence, seemingly not worried that she was late to the festivities. After stowing a huge bag under the table, she set her mini Schnauzer in the pen with the models' dogs.

She glared at Kitty. "This is the place where the dogs are being kept for the Nola contest, correct?"

Kitty brushed away her tears and sat straighter in her chair. "Hello, Lilah. How are you doing?"

The woman held her hand out to Ellie, acting as if Kitty hadn't spoken. "I'm Lilah Perry, one of the four designers. You must be Ellie, the dog sitter."

"She's the dog professional, Lilah," Kitty answered, her voice tight with displeasure. "And one look at the little guys in the pen should tell you where you are."

"Oh, hello, Kitty," Lilah said, as if seeing the girl for the first time. "What are you doing here?"

Kitty's pink-tinted lips thinned. "I guess you haven't heard. NMD and the CFDA hired me to assist for this gig."

"Well, how lucky for you to have a bigwig brother working at NMD these days." Lilah almost sneered. "I'm starving," she announced, her tone demanding. "Is there anything decent to eat around here?"

Lilah's voice was so loud just about everyone within shouting distance turned to stare. Couldn't the woman see the table filled with food?

Standing, Kitty picked up an energy bar. "There's plenty of fruit, and I hear these are good, with lots of flavors to choose from. They even have—"

"Aah! Are you trying to kill me?" Lilah's voice rose to shrill. "There are peanuts in that bar."

Kitty's face flushed red. "Sorry, sorry. I forgot about your allergy. Let me read the list of ingredients. There's got to be one here that doesn't contain peanuts."

Ellie continued to watch the show. The rude designer was as thin as a supermodel and quite beautiful, but she didn't look healthy. Dark circles ringed her eyes, and her wrinkled forehead added years to her face.

The crowd murmured as Lilah kept muttering. "She knows about my food problems . . . clear the night of . . . could kill me . . . Thank God I have my pen."

"That dame needs a conk on the head," Rudy stated, watching Lilah retrieve her bag from under the table and begin to dig.

When she finished complaining, she ignored a flustered Kitty, who was still reading ingredients from the different bars, and flounced to Ellie's side. Narrowing her hazel eyes, she inspected Rudy from head to tail. "I thought all the dogs in this contest were purebreds. This one certainly isn't."

The second Ellie heard the comment she wrapped her fingers around her yorkiepoo's muzzle. "This is Rudy. He's a pound puppy of the best kind, and he's all mine."

Kitty stopped reading the energy bars and glanced at Ellie. "You'll have to forgive Lilah. Besides her peanut allergy, she has another severe affliction. It's called over-inflated ego."

Several of the people standing nearby laughed. As if making a point, the designer put her hands on her non-existent hips and nodded toward her mini Schnauzer. "My baby's competed in conformation shows, so I know something about the canine world. I was assured I'd be fitting a purebred dog."

"Just because a dog isn't a purebred doesn't mean they're bad, or untrainable, or unlovable," Kitty interjected.

Lilah's kohl-lined eyes narrowed. "Poor you, still feeling sorry for yourself because you didn't get one of the design spots." She focused on Ellie, who felt as if she was sitting center court at the US Open. "Have you seen Cassandra or Yasmine? They're my models, and I wanted to take a good look at them before their fitting."

"Uh, no," Ellie said. "But maybe I could—" She stifled a grin as a Bradley Cooper look-alike dressed in a black tank top and well-fitting black jeans strolled to her side.

"Hello," he said, sizing her up from head to toe. "I'm Marcus David. One of the designers." He shook Ellie's hand with a strong grip that matched his generous biceps. "I heard I was getting a new plus-sized model. Is that you?"

Plus-sized model? Ellie didn't know whether to be ticked off or pleased. To this group, plus-sized was a term for anyone who wore a size twelve or larger, but asking if she was a model . . . ? "Um, nope. I'm in charge of the dogs."

He gave her another once-over. "Too bad. Not about the dog thing, but about the modeling. Your hair is fabulous, and so are your eyes. I could do a lot with you, if you wanted to change professions."

"Marcus, really," Lilah began. "She's not exactly model material. Her shoulders are too broad, and her ass, well—"

"Well, nothing," Marcus said, huffing out a breath. "I could do great things with that—"

"Maybe you should stick to designing for chubby women, since they do run in your family." She folded her arms and shifted her gaze to Ellie. "This one reminds me of—"

"Excuse me, but I'm standing right here," Ellie said. She nodded toward two women who had just entered the scene, one carrying a French bulldog, and the other who was dogless. "And I believe these are your models."

Hours later, Ellie's head was spinning. She'd spent the afternoon meeting several more people, all involved with the contest in some way, and heard everything that had led to the competition a dozen times over. The way she understood it, not only had the designers and models been handpicked, but the makeup artists and hairstylists were at the top of their field, too.

The amount of hours the designers had dedicated to this endeavor was mind-boggling. Four designers had been assigned two models each, one who met the fashion industry's strict standards, the other a female of "normal" size, who represented the woman of today. The designer would outfit the two models in identical designs of day wear and evening wear, and finally, a third outfit for both the models and their dogs.

That meant three original designs for two women, and two canine outfits as well. It was, she decided as she watched the models being fitted into the first outfit, a huge task. In between observing the preparations, she'd taken the dogs out twice, made sure they had water and treats, and comforted them when they complained about being cooped up in the pen.

For some reason, the snappish Lilah Perry had added her mini Schnauzer, Klingon, to the group, automatically assuming Ellie would care for him with the other pure-breds. Besides Cheech, there was a second Chihuahua, two Yorkies, two French bulldogs, another mini Schnauzer.

To make matters more complicated, a model named Cassandra had forgotten her dog, which made no sense to Ellie, but the missing animal wasn't her problem. Unfortunately, the no-show had caused a heated flare-up between Lilah and her model, which made things uncomfortable whenever they were around.

Even though all the dogs weren't able to communicate with her in the psychic manner she could employ with dogs she knew well, they seemed easy to work with and didn't have the diva complex from which several of their owners suffered. Lilah Perry's dog in particular had a very sweet disposition compared to that of his bossy mistress.

Jeffery King had also dropped by every so often to make sure things were on track, and Morgan Prince, the other half of Nola Morgan Design, had come to inspect the premises several more times.

On each visit, Jeffery had taken his sister aside for a private conversation. Ellie hadn't been able to hear what they said, but their body language and facial expressions told her it had something to do with Lilah's brash treatment of Kitty.

Right now, several of the models and designers were going through their gift bags, comparing items and guessing their retail worth. Besides the goodies, NMD was using the contest to launch a new perfume line with a product called Forever. The perfume was said to equal the best in the industry, but the unique way it was dispensed was its selling point.

Small pads held waxy strips the size of an address label. All the wearers of the perfume had to do was peel off the strip and place it on any pulse point or warm spot on their body. The strip would dissolve into the wearer's skin while the scent stayed with them for hours.

Lilah picked up her basket and plopped down next to Ellie, as if they were close friends. Then she reached into her gift bag and pulled out her perfume pad. "Mmm. Mine is supposed to represent summer, so it smells like lavender and verbena. Who knew I was a freak for lavender?" Lilah asked as she stuck a waxy strip between her breasts. "Isn't this great? I can smell it already. And look how easy they'll be to carry." She dropped the pad back into her swag bag and tucked it under the table. "I love it. Don't you?"

Ellie dug through her basket, moving past a Bottega Veneta handbag, until she found her scent pad. Hers was decorated in a delicate green with gold leaf and labeled Spring. After giving the pad a quick sniff, she did the same as Lilah—peeled off a strip and tucked it in her bra. Moments later, a soft but refreshing aroma that did indeed remind her of a cool spring rain wafted to her nose.

When someone called out "five minutes," the mob of models and designers scattered, racing to the area behind the runway to get a final review before stepping onto the catwalk. Seconds later, the show's prominent emcee, Kurt Jager, announced the details of the NMD contest and its first design showing: day wear.

Ellie and Rudy tiptoed to the back of the crowd, hoping to sneak a peak at the runway. Music floated from the loudspeakers as the first contestant, Marcus David, began the day wear competition. She wasn't sure she liked the black slacks with their wide cuffed legs and tight waist, but she did approve of the top his models wore, which consisted of a short, fitted red jacket over what looked to be a plain white blouse. But after Patti and Claire Smith did the usual walk to a goodly round of applause, they removed the jackets at the end of the runway and showed the pin-tuck detailing on the front and back that made the blouse interesting and unique.

Designer number two was Anton Rouch, a guy with a dark look in his eyes and a face devoid of expression. She'd only met him once, when he asked her which of the dogs belonged to his models, Lawan and Kate. He made no comment when he was introduced to a white Chihuahua and a Yorkie, so Ellie figured he wasn't dog friendly.

The applause continued as the models strutted their stuff. Kurt Jager made appropriate commentary, even throwing in a few jokes during the walks. Designer number three, Fiona Ray, was introduced. Her models, Dominique and Crystal, both owned French bulldogs. The color scheme of Fiona's day wear, consisting of oranges and yellows, was too bright for Ellie's taste, but the audience seemed to love the pencil-slim, knee-length skirt and wide-shouldered jacket.

Last to show was Lilah Perry. Her models, Cassandra

McQuagge and Yasmine, appeared professional, though the day wear Lilah had created was, in Ellie's mind, far from appealing. The skirt, made of black leather or something like it, showed more thigh than any professional would want to wear, and the jacket looked tight and uncomfortable. When each model slipped off her jacket, the fitted black tee had no special detailing, which only helped to make the suit a bore.

The applause continued as all eight models reappeared and took another strut down the runway and back, lining up along the rear curtain. Then the four designers, the real stars of the event, strode front and center. But when the applause ended abruptly on a sudden gasp, Ellie shifted from behind the curtain to see what had happened.

"I can't see. What's goin' on?" asked Rudy, trying to climb up her leg.

Gazing at the audience, she realized that everyone's eyes were focused on the designers. "I'm not sure," she answered, rising on tiptoe and peering between the heads of the backstage crowd. Then she spotted Lilah Perry, her hands clasping her throat as if she were fighting to draw air into her lungs.

Ellie shoved through the statuelike mob without thinking. The models and designers moved back when the emcee rushed over to lend a hand, and Ellie joined him. Lilah had dropped to the floor, her mouth opening and closing like a fish out of water, her face swelling so quickly one could actually see the changes as they morphed her features into a puffy mass.

"She's in anaphylactic shock," someone screamed. "Where's her bag? She carries an EpiPen."

The emcee rose from his knees. "We need an EpiPen! Does anyone in the audience have an EpiPen!"

Ellie took off running, relieved to find the crowd

parting, and raced to the food table. There, she dragged Lilah's bag out from under it, dug inside, and found what she thought was an EpiPen. After pulling it out, she hiked the bag over her shoulder and shot back to the stage.

Chapter 2

"*I can't believe this is happening to us again,*" Rudy groused while sitting at Ellie's feet. "*We must have a sign hangin' over our heads. Somethin' like 'They're here. It's time to kill somebody.'*"

Sitting on one of the chairs between the water cooler and the food table, Ellie scanned the canine corner. The forensic team was still collecting and labeling everything that had been on the table and under it when the show started. The models had been released from questioning, as well as the designers, and the detectives on the case were finishing up with anyone who'd worked behind the scenes, including the makeup artists and hairstylists.

She'd been told to sit and wait. The man in charge would get to her soon enough.

"I think that's a bit of a stretch. We don't have that kind of power, nor do we want it." Ellie ended the comment with a sigh. She was beat, but she had sat through enough of these murder cleanup sessions to know the cops would take their time to do it right, no matter whom they inconvenienced.

Rudy jumped on the chair to her right. *"Then we must have some bad karma workin' our lives."*

"You're starting to sound like Viv's sister and her astrology predictions," she said, remembering the detailed chart she'd received from Arlene Millman after she'd exposed the person who killed her sleazeball fiancé. She'd been thinking about the chart since Lilah had been pronounced dead on the stage, and had made a decision. "I believe these murders we keep stepping into are accidental. There hasn't been a thing we could do to stop them, yet we end up finding the killer. It's our destiny."

Rudy gruffed a laugh. *"Isn't destiny the same as karma?"*

Ellie shrugged. "I guess, so that's probably the way I'll have to look at it. I don't think we have another choice."

"How about you try tellin' that one to Detective Demento, and see what he has to say."

"Let's keep the idea between the two of us, shall we?"

She was happy that Sam and his partner, Vince, hadn't been called to this case. Sam was going to blow a gasket when he found out she was involved in another murder, even if she really wasn't. "It's going to be difficult enough when he finds out this happened while I was here. And when he learns that I was the last person to come in contact with the body before . . . Well, I don't even want to think about it."

Ellie would never forget touching Lilah's clammy skin and sticking the EpiPen needle in her thigh. Unfortunately, by the time the EMTs in the emergency van stationed outside the event had pushed their way through the crowd and done their best to revive the designer, she was gone.

After they'd officially declared Lilah dead, they asked Ellie questions. That's when she found out the EpiPen she'd pulled from Lilah's bag was a blank. And when she'd told the EMTs Lilah had made a huge deal out of her allergy, they had called the medical examiner and the police. According to them, it was rare for anyone with an allergy as serious as Lilah's to be caught with an empty EpiPen and no backup.

It was then she learned that the pens usually came in a box of two, and people with a severe allergy took pains to carry a full load. In fact, these days the pens were used for so many types of allergies that even the ME, a guy named Steve Bauman, was surprised no one in the audience had responded to the emcee's plaintive request.

The thought that she'd been unable to help Lilah made Ellie's stomach churn. Though she couldn't be blamed for killing the designer, she felt responsible for using an empty pen. If she'd known it was already discharged, she might have been able to do more to locate another one.

While she continued to stew over the tragic event, one of the women from the forensic team, a blonde named Charlene whom Ellie had met before, crawled out from under the table. "What do you know about this?" she asked, holding up her prize.

"That's an orange," Ellie answered, trying to sound intelligent. "What's it doing down there?"

"That's what I'd like to know." Charlene pulled an evidence bag from her pocket. "Considering the amount of stuff stored under there, I doubt it would roll so far to the back without assistance. My guess is someone dropped it back here behind the table, hoping no one would notice until the cleaning crew tossed it out." She bagged and tagged the orange. "We've already confiscated the fruit sitting on top, but I'll keep this one separate. It might be something—or nothing at all. We'll have to wait and see."

When Charlene left, Marcus David ambled over and sat next to her. "I'm not being nosy, but I have to ask. I heard you were a crime solver of some renown. What's that all about?"

"Be careful what you say, Triple E."

She wrapped her fingers around Rudy's muzzle. "Where did you hear that?"

"Just around. You know how people talk." A corner of the handsome designer's mouth curled up in a grin. "I don't like rumors. I prefer going straight to the source." When she didn't answer, he got the message. "Okay, so you don't want to talk about it. Are you willing to answer another question?"

"Depends," she told him. And who was spreading rumors about her past escapades? "What do you want to know?"

"I noticed you talking to your dog. At least, I think it was your dog, or maybe it was to yourself." He gave a full-fledged smile. "I just wondered which it was."

"I told you to watch yourself, but did you—?"

Ellie gave the yorkiepoo's muzzle another squeeze. "Maybe a little of both. I guess I was trying to figure things out—"

"Things about Lilah's death?"

"See, what'd I tell you?"

"About the contest, for one," she replied. "Do you know if it's been postponed, or is it still on for tomorrow?"

Marcus shrugged. "Beats me, but I imagine it will continue on schedule. This is a huge venue with designers from around the world participating. I doubt the powers-that-be will stand for a disruption—murder or no murder."

Murder? Ellie swallowed. "Did you hear something official? Has Lilah's death actually been declared a murder?"

The designer leaned back in his chair. "That's the gossip circulating. As for the postponement, well, I hate to sound like a pompous jerk, but with Lilah gone it gives the three designers left a better shot at winning."

"You mean they won't move down to the next designer in line? The one who finished in fifth place?"

"I have no idea, but that would be a bummer. That fifth-place designer would have to play catch-up with everything."

Before she could comment, her cell rang. When she checked caller ID, she heaved another sigh. "I have to take this."

Standing, he said, "No problem. See you tomorrow," and walked away.

Ellie waved her fingers, then took the call. It was Amber Truly, the fellow dog walker she'd asked to cover her regular customers while she worked this show. "Hey, Amber. Sorry I didn't call you earlier. How were the walks?"

"Everything went great." Amber's cheerful voice made Ellie smile. "I'm exhausted, of course. Adding thirty dogs to my daily schedule wasn't easy."

She'd made friends with Amber about six months ago while doing her rounds. The girl seemed friendly and responsible, and she employed two assistants, which meant she'd probably given most of her regular dogs away and walked those in the Davenport herself, which is where Ellie had met her.

"I'm very grateful for your help. You know I'll do the same for you if you ever need me." Amber was also getting about sixty percent of Ellie's profits for her trouble, but this wasn't the time to quibble about money. The amount she was being paid by NMD was triple what she earned for the walks. "Did they all behave?"

"Everybody except the one you call Mr. T. That Jack Russell acted like he had a stick of dynamite up his butt. Good thing I only have to do him once a day, or I'd be demanding double."

Ellie grinned. Viv's Jack Russell was a trip, and he was never happy when he had to work with someone new. She'd had a long talk with him about Amber last week, and again this morning, but that didn't mean he was going to be agreeable. "Sorry, but there's nothing I can do about him. T has a mind of his own."

"I can see that. Are you still mingling with the fabulous fashionistas or are you home?"

"I'm still at the event. There's been an . . . incident. You'll probably read about it in tomorrow's newspaper." Ellie took a deep breath, hoping to ward off the first of many comments she was sure to receive from her friends. "And before you say anything, I had nothing to do with it."

"Oh, my God. There's been another murder," Amber exclaimed, her high-pitched voice ear-shattering. "I can't wait to hear the details. You owe me a lunch."

"Okay, fine. Just don't make it this week." She spotted the detective she'd been told was in charge talking with Charlene, and figured she'd be next on his list. "I've got to hang up. Have fun tomorrow and be nice to my kids. Bye."

Moments later, a tall, thin man with a shock of gray hair finished his discussion with the forensic technician and headed in Ellie's direction. She had no idea if the lead detective was a nice guy or not, but he'd be in charge, so she decided to make the best of it.

"Ms. Engleman?" He held up his badge. "I'm Newton Vaughn, lead detective on this case. I understand you were the one who tried to revive the victim before the emergency crew arrived."

Ellie moved Rudy to her lap, hoping the extra room would encourage the rangy detective to sit. She'd have a crick in her neck if she had to stare up at him much longer.

"I did, but I had no idea the pen was dead—er—empty until after I tried it."

Detective Vaughn took the hint and parked himself, leaving the middle chair between them for room. Then he pulled out the ever-present spiral notepad. "You know anything about allergies?"

Ellie shook her head. "Not a thing. In fact, I don't believe I know a single person, family member or friend, who's allergic to anything."

"So this pen was new to you?"

"I'd heard about EpiPens, of course, but no, I'd never seen one. When I got there with her bag, I had already pulled it out. Lilah was gasping for breath, her face swollen, her body stiff, so I automatically flipped off the cap, saw the needle, and pushed it into her thigh. Then I saw that the plunger was already depressed. That's when Mr. Jager took a look and told me it was empty. We checked her bag, but didn't find another one."

Detective Vaughn leaned back in the chair, his ruddy face set in a grim expression. "I understand from Mr. King that you were the person in charge of this area. You saw who came and went, who put their belongings under the table, who was inspecting those fancy gift baskets, that sort of thing."

"I was, but not all the time."

"Not all the time? What does that mean?"

Ellie figured he already had this information, and was

just asking to make sure she gave the identical explanation. "My first priority was the dogs. I had to take
them out back on schedule. I also made sure they had
water and treats, and I gave them an ear if anything was
wrong."

"An ear?" Vaughn's generous mouth curled down
into a frown. "Care to tell me what that means?"

*"Smart move, Triple E. That's the way to show him you
have a sensible head on your shoulders,"* Rudy muttered,
nosing her neck. *"Get outta this one."*

"I—uh—I seem to have a sixth sense where canines
are concerned." She crossed mental fingers. "I can usually tell if they have a good life, owners who love them,
that kind of thing."

"I understand Ms. Perry had a dog. Do you know
what happened to it?"

"She has—er—had a mini Schnauzer named Klingon,
and he's a cute little guy. One of the models took him
home with her when she was dismissed." Ellie had thought
about keeping Klingon herself, but Yasmine had claimed
that her own mini Schnauzer, Jojo, and Lilah's dog got
along, so she figured it would be all right. "I hope that
wasn't against the rules," she added, remembering what
Sam always said about taking dogs that belonged to a
murder victim to the city shelter.

Vaughn scribbled a notation on his pad. "I don't see
why not. The dog wasn't near the victim when she died,
so it really wasn't involved. We'll have to notify Ms. Perry's next of kin, of course, so they can claim the dog, but
that might take a while." He tucked the spiral notebook
in his jacket pocket and pulled out a business card.
"There's just one more thing. No one can find both of
the deceased's bags, and I understand they were last in
your possession."

Ellie cocked her head. "Both bags? You mean her personal tote *and* her gift bag?"

"We have her personal bag, but the gift bag is missing, and my people say there's no sign of it. Since you brought her personal bag to the staging area, I wondered if you'd seen her gift bag."

She remembered bringing the bag when she'd found the EpiPen. "I don't recall. Once I found the EpiPen, I was so busy trying to help Kurt revive her I never thought about the swag bag. Then the EMTs arrived and—"

"Somebody took it, of course. Didn't you say it held thousands in gifts?"

She cupped her hand around Rudy's muzzle. "I hate to say this, but I imagine it was stolen. The stuff inside the bag was worth a lot of money, so someone probably saw their chance and grabbed it."

"Hmm." He passed her his card and stood. "One of the officers told me who you were, so you know the drill. Call me if you remember something you think we need to know."

Great. It figured someone would fill Vaughn in on all the investigations in which she'd been involved, and that she lived with an NYPD detective. Resolving to take his remark in stride, she asked, "Do you know if the show will continue tomorrow morning, or is it postponed?"

"The mayor has ordered us to stay here for however long it takes tonight, so this Fashion Week thing can go on as scheduled. I think it'll be safe for you to return at your usual time in the morning."

"Can I clean up the dog pen or is that considered part of the crime scene?"

He gazed at the pen. "The death occurred a good thirty yards from here, and we've taken everything we consider evidence, so do what you have to. Just keep out

of the way of the forensic team." His expression grew
stern. "That means minding your own business, and
staying out of theirs."

With that, he stalked off in the direction of the stage.

Ellie thought about his choice of words as she retrieved the toys and dog beds in the pen and moved
them under the table. Since the tech crew had picked the
table clean, and Charlene had taken care of everything
underneath, she guessed it was okay to stuff the canine
paraphernalia out of the way. She imagined the area
would look good as new in the morning, refilled with
fruit and veggies, identical energy bars, and drinks.

"That dippy dick didn't mince words, did he?" said
Rudy as they left the building.

"Nope, and I plan to do exactly what he said. I'm not
sticking my nose in this one."

"Ooo-kay, if that's the way you want it," he said, walking
alongside her onto the street. *"Just remember that word."*

"Word? What word?"

"Karma."

An hour later, Viv was sitting in Ellie's kitchen, oohing and
aahing over the booty in Ellie's swag bag. She'd shown up
unannounced shortly after they arrived home, and Ellie
didn't have the heart to turn her best friend away.

Fashion was Viv's first love. It always amazed Ellie
that she'd never pursued a modeling career, but as she
grew to know Viv, she began to understand. Vivian saw
everything in black and white, which was the way people
in money dealt. You either made it or you didn't—period.
That's why Viv did so well in her finance career.

She could never sit statue-still while someone fussed
over her hair or makeup. Nor would she be patient with
a designer who did all the picky business that went with
creating a beautiful outfit.

After Viv made a thorough search of the swag basket, she said, "This is fantastic. I can't believe you got all this stuff for free. Thanks so much for letting me grab the Bottega Veneta handbag and the D&G scarf."

"No problem." Ellie moved the basket to the counter. "You sure you don't want to try my perfume strips? They seemed to be the rage with everyone." She sniffed at her chest. "And Nola Morgan Design is right about the long-lasting effect. I can still smell the scent of spring rain from mine."

"I smell it, too, and it suits you, but I like my perfume a little more earthy." Viv went to the freezer, retrieved her half-eaten container of Caramel Cone ice cream, and dug in. "Maybe you and I can go to Bergdorf's over the weekend and I'll decide if there's one that's right for me." She swallowed a spoonful of ice cream. "So what else happened?"

It was then Ellie explained the rest of her day, finishing with Lilah's death. Viv, who was almost through with her frozen treat, stopped midscrape and opened and closed her mouth in silence. "I'm sorry. I don't think I heard you correctly. What happened at the end of the first showing?"

"Go on," Rudy encouraged from his mat. *"Tell her the story. I'm ready for what Vivie has to say."*

Ellie decided blunt was the best way to go. "One of the designers had an allergy attack and died. They think it might have been murder. They're not sure."

Viv plunked her spoon and empty container down. "You're joking."

Ellie placed an elbow on the table and cupped her chin. "I only wish."

"Did you know the victim?"

"Not well. But it was clear she made enemies with her brash personality."

Viv grinned. "Okay, Little Mary Sunshine. What did she do that was so bad someone would want to kill her?"

"Too many nasty comments to count, if you ask me."

After giving her boy a glare, Ellie shrugged. "Nothing specific. But for instance, after we met, it didn't take her more that five minutes to make a negative comment about my build."

"Oh, Lord. What is wrong with those people?"

"Those people?"

"Fashionistas. They pay more attention to the shape of the models wearing the clothes than they do the designs."

"That's why this NMD contest drew so much attention. The designers have to dress two sizes of models, one with a figure like yours, and one with a figure like mine."

"You mean built like you, or Crystal Renn or Kate Dillon," said Vivian. "It's about time."

"They were there. If I remember, Crystal has a French bulldog. He's a very cute little guy."

"I love it when you categorize everyone by the kind of dog they own," Viv said with a laugh. "So this Lilah person, she didn't like working with normal-sized women."

"It was only me she commented on, but she made it pretty clear how she felt about anyone who wore a double-digit dress size."

"And her opinion was so obnoxious that someone would kill her for it?"

"I vote yes on that one."

"Give me a second." Ellie walked to the cupboard, pulled out two of her friend Sara Studebaker's carrot-and-apple biscuits, and gave one to Rudy and one to Mr. T. "You boys need a bedtime snack; then we'll go out for our last walk of the night." She raised an eyebrow. "You got it?"

Mr. T and Rudy started chewing. It was the yorkiepoo's way of saying yes without giving an answer,
and she returned to the table. "I really don't know too
much more, but I'm sure I'll hear the details tomorrow.
We have to be up early, especially if I have to take your
guy for his walk."

"So don't take him. I'll handle it. That'll give you an
extra fifteen minutes." Viv tossed the container in the
trash and set the spoon in the sink. "I'll take my swag to
my apartment, and get my sweater. You bring the boys.
I'll meet you in the lobby."

She collected her gifts and left, while Ellie started
down the hall with Rudy and Twink at her heels. *"Let's
get this show on the road,"* her boy goaded. *"We got a lot
of work to do tomorrow."*

"Excuse me?" She slipped a sweater over her head.
"Why would we get involved?"

"Because we have to. It's in our blood."

She heaved a sigh. "Yours maybe, but not mine. I can
only imagine what Sam is going to say when he hears, if
he hasn't already."

*"Detective Demento? How many times do I have to
tell you, we don't take orders from him."*

They returned to the hall and headed for the door.
Once there, Ellie snapped leashes on both dogs and they
walked down to the inside landing, where Viv was waiting. "Let's make this quick," she said, handing Mr. T off
to his mistress. "I'm too tired to think straight."

"I understand." Viv led the way. "We'll go to the corner and back; then we're through."

The cool night air gave Ellie renewed energy. "Besides those gorgeous baskets, I got another piece of
good news," she said while they watched Twink water a
fire hydrant. "I managed to get you a ticket for the grand
finale."

Gasping, Viv spun around. "What? No! You didn't!"

"I told you I would," said Ellie, smiling. "I'd never let you down."

"What day? What time? What should I wear?"

"It's on Friday. The first catwalk run is scheduled for ten a.m., and you can stay all day, and wear whatever you want."

Viv heaved a breath. "I forgot to ask. Who was in the crowd today? Did you get to meet anyone famous? Name names, please."

"You're asking me? A woman who doesn't even read *Vogue*?"

"*Vogue, Harper's, W*, they're all the bible," said Viv. They stopped at the corner, where the boys did their business; then Viv and Ellie scooped and deposited the bags in the trash can. "Did you meet Anna Wintour or Grace Coddington?"

"The names sound familiar. I did see Michael Kors and Christian Siriano on their way to somewhere."

"Good God, but you're difficult." Viv huffed out a breath. "You met important people, big names in the fashion world, and all you decided to talk about was a 'maybe' murder."

"Keep your voice down, please," said Ellie, narrowing her eyes as they neared the porch. "I think I see . . ."

"Oh, brother."

Sam sat on the cement balustrade of the apartment building, waiting for Ellie and Viv to return from their nightly dog outing. Word of the murder investigation at the fashion event Ellie was working had reached him around six, and he knew that, just like all the rest of the crimes she found herself in the middle of, she'd end up involved in this one, too.

She hadn't pulled the trigger or thrown the dagger, of

course, but she had put herself in a sticky situation. According to department gossip, she was the last ordinary citizen to have contact with the victim.

Now Vivian was laying into her so loudly it echoed up the street, berating her for caring more about the details of the crime than the big names at the event. He'd thought about giving Ellie his usual harangue on how she needed to answer Vaughn's questions and stay out of the rest of it. After hearing Viv give her hell, well, maybe he just needed to slow things down for the night.

Reading the exhaustion in Ellie's eyes, he leaned forward and kissed her cheek when the women arrived at the stairway. "Hi, babe." He pulled her near. "Viv, how are you doing?"

"I'm great, now that I know I have a ticket for the final day of Fashion Week," she said, grinning. "I'll leave you two alone. I think you have a lot to talk about." She headed up the steps with her Jack Russell in tow. "Ellie, see you in the morning."

He waited until the door closed before saying, "I heard you had quite a day. Do you want to talk about it?"

She leaned into his chest. "Maybe for a minute; then I need sleep. Is that okay?"

He took her hand and led her into the building. They climbed the stairs to the third floor. "I'll put on my listening hat, just for you."

Ellie smiled and his heart jumped. In the almost six months they'd lived together he'd done his damnedest to make her happy, and that was a big improvement for him. According to his ex, he'd been a lousy listener, a fact for which Carolanne never forgave him. It was getting easier and easier to sit back and listen to Ellie, to understand where she was coming from, and to enjoy her positive, almost rosy, outlook on life.

It had taken five murders for him to realize his girl was

right. She never looked for trouble—trouble just seemed to find her. And it was his job to keep her safe and happy while things took place around her, which included allowing her to help those she considered her friends.

They got to their apartment and he pulled out his key, but Ellie simply opened the door. "Sorry. I forgot to lock it, but Viv and I were only going to be out for a couple of minutes."

He held back his usual "This is New York. Lock the *effing* door" comment. "And Rudy would protect you if a bad guy slipped inside?"

She knelt to undo Rudy's leash. "I think he's finally getting the message, little man. What do you think?"

Sam waited while she held a short conversation with her dog. When the mutt glanced up at him and cocked its head, he wanted to groan. No matter how many times he saw the hound, he still couldn't get over the almost human expression on its face.

When they got to the bedroom he tugged off his clothes while Ellie brought Rudy and his pillow to the spare room and told him good night. By the time she finished whatever females did to get ready for bed, he was under the covers waiting for her.

She climbed in and he pulled her close, spooning himself against her back. "You don't have to talk about it tonight. I'll get up with you in the morning. You can give me the details over coffee." He circled her waist with his arm. "Unless you need to get something off your chest now."

She blew out a breath. "Just that I had nothing to do with it. Even trying to save Lilah's life was an automatic reaction. I've been thinking: How could a woman who complained about her allergy as much as Lilah did carry an empty EpiPen?"

"I know Vaughn. I'm sure he's already figured that out."

"So how did she come in contact with peanuts?"

"My guess is Vaughn is asking himself that same question. And the ME will probably come up with the answer."

She wriggled her bottom against his growing erection. "So I should keep my nose clean and let the cops do their job?"

"You should," he agreed, nuzzling the back of her ear.

"Uh-oh. It feels like I'm going to owe you a special wake-up in the morning," she said with a smile in her voice.

"That'll be the perfect way to start my day."

She snuggled closer and he felt her muscles relax and her tension ease. That's when he decided there was no reason to begin his usual "no snooping—mind your own business" speech. Ellie was just too tired.

A minute later, just as he was dozing off, he heard her say, "Thanks, Sam, for not lecturing. I appreciate it."

Chapter 3

First thing the next morning, after sharing breakfast and the exact details of Lilah Perry's death with Sam, Ellie and Rudy hopped out of the cab when it stopped in front of the Fashion Center. The same security guard as yesterday waved them through, and she prepared for whatever might be the attitude of those inside.

She hoped the gofers, assistants, and staging folks would be more calm and respectful than the day before, when it had taken her only a few hours in their presence to realize that the people in this industry were manic. It stood to reason the craziness that accompanied said profession would be softened by the tragedy.

But she moaned internally when she arrived in the work area of the show. So much for hoping people would be pondering the tragedy, mourning for Lilah, or worrying if any of them would be a victim as well. This group had lost one of its own under shocking circumstances, yet people raced the floor pushing clothing racks, carry-

ing mounds of shoe boxes, and setting up makeup and
hairstyling stations as if nothing had happened.

She just missed getting whacked by a rolling rack,
darted out of the way of a woman toting an armful of
fabric, and blew out a breath when three girls, carrying
trays of coffee in each hand, jostled past her. Nothing
was toned down or softened. The place was downright
dangerous, and the pace was still frantic.

*"Do you think these guys know they're hangin' tight
with a murderer?"* Rudy asked as he scuttled closer to
her ankle.

"Detective Vaughn wasn't exactly secretive when his
team commandeered everyone and asked questions. If
Marcus David heard rumors, I'm sure everybody else
did, too. And I'm positive word of Lilah's death made
the newspapers. Although I was in such a rush this morning I forgot to check."

She jumped to the side and pulled Rudy with her to
avoid another garment rack collision. "Excuse me," she
muttered when the person passed, head down and pushing determinedly, without one word of warning.

"These humans need better manners."

Ellie tugged her boy to an empty makeup station and
squatted. "We'll talk about good manners some other
time. For now, just stay close. I don't want to lose you."

Regrouping, they walked by a girl sitting patiently
while a striking man, his hair gelled in a bright red Mohawk, transformed her into a dark and dramatic beauty.
Just past that, two pencil-thin girls of no more than six-
teen stood on round podiums in nothing but silk bikini
bottoms while designers draped them in fabric. Vivian
had told her about young girls, children really, who were
making it big in the fashion industry, and these scenes
supported Viv's view.

"I thought humans were supposed to wear clothes in public," Rudy said, his tone a snigger.

Ellie cleared her throat. "We are, but this is the fashion world. The way I understand it, the body is nothing more than a hanger with a heartbeat, made to show off designer creations. Since they think they're behind the scenes right now, it's private to them. Public is when they're out on the catwalk."

"Those kids should be runnin' on a soccer field or taking piano lessons, not getting dressed up to look like hookers."

"I wouldn't say hookers. They're more like kids playing dress-up with their mom's clothes and cosmetics."

She kept walking as she pondered Rudy's observations.

So much of what she'd seen backstage was like make-believe. Most average women couldn't afford what these high-end hairstylists and makeup artists charged, ditto what the fashion houses were selling, which was why she appreciated the concept of Nola Morgan Design's contest. The designers in the competition were creating clothes for real women, and real women were the ones who spent most of the money and did most of the buying.

Deciding she'd never understand the minds of those who ran this industry, she was relieved to find their station just as she'd predicted. The table was filled with the same setup as the day before, and the puppy pen already held a Yorkie and both mini Schnauzers.

She stored her tote under the table and gave her boy a nod. "How about if I put your travel mat in the pen and you hang with the other dogs? Maybe you can find out how Lilah's baby is doing. No matter how nasty she was to people, Lilah was his mom and he lost her, so I'm sure he's sad."

Rudy curled up on his mat and eyed the other canines. *"No problemo. I can keep watch on them and the table from here."*

A minute later, jumping like a crazed grasshopper, Kitty King ran over. "Oh my God! Oh my God!" She threaded her fingers through her spiky blond hair. "Have you heard?"

"Heard?" Ellie grabbed her assistant's shaking hands and pulled her to a chair. "Is this about Lilah?"

"What?" Kitty shook her head. "Lilah? No." She heaved a sigh. "Well, sort of. I still can't believe it."

Had someone confessed to emptying Lilah's EpiPen? Had the cops figured out how she came in contact with peanuts? "Sit and relax for a second. If it doesn't concern Lilah, I have no idea what you're talking about."

Kitty breathed slowly, in and out, in and out. Then she grinned. "The NMD officials have moved me into Lilah's place in the competition."

In the design contest? Ellie knew the young woman wanted to be a designer, but she had no idea that Kitty had even entered the competition. Or was she taking Lilah's place with the help of her brother, Jeffery? "Really? I mean, you didn't say a word about entering. How did it happen?"

"I got a phone call last night," Kitty said, inhaling. "I did enter, but no one ever mentioned how the losing designers stacked up, so this was the first I realized I must have been number five." She raised her palms to her temples. "I'm a wreck. I have a ton of stuff to do. I spent all of last night going over my designs, trying to choose the ones that were best, but easiest to do on such short notice." She shrugged. "I guess that old saying 'what goes around comes around' is really true."

"Sorry. I'm not sure what you mean by that."

"I never found the time to tell you." Kitty ducked her

head and lowered her voice. "Lilah stole my designs and used them to win a spot in the competition."

Ellie blinked her surprise. "She copied your work?"

"Worse than copied." Kitty nodded a hello to the model dropping off her tiny Yorkie, and waited until she left before continuing. "She actually found the drawings of what I planned to submit in my brother's home office."

"Your brother's home office? What was Lilah doing at his place?"

"He threw a party to celebrate his promotion and invited NMD people along with friends. Lilah hadn't been invited, but she showed up as someone's date, and Jeff didn't want to make a scene so he ignored her most of the night. I'd brought a folder holding the designs I planned to submit and left it sitting on his desk. After the party, while he and I were cleaning up, we realized it was gone. We figured somebody had taken it, so I pulled out my second choices, worked them over, and sent them in instead."

Kitty took another deep breath. "They weren't as good as my first choice ones, of course, but the next business day was the deadline, so I had to submit them."

"When did you find out it was Lilah who took them?" Ellie had a sinking feeling the episode would come back to haunt her assistant, but she wouldn't say anything until she heard the whole story. "Did you confront her?"

Slumping in her chair, Kitty sighed. "I didn't, but Jeff was on the recommendation committee and he knew she was the thief the minute he saw Lilah's entry. Even so, he couldn't accuse her until he talked to her." She hugged her arms around her chest. "According to him, it got ugly."

"Ugly how?"

"He asked Lilah and she denied it. They argued and a

few people overheard the fight. Word went round that he only accused Lilah because he was trying to get me in. When he heard that, he excused himself from the committee. Since there was no real proof that Lilah stole my work, she won a spot."

"I see." Ellie smiled a hello to the model dropping off her white Chihuahua and adding her tote to the growing pile under the table. "Then I guess you're happy Lilah is gone."

"I'm happy she's out and I'm in, but I never wanted her dead," said Kitty, raising her button nose in the air. "I have no idea how it happened, but I'm glad it did . . . sort of. You know what I mean." She heaved another sigh and shot to her feet. "I have to get moving. My models will be here any minute, and I have to start creating."

Kitty raced off and Ellie slumped in her chair. So that's what the girl had meant yesterday, when she mentioned design theft and backbiting. But it had to be a coincidence that Lilah ended up dead. Kitty didn't strike her as the type to commit murder. Then again, according to Sam, murderers had no particular type. Anyone could kill if they were desperate enough or pushed in the wrong direction.

"Are you thinkin' what I'm thinkin'?"

She dropped to her knees and kept her voice low. "There is no way Kitty could kill anyone. I saw her with the dogs yesterday, and nobody as kind to animals as she is would ever commit murder."

"I don't think so either, but you know the cops. They'll suspect her."

Before Ellie could answer, a pair of long legs approached them, and she rose to greet Marcus David.

"Talking to yourself again?" he asked, his handsome face wearing a grin.

"I'm—I was—talking to my dog."

He cocked his head and his sandy brown hair feathered his forehead. "I bet that little guy knows a lot of your secrets."

"He's more like my sounding board," she answered. "Are you ready for this afternoon?"

"Me? Sure, but I bet Kitty is having a fit." He stuck his hands in his pockets. "She's got to show both outfits to the committee today, and to the press, and with the murder and all, she'll be in the spotlight for sure."

"Then you heard something from the police? They're certain Lilah was murdered?"

Marcus lifted a broad shoulder. "Has to be, no? Lilah was always blabbing about her EpiPen. She'd instructed the few friends she had on how to use it in case she was stricken. She'd never have carried one that was discharged, which means someone emptied it, then made sure she came in contact with peanuts."

Ellie raised a brow. "The few friends she had? Is that a nice way of saying Lilah had enemies?"

"You saw her, heard how she talked, and it wasn't a joke. She had a gift for hurting people's feelings, like when she argued with me about your figure, which is perfect for the plus-sized gig, by the way." His lips thinned. "She had a way of saying things that cut right to the bone, and I should know."

She couldn't imagine Lilah saying anything rude about a tall, handsome man like Marcus David. As far as she could see, he was a talented designer, and he'd been polite and friendly every time they spoke. "You should know? I'm sorry, but—"

"It's personal, so don't worry about it. I shouldn't have said anything." He glanced at his watch, then scanned the room. "The first show on the schedule—I think it's Richard Chai—is set to start in fifteen minutes. I've got to run."

Ellie checked out the room when he left and spotted Detective Vaughn speaking with Kurt Jager, last night's emcee and the person who'd begged audience members for an EpiPen. They made eye contact and both men headed in her direction.

"Ms. Engleman," said Detective Vaughn when they reached her, "I have to ask you a few more questions."

"Here? Now?"

Vaughn took a quick scan of the area. "I don't see anything happening here right now, so yes."

Kurt Jager, wearing a George Hamilton tan, smiled, and his handsome face looked ten years younger. He was a retired model who'd been featured in Ralph Lauren's Polo ads back in the eighties, where he'd made his fortune. He'd been kind to her during and after last night's incident, and they'd shared a joke or two about his own dog, a Spuds MacKenzie look-alike named Mavis Davis, who was an English bull terrier.

"It's all right, Ellie. He has news," said Kurt.

"News?" she asked, hoping the police had ruled out murder.

When Detective Vaughn said, "I can take it from here, Mr. Jager," she knew she was wrong.

Giving a snappy salute, Kurt left, and Ellie took a seat. "Have you found out what happened to Lilah's EpiPen?" she asked when Vaughn sat across from her.

"As far as we can tell, the pen was drained on purpose," he answered, his tone subdued. "We found epinephrine in an orange one of the CSU techs found underneath this table."

Then Charlene had been right. That orange was something special.

Vaughn continued. "Testing showed it held the usual amount found in an EpiPen of the type the victim carried." He crossed his long legs and his pants crept up, showing his faded red socks. "Unfortunately, the rough peel on the orange makes it impossible to lift a print."

"So whoever emptied the pen knew what they were doing."

"There's no doubt in my mind that they did. But we're having less luck finding out how Ms. Perry ingested or came into contact with a peanut." He pulled out his spiral notepad. "That's where you come in."

Ellie swallowed. "Me?"

"You spent time with her, and her bag was under your surveillance most of the day." He raised an iron-gray eyebrow. "Besides that, you saw whatever anyone ate or drank, if they did it here."

"Sure, I watched, but I didn't take notes or anything personal. People came and went all day, and a lot of them brought their own food. You know the joke about models eating a lettuce leaf for lunch? Well, that's just about what they did."

"But Ms. Perry wasn't a model. We ran tests on everything she carried in her bag, and it was all peanut free. And we heard about the fuss she made when Ms. King offered her an energy bar. If she didn't come into contact with peanuts from something on this table, then where did it come from?"

She couldn't figure out if he was asking her or talking out loud to himself. This was the first time she'd dealt with Newton Vaughn, and she had no idea if he had a sense of humor. It was something she needed to find out from Sam, if he was off duty tonight.

"Do you expect me to answer that?" she finally asked when his sharp eyes continued to scan her face.

"I heard you were a good observer. Now that you've had time to think about it, I hoped to hear more about what you noticed."

Ellie stifled a groan. Her life had been so much simpler before she started her dog-walking business. Of course, it had been boring, too, and she'd been broke most of the time. Now she had money and great friends. But was it a plus when she added murder to the mix?

"Dozens of people came and went during the day. It was impossible to keep track of just one person. Especially one who was . . . um . . . difficult."

"Difficult?" He crossed his arms, his posture relaxed. "That's one of the most kind descriptions anyone has given of Ms. Perry to date."

"Oh, well, I really didn't have much personal interaction with her."

"Of course you did," Vaughn said. He flipped through his notebook. "She insulted you when another designer commented on your figure, and she insulted your assistant, too. Accused Ms. King of trying to poison her when she offered her that energy bar, if what a few people told me is correct."

Ellie shrugged. "It didn't bother me much, and I got the impression Kitty was used to her negative comments."

"What about Ms. King's brother?"

"Jeffery?"

"That's the one."

"I'm not sure. I barely know him."

"I was told he held a party a few weeks ago, and Ms. Perry showed up, even though she wasn't invited."

Ellie sat straighter in her chair. This guy was asking her the questions Sam had warned her about—the ones that implied she was part of the investigation. "Look, Detective Vaughn. I'm really not the person you should be speaking to. I wasn't at the party. I don't know a thing about him accusing Ms. Perry of—I mean—"

"Way to go, Triple E," Rudy yipped from the pen.

Vaughn narrowed his steely eyes. "Accusing her of what?"

"He's testin' you. Just wants to see if you know what he knows."

"I met Ms. Perry and the Kings yesterday, so I have no idea of their past interactions," she said, still pondering his interrogation.

"But you've heard?"

"About an incident. Jeffery King accused Lilah of stealing his sister's designs and using them to win a spot in this competition." She swallowed a grin. She had him on this one. "But I believe whatever I tell you, as you people in law enforcement call it, would be hearsay."

Vaughn ignored her perceptive comment. "And you'll tell me if you hear or observe something you think I need to know?"

"Of course. I always cooperate with the NYPD." She heaved a sigh. "If I may ask, why are you looking for answers from me?"

He smiled, but his eyes remained serious. "Because other than my men and me, you seem to be the only normal person on staff here, and I need normal to run a clean and sensible investigation. Not crazy."

At that moment a model Ellie had met the day before showed up and passed over the leash to her Greyhound. "Look at me," she wailed, pulling at her hair. "Reynoldo promised me the color would be stupendous, beautiful, a work of art. Look what he's done to me."

Ellie glanced at the Greyhound, a large and seemingly peaceful dog she'd never encountered before. She'd been told the models chosen for this competition had pocket pooches, not ponies. Did this girl think she was running a canine day care center? The model tugged at her hair while she moaned, and when Ellie glanced up she found Vaughn grinning.

The girl whirled in place and Ellie fought to remember her name. Katherine ... Cassidy ... Cassandra? "Ah, it—it looks fine to me," she stuttered, trying to see the flaw. The model's hair was long and lustrous, with a slight curl at the ends.

"It's brown. Mud brown, if you want the truth." She dragged the hair up until it stood on end. "It's ruined!" Dropping into a chair, she slapped her hands over her face and began to cry.

Ellie anchored the Greyhound's leash under a table leg, and the dog sat patiently next to his mistress. When she turned around, Detective Vaughn was gone.

"I need Karen Hood," the model sobbed. "I never should have let anyone else touch it. I'm due to be in a show in an hour, so I came in early to see Karen, but she was busy. So this other hairstylist, Reynoldo, convinced me he could do the job just as well. And like a dope, I said okay."

Karen Hood? It was a name she'd heard yesterday. All the models wanted her to do their hair, but only a few were worthy of the special treatment.

"Please, please find her for me," the girl continued.

"I'm afraid I can't help you with that. All I can do is keep your dog." It was then her memory kicked in. "You're the model who didn't bring one yesterday," said Ellie. "But this can't be— Is this the dog you plan to use for the show?"

Cassandra raised her head and blinked through teary eyes. "I know, I know, he's too big, but he's all I have now. I lost my Yorkie. He died and—"

When she sobbed again, Ellie felt her pain. Saying good-bye to a dog you loved was one of the most difficult things a person could do. She found a tissue in her tote and passed it over.

"A friend took me to a Greyhound rescue event last weekend and I couldn't resist. I took one look at this big boy and saw my Reggie in his eyes."

"But you didn't tell the committee?"

"I was afraid I'd be dropped if I gave them the news. That's why I didn't bring him yesterday. I figured if I'd already had a fitting and worked with the designer for a day, I'd be safe. They'd never ask me to leave. And now that Kitty is here, it'll be so much easier. Lilah was a bitch, plain and simple, but Kitty—" She sniffed. "I just couldn't leave my new baby home alone again. Ranger's such a good boy." She gave her four-legged pal a wobbly grin and the dog licked her face. "I can leave him here, can't I? He won't make trouble. I promise."

Ellie frowned. "But I don't think he'll fit in the pen. And I don't have large biscuits or—"

"I brought everything you'll need." She picked up her tote and dug inside, then passed Ellie a plastic bag filled with king-sized treats. "See, here it is." She blinked her green eyes. "If you want extra, I'll pay whatever you ask. It's too late for me to bring him home. I have a fitting for Max Azria in—in—" She focused on her watch. "Twenty minutes, and I'm nowhere near ready."

A man—the evil Reynoldo?—strode through the crowd, shouting, "Cassandra? Cassandra McQuagge? Where are you? We're not finished!" Spotting her, he boomed out an order. "Get your bony ass in that chair or I'll see to it you're dropped from the list."

Swallowing a sob, Cassandra stood. "I'll be back in two hours." She hugged the Greyhound, then raced after the dreaded Reynoldo without a backward glance.

"Are we really gonna watch that retired racehorse?"

asked Rudy from his mat. He gave Ranger a once-over. *"He'll squash us like bugs if he comes in here."*

Ellie had already walked a Ranger, but he was a hypochondriac miniature Poodle who mimicked his opera-star owner's every ailment. This dog was much larger, but he seemed calmer and easier to control.

"I'll keep him under the table," she said. Crawling underneath, she moved a few of the bottled water and energy drink cases. Then she pulled a throw from her bag and made the dog a bed. Backing out on her hands and knees, she stopped to rub Ranger between the ears, then stood and pointed to the throw. "Think you can stay on that for the next couple of hours, big boy?"

The Greyhound sneezed slobber over her shoes and gave a pathetic-sounding whimper, but he did as he was told. Then, as if answering, he curled into a ball and tucked his nose between his rear legs.

"See," she told Rudy. "He won't be one bit of trouble. If only I had a—" She saw Vaughn in the distance, talking on his cell phone, and hoped whatever news he was receiving would send him on a different course. But she didn't get her wish, because he closed the phone and headed her way.

She blew out a breath as he neared. "Detective? Something more I can do for you?"

He skipped the formalities, continuing as if he'd never left her. "Did you see everyone who received one of those swag bags yesterday morning? And who dealt them out?"

"Mr. King was the one who handed them out to the models, designers, and myself."

"Can you tell me what they contained?"

"Freebies. You know, merchandise companies use to promote their line of clothing, jewelry, handbags, that sort of thing."

"What about perfume?"

Ellie thought quickly before answering. Yes, there was perfume. Hers had been labeled Spring, and Lilah's had been Summer. They'd sat side by side and applied the waxy strips together.

"Is your bag here?" he asked, after she told him what had happened between her and Lilah.

"My bag? Why no, I took it home last night, and I assume everyone else did the same with theirs."

"Were all the bags identical—filled with the same stuff?"

She racked her brain, remembering her exchange with Lilah as they'd checked their baskets. "I think so, but I only saw what was in Lilah's because we were sitting side by side. Everything looked identical—except for the perfume."

"And you didn't see what happened to her gift bag?" he asked her again.

"I've already told you no. I have no idea where it went." Was he accusing her of stealing Lilah's swag bag? "Like I said yesterday, I dropped her bag when I brought it onstage and used the pen. As for the swag bag, I just assumed someone from the forensic crew eventually found it and tagged it as evidence."

"I wish that was the case, but—" Vaughn tugged on his lower lip, as if pondering her answer. "Did you see anyone carry out two of those bags, or spot someone taking a bag they shouldn't have?"

"If you'll remember, things were a little panicked around here after Lilah died. People scattered, even though Mr. Jager told them to stay in place. Some of the models raced back here, collected their things, and took off. The others snacked on food, or just took a breather because they knew the police would be called."

She raised her eyes and locked gazes with Rudy.

"Don't you get it, Triple E? He's tryin' to clue you in. The peanut stuff was in that bag."

As soon as she heard him, the words sunk in. Each bag had a booklet of Forever strips, with a scent chosen especially for the recipient. The perfume melted into the wearer's skin, and its scent lasted for hours. Plenty of time for the peanut oil, or whatever it was, to sink in and do its dirty work.

"It was the perfume strip, wasn't it?" she asked him. "That's how Lilah came in contact with peanuts. Someone dipped her strips into peanut oil, or something like it. When she put the strip on, it—"

Detective Vaughn held up a hand. "Right now, that's merely speculation. The ME is still running tests to find out what the compound is. We'll know more by the end of the day." He cleared his throat. "But I do have a two-part favor."

"From me?" His request was a first, and she wanted to be sure she got it right.

He smiled, and she realized Newton Vaughn was a nice guy. "If you don't mind. I need an exact duplicate of that bag, and you've told me that, except for the perfume strips, yours and the deceased's were identical." He cleared his throat. "I can't go to Nola Morgan Design for a bag, because I don't know if I can trust whoever would put it together."

"Jeffery King would be the person to—"

He held up a hand. "Like I said, I don't know who at Nola Morgan Design can be trusted, and since I believe you're an innocent observer, and you know how we work, I'd like to examine yours."

Ellie thought about her swag bag and what was left after Viv had gone through it. "I can pull some strings to get mine here, but it might take a while. I really think it would be faster if you asked Mr. King."

"That's the second part of the favor," Vaughn said, lowering his voice. "I don't want Jeffery King or anyone else to know we're examining the bags. If you see him, don't mention it. Just tell him I'm looking for him."

Chapter 4

Ellie decided to phone Vivian. Her best friend worked on Wall Street, but her schedule was flexible and she could take time off during the day for a variety of reasons. If she had a free morning, she could laze in bed. If her afternoon luncheon appointment was over, she could shop. Some days she had a dozen meetings, other days not so many. As long as her projects were finished, she could do whatever she wanted.

Sitting on a chair next to the water cooler, Ellie snapped open her phone and made the call. "Hey, Viv, it's me. Do you have a couple of minutes?"

"For you? Of course I do. What's up?"

"Remember the swag bag we went through last night, the one with the Bottega Veneta handbag?"

"Yep, and thanks again for the goodies. What's the favor?"

"I need the bag, including the stuff I gave you. Can you go to my apartment and collect it? It's on the kitchen counter, exactly where I left it before going to bed."

Silence on the other end of the line told Ellie Viv's wheels were turning.

"Are they asking you to give it back? Because I really like that handbag."

"Not for good. But the police want to look through one that's intact and holds the same stuff as Lilah Perry's. And since she and I compared bags yesterday, except for the perfume, I know ours were identical."

"So I'd get the Bottega Veneta back in a couple of days?"

Ellie breathed out a laugh. "Of course you'll get it back, but I can't promise when, especially if it's being confiscated as evidence. And if that's the case, I'll ask Jeffery King to hook me up with another one. I don't see why he'll say no if I tell him the cops took it."

"Really?"

"Really."

"All right, give me a minute." The pages turned in Viv's appointment book. Then she said, "I have a ten o'clock that should last about an hour. After I finish, I'll go to your place and gather things up, then get down to the Fashion Center around one. I don't have anyone else coming in until five for a dinner meeting."

"One o'clock is good, but don't rush. Detective Vaughn didn't say it was urgent or anything. He just wants to take a look, and apparently Lilah's is gone."

"Gone? Like disappeared?"

Viv could be trusted. She'd never repeat a secret if she was told it had to do with a case. "Keep it to yourself, but it's gone, though they have her personal tote. Vaughn thinks the killer took it because he or she didn't want the police to know how Lilah came into contact with peanuts."

"What! Wait a second. I don't remember seeing peanuts in your bag."

"Not real peanuts—something *like* peanuts."

"*Like peanuts?* Is this a game, like find the item that's a peanut but isn't a peanut?"

Ellie sighed. "I'll explain when you get here. Just bring the bag and make sure everything is in it, okay?"

"Okay, fine. So where do I meet you?"

She gave Viv directions to the rear door she used to take the dogs out. There was no security guard, so Viv could enter without an ID or pass, and she'd be right at the site instead of walking the fashion gauntlet. Knowing Vivian, if she entered through the main door, she'd get so distracted by the hair, makeup, and clothing circus going on around her, she'd never find her way to the dog pen.

After tucking her phone back in her bag, Ellie slumped in her chair to think. As usual, it appeared that her four-legged buddy was right. No matter how hard she tried to mind her own business, something always seemed to find her. She hadn't done a thing to encourage it, yet her gift bag would become part of the investigation, and Vaughn was already using her as his inside informant.

"*Er—your charges need a quick outside, Triple E,*" came a familiar voice from down below. "*A couple of 'em are lockin' their rear legs together, me included.*"

Standing, she slipped on her jacket, and collected leashes. "We'll go," she told Rudy, "but with eight of you and a Greyhound, it will have to be in two shifts." She scanned the canines. "Okay, paws up if you need to go outside right away."

Muffin, a Yorkie, and Kiki, a French bulldog, and Jojo and Klingon, the mini Schnauzers, all barked a "yes" so they were first out of the pen. Just then, Patti Fallgrave sidled over dressed in a red kimono-like gown, and Ellie decided to take advantage of her visit. "Please tell me you have some free time."

"I can spare about fifteen minutes; then I'm due at a styling station," she answered, pointing to her wrapped-in-rollers hair. "According to Karen Hood, I'm being completely transformed for my next trip on the catwalk."

Ellie decided she had to meet this Karen person, who seemed to be the hairstylist of the moment. Since everyone wanted the woman to do their hair, she was super-curious. Filing the task away for later, she said, "I guess you heard, Kitty's the new competitor for the NMD contest."

"The news is out, and I think it's great for her, but not everyone agrees. There's a ton of gossip going around about who killed Lilah and why, and she and her brother are at the top of the list. Worse, you lost your assistant, but I'll find someone else by this afternoon, I promise."

Ellie figured anyone with a brain would accuse Jeffery King eventually, but Kitty? "Talking that way about Kitty is ridiculous; her brother, too."

She crossed mental fingers over her last pronouncement. She'd heard a lot of stories about brothers who did everything and anything to right a wrong someone had committed against their sister.

"And losing Kitty is why I need you now. Keep an eye on the dogs and the table until I get these guys out and back. I have to do it in two trips. Is that okay with you?"

Patti took a seat and nodded. "Fine. I'll be here. Just hurry up."

Ellie stepped out the door and took a deep breath of the fresh autumn air. She hadn't realized until she was released yesterday how cloying the scents of cosmetics, hairspray, perfume, and whatever else was used to put the shows together were. Not only did the stuff smell—each fabric seemed to carry an odor, as did the models.

Many were doused in cologne, but a few others had plain old BO, and there was no way she could bring that up with them.

The dogs were quick with their business, so she returned inside, where she found Patti deep in conversation with Jeffery King. "Here she is now," said Patti, smiling. "Ellie, Jeffery needs to talk with you."

"But I don't want to get in the way of your canine duties," he told her. "Though I do have to ask, who owns the Greyhound?"

While he talked, Ellie unleashed the first round of dogs and clipped up group two, which included her boy. She wanted to ask Jeff about the swag bags, and Rudy's observations were always helpful.

"One more out," she said to Patti. "How about you come with me, Jeff? We can talk while we walk. It should save some time."

He followed her and opened the door. Again in the fresh air, Ellie took another deep breath and guided the dogs down to the grass. "This part of the job is really the best for me. I'm not sure I can take much more of the craziness inside."

Dressed in a beautifully cut suit, matching shirt and tie, and Testoni shoes, Jeffery King could have been a model himself. "Here, give me the big guy."

He held out his hand and she passed him Ranger's lead. "Maybe you didn't hear me. The first thing I need to know is who owns this Greyhound?"

"Cassandra McQuagge, one of the plus-sized models," she told him, waiting for her crew to take care of business. "Apparently he's a rescue she found to replace the dog she had to put down last week."

His expression grew grim. "Did she say anything about her contract? Because the models who signed on for this contest were told their dogs had to be small—no more than fifteen pounds. I'll have to look up the agreement, but I think Cassandra said her dog was eight pounds, and that sure isn't this boy."

Worried that Cassandra might be in trouble, Ellie used her pickup bags to take care of the dog droppings while she thought. "I don't believe she lied when she signed the contract. It sounded as if losing her own little pal was a surprise. Besides, I didn't think policing the models was a part of my job."

Jeffery straightened his red-and-tan striped tie with his free hand. "NMD made this entire contest my responsibility, and I have to ask. Since I contracted the models, I'll be the one in trouble if the rules aren't followed, but don't worry. I'll find her and we'll discuss it." Glancing down at the dogs, he cleared his throat. "I just needed to ask you something."

"Sure, go ahead."

"I figure by now you've learned that this business lives on gossip, and I assume that since you're the one keeping an eye on the snack table you hear it all."

"Sometimes, but I do spend a lot of time talking to the dogs. They miss their caretakers and this place is crazy loud. Plus the wild smells make them nutty."

"Stop right there, Triple E, or you'll be in trouble."

"Talking to the dogs? You mean giving them treats, taking them out, correct?"

Smiling, she glanced at Rudy. She could get out of this one on her own. "I do all that, yes, but I talk to them, too. It makes them more comfortable when I treat them like their owners do."

"Ah, I see." He put his hands in his pockets. "Back to the gossip. Have you heard anyone talking about Kitty and how she got into the competition? Or the argument I had with Lilah a few weeks ago?"

"Argument?" asked Ellie, playing dumb, something she did really well.

"Kitty said she told you about the fight Lilah and I had after I realized she'd stolen Kitty's designs."

Which meant he had to know how bad it looked that Kitty was the one taking Lilah's place, especially since he'd accused Lilah of thievery.

"Oh, that argument. Sure, Kitty told me about it, but it didn't sound bad to me. And I almost forgot. Detective Vaughn asked me to give you a message. He wants to talk with you again, so please find him," she said, gauging his reaction.

Jeffery's eyes narrowed. "Did he say what he wanted?"

"Uh-oh," said Rudy. *"I think you pushed the wrong button."*

"Um, not exactly. Just something to do with the gift bags."

"What does he want to know?" His nostrils flared. "Did he hear about Kitty's promotion?"

"Yes, he knows about Kitty taking Lilah's place in the competition."

After muttering a curse, he heaved a sigh. "What do you think I should do?"

Ellie swallowed a gasp of surprise. It was clear that Jeffery King *did* know something was up with Detective Vaughn, but why did he care about her opinion? "You're asking me? I'm a professional dog walker, not an attorney or a—"

"Do you think I need a lawyer?" The words rushed out as he began to pace, dragging Ranger along behind him. "Damn, I knew this was going to happen."

"You knew *what* was going to happen?" she asked him. *And why?* She grabbed the Greyhound's leash. "I'm sure it's just more routine questioning. That's what the cops do when they investigate a murder."

He swung around to face her. "Then they do think Lilah was murdered?"

She held back a groan of frustration. How much could she tell him before she broke her promise to Vaughn? "Her EpiPen turned up empty, Jeffery, and since that's something Lilah would never let happen, well, it's fairly damning evidence. Since you were a part of the committee that chose her as a competitor—"

"I excused myself from the selection committee as soon as I figured out that Lilah stole my sister's work."

"Kitty mentioned it, but still . . ."

He ran his fingers through his hair, much like his sister did when she was upset. "I know we just met, but Kitty told me she heard from Patti that you have some experience with episodes like this."

"Episodes? I'm not sure what you mean."

Before he could answer, Patti stuck her head out the door. "Ellie, my time is up. I've got to run. I'll talk to you later."

Ellie straightened her shoulders. "We have to go in. I'm shorthanded and I need to be with the dogs." She hurried her charges inside, with Jeffery and Ranger following behind. "If you want to talk about this, you'll have to hang with me, but I think that, for your sake, you need to find Vaughn first."

"I can't believe anyone would murder Lilah. Want her dead, sure," said Cassandra McQuagge. "Marcus, Claire—even I wished she was gone from the planet a couple dozen times, but I didn't hate her enough to actually do the deed."

Ellie eavesdropped on Yasmine and Cassandra, the two women who'd modeled Lilah's creations yesterday, as they picked through the hospitality table's offerings on their break. Was it Marcus David they were talking about?

"What's so odd is that Lilah seemed to do a complete turnaround when she entered this contest. The designs she submitted were nothing like her usual tough-edged work," Dominique added. "Which only backs up Jeffery's accusation. She stole Kitty King's designs and called them her own. I just hope Kitty's new pieces are as good."

"So who do you think managed to get her close to a peanut?" asked a third woman, African-American and beautiful, who went by the single name of Lawan.

"I have no idea, but whoever did it, well . . . they have my congratulations," said Dominique. "I just hope Kitty will create the same fabulous styles and finish them by four o'clock."

Ellie glanced at her watch. It was close to one and Viv was due any second. She'd probably think listening to these women gossip was a wonderful experience. And it was, if you liked the dirt on the street.

"I hear she slept with someone on the committee, just so she'd get chosen," Lawan continued. "Maybe he's the one they should look for as the killer."

"I think they're going to go after Jeffery King," said Dominique. "He and Lilah never got along. They got into a huge argument when he accused her of submitting designs created by his sister."

"I heard about the fight, too." Lawan started peeling an orange. "He pulled out of the selection committee right after he confronted her."

"Maybe so, but isn't it strange that his sister now has Lilah's spot? Makes you wonder if he wasn't the one who found a way to get Lilah close to her allergen, then *bam!*" Dominique smacked her right fist into her other palm. "She's having an attack and her pen is conveniently empty."

Ellie swallowed a protest. She assumed Detective

Vaughn was already on this same track. He didn't need to hear it from the models.

Cassandra, dressed in nothing but a sheer robe, took a seat, opened an energy bar, and gave the first bite to her Greyhound. "Jeffery wants to throw Ranger out of the competition. He says he'll find me a little dog to use as my companion, but that's not going to fly." She gave her boy a hug. "No one is going to kick my baby out of the running."

The models, all in various stages of undress, started throwing out ideas about a dog Cassandra could use. Ellie wanted to chime in. The girl had to have a friend that owned a small dog. If Cassandra had signed a contract that said "a dog under fifteen pounds" she was in trouble unless she complied. As far as Ellie was concerned, a contract was a written handshake, and NMD had the right to demand she stick to the deal or they'd use another model.

Fingering Jeffery King for the murder was another matter. Didn't the women realize that the more they spread the word, the more the cops would listen?

Kitty took that moment to walk on the scene, and the topic of conversation automatically switched channels. Carrying an armful of fabric, she grinned at her supermodel. "Yasmine, I need you to try on my creation for evening wear. Do you have time or are you working for another house this afternoon?"

"I have a couple of minutes; then I'm due at Karen Hood's station. How about holding up the gown and giving us all a peek."

Kitty rolled her eyes. "You're kidding, right? I'd have to stand on a chair to get it up off the floor. How about you help me," she asked Ellie, shooting her a grin.

"Uh, me? Okay sure." Standing, Ellie took the dress

Kitty passed her and raised it to her chest. When the material, a soft silky weave, slipped from her fingers, the models gasped.

"Wow, that's beautiful," declared Yasmine. "I'm gonna look like a million bucks in it."

"I'd kill to wear it," Cassandra muttered.

Another tall, thin model said, "Where did you get the idea for that?"

The crowd murmured their approval, which encouraged Yasmine, in typical model fashion, to slip off her robe and shimmy the gown over her head. That's when the dress transformed from a lovely piece of cloth to a work of art. It had no shoulder straps, just a bodice dusted with pale pink feathers that ran down over the bust to a high, fitted waist that dropped to the floor in a fall of pink mixed with shades of purple and every color in between.

A few inches shorter than Yasmine, blond-haired and blue-eyed Cassandra swooned. "Oh, my God, I'm going to look like royalty." She arched a brow and stared at Kitty. "Mine is exactly the same as this one, right?"

"Almost. Not as long, of course, and the belt is a bit wider, but that's it."

Yasmine twirled and the girls grabbed at the fabric, letting it slip through their fingers and gushing over its lush feel. While they muttered comments, Kitty turned to Ellie.

"Looks like I did good on this one, huh?"

"I'll say," said Ellie. "Now what else do you have?"

"The outfit I'm using to replace Lilah's from yesterday." She held up a one-piece jumpsuit in cream wool with rust-colored buttons, a wide rust suede belt, and matching collar and cuffs. "What do you think?"

"I love it," said Ellie, imagining herself dressed in it. "The color coordination is perfect."

"I'm glad you like it. I made it with you in mind."

"Me? But why?"

"Marcus David was right yesterday when he was arguing with Lilah. You could be a model like Cassandra or Claire Smith, so I imagined you wearing it while I drew the design."

Ellie admired the line of the fabric and the slash-cut pockets trimmed in the same rust suede. If this ever came to a ready-to-wear store, she would buy it, no matter the cost.

"That is an incredible piece."

Ellie heard a voice coming from behind her and turned.

"You're here. I'm glad you found your way over."

"Are you kidding?" said Viv. "I wouldn't miss this chance for the world." She handed Ellie the swag bag. "And here's what you asked for."

Ellie took the basket and set it on a chair. "Kitty, this is my best friend, Vivian. Viv, this is Kitty King, one of the participants in the Nola Morgan Design contest."

The women shook hands, and Viv asked, "Is that one of your creations?"

Though focused on the swag bag, Kitty heard the question. "It is. Do you like it?"

"It's beautiful," said Viv. She followed the designer's gaze. "Oh, that's just something Ellie asked me to drop off."

Kitty glanced at Ellie. "I hate to be nosy, but is there a reason you need the gift bag here today?"

"Ah, sort of."

"You're a terrible liar, Triple E. Might as well tell her the truth."

"I mean, yes, someone needed to see it." Ellie figured she could get away with a lie within a truth. She grabbed

Viv's hand. "Come on. Let me introduce you to the models."

While they'd been chatting, a few more of the NMD girls had shown up, and they were still admiring Kitty's feathered dress. Ellie made introductions while Yasmine stepped out of the dress and returned it to Kitty.

"My designer is Marcus David, and I haven't seen his evening wear yet," said Claire. "My guess is it'll be some kind of tribute to his younger sister. She died a year ago, and it took him a while to get back to work on his designs."

The sentence made Ellie think about what Kitty had just told her. Other artists, like painters and sculptors, sometimes had a person in mind when they did their work, so why not a designer?

Since Viv fit right in with the cluster of models, Ellie pulled her old assistant aside. "Is something bothering you about the swag bag?"

Kitty folded the dress and jumpsuit carefully over her arm. "Not exactly. I heard a rumor, is all, and I'm worried."

"Care to tell me what the rumor was about?"

"About my brother. Word is going around that he's the one who did Lilah in, and it was all because of me. They're saying he somehow found a way to put peanuts in her bag and contaminate whatever she touched. Then I heard the cops were trying to find her bag, and it was missing. Now yours is here and—"

"You're worried there might have been something in it? Something Jeffery didn't tell you about?" Ellie raised an eyebrow. "Do you really think your brother would stoop that low, would kill someone so you could compete in this contest?"

Kitty dropped to a chair, the clothes folding into

her lap. "I don't want to believe it, but I know he hated Lilah for what she did to me. Whoever killed her was calculating, and I cannot see my brother in that light."

Rudy walked over and nudged her hand up, then stuck his head under her palm. She smiled and scratched his ears. "You're so lucky you have this little guy." Kitty sniffed back a tear. "I know you love him, and I love my brother. He's all I have in my life. If anything happened to him, I don't know what I'd do."

"I wouldn't worry about it. If you don't think he did it, I'm sure he didn't. Besides, I agree with you. He doesn't seem the type. I mean, whoever did it had to make sure Lilah came in contact with the allergen; then they had to empty her EpiPen. That would take a lot of planning, and I don't see your brother being such a psycho."

"He isn't," Kitty whispered. "It's just that the rumors are hard to take. That's why I put my all into these designs. So people would say I got here on my own merit, and not because my brother killed someone to get me in."

Over the past few minutes, the group of models had scattered. Viv took a chair next to Ellie and sighed. "I could sit here all day. I'd watch the models, the makeup artists—" The hairstylist with the red Mohawk sauntered by. "Even guys like him. I bet he'd be fun to joke with. And I bet he could show me how to do a better job of putting on my eyeliner at the same time."

Glancing in the distance, Kitty sat up straight in her chair, which made Ellie and Viv pay attention, too. Detective Vaughn was approaching with Jeffery King, who was flanked by two uniformed police officers.

As they neared, Ellie could tell that Jeffery's arms

were behind his back, a sure sign of handcuffs. Vaughn stopped in front of them, his face set in a frown. "I wouldn't normally do this, Ms. King, but your brother begged me to find you. I'm here to tell you that he's under arrest for the murder of Lilah Perry."

Chapter 5

"Wait, no!" Kitty raised her hand, but it was too late. Detective Vaughn, Jeffery, and the officers disappeared around the corner that led to the door Ellie used to take out her charges. More tears sprang to Kitty's eyes as she sobbed out a weak farewell.

Viv sat upright, her mouth open, her eyes wide.

Kitty gasped, then fell into a deflated heap.

Ellie raced after the police brigade and caught up with Vaughn at the rear door. "Really, Detective, are you sure about this? My swag bag is here. Maybe you could find something in it that would—"

"Incriminate Mr. King further?" His gray eyes darkened to pewter. "We have a close-to-airtight case, Ms. Engleman, so there's no need to examine a bag that merely resembled the bag of the deceased, though I'm sure Ms. Perry's will turn up somewhere." He narrowed his gaze. "Mr. King will be booked on Green Street. Thanks for being so cooperative. We're through for now."

Ellie raced back inside, hoping to calm Kitty. When

she arrived at the dog pen she found Viv tugging on the newly designed clothes that were crushed in Kitty's lap.

Viv stood and shook out the wrinkles, then draped the garments over the water cooler. "No matter how miserable Kitty is, these creations are part of the biggest event in her life. She shouldn't ruin them, even for her brother."

Realizing Viv was correct, Ellie nodded. When Viv scanned the area, she asked, "What are you looking for?"

"Something to hang these on. You take care of Kitty. I'll be back."

Kitty continued to sob, and Ellie had no idea what she should say or do. She felt like a traitor. She'd suspected the arrest was coming. Vaughn had given her enough of a heads up, and she'd spoken to Jeffery, too. But she had no business messing around in this investigation. She didn't know either of the Kings well enough to stick her nose in their lives, especially when she had promised Sam she would steer clear of any and all things criminal.

She searched her tote bag and passed Kitty a tissue.

The girl blew her nose. "I heard the detective mention Green Street. Do you know where that is?"

"Downtown somewhere, where they take most people who are arrested. They get booked, fingerprinted, that sort of thing." She realized the description sounded harsh, and tried to soften the words. "It's not a big deal."

The designer inhaled a gasp. "Oh, Lord. I don't know what to do. Jeffery is all I have in the world." She dabbed her watery eyes. "We've got to help him."

Ignoring Kitty's last sentence, Ellie checked her watch. "It's close to two. How far along are you in finishing your pieces?"

"I don't know. I can't think." She shuddered, holding

back her tears. "Jeffery will need a lawyer, right? Someone to bail him out of this mess."

"If he doesn't have a lawyer, the court will appoint one. Attorneys cost big bucks in this city, especially when they're representing someone accused of murder."

The words set off another round of Kitty's tears. Rudy put a paw on her knee, so Ellie wrapped an arm around her shoulders and squeezed. "Hey, it's gonna be okay, really. You said Jeffery was innocent, so things will work out."

"You've been involved in this kind of thing before. Patti said you live with a homicide detective. Can you maybe recommend a lawyer? Someone you know who can get him out on bail?"

"Think before you open your mouth, Triple E," said her boy. *"I smell trouble rollin' our way."*

Ellie heaved a breath. Rudy was right. She had to tread carefully or she'd be up to her eyebrows in murder . . . again. Joe's uncle, Sal Cantiglia, was capable enough to handle the small stuff. And her stepfather still had enough connections from his time on the bench to recommend someone, but her mother would skin her alive if she knew her daughter had gotten the older judge involved.

When she drummed her fingers on the chair back, an idea struck. "The only attorney I can think of is a guy called Keller Williams. He represented a friend of mine last February, and things turned out in his favor." She didn't know Mr. Williams personally, but Rob could probably relay the message and get the man to at least take care of Jeffery's arraignment. It couldn't hurt to get things moving in the right direction.

"I could put you in touch with a customer of mine named Rob Chesney, and maybe he could contact his attorney."

Kitty's lower lip quivered. "Would you please?"

She found her cell phone and flipped it open. Rob picked up on the third ring. After the pleasantries were over, she steered the conversation around to Keller Williams. "Would you call him for me, and help pave the way for Kitty?"

When he answered yes, she said, "That would be great. Here, I'll let you speak with her. She'll give you the details."

Ten minutes later, things were under control. Kitty passed the phone back to Ellie. "Rob seems like a nice guy. I think I remember reading about him in the newspaper. He said you were the one who proved him innocent. He claims you saved his life."

"Uh-oh," said Rudy, still sitting with his paw on Kitty's knee. *"Leave it to Bobbi-Rob to dig the hole deeper."*

She ignored her boy and continued doing as much for Kitty as she felt she could, without actually getting involved. "He's just saying that. It really wasn't much."

"But Patti told me the same thing. About how you've helped a lot of people who were accused of murder and were innocent. She said you found the real killers."

"She makes it sound like we got nothin' better to do than go on a psycho search."

Ellie frowned in Rudy's direction and explained. "It isn't quite like that. I'm not a private investigator. I don't have a license, or a badge, or a gun or anything. Sometimes I get lucky and figure things out on my own."

It was then Viv appeared with a couple of padded hangers in hand. "Good Lord, these people are ridiculous. You'd think hangers, especially the plush kind, were made of gold." She picked up the jumpsuit and arranged it on the first hanger. "Now what am I supposed to do with this beautiful baby?" she asked, holding up the feathered evening gown.

Kitty swiped the tissue under her eyes, smearing mascara over her reddened cheeks. "I have to sew on the strings so we can secure it to the hanger. I'll bring it to my station."

She stood and Ellie gave a discreet nod.

"I've got an idea." Viv held both creations high. "I have a little extra time. How about if I carry these for you, and lend you a hand getting settled?"

"Oh, gosh. Would you? That would be great." Kitty managed a timid smile as she stood. "Ellie, thanks again for the lawyer thing." She gazed at Viv. "This should only take about fifteen minutes."

The two women left, walking side by side. Kitty was so petite she didn't even come up to Viv's shoulder, but they looked like a team. Ellie heaved a sigh. "That takes care of that," she told Rudy. "Once Kitty gets busy, she won't have time to pester me, and Rob will get Keller Williams to help Jeffery. This event will be over in a couple more days. Then we're out of here."

Rudy jumped on the chair next to her. *"Can I get a word in edgewise, please?"*

"Not if it's a lawyer joke."

"Nah, not one of those. It's just that Kitty's a nice girl, and Jeffery seemed like an okay human, too."

She ruffled his ears. "I agree. And Mr. Williams is a professional. He'll do right by them."

"So you're not curious?"

"Curious?"

He cocked his head and broke out in a doggie grin.

"Oh, no. Nuh-uh. Do not even think about getting me involved. I don't have the time, and neither do you."

He put both paws on her chest and gave her cheek a sloppy lick. *"Aw, come on. This one isn't like the others. There's no poison, no scissors, no gun, not even a handheld battery charger. The victim was killed by a peanut.*

Detective Demento can't say we'd be in danger from a peanut."

"But Sam would complain about me sticking my nose in police business. After our adventure in the Hamptons, he asked me to control my urge to snoop, and I told him I would try."

His next lick hit her chin. *"You said 'try,' and that's the magic word. You're tryin' now, and I'm encouraging. It's not your fault. It's mine."*

"Somehow, I don't think that will fly with Sam." She glanced at her gift basket, sitting on the edge of the snack table. "But I would like to know how the killer did it. And since it seemed so important to Detective Vaughn . . ." She grabbed the bag and started digging, placing each item on the chair next to her. "I know this bag is mine, not Lilah's, but maybe something will give me a clue."

She raised the scarf to her nose and sniffed. "No scent here." She pulled out a pair of red suede gloves and held them to her nose. "Hmm, nothing smells as good as real leather." She peeked at the designer label. "And they're outrageously expensive. Lucky for me Viv already has two pair, or she'd snap them up."

Rudy nosed each item after she did. *"I'm double-checkin'. You humans don't have the same sniffin' power we do."* Then he reared his head. *"But I'm confused. Why are we smellin' your stuff, when it was that designer's bag that held the peanut juice?"*

Ellie shrugged. "I guess it's a dumb idea. Lilah and I compared baskets, so I was hoping something she had could have rubbed off on my stuff." She passed him a pair of Dolce & Gabbana sunglasses, a tan clutch from Tod's, a three-pack of Tom Ford lipsticks that normally rang up at forty-five dollars a tube. Then came a real prize: Viv's mustard-colored hobo bag from Bottega Veneta.

Now at the bottom of the basket, she pulled out her package of Forever, and held the thin strips of a scent titled Spring. After again smelling a page, she pulled off a strip and stuck it under her pale blue sweater between her breasts.

Then she held the packet up to Rudy. "Take a whiff of this and tell me what you think."

He cranked out a huge canine sniff and sneezed, smattering her with dog spit. "Thanks a lot," she muttered, brushing off the droplets. "Do you think a peanut scent could be hidden in something like this?"

"Maybe yes, maybe no. You did say Lilah's perfume was stronger than yours."

She recalled sitting next to Lilah as Lilah secured her own strip of perfume entitled Summer. Her scent had notes of lavender and verbena, too overpowering for Ellie's taste. Finally, it all made sense.

"Duh! I just figured it out. I bet the killer somehow soaked Lilah's strips in peanut oil. She couldn't smell it, so she put a strip on, and bingo—ten minutes later she had the attack. If she'd waited until she was home to use a strip, there wouldn't have been a thing she could do, even if she reached her empty EpiPen."

Rudy took another strip sniff. *"Hmm, that might fly, but it's a sneaky thing to do. The killer had to plan it all out and not get caught messin' with those strips or her pen thingy."* He sneezed again. *"Would the strip have to be soaked in oil, or would a single drop do?"*

"That's a good question." She began loading the goodies into her bag "I'll see what I can find out tonight on the Internet."

"I did tell you these people were crazy, didn't I?" said Viv later that afternoon, when she took a seat next to Ellie on one of the chairs.

Ellie cracked a smile. "Yes, you did. So what happened to reinforce your decision?"

Viv crossed her long legs. "First off, Kitty's models. They're two of the most self-absorbed women I've ever met. That Cassandra person? All she could talk about was her dog. The one that died." She sneaked a peak around Ellie and stared at the sleeping Greyhound. "I assume that's Ranger, the pet that's got her so worried?"

"Do you see another three-foot-tall canine here? Yes, that's him, and he's a sweetheart. Quiet, easy to get along with, a real peaceful guy. Trouble is, Cassandra signed a contract and in it she promised she'd bring a small dog to this event. Something Ranger clearly isn't."

"She's looking for a way to convince Nola Morgan Design that her boy can do the job, but now that Jeffery King is in jail, I'm not sure who she'll talk to." Viv stretched her arms over her head. "Then, when Yasmine didn't show to try on the jumpsuit because she was on the runway with another designer, Kitty talked me into being her model. I said yes, thinking she'd take me into one of the changing rooms, but did she?" Viv shook her head so hard her fall of straight and shiny mink brown hair hid her face. "No-ooo. She had me strip right there in front of everybody."

Ellie laughed out loud. She'd watched the behind-the-scenes action for two days now. Models ignored whoever was around and seemed to have no problem standing nearly naked for the entire event. "Oh, Lord, why didn't you call me? I'd have given a thousand dollars to see the look on your face."

"Yeah, well, it wasn't so bad once we got started. But it's a good thing I wore a matching bra and panties, because Kitty stripped off my Donna Karan suit before I could say a word. People walked by and stared as if I was made out of plastic. Then some short bald guy wearing a weird pair of shoes stopped and watched the rest of the fitting. He even took out a notebook and scribbled something before he sauntered away."

"Who was it?"

"I have no idea." Viv sniffed. "And apparently, they expect all the tall models to be the same size. I'm a four, but I'm not stick thin, so Kitty had to let out the bust, but the rest of it was okay. It gave her one less thing to worry about. Both of the day wear items are finished, and I left her fitting a whining Cassandra into her evening wear."

Ellie could have sat and people-watched with her best friend for the rest of the afternoon, but she knew it was getting late. "Don't you have to be somewhere right now?"

Viv looked at her watch and jumped to her feet. "Yikes! I have thirty minutes to prepare for my five o'clock. I gotta run."

"And I have to take the dogs out, so I'll follow you. The second showing will start soon." Ellie took half the group, with Rudy in the lead, and went to the rear door. "Will I see you tonight?"

"I don't think so. It's a dinner meeting, and those can drag on and on. At least we're going to a trendy new place. I'll let you know how it is, and we can talk Dave and Sam into taking us out one night next week."

Ellie waved a good-bye, then, standing on the grass, let her charges sniff and explore. The day had been eventful, and she hadn't paid them as much attention as she should.

"Earth to Ellie," came a voice from below.

She locked eyes with her boy. "Yes?"

"I got a bad feelin' about all this. If Jeffery didn't kill Lilah, who did? And why?"

"I don't know who, but the why is fairly obvious. Lilah was rude and pushy, and she was a thief. She must

have offended someone so badly they wanted her dead."
She rubbed her nose while she thought. "The part that
I'm really curious about is how someone did it. If the
peanut oil was on Lilah's perfume strips, well, that was
genius. Imagine finding a way to get hold of those strips,
put on the oil, and get the strips back in her gift bag
without anyone noticing. I can see why the cops think
it's Jeffery. He was the one in charge of the bags, and he
had a motive."

*"Yeah, but those swag bags were on the table all day. I
saw lots of people peeking inside."*

"Really? Do you remember who they were?"

He parked his bottom on the lawn and gazed up at
her. *"Marcus David, for one. He said he was a guy and he
wanted to make sure there were guy things in his bag, so
he dug in there whenever he could, but mostly when you
took the dogs out."*

"Who else?"

"That Dominique girl, and that Claire person."

"I haven't had much chance to talk to them, but they
seem to be as popular as Patti. And I did hear a couple
of the other models saying they were happy Lilah was
gone. They said—"

"Hey, Ellie. You're needed in here ASAP." Patti stuck
her head out the door. "The dogs are rioting."

"Oh, Lord, now what?" She gathered the group.
"Stick together, guys. This ought to be good."

When Ellie returned inside, she saw that Ranger had decided to get in the pen with the Yorkies and the rest of
the small dogs. He'd dragged the table from the wall and
aimed for their holding area, crowding the circle until the
little guys were in a panic. They didn't want him there, so
they were yowling up a storm. It was the first time she'd
heard all the voices talking at once.

"Hey, get back on your own side of the fence," complained a snooty French bulldog.

"He stepped on me," grumped Daisy, the white Chihuahua.

"Get a keeper, ya big bozo," said Muffin, the tiniest Yorkie.

Patti held Cheech in her arms. Small, sharp growls and barks rang out, continuing until the Greyhound let out a huge woof that ended with a shout. *"Qui-et!"*

"Okay, okay, that's enough," Ellie added, surprised the big boy would take such a stand.

Still muttering, the herd piped down, but apparently not in time. Because, in the distance, an officious-looking man dressed in a black-and-white pin-striped suit, wearing a red tie and spats, was headed their way.

"Thanks, I can take it from here," Ellie told Patti, keeping her eye on the quickly approaching observer. The supermodel passed Cheech to Ellie, while Rudy stood guard at her feet when the fellow neared.

"This racket is absolutely not allowed," the rotund man pronounced, glaring at her and the milling dogs. His face shined with sweat and his round cheeks and chin needed a shave. "Another outburst like this and you'll have to put these animals in cages."

"Who you callin' an animal?" demanded Muffin.

"We got a right to our opinion, just like you do," said a mini Schnauzer.

"Cage? Who do you think we are?" asked Daisy. *"Monkeys in the zoo?"*

While the rest of the pack continued to complain, Ellie was still trying to figure out who he was. She dropped her gaze and gave the crew a warning glance. She wanted to stay calm and polite, but where in the world did he expect her to come up with that many dog crates? Did he have any authority where she was concerned?

"I've got them quieted down now," she said as she straightened out the pen and put in the last dog. "But I do have to sort out the ones who still need a walk, so if you'll let me do my job . . ."

"I'm Clark Fettel, the new head of promotions for this contest, and my rules are now in place." The guy straightened up and stepped closer, as if demanding her cooperation. "We have to talk."

"Fine by me, Mr. Fiddle, but it'll take some time. I have work to do. Now if you'll excuse me." She opened the clips holding the pen together, hustled the group she'd taken for a walk in, and led the second group out.

"That's Fettel," the man called as they left.

Once they got outside, Rudy sniggered. *"Clark Fettel? Is he for real?"*

"Sounds like," said Ellie, letting the dogs take their frustration out on the lawn. She bent and scooped poop twice before things got a bit more under control. "It didn't take long for Nola Morgan Design to replace Jeffery, did it?"

"Just a couple of hours. And I don't like that fiddle-faddle guy. He's gonna be trouble. I feel it in my bones."

"Could be. He's not as nice as Jeffery, and doesn't seem as understanding, either. From the way he acts, I'll bet he doesn't even like dogs."

"I'm with you there."

"So we have to find a way to placate him until this event is over."

"You think he could really call off the canine part of this competition?"

"I don't see how. NMD has promoted the heck out of this show, especially the finale with the dogs dressed to match their owners. I hear there's going to be special news and television coverage, an interview with some big shot at NMD, the works." She heaved a sigh. "But even with all that, he could find a way to make our lives miserable."

"Then I say we let the blowhard blow, yes him to death, and do what we want." Rudy snorted, then scratched his back legs over the lawn, throwing up blades of grass and tiny clods of dirt. _"We're in charge here, not him."_

After gathering the pack, she opened the door. "I'll do my best to keep him off our case, but you stay quiet. I can't concentrate when I hear you giving orders in my head."

Back inside again, she spotted Mr. Fettel, hands in his jacket pockets, pacing the far perimeter as if distancing himself from the dogs. When he locked gazes with Ellie, he acted as if he wanted her to march directly to him.

"Make him work for it, Triple E," Rudy advised.

She blew out a breath. So much for her boy obeying orders, though she had to agree. This was her gig. She'd been told by Jeffery that she had the final say on anything to do with the dogs, and NMD trusted her completely. She'd already been paid her exorbitant fee, so it was too late to fire her. Besides that, she doubted they'd find someone to take over her job at this late date.

Feeling empowered by her thoughts, she took a seat and opened one of the fashion magazines she'd left on the snack table. A moment later, when she glanced at the floor, she saw shoes with spats and let her gaze wander upward.

"Can I help you?" she asked politely.

Mr. Fettel pulled his shoulders back. "What you can do is cooperate, young lady. I've been thrown into a position with which I'm uncomfortable, so please don't take advantage of me."

"Aw, he's askin' so nice," said Rudy, snorting.

She closed the magazine. "I'm sorry you're in an unappealing position right now, and here in the canine area we're very understanding. Tell me what you need and I'll try to comply."

He crossed his arms and let them rest on his paunch. "That's a little more like it."

"Hey, don't let him talk to you like that."

Biting back a snarky response, she smiled. "If you'd just get to your point . . ."

"May I sit down?"

Ellie set the magazine on the middle chair to make certain they'd be a few feet apart.

He took the far chair and straightened his tie. "We have a problem, and I'm hoping you can help."

"A problem?"

"It's about one of the models."

"One of the NMD models?"

"Yes. And I was hoping you could shed some light on the issue."

He wanted her help? Well, he certainly had an odd way of showing it. "I was hired to care for the dogs, Mr. Fettel. I don't have a thing to do with the models."

"I'm aware of that, but you were the only person I could think to ask." He cleared his throat. "If you don't mind."

Great. She'd always wanted to be someone's last choice. "I'm listening," she said instead.

"It's about Cassandra and her dog."

Ellie had figured as much.

"He has to be replaced."

She heaved a sigh. "I'm sure Cassandra knows someone who'd be happy to let her borrow their dog. Especially since the dog would be featured in an event of this magnitude."

"I've suggested as much, but she isn't willing to cooperate." He pulled a handkerchief from inside his jacket and dabbed at the sweat beading his forehead. "Her uncooperative attitude is quite disturbing."

"I don't think she's being uncooperative, exactly. She's still in mourning."

"Mourning?" His stern expression didn't change. "Who died?"

"Her other dog, a Yorkie, if I understood her correctly." And why not? Losing a four-legged buddy was like losing a dear friend or a member of your family. "She's convinced Ranger is the perfect dog to take his place, and she doesn't want to let him go."

"Ranger?" Fettel looked confused. "Who is Ranger?"

Was this guy for real? "Ranger is the Greyhound we've been discussing. She rescued him after the Yorkie died, and they've formed a bond."

"But—but that's ridiculous. She lost a dog, not a parent or sibling." He swiped the hankie over his upper lip. "No one to be depressed about."

Ellie's patience was all but gone. "That might be your take on losing a dog, but it's not Cassandra's, and I completely understand. Anyone who loves their four-legged friend loses a bit of themselves when that pet dies. They grieve, just like they would if it were a human."

He opened and closed his mouth, as if unable to form the words. Then he shook his balding head. "But we have a contract."

"I understand that, too." She hated to see Cassandra burned, but . . . "I gather you already reminded her that she can be replaced."

"Of course, but she pulled a fast one. Didn't bring him on the first day, and by the time we found out . . . well, it was too late."

Cassandra had told her the same thing, so she knew he was correct. "I'm not aware of anyone who has a canine we can borrow. And even then, you need to find a dog that Cassandra would accept as her Yorkie's replacement."

"What about these dogs?" He gestured toward the pen. "There are eight models, but ten animals. Who owns the extras?"

Ellie nodded at Rudy, who was sitting at attention and following the conversation. "The small gray and white dog is mine, and the mini Schnauzer was Lilah Perry's. Another model is taking care of him until Ms. Perry's family can be contacted."

"That little one is yours?" He narrowed his eyes. "Hmm, I see." He studied her boy for a half minute. "Is he a purebred?"

She grinned. "Rudy is all pound puppy, but they're the best. He's smart, playful, obeys commands—"

"Hey, I wouldn't go that far."

Fettel stood. "Then it's settled."

Rudy cocked his head. *"Oh, no. No, no, no, no, no."*

"Settled?" asked Ellie.

"I'm giving Ms. McQuagge an ultimatum. Either she uses your dog, or she's off the show."

Chapter 6

Ellie peeked around the curtain shading the near side of the stage about five minutes before the second competition began. The showroom was so crowded many of the attendees had to stand along the perimeter, fighting for space with members of the pushy press. And the press didn't care if they were in the way. All they wanted were photos or quotes from the big shots of the fashion world.

She knew from yesterday's contest debut that Nola Morgan Design drew important names, but the number of people attending this second review had doubled, maybe tripled in size. It was, of course, because of Lilah Perry's demise that so many people were in attendance. Though they would never admit it, she had a suspicion they'd come on the off chance there might be another murder.

She watched as the paparazzi snapped photos of anyone who appeared important. Two women sitting to the right side in the front row had to be on the A list, because the press hovered over them like flies on honey, but Ellie had no idea who they were. She had better luck recognizing Heidi Klum, Tim Gunn, Mondo Guerra, and a bevy of past *Project Runway* contestants, mainly because Rudy had forced her to watch the show's reruns after she told him about this job.

And Viv had coached her, too, encouraging her to read the weekly Style section in the *New York Times* and check out the daily advertisements for additions to the latest collections from Dolce & Gabbana, Lagerfeld, Marc Jacobs, Michael Kors, and all the other famous designers with a new line.

"See anyone interesting out there?"

Jumping, Ellie spun around and faced a grinning Marcus David. After heaving a breath, she said, "Sneak up on a person, why don't you?"

His smile widened. "Sorry, but I couldn't resist. You looked like a kid peeking down the stairs to spy on Santa Claus or maybe the Easter Bunny."

"I'm just scanning the crowd in hope of recognizing someone. My best friend is a fashion addict, and she'll expect me to name names next time we talk. Unfortunately, aside from the popular reality show participants, I don't know a single person out there."

He moved next to her, took stock of the crowd, and gave a low whistle. "Wow. The place is definitely filled with movers and shakers."

Pulling the curtain aside, she cocked her head. "Who?"

Marcus nodded. "See those two women in the center of the front row, right side of the catwalk?"

"I figured they were somebodies, but I can't place them."

"Trust me, if you were in this business you'd be in awe. The one on the left is Anna Wintour, editor in chief of American *Vogue*. Meryl Streep portrayed her in *The*

Devil Wears Prada. And to her right is Grace Coddington, their creative director. Word is they don't both
cover an event unless it's the biggest of the big." He ran
a hand over his chin. "Seeing them out there makes me
more nervous than I was yesterday."

Ellie gave his arm a playful punch. If she remembered correctly, Marcus had yet to act nervous about
anything. "Oh, come on. A big boy like you, afraid of a
couple of magazine editors?"

He stuck his hands in his pockets. "They're not just
magazine editors, they are *the* editors. And guess who's
sitting across from them."

She spotted a well-dressed man and woman chatting
with each other while they nodded at members of the
crowd. Ellie hid a smile when she realized they reminded
her of a king and queen. "I haven't a clue."

"Glenda Bailey of *Harper's* and Stefano Tonchi, the
managing editor of *W.* With them here, this competition
could only get hotter if you poured on the gasoline and
lit a match."

She recalled Vivian mentioning their names, but
never thought she'd actually see these gods of fashion in
person. "And since their seats are front and center, I
imagine whoever is running this event sat them there as
a tribute to their importance in the industry."

"*W* is the most influential fashion magazine in the
world today, so more than likely Jeffery King took care
of it, though I'm sure he got his orders from someone at
the top of NMD," Marcus said, his tone serious.

Ellie had tried her best to get a handle on the hierar-
chy of the fashion world in the week before the contest.
Having Marcus there to explain things made it easier.
She only wished he'd been around earlier, when Clark
Fettel had been badgering her about Cassandra and
Ranger.

"Where have you been, by the way?" She turned to face him. "Hard at work for the evening wear part of the competition?"

He moved so close to her she smelled his cologne, a light outdoorsy scent that made her think of pine trees. "Why? Did you miss me?"

"What? No." She took a step of retreat. "I'm just trying to figure out where people were when Jeffery King was arrested."

"Oh, that." He raised an eyebrow. "I was helping Jeffery referee a disagreement between Anton Rouch and one of his models when the cops showed. But the arrest didn't take anyone by surprise. The way I see it, King was careless and he got caught, which is probably the way everyone else felt, too."

"You think he's guilty?" Miffed that everybody would be so callous, Ellie said, "That's cruel," and headed back to the canine area.

Marcus stayed on her heels. "Hey, he had a motive. Lilah stole Kitty's designs. He was paving the way for his sister. As an older brother, I can understand that." He grabbed an energy bar from the table and peeled off the wrapper. "I'd do the same if anyone hurt a sister of mine."

Ellie sat in a chair, and opened a bottle of water. "I didn't realize you have a sister."

"I had three." When he used the past tense, she wanted to ask what happened, but he'd finished his snack and tossed the wrapper in the trash. "Sorry, no more time to talk. They should start calling the lineup in about fifteen minutes, and I have to put the finishing touches on Patti and Claire Smith."

He took off at a fast clip, waving good-bye as he walked, and Ellie muttered a curse. She'd let time slip away from her. The dogs had to go out and she only had a few minutes to take care of it if she wanted to see the evening wear competition.

After gathering her charges, she searched for her boy. Rudy was smart. He was supposed to stay close and he knew it, but he'd blown a gasket when Clark Fettel declared him the dog to take Ranger's place. She planned to talk to Cassandra when today's show finished and remind her that it was her responsibility to find a small dog to sub for the Greyhound, and it shouldn't be Rudy. She could borrow a canine from a friend, or foster one for the week from a small dog rescue, but she wasn't automatically welcome to Rudy.

"Okay, guys," she said to half the pack as she led them out. "Make it quick, so I can watch the show."

They did as ordered and calmly followed her back inside, where she picked up the remainder of her crew. "Ranger," she began, hoping to cheer up the sulking Greyhound, "you do understand why you can't be in the big finale, right?"

He sniffed, then shook his elegant head. *"Uh-huh, but that doesn't mean I have to like it. Cassandra is my new mom, and I should be with her while she's doing her job."*

Ellie smiled at his even tone. Ranger sounded like one of Great Britain's aristocrats, so different from the little guys she usually walked. "I understand, but we'll find her a dog she can work with. And don't worry. She wouldn't let anyone take your place in her heart."

She led the second group of canines outside, still wondering about Rudy. If he got in the way of someone who didn't like dogs . . .

When she returned, she heard the first call for the start of part two of the Nola Morgan Design show.

"Could you bring me to the stage when it's Cassandra's turn to walk the ramp? If I can't be with her, I'd like to see how she looks in full gear," Ranger asked politely.

"I'll try, but it gets tight up at the front. Let me see if I can find my guy." She scanned the area and, with no sign of him, decided she would find someone to stay with her charges while she began a search. Music blared as a last call went out over the loudspeaker, and she locked gazes with Cheech. "Any idea where my boy is, little buddy?"

The Chihuahua raised his nose toward the snack table and she backed up, then lowered to her knees and gazed at Ranger's lumpy throw. After picking up a corner, she found Rudy curled in a tight ball. With her heart in her throat she asked, "Hey, are you all right?"

No answer.

She tapped his nose. "Rudy, are you okay?"

Still no answer.

Sensing his unhappiness, she rubbed his ears. "Do I need to make an appointment with Dr. Dave?" she asked, referring to Viv's boyfriend and the veterinarian who took care of her dog.

He buried his muzzle between his paws and Ellie swallowed hard. "Rudy, this isn't funny. I know you're mad, but I told you I'd talk Cassandra into finding another dog."

The music rose, signaling the start of NMD's big event, and she heard Kurt Jager call out Kitty King's name. Kitty had to display both evening and day wear for this show, and Ellie imagined the jumpsuit she'd admired would be first.

"All right, be that way," she said to her boy. "But don't go anywhere else. We'll discuss this at home."

Ellie and Ranger weaved their way through the crowd and managed to arrive at a half-decent spot with a view that showed most of the catwalk. After Kurt explained to the audience that Kitty had replaced Lilah Perry, he introduced her day wear design and allowed the music to take over.

Yasmine and Cassandra appeared, one at a time, in the jumpsuit Ellie admired. On Yasmine, who was tall and slim, the suit was all legs worn with a pair of rust-colored boots that perfectly matched the suede on the collar, belt, and pockets. Cassandra's look took a different turn when she did her catwalk run wearing spiked, platform heels in a cream color that blended with the body of the suit.

There was no applause meter, but from the amount of clapping Ellie heard she felt certain the audience would choose Kitty's design today over any of the outfits shown in the competition yesterday. Her creation was definitely more wearable than Lilah's tight black skirt and tighter jacket.

But the winner would be chosen by Nola Morgan Design alone, and she imagined they would take into account the audience's reaction to each piece as well as the way the creations would appeal to a normal woman who bought her clothing on a budget.

Kurt Jager broke into the still pounding applause and began the second part of the competition by informing the audience that the next group of designs encompassed evening wear.

Marcus David's models began the show, the same as the day before. His evening gown appeared regal yet simple, with a white, fitted bodice overlaid with crystal beading. When the models, Patti and Claire, began to strut, their gowns swirled from the waist down with inserts of white, pale green, soft pink, and sky blue. Applause rang out, and Ellie agreed with the audience. The dress reminded her of a walking rainbow, complementing each model's coloring and figure. Ellie grinned. Marcus was a nice guy, and his work deserved to be appreciated.

Designer number two, Anton Rouch, had a serious demeanor and a fear of dogs. She hadn't heard a word from him since yesterday morning, when he'd talked to her about his models, and Kate and Lawan didn't have much to say about him either.

His gown, unlike him and his day wear creation, was playful and interesting. The silver-shot fabric draped over the left shoulder and tapered to the wearer's waist while the bodice dipped low over her bare right shoulder. The fabric fell from the wide-belted waist in a slash of sparkling silver threads covering a sheathlike skirt of deep magenta with a leg-baring slit that ran to the thigh.

Both models looked comfortable and ready to go out on the town, maybe to the opera or an upscale party, and the audience seemed to enjoy the way the gown flashed in the flood of lights gleaming from both overhead and the walkway.

The applause continued as the third duo of models appeared. Kurt Jager made appropriate commentary, even throwing in a few jokes when he introduced Fiona. Dominique and Crystal, her models, wore an over-the-top flashy orange gown covered in sparkly sequins in varying shades of green, with a flowing cape that hooked onto the bodice by a huge yellow flower that Ellie expected would squirt water at any moment.

Again, Fiona's design was too bright and silly for her, but someone like Lady Gaga, or maybe a circus clown, would find the ensemble wearable.

Finally, it was Kitty's turn. Ellie knew the girl was under a huge amount of pressure. Kitty felt undeserving of her place in the competition. She was only here because the woman who had stolen her designs was dead, and her brother had just been arrested for the murder. How sad that the biggest moment in the young designer's life was so tainted she was unable to enjoy the ride.

The music blared as Yasmine appeared first, dressed in the stunning feathered gown. After making a two-part turn in place, she sauntered down the runway, her tall, slender body swaying in perfect time to the beat. The crowd gasped, then showed their approval with thundering applause as she sashayed back to the top of the stage.

A moment later, Cassandra began her dip and sway. She wasn't as tall as Yasmine, and she was broader across the shoulders and waist, but the feathered bodice fit her perfectly. When she turned in an elegant circle at the bottom of the catwalk, the gown's color palette floated from pale pink to purple with every color in between getting a chance to shine. She did her own gracious saunter as she returned to the top of the ramp, where both models again swung in a circle, then disappeared through the curtain.

Ellie smiled. If Kitty were next to her, she would have hugged her. Both models had done the spectacular dress justice. In the face of Jeffery's arrest, that had to count for something.

It took a while, but the audience finally filed out, and Ellie led the Greyhound back to their area. She had to make sure the dogs were returned to their proper owners and the toys and treats were put away for the next day. One by one, the models appeared to collect their charges, and she sorted out the carriers and helped the women store their pets inside.

After Yasmine put a leash on her own mini Schnauzer, Jojo, and Lilah Perry's dog, Klingon, she asked if Ellie had the time to talk with her privately. Ellie said yes, but when she turned around, she came face-to-face with three people who gazed at her as if she was at their command.

"Hi," she said, putting on a smile.

"I've brought some people here to speak with you," said Clark Fettel, his face a mask of superiority. He nodded toward the woman beside him. Nola McKay was short but undeniably elegant in dress and manner. They'd been introduced earlier, but Clark must not have been told. "This is Nola McKay, CEO of Nola Morgan Design."

Ms. McKay held out her hand and Ellie shook it. "It's so nice to see you again."

Before the woman could answer, Clark continued, "And this is Morgan Prince, the company's CFO."

Ellie grasped his outstretched hand. She'd seen him that first day, studying the activity around the food table, but they hadn't been introduced. "They wanted to meet you, to discuss the . . . um . . . matter we talked about earlier."

The matter we talked about earlier? Ellie wasn't quite sure what to say until she saw Cassandra standing behind the tall, broad Mr. Prince. "Oh, you mean Ranger. The Greyhound."

"It's all right, Ellie," said Yasmine, who'd been waiting for a private moment. "I'll catch you tomorrow."

After the supermodel walked off with both mini Schnauzers, Ellie expelled a breath of frustration. If she'd known she was going to get stuck in the middle of a contract negotiation, she might not have accepted this gig.

Taking a seat, she continued to smile while she sized up the NMD biggies now sitting across from her. Both appeared to be in their mid-fifties and well taken care of. When she glanced at their hands she saw that they wore matching rings, though Ms. McKay's was smaller and more feminine than her partner's. When Fettel brought over three more folding chairs and set them down, he and Cassandra took their places.

"Dontcha kind of wonder who the sixth chair is for?" came a voice from beside her feet. *"Reminds me of the first time Detective Demento brought us in for questioning."*

She reached down and patted Rudy's head. This wasn't exactly the best time for her pouting pooch to awaken from his sulk and start talking.

"Don't answer any questions without the judge here, Triple E. He wouldn't let them get the best of you."

She circled his muzzle with her fingers and gave a gentle squeeze.

"Hey, I know. How about we just get up and walk outta here?" he mumbled. *"What are they gonna do? Fire us?"*

Unable to think straight, she gazed at her visitors. "Would you excuse me for one minute? I have to take my dog outside to ward off an accident." She grabbed her boy's leash and pulled him from under the table. When he dragged his feet, she bent and picked him up. "We'll be right back."

"Hold it a second. I don't hafta do business."

She ducked around the corner leading to the back door. "But you do have to shut up. There's no way I can concentrate with you sticking your two cents into the conversation."

He gave a doggie grin. *"My comments are worth more than that, and you know it."*

"You do realize they're here because they want you to be Cassandra's dog in the show on Friday."

"Hah!" Rudy struggled to get out of her arms. *"I'm no swishy canine. No way they're gonna get me to wear those sissy designer duds."*

Ellie set him on the floor. "And you don't want to help Cassandra or Ranger?"

He scratched his hindquarter. *"No."*

"Not even to get your face in a magazine or newspaper?"

"Nope."

"How about a cover?"

"A cover?" He perked up his ears. *"A cover of what?"*

Ellie shrugged. "I don't know, but with so many of the big fashion magazine editors sitting out there I'm sure one of them will give this contest a cover. Heck, NMD could already have that worked out. If you and Kitty won, there'd have to be some recognition."

"Me and Kitty?"

"Yes, you and Kitty. Cassandra is her model, but Kitty would be the winner of the contest."

"Oh, I—uh—forgot about that."

"It's really Kitty that you'd be helping. If they fired Cassandra, Kitty would need to start all over again. Re-measuring, redesigning, doing all the work that goes with creating one of those sample outfits for a new model. She's already at a disadvantage, coming into this on the second day. Working with a canine model who's a stranger could make it worse."

"I didn't think about that."

"Tomorrow is an off day, to give the designers a chance to complete the set of third outfits for each model, and sew one that matches for their dogs." When his head cocked, she decided to offer him a choice. Something she'd been thinking about all afternoon. "I do have another idea. One that might take you off the hook and give Nola Morgan Design more good publicity."

"Ah, okay. I'd still be happier if I didn't have to make like a pretty boy."

"Great. We'll worry about it after I give my thoughts to Nola and—"

"Ms. Engleman?" Clark Fettel stuck his head around the corner. "Who are you talking to?"

"Uh, no one—just myself—and my dog."

His eyebrows mimicked question marks. "Your dog?"

"Yes, my dog. Do you have a problem with that?"

He frowned. "No, of course not, but Nola and Morgan are waiting, and since they're sponsoring this event and your paycheck, it might be nice if you paid them some attention."

"He's got you there, Triple E."

Rudy was correct, of course. She put on a happy face. "We're done here, so lead the way."

He turned and Ellie gave her boy a look. "Remember, no additional commentary. There still might be a way to get you out of this," she whispered.

They arrived in the dog area, where Nola and Morgan had helped themselves to bottled water and energy bars. Ellie took a seat and Rudy stationed himself at her feet. Since the two bosses looked so approachable, she decided to pour on a little charm. "I've been meaning to thank you for giving me the chance to be a part of this event," she began. "It's very exciting to be in at the start of something this huge."

"Patti Fallgrave spoke so highly of you, we had no choice but to take her suggestion," said Morgan. He glanced at Clark. "I believe you already know about our problem with Cassandra and her dog."

"I'm aware of it, yes."

"But we've come up with an idea that might work, if you and your own dog are agreeable." He went on to ask if she would allow Rudy to be Cassandra's canine for the finale. "We'd be sure to mention your dog-walking service in future ads as a thank-you. Or would you want an additional fee?"

"Gosh, no. You've already taken care of that. I just have one worry."

"And that would be . . ."

"My boy isn't a purebred. He's a pound puppy, and the ASPCA could only guess his lineage."

Nola bent forward and chucked Rudy under the chin. "And what do they think he is?

"A yorkiepoo. That's half Poodle—"

"And half Yorkshire terrier. I thought so. He looks a lot like my own little man." She sniffed back a tear. "I lost Eddie six months ago, but it seems like yesterday. The feelings are still so raw, I haven't been able to replace him."

Morgan patted her hand. "So you see, we're in sympathy with Cassandra's feelings, but we know it will also put Ms. King in a bind. There really isn't time to search for another small dog that's agreeable and at ease with both the women."

"There is one alternative," said Ellie. Seeing Yasmine earlier had made her think of it. "With Lilah Perry gone, her dog, Klingon, is an orphan."

"What a frightful name," said Nola, shuddering. "Though it does match Lilah's personality."

"I guess that means you knew her fairly well?" said Ellie.

"Unfortunately, yes," she answered. "And we didn't much care for—"

"Now, Nola, that isn't professional," her partner interrupted.

"I know, but this isn't a public outing. And anyone who knew her will tell you the same thing." The CEO leaned back in her chair. "Knowing Lilah had a fresh mouth and a nasty way of treating others, I wasn't surprised when Jeffery accused her of thievery. But he had no proof, so we had to go with the designs that were submitted, and hers were definitely at the top of the list. When we saw what happened onstage, we were more than happy to give Kitty a chance to prove herself."

"But what do you think about Jeffery King being accused of killing Ms. Perry?" asked Ellie.

"Jeffery? We believe he's innocent." Nola clutched Morgan's hand. "That's another thing we need to discuss."

"Hey, aren't we gettin' a little off topic here?"

Ellie bit her lower lip. She didn't like the sound of Nola's last sentence and decided to wrap things up as fast as possible. "So, Cassandra, do you think you could work with Lilah's dog? He seemed sweet and easy to handle. Call Yasmine and ask her about him, why don't you?"

Cassandra exhaled a breath. "Okay, yes. I have her number, and I'll call her tonight. If she thinks Klingon will walk the runway with me, I'll use him. In a way, it will be a tribute to Lilah. That should make Nola Morgan Design look sympathetic in the press, don't you think?"

"Exactly," Clark Fettel agreed. "Stellar promotion for NMD. We're honoring Lilah Perry's memory. No one need know she was a bitch."

The three women gasped in tandem. "Really, Fettel, was that necessary?" asked Morgan.

"I dealt with the girl myself, plenty of times, and more after she was chosen for this contest, so the answer is yes. I tried to keep our disagreements quiet, but half the world—"

"It wasn't that bad, Clark," said Cassandra, acting the peacemaker. "Just a few of us heard what she was saying."

Considering Clark Fettel's angry expression, and the fact that he worked for NMD and could have had access to the gift bags, Ellie added him to her list of suspects . . . just because she was curious, of course. Not because she had any intention of delving into the murder investigation.

"Okay, then I guess that's settled," she said, hoping to close the meeting.

Cassandra said good-bye, promising to phone Yasmine, and Ellie stood. It was then she saw a teary-eyed Kitty walking toward them.

"Uh-oh," said Rudy. *"I know where this is headed."*

Ellie agreed with her boy, which was why she eyed the rear door, but it was too late.

"Nola, Morgan," said Kitty, giving a watery smile. "I'm so happy you're still here."

"Of course we are," said Nola. She clasped Kitty by the hand. "Now take a seat. We were just about to ask Ms. Engleman the question."

The question? "I really don't have time for any more questions. It's late and Rudy and I have to get home. He's cranky when he doesn't get his dinner on time and—"

"This will only take a moment," said Morgan, his expression grave. "Kitty told us about your success in solving murders, as did Patti Fallgrave." He cleared his throat. "We put our faith and trust in Jeffery, and you know we think he's innocent."

She was going to smack Patti upside the head the next time she saw her. "I agree with you about Jeffery, but I'm afraid Patti exaggerated my ability. I have no formal training or—"

"That's not what we heard," Morgan cut her off. "So we'd like to make a request."

Ellie raised a hand. "I've already explained to Kitty—I'm not a private investigator. The police are the experts. They have all sorts of techniques and scientific processes at their disposal. Not me."

"Perhaps, but we know how the police work. Once they arrest a suspect they do all they can to amass evidence against that person. They don't continue to look for other possibilities."

"They must watch CSI," Rudy muttered.

Ellie heaved a sigh. Her boy was probably correct.

"We're willing to offer you a fee. Just name your price."

"Oh, no. I could never—"

"All right, if there's no fee, we'll find another way to repay you." Morgan locked eyes with Nola, then Kitty, then again gazed at Ellie. "We're making you a serious offer. Not only do we believe Jeffery King is innocent, we also feel the need to rescue our company from bad publicity. His arrest will surely have the daily rags and gossipmongers in an uproar, as well as the TV tell-alls and the Internet magazines. We don't know where else to turn. Please look into Lilah Perry's murder and find the real killer."

Chapter 7

Ellie set her take-out bag from China Jewel on the counter, and walked to the front hall closet with Rudy beside her. After hanging up her jacket, she returned to the kitchen and sat at the table, where she pulled her phone from her tote bag. She listened to three messages from Sam, erased them, and looked at her boy.

"Did you hear? Sam said he'd be home by seven. Should we believe him?"

"Sure, if you're willin' to starve. How about rattlin' those pots and pans, 'cause I could eat a horse."

"There's no need to exaggerate. I live to serve you, my friend," she joked as she went to the sink and retrieved his food bowl. "It'll keep my mind off this latest quandary."

Rudy stretched out his front legs and yawned. *"Yeah, so what else is new? Seems like we're in the murder business whether we like it or not."*

She dropped a quarter cup of his high-end kibble into the dish. What was it that made her so cost-conscious when buying clothes for herself, yet more than willing to pay a premium price for her four-legged pal's upkeep? The money she spent for his grooming, food, and the time she used to cook his organically grown veggies would probably get her one designer dud a month.

Grinning, she went to the fridge and pulled out his canned food, Grammy's Pot Pie, and vegetables: a ground mix of baby carrots and green beans. At the counter, she added a heaping tablespoon of each to his bowl and began to stir while her mind drifted back to the questions she'd been mulling since her meeting with the NMD big shots.

Both Patti Fallgrave and Kitty had passed along what they knew about Rob's case and how she'd helped him. But why did their opinion make Nola McKay and Morgan Prince think she was expert enough to rescue Jeffery King and keep their company off the radar screen in this murder?

Lilah had been killed at one of their events. The designer had so many enemies, Ellie didn't know where to look first. How was she supposed to investigate when she was shut in the Fashion Center for ten hours a day?

Still mixing, she shook her head. Sam would tie her to a chair for the rest of the week if he knew she'd considered saying yes when they asked her to run her own investigation into Lilah Perry's murder. Especially since the cops had already nailed a suspect.

"'Scuse me, but if you keep on stirring I'm gonna be eatin' baby food instead of canine chow," came a voice from below.

"Oops, sorry." She stopped mixing and gazed at the pulpy mess. "It is a little on the creamy side. Still want to give it a try?"

"Of course. Grammy's Pot Pie rocks. Just set 'er down and stand back."

Ellie did as directed, and he dived in with gusto, which gave her more time to think. She'd brought Sam's standard dinner order home from their new favorite restaurant, hoping to soften the blow when she told him about this latest development in her life. Slumping forward, she drummed her fingers on the table. Did she really have to share exactly what had happened in the after-hours meeting? She was a terrible liar, but maybe she could circle around Nola and Morgan's direct request and ask him what he thought about her lending a hand to a new friend.

A soft belch from below told her that time was up for thinking alone. She had a second opinion waiting from a tried and true veteran of what she'd begun calling "the great Sam debate."

"So, any advice on what I should tell Sam?"

"Detective Demento won't like whatever you say, so play it by ear." Rudy circled his mat, then curled in a ball. *"Start small and keep movin' until you know you should stop."*

"Gee, thanks. You're a big help." She checked her watch and realized she had no idea when her boyfriend would arrive home, and Viv had already told her she wouldn't be back from her appointment until late.

"Your face looks all flat and squishy, like one of my squeaky toys after I killed it. If you're that worried, call the judge," Rudy suggested. *"He's one of the smartest humans I know, and he always comes up with a good answer for everything."*

Ellie thumped her temple with the heel of her hand. Geez, why hadn't she thought of that? She heaved a sigh. Sometimes it was hard to admit a dog was brighter than its owner, though she knew a couple of dozen who were.

She dialed her mother's number and gave a silent

thank-you when Corinna, Georgette's faithful house-keeper, answered. "Ms. Ellie, how you doing? Your mother asked me yesterday to make sure we phoned you by Saturday. She said she wants a complete report on the fashion lines for the coming year."

Ellie's groaned internally. There'd been so much going on behind the scenes with NMD that she hadn't had time to pay attention to the other houses unveiling their new spring lines on the runway.

"I really called to speak to the judge. Is he free and out from under Mother's thumb?"

Corinna laughed. "That man is never out from under Georgette's thumb, but your mother isn't here, so the coast is clear. But I expect her home any minute, so don't keep him too long."

She imagined the housekeeper trekking across the penthouse suite from the kitchen to the library to tell her stepfather, Judge Stanley Frye, that she was on the phone.

"My darling girl," the judge began when he finally came on the line. His voice was especially strong for an eighty-five-year-old wheelchair-bound man. "We haven't heard from you all week. It's so nice of you to phone me. How are things?"

"Things are just fine, you charmer, and Corinna said you were alone, which is perfect. I called because I need an opinion, and you're the first person I thought to ask."

"After me," Rudy reminded her.

"Fire away, but keep it short. Your mother is due to arrive any minute, and from the sound of it this is something you'd rather keep between the two of us."

"You're right, but not because I'm in trouble or anything."

"When it comes to her only daughter, I think it's the

'or anything' that disturbs Georgette the most," he said with a chuckle. "So let's hear it."

"Well, I'm sure you know where I am this week. Mother probably told you, right?"

"You're at Fashion Week, that big show where the premier design houses give a preview of the upcoming season's clothing. If I remember correctly, Georgette has a list of questions she plans to ask you about it."

"Then I guess I'd better start paying closer attention to what her favorite houses are pushing for next year. In the meantime, I assume you read about what happened there yesterday. One of the designers in the contest I'm working died in the middle of the event."

"I saw it in the paper. Terrible business that." He *tsk*ed. "They hinted that it was deliberate, a possible homicide."

Ellie imagined the judge shaking his balding head.

"It would take someone completely diabolical to think of a plan that would cause an allergic reaction, then make sure no antidote was available. It's a capital murder offense if ever there was one."

Great, thought Ellie. People arrested for murder in the first degree were rarely granted bail, and if they were, the amount needed was sky-high. Kitty was going to fall apart when she heard that it was more likely her brother would be tried for capital murder. "I know how it sounds, but I have a gut feeling they've got the wrong man," she began. "I've met him, and his sister, and I just can't see him doing all that."

"Me neither."

"Ah, well then. I guess that means you'll be on top of it, righting the wrong done to someone you consider innocent."

She heaved another sigh. "Sometimes, I think you know me better than Rudy does."

"How is my boy?" he asked, never missing a chance to talk about his favorite yorkiepoo. "We haven't seen either of you in too long."

"Rudy's fine, and you'll see him soon. I'm fairly certain we'll be at Mother's monthly Sunday brunch."

"Ah, yes, she did mention it. Now back to the matter at hand. You still haven't asked me a question."

"Okay, here goes." She inhaled and let her breath out slowly, aiming to be as truthful as possible. "The people the accused works for—that's the man and woman who own Nola Morgan Design—want my help in finding the real killer. They're as certain as I am that their favorite employee, Jeffery King, isn't guilty, and they think I can do the job of nabbing the guilty party better than the cops."

"Hmm, I see." He paused for a beat. "What makes them so certain their fair-haired boy isn't the killer?"

"His work ethic and his dedication, I think. They're also worried about the negative publicity they're sure will haunt NMD if he's proven guilty—which he isn't."

"You're certain?"

"As certain as I can be." She imagined the judge tapping his chin as he thought. "At least I feel it inside."

"And what makes them think you're more capable than the police? Have they been talking to someone who knows about your investigative success?"

"I asked them the same question, and they admitted they'd spoken to one of their models, whose dog I walk, and I know Jeffery's sister talked to Rob, the client I helped a few months back."

She could almost hear the judge's wheels turning. Then he asked, "Is there any chance you'd be in danger doing as they ask, the way you've been in the past?"

"I doubt it. With the other crimes there was a weapon—you know—a gun, poison, scissors—to contend with," she told him, echoing Rudy's logic. "I'm not allergic to anything, so I can't imagine how I'd be hurt."

"And you want someone to rubber-stamp your involvement in the case," he said bluntly. "You know Detective Ryder won't condone it, so you'll use my permission as your cover."

Glancing at her boy, she rolled her eyes. The man might be well into his senior years but his mind was still razor sharp. "I hate it when you read me so well, Judge Stanley."

"Want to know how I do it?" he asked, his tone teasing.

"Um, sure, clue me in."

"Because you and I are very much alike. We hate seeing injustice done to anyone, whether we approve of them personally or not. We believe in being fair in all things. If we see a wrong, we feel the need to right it, come what may."

"You make it sound as if I'm running for sainthood."

"Nonsense. You're no saint and neither am I. We merely want to see things done as fairly as possible."

"So you think I should do what they want and look into the matter?"

"I think you will whether I say you should or not. Just be careful and stay out of harm's way." He cleared his throat. "Now, I have a question for you."

Ellie gazed at the ceiling. What was one more question? Her day had been full of them. "Um, okay."

"Actually, it's more of a favor," he admitted.

She loved the man like a father. She doubted she could say no to whatever he asked. "If it's in my power, I'll be happy to grant it."

"It's for your mother." He stopped, knowing full well that she and her mother were not always in harmony. "I'd like to give her something special for her birthday.

It's coming up, you know, and she's so difficult to buy for."

On that topic, Ellie couldn't agree more. "I understand. What do you want to give her?"

"A pass to the final day of the shows. Something that would allow her into all the design exhibits, plus the big contest you're working. I called the main office and they said they were out of tickets, so I hoped you might have some pull. I'm going to give her carte blanche on the design of her choosing, and I thought the ticket could be from you. It would make a fine birthday gift from the two of us, don't you think?"

Wow, thought Ellie. That would sure take a load off her shoulders. Finding a gift for Georgette was like finding the next new planet in the solar system. But that meant her mother would be there when she did her thing with the dogs.

"Ellie. Is it too much to ask?"

She bit her lower lip, then plowed ahead. "Of course not, Judge. I'll find a way to get her a ticket and I'll get it to you sometime Thursday. If you have Corinna buy a card, you can tuck the tickets inside and give them to her so she and a friend can show up first thing Friday morning, and stay for the big finale that afternoon."

"Excellent. I don't know how I can repay you. Just promise me one other small thing: Please don't tell your mother we had this conversation."

"Georgette's holding her monthly brunch on Sunday and she expects us to be there," said Ellie later that evening as she set a steaming plate of beef and broccoli with fried rice at Sam's place.

He removed his shoulder holster and hung it over the back of his chair. Sitting, he raised an eyebrow and gave a cocky grin. "And you told me this when?"

She joined him at the table with her plate of shrimp, snow peas, and brown rice. "Last weekend. Sunday morning, right before you left on the Lombardi case."

"It's the Lombard-*o* case, and I don't remember hearing Georgette's name or a mention of the invitation." He speared a chunk of beef and held it up to cool. "Are you sure?"

She glanced at Rudy and made a silent plea. *I did tell him, didn't I?* When his answer was a doggie shrug, she said, "I know I did. You nodded, so I assumed I broke through the Dick Tracy barrier."

"Hah! Very funny." He scooped up another forkful of beef and broccoli, then washed it down with a swallow of beer. "Just remember, if I have a lead on a case or something important comes up, I'm off the hook with the ex-terminator," he warned, using Viv's favorite name to describe Ellie's many-times-divorced mother. "How are things going with that Amber woman, by the way? Is she doing an okay job with your charges?"

Ellie dropped her fork. "Oh, crap. I forgot to call her when I got home."

"Is that the plan? You call her and check in?"

"Kind of. She phoned me yesterday, so it was my turn for today, but something happened and I forgot."

He raised an eyebrow. "Something happened? What kind of something?"

"For one thing, they had to choose a designer to take the place of the girl who died, and they picked my assistant. That meant I had to take care of the dogs and watch the food table and bags by myself. It wasn't a big deal, but I did have my hands full."

"What about the contest? Did part two go off as planned?"

"As far as I could tell, yes. Though poor Kitty was a mess. She only had one night to get her day wear outfit ready, and that was tough." Ellie pushed a shrimp around her plate. "But the design was great. It was a cream-colored lightweight wool jumpsuit with burnt orange suede trim, and I really liked it. So much, in fact, that I'm thinking of purchasing it."

"Hmm. That says a lot." He narrowed his eyes, as if reading her from across the table. "If you like it that much, maybe I could buy it for you."

Sam hated that she made more money than he did, and he tried to gloss over it by paying his half of her mortgage every month. And his buying her presents was always a sticking point. He thought he had to get her the same things Viv wanted or, heaven forbid, go along with her mother's over-the-top suggestions for her birthday or Christmas gift.

"I'm not sure what will happen to the outfits created by the designers who don't win the contest, but I heard NMD will own all the designs when this is through." She topped the shrimp with rice and lifted her fork. "Even the ones created by the losers."

His noncomment told her Sam really wasn't interested, but she continued to talk about the contest, hoping to work her problem into the conversation. "I do have my fingers crossed for Kitty. Both of the designs she showed today were great, and she deserves to win after all that's happened to her."

He took another swig of beer. "What was her name again?"

"Uh—King—Kitty King."

Sam leaned back in his chair. "Any relation to Jeffery King?"

Ready to take the plunge, she sucked in a breath. "So you heard about the arrest."

"Word spreads quickly around the department."

"Well, Jeffery is Kitty's older brother and a really

nice guy." She sipped her tea, composing her words carefully. "Kitty says he's innocent, you know."

"What else would a sister say?" He scraped up the last of his dinner. "Word is the case is a lock, but you didn't hear that from me."

Ellie knew better than to break a confidence. She and Sam had developed an unspoken agreement over the months they'd lived together. She kept whatever he told her private, and he didn't toss her in a padded room when she bombarded him with questions.

"Have you talked to Detective Vaughn?"

"Not me, but Vince spent some time with him. He told me Vaughn asked some specific questions about you."

"Me?"

Sam grinned. "Yeah, but Vince did his best to convince Vaughn you'd keep your nose clean."

"Sounds to me like you're toast, Triple E."

She glared at her boy, then said, "He did, did he?"

Sam cocked his head, much like Rudy did when he was confused. That's when it dawned on her that some of their mannerisms were identical. If only they knew ...

"Something funny?"

"Not exactly. It's just that Vince really shouldn't speak for me."

"Hold on. Is this your way of telling me you *are* going to stick your nose in this murder?"

She took another swallow of tea, hoping the warm drink would give her courage. "I planned on discussing it with you, so now is as good a time as any. I've been formally requested to look into ... things."

He sat up straight in his chair. "Formally requested? By who?"

"By Jeffery King's employer, Nola Morgan Design. I met the owners of the company today, and they believe he's innocent. To be honest with you, so do I."

"Oh for—" He stood and carried their plates to the sink. "Ellie, I'm telling you now, do not get involved." Turning, he leaned back against the counter. "Vaughn is a good detective, and he follows the rules. He won't go easy on you if you fuck up his investigation."

"I don't intend to—to—do what you said," she answered, avoiding the raw language that came out when he talked cop. "But I do think he has the wrong man. I may ask around, see if there's anything I can find that will give Jeffery a leg up."

"That's a nice way to put it," Rudy added.

"A leg up?" Sam frowned. "I don't think you should help him in any way. Let Vaughn do the work."

She stood and started boxing up the leftovers. "But Jeffery is already in jail. You know what that means as well as I do."

When he didn't answer, Ellie gave herself a mental high five. Once the cops thought they had the killer, the investigation for fresh leads stalled. "How about if I play by our new rules. I'll ask around and if I find anything odd or suspect, I'll tell you about it before I try to go further by myself. You offer guidance, and look into it if you think I'm on the right track."

"When did we make that a 'new' rule?" he asked, pouting like a three-year-old.

Hiding a grin, she stored the cartons in the fridge. Then she walked to him and put her arms around his neck. "We made it a rule after Rob was arrested—remember? You set up guidelines and I agreed." She rested her head on his shoulder. "I thought that was very reasonable, and now we can work it out. It's a no-brainer, really."

He blew out a breath, a sure sign that, this time, it was his turn to agree with her. Then he slid an arm around her and moved his hand under her sweater, where he rested his palm flat against her back. "Just promise me one thing: You won't do anything stupid or dangerous."

Shivers raced up her spine as his gentle touch brought her senses to attention. "There's no way I'd be in danger with this one. Death by peanut is an off-the-wall way to kill someone, and since I don't have any allergies . . ."

Pulling her closer, Sam nuzzled her neck. "I'd fall apart if anything happened to you." Following the line of her jaw with his lips, he found her mouth. "Be careful, and if it looks like there might be trouble—"

His kiss made her knees weak and her heart hammer. She moaned, melting into his chest. "Sam, I—"

"Promise me, Ellie," he said, biting her lower lip.

She nodded. "I promise." But the words got lost when their mouths met in another mind-bending kiss.

Sam took her hand and led her down the hall. "I know it's early, but I'm beat. You ready to call it a night?"

"Hey, what am I? Chopped liver?" said Rudy, walking behind them. "*I need an out before we turn in.*"

She crooked her arm in Sam's, aware of how patient and quiet Rudy had been while they were talking. "I hate to tell you this, Mr. Romance, but I have a dog that needs a trip outside before we call it a night."

He stopped at the bedroom door. "Not a problem. You get ready for bed and I'll take the pest for a walk. How does that sound?"

"Lame."

"Like a plan." Ellie cupped his cheeks and drew him near. "I'll be ready by the time you get back." She rubbed her nose against his chin. "Just don't be long."

"Don't count on it," Rudy muttered, following him back to the kitchen. "*I got a lot of business to do tonight.*"

Ellie brought Rudy's favorite pillow to the spare bedroom and exchanged it for one from the guest bed, which she would give to Sam. It was a habit she'd developed whenever Sam spent the night, and now that he'd moved in she continued the practice. Ever since she'd brought her boy home from the ASPCA shelter, he'd claimed the pillow next to hers, and he'd never expected that to change. But after they had a long talk, and she told him how important Sam was to her, he'd taken the move in stride.

And it really wasn't so often they slept apart. Sam got called out at all hours several times a week, so Rudy had plenty of chances to sneak back into her room and reclaim his spot. To date, the pillow transfer was working so well, even her macho detective didn't complain when he realized Rudy slept on his side of the mattress whenever he could.

Back in her room, she slipped her cell into the charger on her nightstand, then changed into a sleep shirt and headed for the bathroom to wash her face and brush her teeth. According to tomorrow's NMD timetable, she had the first few hours of the day free, which meant she could do her morning runs and check in with her regular charges.

Back in the bedroom, she phoned Amber and gave her the news. It was early enough, Amber assured her, that she could call her helpers and shift the responsibility around.

A few minutes later, the door opened and Sam's footsteps sounded in the hall. When Rudy trotted in and put his front paws on her knees, she bent down and whispered, "That was fast. I assume you were a good boy."

He huffed out a breath. "*Sure, why not. The daffy dick took it easy, no draggin' me up the street and back like he usually does, so I cooperated.*"

Hugging him, she kissed the top of his head. "You are such a good dog. So good, in fact, that there'll be a surprise tomorrow morning."

He dropped to all fours and spun around. *"A surprise! Tell me now! Tell me now!"*

Sam came into the room and walked to the closet. "What's up with your furry friend?" He unbuttoned his shirt and dropped it in his hamper, a routine he'd agreed to when they made up their "house rules." "He acts like he wants food or playtime."

"He knows he's going to be doing something special tomorrow morning, that's all."

"Special how?" Sam stepped out of his slacks and hung them on a hanger, slipped off his T-shirt, and removed his socks and boxers. "Tell me. I can keep a secret."

"Get me out of here," Rudy said, staring at a well-muscled and naked Sam, who was clearly ready to take his woman to bed. *"I'm getting testosterone overload."*

Ellie bit back a grin. "I called Amber because I have time to do my regular first run in the morning. That means Rudy will be seeing all his pals."

"That's it?" Sam grasped her hands and drew her to her feet. "He's a nut job."

"He's just a normal dog, happy when I'm happy, sad when I'm sad. . . ." She moved near and he pressed his hips against her. "You know how much I love him."

Sam kissed the side of her neck while his hands cupped her bottom. "As much as you love me?"

Their lips met and he coaxed her mouth open for more intimate contact. The heat from his body traveled through her, warming her to her toes. When he inched a hand up her back and around to her breast she sank into his touch and—

"'Scuse me, but I'm still in the room," a voice called out.

Ellie untangled herself and heaved a breath, then picked up her boy. "I'll be back in a minute."

"Don't be long," said Sam, climbing under the covers.

"Ewww," Rudy gruffed while she carried him. *"Why did I have to see that?"*

"Because you have a bad habit of hanging around when Sam and I are ready for private time." She plopped him onto the mattress. "I always move your pillow, so you could have just gone straight to bed instead of asking questions."

He gave her cheek a sloppy lick. *"And I heard the answer."* He circled his pillow, then lay down. *"We're gonna see the gang, right?"*

"Right." Ellie stood. "Now get cozy and have a good night. We have a lot to do tomorrow."

He tucked his nose under his paws. *"I heard him ask you a question, too."*

She knew where he was going with the comment, so she rubbed his ears. "I love you both very much, but you'll always be first in my heart." Standing, she blew him a kiss. "I promise."

Chapter 8

The next morning Ellie started her regular walk routine backwards, hoping to spend some time talking privately with Patti Fallgrave before she arrived at the Fashion Week facility. In order to do so, she and Rudy had to make the Cranston their first stop and work their way south, taking care of the dogs in Sara Studebaker's building, then those in the Davenport, and finally her charges in the Beaumont.

"Good morning, Natter," she said, greeting the doorman when they walked into the foyer.

"Ms. Ellie. What happened to Amber? I thought she was taking over for you this week."

"She is, but I had some extra time this morning."

"Well, it's good to see you. You too, Rudy. Ms. Amber, she's a nice lady, but you two always give me something to talk about with the missus." His bushy eyebrows rose to his hairline. "Like the latest thing I read in the paper."

Ellie headed for the elevator. She knew what the doorman was saying, and she didn't want to comment.

But he continued talking as she walked away. "Did I read the headline right? Was somebody killed the other day during that show you and Ms. Fallgrave are working?"

"Um, yes, Patti and I were there." She stood in front of the elevator and pushed the button. "I have to get moving."

"The paper hinted it was a murder," he said, his tone questioning. "And I was just wondering if you'd be mixed up in the investigation, like usual."

Hearing him say "like usual" was bad enough. If Natter knew how she'd helped Viv's sister find her fiancé's killer in the Hamptons this past summer, she was certain he'd think she was ready to hang out a shingle reading ELLIE ENGLEMAN, PRIVATE EYE.

"Uh, no, no. Not me. Helping that client in the Davenport was my last brush with anything that has to do with murder." Not wanting to be rude, she continued waiting for the door to open. "But I have to speak with Patti Fallgrave, and I don't have much time."

"Haven't seen her yet, so she's probably still at home." He opened the main door for a tenant. "Go right up. I'm sure you'll find her."

"Thanks. I'll be down with the gang soon."

The young woman who entered the building needed the elevator, too, so Ellie let her in first. The woman, little more than a girl, really, had a pale face, made even paler because of her coal black eyebrows and deep red lips. Dressed as if it was a freezing day in January instead of a cool day in September, the woman eyed Rudy. "Are you one of the dog walkers in this building?"

"Yep, but this is my boy. Do you have a dog?"

She shook her head and her dark scarf slid to the back of her head, revealing pitch-black hair parted in the middle a la Morticia Addams. "Not me. They're too much work."

"Doesn't sound like you'll find another customer in this babe."

Ellie figured Rudy was right, but that didn't mean she couldn't make polite conversation. "They can be, but that's why people who love dogs hire me."

"Then how about talkin' to someone who cares, like me," Rudy ordered. *"Or Natter. He's okay—for a human. Gives me the respect I deserve."*

"Oh, well, that won't make me want one."

"No problem," said Ellie. She waited to answer Rudy until the *Addams Family* wannabe got out and the door closed. "Natter is definitely a good guy, but don't you think it's odd that he'd automatically assume I was involved in another murder investigation?"

"You're kiddin', right?" He snorted a laugh. *"Since Patti's been singin' our praises, I'd worry if he didn't think it. If you ask me, she's doin' a good job drummin' up business, too."*

"Why do you suppose she's so determined to get us on her bandwagon?"

"Beats me, but you oughta ask her. Maybe there's somethin' else cookin' in that picture-perfect brain."

After stepping on the Fallgrave sisters' floor, they headed down a wide hallway. "Maybe I'm being too suspicious. Could be she was simply making polite small talk, not encouraging the NMD people to ask for our help."

After knocking on the door and receiving no answer, she used her key to enter the apartment. A gentle wash of jazz filled the air along with the sound of a woman's exceptional contralto. "I bet that's Janice's new album."

A moment later, Janice Fallgrave appeared from the

rear of the apartment cradling Chong, her ever-silent Chihuahua. She gave Ellie a grin and speed-walked to the wall of bookcases that housed her stereo system. Dressed in black slacks and a red top, the singer was the polar opposite of her tall, dark-haired supermodel sister. With curly blond hair and a petite but full-figured body, Janice had the face of an angel and a voice to match.

"I'm sorry about that," she said after fiddling with the controls. Her cheeks flushed pink. "I don't usually listen to myself, except in the studio, but this is a demo of my first album, so I thought I should hear it as if I were a paying customer."

Ellie advanced with her arm outstretched. "Congratulations. You sound fabulous." When she took Janice's hand, the two girls automatically hugged. "You've worked so hard to get here."

"I feel like I'm living in a dream world. This can't be real." She blinked back a tear. "It's what I've wanted my entire life, and now that it's going to happen I'm— I'm—" She snuggled her nose in Chong's neck. "I'm terrified."

"Terrified?" Ellie sat next to her on the sofa. "What's there to be afraid of? Fame? Success? Heck, you can handle that. Just use your older sister as a guide."

"I know. Patti's face and figure have been on the cover of some of the biggest fashion magazines in the world. In her business it's all about the look. But in the music world . . . well, it's not just your 'sound.'" She used air quotes to emphasize the word. "You need something to draw people to you. Take Lady Gaga for instance. She's a complete package—"

"And if you ask me, not a very good one. She pulled some stunt that got her thrown out of Yankee stadium last summer, and she did that disgusting meat thing at an awards show. Gross. Besides, you already have the perfect gimmick."

"I do?"

"Sure." She nodded at the tiny, fawn-colored canine Janice was cuddling. "You have Chong."

"The hairless wonder?" grumped Rudy. *"Oh yeah, he'll be good. And when those immigration guys see him, out he'll go."*

Ellie ignored the snarky comment and concentrated on her client. "Instead of being absurd or quirky, your push could be helping homeless animals. Give a concert for Best Friends, that wonderful animal rescue in Utah, or maybe find a shelter around here looking for a spokesperson or—or—"

The singer set her bitty baby on the sofa and covered her ears. "Stop. I can't hear any more. Maybe you could take the place of my manager. All Jackson has suggested is buying a billboard in Times Square and getting me a gig singing 'The Star-Spangled Banner' at a Mets game." She leaned back against the sofa. "It's scary enough that I'll be reviewed in *People* next month, and the album is on sale for Christmas."

"Don't worry. You have lots of time to work up a unique promotion idea." Ellie scratched Chong's pointy, oversized ears. "I don't mean to be rude, but I have to talk to Patti. Is she getting ready to go to the show?"

"Yep."

"How about if I do my usual run and you tell her I need to speak with her when I return? We can cab to the Fashion Center together while we talk."

"Sounds like a plan," said Janice. "I'll help you hook up my boy; then I'll give sis the message."

The two women and their dogs went to the foyer,

where Janice attached Chong's leash and passed it over. "See you in about thirty minutes," said Ellie.

She and her charges walked to the elevator in silence. When they got on and the door closed, she said to Rudy, "What? Now you're holding out on me? How come you're not spouting your normal string of insults at poor Chong?"

He gave a head to tail shake. *"Why should I when that Shrinky Dink bean eater won't bother to answer?"*

"You're not being fair. There are plenty of dogs on our customer list who don't talk. That doesn't mean they can't. Could be they're uncomfortable with the idea of speaking to a human—or you." They got off on Lulu's floor and aimed for the spoiled Havanese's luxury apartment. "It doesn't matter. Now that we're here, you can chat with Ms. Pickypants to your heart's content."

Nelda let them in with her usual cheerful hello and passed Ellie the champion Havanese's lead. As suggested, the canine lovebirds gabbed up a storm while Ellie continued her stops, picking up Bruiser, a sulky Pomeranian; Ranger, the hypochondriac toy Poodle; Harvey, a stoic mixed breed; and Satchmo, a nosy Japanese Chin.

After strolling through Central Park and doing her lawful clean-up duty, Ellie returned to the Beaumont, dropped off the dogs, and hurried to the Fallgrave apartment, where she found Patti waiting.

"You're ready," she said, noting the supermodel wore a lovely camel coat over her clothes. Since working in the heart of the fashion industry this week, she'd learned a lot about identifying designers, and this coat looked very much like the star of Calvin Klein's spring line.

"Cheech and I are all set. Once we're downstairs, Natter will call us a cab."

Ellie gave Chong his morning biscuit, grinning when he took it and trotted down the hall. "Guess he's going to find Janice."

"Oh, yeah. That little guy is totally devoted to his mom, just like Cheech is to me." She kissed her Chihuahua on top of his head and set him on the tile. "Let's get moving. I'm scheduled for the second round today, a Zac Posen spring showing. Then a Donatella Versace."

They entered the elevator and slipped to the rear when another couple followed them in. "So, what do you want to discuss?" asked Patti. "The big finale is tomorrow. Are you getting cold feet?"

"Why should I? I'm not the one who has to parade the catwalk with hundreds of people watching."

"Don't try to fool me. I know all about your fear of performing in front of an audience. You're in charge of the dogs, so you'll be a bundle of nerves when they go out to do their thing. You're the one who has to make certain their outfits are on and will stay on, and that each is groomed to look their best."

"Gee, thanks. I wasn't worried until right now," said Ellie, frowning. "You've given me a lot to think about."

"I know you'll do a great job. I wouldn't have recommended you to Nola if I didn't believe in you."

They arrived on the lobby floor and headed for the exit. "Which brings up what I want to talk to you about," said Ellie after Patti asked Natter to hail a cab. "Besides my excellence at canine care, what else did you tell her about me?"

The taxi arrived and Patti and Cheech slid inside with Ellie and Rudy following. When the supermodel didn't answer, Ellie cleared her throat. "Patti? I'm grateful for this job, really I am, but what else did you tell them?"

Patti rubbed her perfect aquiline nose. "Promise you won't be angry?"

"I'll try, but—"

"Okay—well—then—"

"Just start at the beginning, and I'll—" The cab made a quick, tight right turn. Gasping, Ellie slid to the side. Both women clutched their dogs as they fought to stay on the seat. "Hey, take it easy," Ellie shouted over the jostling.

"Sorry, sorry," the driver answered, though his grumbling tone belied the apology. He steered the racing cab past the Plaza Hotel to Columbus Circle, then veered around to make a left onto Broadway. Once they were heading south toward the Fashion District his riders exhaled a breath.

"Geez," said Ellie, rolling her eyes.

"Ditto for me," said Patti. She glanced at her watch. "One good thing, at this rate I'll be on time."

When the driver finally settled down to a reasonable speed, Ellie called out a thank-you and ran her fingers through her mop of curls. "So." She focused on Patti. "What did you tell Nola?"

Patti swallowed, then gave a sheepish grin. "Not much."

Ellie narrowed her eyes. "How much is not much?"

Snuggling Cheech to her chest, Patti bit her bottom lip. "Just that you had a reputation as a crime fighter." She held up a hand. "I know, I know. You hate when your clients talk up your success in the investigation business, but you have to admit it's true. People who love you are proud of you, plus we're jealous. Interesting things are always happening to you. And you're dating a sexy detective, too. Let's face it, you have more going on in your life than almost anyone I know."

Okay, so Sam was a sexy guy, but that was about the only thing Patti had right. "More going on—in—in *my* life?" Ellie stuttered. This from a woman who had done fashion shoots in Spain, Morocco . . . Fiji? "You've got to be kidding." It was her turn to hold up a hand. "Oh, no. You're not going to get me off track about this. Just tell me what you said to NMD."

The cab pulled in front of the Fashion Center and Patti paid the fare. "I think we still have a few minutes, so let's stay out here. Once we get inside, people will start clamoring for your attention, and we won't have any privacy."

They walked the boys to a strip of grass, where Ellie continued the conversation. "Patti?"

The model shrugged. "I'm not sure why, but Nola and Morgan were distraught over Jeffery's arrest, and I thought I should say something to make them feel better, so I told them you'd probably be happy to help exonerate Jeffery. Then there's Kitty. She's such a sweetheart, and she and her brother are pretty much alone. They need help, and I thought that you, being such a fighter for the underdog, would want to see the right person arrested."

Ellie raised her eyes to the morning sky. Patti had hit plenty of the correct buttons in her explanation; in a way, she'd even echoed Judge Frye. She did like Kitty— and her brother—and she did have a gut feeling Detective Vaughn had nabbed the wrong guy. But the evidence against Jeffery was overwhelming. Unless . . .

"Okay, but if you want me to lend them a hand I'll need your help."

"Who, me?" Patti blinked. "What can I do?"

Hands on hips, Ellie said, "First off, give me some info on the other designers and models working here. I got the impression Lilah had plenty of enemies. Who were they and why?"

"Do you really think one of the models had the balls to kill someone?" She shook her head. "I can't see that."

"You'd be surprised what might drive a nice person to murder. Anger, greed, frustration, jealousy . . . Those are just a few of the negative emotions that erupt if someone is pushed hard enough." They headed toward the protected rear entrance side by side. "The easiest way to prove Jeffery innocent is to find the real killer, and for that I need a hand."

Patti's peaches and cream complexion paled. "But I don't have a clue where to begin."

"Sure you do. Just think a minute."

"But—"

"How's this for starters? I heard rumors about spats between Lilah and some of the models, and those are the ones who had the opportunity to do the deed. Who could have taken her EpiPen or screwed with her perfume strips?"

"So that's what the cops think happened? Someone doctored her perfume strips, then stole Lilah's EpiPen and emptied it?"

Ellie eased out a breath. "I believe that's the general idea. Detective Vaughn and I talked a time or two, and Sam heard some gossip at the precinct about Jeffery and the killing."

"And they're sure he did it?"

"They're never sure. It just depends on the evidence, which I think they're still gathering. Then it's up to the DA to make a case with what they find." Ellie wagged a finger and they walked through the door, where she peeked around the corner and saw three dogs already waiting in the pen. "That's why I need you to do a little spying. Give me a reason to suspect someone other than Jeffery, so I can look into their actions, see if they had a motive, so I can convince the cops they need to head in another direction."

"Like Dominique and Lilah's feud."

"Just like that." When the supermodel continued to worry her lower lip, Ellie put the pieces together. Patti's continued interest in Jeffery King, the fact that she was willing to help in his defense, the way she'd gone to Nola Morgan Design and encouraged them to ask for her help . . .

"Patti, is there something you're not telling me? Something I should know?"

"Something you should know?" Her hazel-green eyes grew wide. "Like what?"

"Like maybe you and Jeffery are dating?"

"Dating? Why, no. But—"

"But you want to?"

Patti frowned. "Am I that transparent?"

"It took me a while to figure it out," said Ellie, "but now I know for sure. You're hoping to prove him innocent because you want to get to know him better. In a more personal way, correct?"

"Okay, yes, I'd like to get to know him better. We started talking after I signed the NMD contract for this event and he hinted that, when this gig was over, we might hook up. He seemed sincere—straight, too." She raised a brow. "And in this business, straight is the hardest kind of man to find."

"I see," said Ellie, still grinning.

"And I'd like the chance to follow it up, but that won't happen if Jeffery's spending time in prison for a crime he didn't commit."

"You're right about that," she said in a comforting

tone. "So, with your help, I'll do my best to prove he's innocent. It can't hurt to poke around a bit while I'm here." The conversation she'd had with the judge popped into her head, and Ellie realized her "in" with the fashion industry was standing right there in front of her. "Think you can do me a favor in return?"

"Sure, yes, anything," Patti said, her six-foot frame visibly relaxing.

"I need two tickets to all of tomorrow's final events, including the NMD competition. I heard they were sold out, and I was wondering if you had—"

"Tickets for tomorrow?" Patti's expression brightened. "No problem. I got four freebies as part of my contract. Janice is using one, so I have three left. If you want them, they're yours."

Ellie almost jumped with joy. She'd just gotten Georgette's birthday gift and her favor for Judge Frye taken care of in one easy move. Taking a step forward, she gave Patti a hug. "You're the answer to my prayers. Thanks so much."

They entered the main part of the building, where Patti said, "I'll get them to you later today."

"Great. Now, back to your assignment. I have to get to my crew, 'cause they're waiting for their midmorning outing. You make the rounds, write down all you can remember about anyone who had a disagreement with Lilah and why. If you get a chance, ask questions. We can talk after this is over."

"Sure, fine, but wait a second." Patti stood and waved a hand at a young woman walking toward them from the other side of the dog pen. "Hey, Julie, I'm glad you made it." The orange-haired girl, who might have been in her early twenties, flashed a cockeyed smile. "Ellie, this is Julie Spinoza, your new assistant."

They shook hands while Julie gushed. "Oh, gosh, I'm

so happy to meet you. Kitty says you're wonderful, and I love dogs." Her brown-eyed gaze locked on to Rudy. "Is this your dog? Kitty says he's a real sweetheart. Hey, little man, are you a good boy?"

Julie bent and scooped him up. Her curly hair was so long it covered Rudy like a curtain when she straightened. "You are a charmer, yes you are. And so handsome."

"I don't know whether to nip her nose off, or just barf on her traffic-cone hair," Rudy said, giving a doggie eye roll. *"But you'd better rescue me fast."*

"I'm glad you like him, but you should probably put him down," Ellie advised. "He's not friendly until he gets to know you."

"Good advice," Rudy yipped, jumping from their new assistant's arms.

"How about if I introduce you to the dogs that are here, and you can take them outside for me?" Ellie suggested.

"Oops. It sounds as if you two have work to do, so I'll leave." Patti edged around the pen. "Julie, be good and do what Ellie tells you. Ellie, I'll catch you later."

"Are you ready to begin training?" Ellie said to the young woman when Patti disappeared.

"Sure am. I can't wait to get started."

"Great." She pointed to the dogs one at a time and gave the girl their name and breed. After that, Julie bent and hooked leads to the dogs' collars.

When the assistant left with the pack, Ellie let Rudy curl onto a folded blanket while she straightened the available foodstuffs, righted the dog beds and bags the models had tossed under the table, and thought about Patti and Jeffery King.

It made perfect sense. She and Patti had discussed men a time or two, and the supermodel had made it clear she'd love to find a partner, but in her line of work, it was a near impossibility. Jeffery was a good-looking guy, and he was tall. She remembered seeing Nicole Kidman walking the red carpet at the Oscars with Keith Urban—at least Patti and Jeffery wouldn't have that silly height problem.

But was Jeffery truly innocent, or was he hiding a serious flaw? Had he thought he could fool everyone, including the savvy Morgan Prince, into believing he had no part in Lilah's death, even after the woman had stolen his sister's designs and won a spot in this contest?

She recalled the heinous way Lilah had died; how her face had turned apple red and swollen to double its size while her airway had constricted until she choked. Other details had been explained to her in medical jargon, but Ellie would never forget the torture the designer had experienced as she'd expired.

If Jeffery hadn't done it, then who could have been so—so—the word Judge Frye had used came to mind. So *diabolical* as to have planned Lilah Perry's tragic demise?

If only she could find a link to someone else working here. A model who knew the importance of having an EpiPen on hand. A designer who knew what a severe peanut allergy could do to someone like Lilah. A person the designer had annoyed so much that they'd planned to kill her in an ugly and lurid way.

Heaving a sigh, she glanced down at her boy. "I'm at a loss on this one. How about you?"

"It's tough goin', but there's got to be a way." Rudy sneezed, a sure sign he was thinking. Then he stood and gave a head to tail shake. *"I got an idea. We could do it, and it'd even be legal."*

"It has to be legal. Gathering evidence illegally won't

fly in a court of law. And we could—I mean I could be tossed in jail."

"Okay, okay. How about if I explain my idea, while you think on it." She dropped into a chair and he sprang onto the one beside her. *"So here's my plan."*

Chapter 9

It was just after twelve and Ellie was exhausted. Models had visited the area time and again, not only to see their babies, but to check on the designers and the creations they were coming up with for the dogs. Julie did the best she could to help, but she had yet to endear herself to the pack, though she didn't seem to realize it.

The designers had come in and out of the dog area, too, with tape measure and drawing book in hand. Most of them liked dogs and didn't have a problem working with them, but Anton Rouch appeared to be a no-go when it came to dressing canines. He'd been onsite all morning without touching Daisy or even checking her over. Instead, he'd stalked around the ring, his dark eyes narrowed, staring at all the dogs as if they were vermin. Just as he was doing right now.

"I can't do it, I tell you. I just can't do it."

Ellie waited for Anton to finish mumbling as he paraded back and forth in front of the pen. His latest fuss had gone on for the past fifteen minutes, and she wasn't quite sure why. The man hadn't said five words to her since they'd met three days ago, and now he seemed up in arms, as if forced to make a life-or-death decision.

Quick as a blink, he stopped pacing and ran his hands through his generous thatch of coal-black hair, pulling at it until it stood on end. She took that as an opportunity to step in and stop his ridiculous tirade.

Circling the pen, she dodged Dominique and a few of the models, who seemed unimpressed by the designer's show of distress. Standing next to him, she called his name as gently as possible. "Anton."

The diminutive designer continued to gaze at the pen of pint-sized pooches, chewing on his lower lip.

"Anton," she tried again. "Maybe I can help?"

"You aren't reachin' him, Triple E. He needs a hammer to that head of his Miss Clairol–dyed hair if you want to get his attention."

Ellie, taller than the designer, was able to get a good look at chunks of four-inch spikes standing on end on the top of his head. Sure enough, he owed the jet-black color to a drugstore box, or maybe a professional hairdresser, possibly the infamous Karen Hood.

When he continued with his statuelike stance and vacant expression, she blew out a breath. Raising her hand, she snapped her fingers in front of his face. "Anton." *Snap!* "Anton! Get hold of yourself." *Snap! Snap!*

"How about tossin' a glass of cold water in his face?"

"Lord, no," Ellie said. "That would get us fired for sure."

"Fired?" Anton said with a shriek. "Am I being fired?" He whipped his head around to look at her. "If you have me fired, I'll see you in court, bitch. I swear I will."

Taken aback by his outburst, she crossed her arms, ready to let him know she wasn't about to accept any of his smart-assed comments. But before she spoke someone came up on his other side and broke into their almost-brawl.

"That's no way to talk, Anton. Try to control yourself," Clark Fettel ordered. Cocking his head, he glanced at Ellie. "I can handle it from here, Ms. Engleman. Go back to whatever it was you were doing, please. We'll speak in a few minutes."

"Great! Now Fiddle-faddle is treatin' you like a servant. What's up with these bozos? If I didn't know better, I'd say they all needed a go-round at getting their anal glands expressed!"

Swallowing a laugh, Ellie walked back to the chairs between the water cooler and food table. Leave it to her boy to give excellent but totally irreverent commentary. "How about you do some scouting work, instead of instigating a riot? Scope out the dogs who are with their models and see if there's anything new we should know before we take on our next task."

"You got it," Rudy said.

She watched him pad into the crowd, a mountain lion stalking prey. Intent on his mission, he appeared to be on the hunt, prowling in a low crouch, and she pitied the poor human or canine that got in his way. Then she walked to the other side of the pen, dropped to her knees, and ran her hand over the head of the white teacup Chihuahua named Daisy.

"Hey, little girl, what do you know about all this? Did you do something to upset Anton?"

"Nuh-uh," said the tiny dog, giving a body shake. Then she yakked for a full thirty seconds. *"I hardly met him. He hasn't measured me or anything. At the rate he's going, I'll never see a costume or a photo spread, never mind a biscuit."*

"You didn't bite him, did you?"

"Not really. I just growled a little. He's not a nice man."

"If I'm there with you when he does his job will you promise to be a good girl? No snarling or snapping?"

Daisy sighed. *"I guess."*

Ellie picked up her charge and carried her to where Clark Fettel and Anton were still in discussion.

"I know I was told that part of my job would be dressing a dog, but I thought it would be a full-sized one, not a rat." Anton's mouth turned down at the corners. "It showed me teeth."

"But it's a tiny thing. A bite couldn't be that bad," said Clark. "Besides, you will definitely lose the competition if you let Lawan walk the runway with a naked dog. Think about your career, man."

"Gentlemen," said Ellie. "Daisy is right here, and I promise she won't bite. She won't even growl, will you, baby?" she asked, nuzzling her nose into the Chihuahua's neck.

Anton quirked an eyebrow. "Oh, and how do you know that? Did she tell you?"

"As a matter of fact, she did."

The two men exchanged smug looks; then Anton spoke. "Really? Well, if that little rat even bares its teeth, I'll have you in court faster than a—" Clark put a hand on the designer's arm, but Anton shook him off. "That goes for Nola Morgan Design, too."

"Now, now. There's no need to get nasty," Clark said, puffing out his chest like a rooster strutting the barnyard. "You signed a contract for this event, and we expect you to stand by it."

"And he calls me a rat?" Daisy asked. *"Why, I oughta—"*

Ellie clamped her fingers around the Chihuahua's muzzle. "Look, Anton, neither Daisy nor I appreciate your surly manner and rude comments. Just take out that tape measure and get to work. As long as I'm here—"

"I'll be good as gold."

The designer shook his head, glared, and pulled the requested item from his tote bag. Ellie bit back a gasp when she got a good look at the carryall, noting it was exactly like Lilah's, or at least what she remembered of the dead designer's tote. Did he and Lilah buy the bags together, as friends would?

Hands on his hips, Anton continued to glare. "All right, let's get this over with."

Ellie led him to the food table, where she had cleared an area for Kitty earlier. Marcus David and Fiona Ray had measured their canine models in the same spot, and it worked out well. Anton Rouch could use this space while she tried to make peace and ask about his relationship to Lilah Perry.

She set the Chihuahua on the table, touched Daisy's nose, and, when she had the dog's complete attention, said, "Remember, you promised."

Daisy sniffed.

Anton stood in place. "You really do talk to them."

"If by 'them' you're referring to my charges, then yes, of course I do."

He gave Ellie a tentative smile. "Sorry for the outburst. Something happened when I was a—a while back— and I've never been fond of dogs since, especially the small ones."

"So you wouldn't mind working with a larger canine?"

"Maybe so. The little ones are—they—" His cheeks turned a ruddy red. "Listen to me. I sound like a kid. Sorry about that." He held out the tape measure. "Just hold it still—"

"*Its* name is Daisy, and I'm sure she'd like you to call her by name."

He shrugged. "Hello, er, Daisy."

Ellie smiled encouragement.

As promised, the Chihuahua stood quietly in place. Anton ran the tape from her neck to the start of her tail, and from paw to shoulder. Then he wound the tape around her chest, after which he wrote each number in his notebook. When finished, he hoisted his tote onto the table and tucked the notebook inside.

"That's a nice bag," said Ellie, picking up Daisy.

"Thanks. It's new. And I appreciate you not calling it by one of those stupid names, like a man-purse or a male-pail."

"I've been watching these past few days and I know how important a carryall is to someone in your line of work. It holds everything you need to do your job, just like mine. At least that's what Lilah Perry told me when I spoke with her." Ellie set Daisy in the pen, and returned to talk. "Your bag looks a lot like hers. Did you know Lilah well?"

He grimaced. "Well enough."

Surprised by the vehemence in the two simple words, she said, "It sounds to me as if you felt about her pretty much the same way everyone else around here did."

Anton stuffed the tape measure in his bag. "Probably."

"Which means you weren't thrilled to have had to deal with her." She kept her expression understanding. "Being Lilah must have been difficult."

He hoisted the carryall over his shoulder. "Lilah had no trouble being Lilah. In fact, she reveled in it." He glanced around the circle, taking in the models, stylists, assistants, and gofers. "I doubt there's a single person here that she didn't abuse, annoy, or anger in one way or another."

"It sounds as if you knew her fairly well," Ellie continued to prod. "On a personal level."

"Not that kind of personal." He gave a cocky grin. "I

play for the other team. Now thanks for helping with the do—I mean Daisy. I've gotta run."

Ellie dropped to a seat on one of the chairs. Rudy immediately popped up beside her, and put his paw on her knee.

"Are you back already?"

"I sure am, and you wanna know what I just heard?"

"Ah, sure. What did you hear?"

"Muffin's mom hated Lilah. She even said she was glad Lilah was dead."

"Muffin's mom? Do you mean Claire Smith?"

"That's the one."

"Really?" Ellie hadn't talked with the model often, but she knew the woman was a friend of Cassandra, the girl who owned the Greyhound. "Did she say why?"

"Something about a guy. Lilah dated him first; then he met Claire and took up with her. That's when Lilah spread a lie, and the guy dumped her."

"Who was she saying this to?"

"Nobody in our crowd. A makeup person?" Rudy sneezed, then jumped to the ground. *"Karen Hood, maybe?"*

Karen Hood? That name kept coming up, and Ellie had yet to meet the woman. "I think she does hair."

"Makeup, hair, whatever you humans do to beautify yourselves, it's all the same to me." He scratched his side with a rear leg. *"Seems this Karen person had a beef against Lilah, too."*

She shook her head. After hearing Rudy's report, Ellie realized something. Lilah had ruffled the feathers of just about everyone in this business, and there was no way she could sift through the past of each person in the fashion world to check out their gripe against the dead designer.

She rubbed the spot between her boy's ears. "Thanks for the report. I have a lot to think about, and I still have to tell Patti about our idea."

She needed to draw up a list of names and add whatever problem each person had with Lilah. Then she had to figure out if they were here that first day, and if so, when they'd arrived at the snack table. More important, she needed some kind of proof against someone clever enough to steal the EpiPen from Lilah's tote, empty it of epinephrine by shooting it into an orange, and doctor the perfumed pages. Then, for a last trick, they'd stolen her swag bag without anyone seeing them do it.

She was dizzy just thinking about the steps the killer had taken, because as far as she remembered at least a hundred people or more had picked up refreshments during the day. She'd been outside with the dogs part of the time, but it was useless grilling Kitty about what she might have seen. The girl was upset enough about her brother. Any more questions and she might fall apart, which was something Ellie didn't want to see.

She tried to help anyone who asked, especially if they were Rudy approved, and Kitty fit the bill. With her career hanging on the line, she deserved some attention.

"I'm gonna do more scouting. Maybe I'll hear more."

"Sure, fine, whatever," Ellie said as he trotted away. "But be careful, and don't get underfoot or annoy anyone."

"It's obvious you really love your dog."

Ellie whirled around when she heard her new assistant's voice. "Oh, hi. All done taking out the trash?"

"Yep. What else can I do to help?"

"Um, how about giving the guys a treat? I have biscuits in my tote under the table. You know the one?"

"Sure, and I can handle it. You take it easy."

Julie dug in Ellie's bag, pulled out the plastic container, and began passing out biscuits. A moment later,

Patti, dressed in an outrageous purple gown with a silver high-back collar and tightly fitted silver sleeves, darted through the crowd.

"I thought you were doing Zac Posen. This looks like something Ming, that creepy guy from the old Flash Gordon films, would wear," said Ellie.

Patti turned in place, showing off six-inch, silver stacked heels with lace-up straps. "Ugly, isn't it?"

"The worst," Ellie whispered in return. "So why are you here?"

The supermodel held up an envelope, and Ellie recalled the model's promise.

"I told you I'd bring you these, remember?" Patti said, still whispering.

Accepting the tickets, Ellie asked, "Are they a secret?"

Patti shook her head. "Not in here, but, out on the street? I heard people are selling their extras for five hundred a pop. Can you believe it?"

"Wow." If that was true, she was giving her mother and the judge a thousand-dollar gift. She couldn't wait to tell Viv that the single ticket she'd received was worth that much in cash. "Then I guess I'd better tuck them away."

"Who are they for?"

"They're a birthday present for my mother, one for her and one for a friend or my stepfather. Whoever wants to join her."

"I'd get rid of them fast, if I were you, before someone rifles through your bag," Patti advised.

"Do you think Julie can be trusted to deliver them for me? Because Rudy gave me— I mean, I've come up with an idea for something the two of us can do tonight, which means I won't have time to deliver them myself. If I tell you what it is, you can tell me whether or not you think you can carry it off."

"Just make it fast. I'm up soon with this rag; then I'm onstage for another designer. I won't be finished until four."

Ellie quickly ran through her idea for later that night, giving Patti the new orders in a hushed tone. "I keep telling myself it's legal because we'll have permission, but ..."

"It sounds perfectly legal to me," said Patti.

"Okay, then. Will you take care of it?"

"I'm going to give it my best shot."

The supermodel sidled away, and Ellie crossed her arms in thought. Digging in her bag, she found a pen and wrote her mother's name and address on the envelope. When Julie returned with the treat container, she pulled out two twenties to offer to Julie as a thank-you.

"All finished," said her assistant when she arrived, looking pleased with what she'd accomplished.

"How would you like to get out of here for a while, and run an errand for me?"

"Out of here? You mean *outside* out of here?"

Ellie quirked her upper lip. "There is another world out there, you know. One where the poor folks who wear off-the-rack live."

Julie elbowed her in the ribs. "I know that, silly. And yes, I could use some fresh air."

"Good." She passed her the envelope and cash. "I need you to drop something off for me. This should cover cab fare, and you can keep the change. If traffic's bad and it gets close to five by the time you finish, go home and I'll see you tomorrow."

"Gee, thanks," said Julie, removing her jacket from the back of a chair. "That's very nice of you."

When the assistant left, Ellie sat and assessed the job before her. Just about everyone in this business liked animals, a plus in her mind. Too bad they were so wrapped up in a person's outer appearance that they ignored what was on the inside. If Lilah had tried to look at the world in a deeper way, she might still be alive and well, not—

Someone tapped on her shoulder, causing her to turn on the chair.

"Nice to see that you found another assistant. That must give you more free time to talk to your dog."

It was Marcus David, dressed in his usual sedate-yet-sexy manner. The blue of his long-sleeved shirt set off the color of his eyes, and its cut perfectly accentuated his rugged form.

"I—uh—yes—I guess so."

"Well, at least you're honest about it. The talking to your dog part, I mean."

His cheeky grin made him look even more charming than usual. She was certain he'd have a successful career as a male model if he wanted a change from designing clothes. "There's nothing I can do but be honest when I'm caught red-handed."

"I admire that in a woman. Now, not to change the subject, but are you going to the party?"

Ellie sighed. "Do you mean the one tonight, after the Isaac Mizrahi show?"

"No, I'm talking about Saturday night, the evening after the NMD winner is announced. The designers, models, and dogs will be stuck here all evening posing for the press, and the next day is scheduled for more schmoozing and picture-taking, but Saturday night is another story. There's going to be a big private celebration at Nola and Morgan's penthouse." He cocked his head. "And I'm looking for a date."

Ellie gazed at the models talking in groups, most of them wearing little more than sheer dressing gowns that showed off their first-class figures. "I'm sure you'll find one. You have plenty of women to choose from."

He took a step closer, his lips stretching into a wide smile. "Actually, I was hoping to find someone who wasn't wrapped up in the fashion world. Maybe someone more interested in, say, dogs."

Heat rose from Ellie's neck to her face, a sure sign she was blushing. "Dogs?" she repeated. Duh! "Oh, sorry, but I don't date. I'm living with a guy, and we're pretty tight."

He reached out and ran a thumb over her jaw. "What's wrong with two friends spending an evening out? It's almost business, and we're going to the same place, so why not go together?"

"Since I doubt I'll be invited to the party, I'm fairly certain it would be a date. And I'd have to make sure Sam didn't mind before I gave you an answer. Besides, he might be free, and if he is I want to spend the time with him."

"Ouch, that hurt," Marcus said, his grin less enthusiastic.

"Sorry, but I tend to say what I mean. It's not that I don't find you attrac—er—I mean you're nice to look—" Positive she was blushing again, Ellie ran her fingers through her hair. Would she ever learn?

"Don't worry, because I think the same about you, only I don't have a girlfriend right now, so I'm in the market for someone to hang with." He shook his head. "And I was certain a girl like you would have an open mind."

He said it so sweetly, she couldn't get annoyed. "I do have an open mind, but Sam and I *don't* have an open relationship. We've been living together for six months, and I don't want to rock the boat."

"Hmm."

Unsure of the meaning of his noncomment, she narrowed her eyes. "Is there something else you wanted?"

"There is." He straightened to his full height. "I've

finished the outfits for Muffin and Cheech. Can I bring the dogs to my station for a fitting, or do you need to be with them while I work?"

Did she? So far, no one had given her that rule, but now she wondered. She was responsible for the daily maintenance and care of the canines. It was her job to make sure they were groomed to look their best and their duds fit correctly at the grand finale. But what if one of them disappeared before then, while they were in a designer's hands? Would she be held accountable?

Of course, now that she had Julie she could handle it, but she'd just given the girl the rest of the day off. Should she stay here and look after the dogs, or leave them and bring those that were ready for a fitting to the designer's booth?

She eyed Clark Fettel, dressed in a winter-white jacket, red slacks, and a matching shirt, still hanging at the edge of the crowd as if waiting for a problem to arise. As her NMD contact, maybe he could give her a hint on what to do.

Lost in thought, she snapped to attention when Marcus touched her arm. "Sorry if the question is a difficult one. I just didn't want to do something NMD wouldn't approve of."

"I'm the one who should be sorry. There's a lot going on today, so I'm trying to get my priorities in order. Give me a minute with Mr. Fettel before you take the dogs."

"Sure, fine." He grabbed a bottle of water and started perusing the food table. "I'll just hang here."

Glancing at the pen, she tallied canine heads, then made her way toward Clark. "Do you have time for a question?" she asked when she came up beside him.

"I've been waiting for you to finish with Marcus. I was

sent by Nola and Morgan specifically to speak with you, so hear me out first, please."

Had she done something wrong, or was he here to find out if she was accepting NMD's plea to help clear Jeffery King's name? Steeling herself, she focused on Clark, who was staring at her as if she were an unsavvy shopper at a blue-light special. "What was it you wanted to speak to me about?"

"It's two things, really. First of all, you're invited to the NMD party being held Saturday evening at their penthouse." He took a step back and ran his gaze over her from bottom to top and back again for the fifth—or was it sixth?—time. "It will be a fancy affair with the major movers and shakers in the business in attendance, so you might want to, um, change into something more, ah, formal before you arrive."

Ellie's cheeks filled with heat again, but this time the blush came from anger. Her clothes weren't Versace or Posen, but they were clean and up-to-date. The jeans were her new Calvin Klein's, and her jacket was a year-old DKNY she'd found on a markdown rack.

"I know how to dress," she began. "And since I don't walk my charges on Saturday, I'll have plenty of time to clean up right." She added a Southern accent to the last three words to let him know what she meant. "In my line of work, wearing Gucci isn't exactly the smartest thing to do."

"Of course, of course," he offered in a sour tone. "Oh, and Nola and Morgan wanted to speak with you at six. They know it's beyond the time they hired you for, but they were hoping you could make it." He raised an eyebrow. "Personally, for the outrageous sum you've been paid, I'd do whatever they wanted. But it's your call."

Ellie bit back a snarky retort. Ceasing to deal with the odious Clark Fettel was another reason she'd be happy to see Jeffery King again in charge. "I'll be glad to wait here for them," she said, continuing her forced smile. "Please let them know.

"There's one more thing—" she started to say.

She closed her eyes when Clark walked away without answering. How much more rudeness could the man pack into one day? Seconds later, he returned leading two men she assumed worked backstage, each carrying a large wooden platform. When they set the platforms up, one on top of the other, it was clear they were sized to form a two-tiered stage.

Behind them trotted a gofer hoisting an armload of fabric. The woman and the two men spread the fabric over the staging area, covering both levels with a bright red cloth. The woman continued arranging the fabric and the men disappeared, only to return a minute later with a huge piece of plywood, onto which was painted an iron fence and flowers surrounding a lovely bucolic scene.

"Exactly what are you planning to do?" she asked Clark, one brow raised.

"Isn't it obvious? We're setting up for a photo shoot."

Before Ellie could speak, the two stagehands returned with lights anchored on the top of tall poles, the type she'd seen whenever a talk show panned to a wide audience view. When they set the poles in place and plugged in the light cords, the area was bathed in a brilliant wash of pale gold.

"Well, don't just stand there," said Clark. "Get the dogs in position."

"You want me to do what?" asked Ellie. *The man was insane.*

"For their photo shoot. Their jumbo pictures are going to be posted on the walls around the viewing area when the runway walk takes place tomorrow." He clapped his hands. "Hurry up now. Get these animals lined up on the tiers and sitting in place."

Ellie heaved a breath. No one had told her this was a part of her job. How in the world was she supposed to—?

"Chop, chop, Ms. Engleman. Time's wasting." Clark circled the dogs and pointed. "Let's take that tiny white one and the fuzzy brown one and set them side by side. We can put the two with the—"

"Hang on a second," she cried. "I need to think." What she really needed was a short huddle with the dogs, so she could tell them what was needed and ensure their cooperation. She had no idea which dogs, if any, were able to follow a sit-stay command or would tolerate being seated next to a fellow dog they didn't like. She had to be careful or there'd be canine chaos.

"Think? About what? It's simple enough," Clark huffed out.

She held up a hand. "If you want this to go right, I'll need five minutes alone with my charges."

Fettel frowned, then gazed around the area. "All right. Five minutes. The photographer has yet to arrive, so I'll find him and make sure he has all that he needs."

She waited for the space to clear, then sat on the lowest riser and called her charges over. They obeyed and she smiled. This might work after all.

"Okay," she began. "You heard the man. It's time for your glamour shot."

Doggie voices rang in her head, so many she wasn't sure which animal was saying what. Speaking in a low tone, she said, "Hang on a second. Let's do this one at a time." She gazed at the two smallest dogs, Muffin and Daisy. "He wants the two of you front and center. Can you sit still long enough for me to arrange the others around you?"

The Yorkie yipped, while Daisy spoke. *"For you, anything."*

"Oh, that's so sweet. So, you know your places." She gazed at Klingon and Jojo, the mini Schnauzers. "Think you can hold up the outer edges on the first tier?"

Jojo sneezed. *"Yes, ma'am. I know we can."*

"Great. And for the rest of you . . ." She eyed the French bulldogs, a second Yorkie, and Cheech. "You four will be on the top. Are you ready to cooperate?"

Baby raised her tiny nose in the air. *"Not unless I'm front and center on the top tier."*

"What makes you think you should be the star?" asked Kiki, the French bulldog. *"Isn't it obvious who the star is in this group?"*

Ellie suppressed an eye roll. "How about if I move you around for each picture, so you'll each have a turn sitting front and center?"

"Nuh-uh. It's me or nobody."

"You're kiddin', right?"

Other dogs joined in, each one voicing a complaint.

"What about me?" barked the Greyhound, his shout drowning out the other dogs' complaints.

"Sorry, big boy, but I don't think you'll be allowed in the photos," Ellie answered, happy to see that the grousing had stopped.

The dogs' attention had snapped to the left and she turned to find Clark Fettel and a bored-looking guy holding a camera staring at them.

"What in the world are you doing?" Clark asked Ellie.

The shorter man gave a shrug and answered before she could. "Isn't it obvious? She's getting the subjects ready. I see it all the time in animal sittings."

Ellie stood. "Thanks for understanding. I think we're ready, but I have a suggestion. How about we move the dogs around in each photo? That way they'll look different. You know, break up the scenes."

"Whatever floats your boat," said the photographer.

Taking her time, Ellie set the dogs in place for the first photo and stood back. "There, what do you think?"

"Hmm. I'm not sure." Clark tapped his chin. "I know. We have an even number. We need another dog to sit dead center on the bottom tier." She followed his gaze and saw Rudy curled on his mat, wearing a grumpy expression. Clark pointed. "That's the dog I want."

Before Ellie could get him, Rudy wrapped himself into a tighter ball. *"No way, no how,"* he mumbled, his voice a growl. *"Touch me and I'll howl the house down."*

Chapter 10

"You've been a very good boy," Ellie told Rudy after the photo shoot she'd coerced him to participate in.

"And I'll get a meaty bone, right?" he asked, gazing at her with a doggie frown.

"As soon as I'm free to go to the butcher. Now take a nap." Her gaze slid to Clark Fettel, standing a few feet away and talking to the photographer. "I have to see to Marcus."

She waited for Clark, and they walked to Marcus's station together, where he was chatting with two scantily dressed women who acted as if their nearly nude presence was completely normal. But after three days of watching models stand at attention hour after hour while they were dressed like oversized Barbie dolls, Ellie realized it was simply a part of their job.

"Ms. Engleman tells me you want to take the dogs that belong to your models over to your station to make sure they're properly fitted," said Clark, breaking into Marcus's conversation. "She'll hook up their leads so you can do what needs to be done, and Ms. Spinoza can go with you in case there's a problem. All I have to say is be careful you don't lose them."

"Sorry, but Julie is running an errand for me," said Ellie, bending to attach leashes to the two dogs. "That's why this decision is important."

Hands on his hips, the NMD overseer tapped his spats. At this rate, she was certain he'd about had it with the way she handled her job.

"And who gave her permission to leave the area?"

"I did. It was something that I needed to have done," she answered, leery of telling him the errand was personal. Tired of Clark Fettel treating her like an indentured servant, she made an executive decision. Standing, she passed him the leashes. "Here you go. Just bring them right back when you're through, and be careful how you treat them or their moms will come after you with guns blazing."

Marcus gave Clark a small salute, then winked at Ellie. "We'll talk later about my offer." With that, he, Clark Fettel, and the dogs disappeared into the crowd.

"Wasn't there somethin' else you needed to ask him?" said Rudy, who suddenly turned up at her feet. *"Like where was he when Lilah had her attack? Or maybe why the two of them were on the outs?"*

Ellie wanted to bang her head against a wall. Some investigator she was. She'd been so wrapped up in getting her afternoon straight, she'd completely forgotten to quiz Clark about his relationship with Lilah Perry. But she didn't remember seeing him around the area until after Jeffery King had been arrested, so maybe . . .

"Oh, well. There goes your chance, but I say good riddance," Rudy ruffed out before she could answer.

When she dropped onto a chair and he hopped into

her lap she gave him a big hug. "I'm such an idiot. How do you put up with me?"

"Easy. You're my girl." He licked her cheek. *"Fiddle-faddle is a jerk. You should'a smacked him before he left."*

"Believe me, I thought about it. But I decided he isn't worth the trouble."

"It's just too bad you didn't ask him any questions."

"I know he and Lilah were at odds, but from the way it sounds, half the fashion world hated her. Besides, I don't recall Clark being here until after Jeffery was arrested."

"Does it matter? He worked for NMD and he had a beef with Lilah. He could have pulled a fast one, doctored the strips before they got here, and found a way to empty her EpiPen without us knowin' about it."

"You're right," she answered, sighing. "I'm a ditz."

He gave her cheek another sloppy lick, then gazed at their suddenly quiet surroundings. *"Guess lots of humans went to see what that Maserati guy has to offer. That means we got time to kill."* He snorted out a laugh. *"Oops, that didn't sound so good."*

"First of all, get the name right. It's Mizrahi, Isaac Mizrahi, and he's one of the biggies in the industry." She touched him nose to nose. "His show is the grand finale for the day, and he's hosting a party afterward, during which time Patti and I will do our spy work. Now, how about telling me what you learned while you were on this latest surveillance outing?"

"Not much, but I do have an observation."

She drew back and looked him in the eye. This was going to be good. "Okay, let's have it."

Buddhalike, he gazed at her. *"This is the most self-absorbed group of humans I ever met. All they do is talk about clothes and how they fit, or complain about their hair, their makeup, their nose jobs. And they never shut up about the size of their butts."*

Ellie bit back a laugh. "Looking good is their reason to exist. Glamour is a big part of their life. "

"And the size of their butts?"

"Is none of our business." She set him on the floor and began straightening the food table, noting the crowd had dwindled to a few gofers. "From the look of it, there's more going on than the Isaac Mizrahi showing, which means I have time to organize my plans for later." She pulled a notebook from her tote bag. "Take a nap while I get my thoughts on paper. Things are going to get busy in a very short while."

A few hours later, Patti and Ellie were sitting next to the water cooler, while the catering company restocked the table of snacks for the next morning. Cheech perched on his mistress's lap, watching the other dogs mill around the pen.

Ellie, notebook open and pen in hand, was ready to do business, but first she had to say, "Julie's a nice young woman. Thanks for finding her for me."

Patti smiled. "I guess she told you, she wants to be a professional stylist."

"She said she's hoping to make a name for herself in the world of accessories. She plans to match the designers' creations with the perfect bag and shoes to style the best photo shoots. In truth, I had no idea you could make a living doing that."

"You certainly can, and a good one. The best accessory assistants are sent to the shoot by the designer or travel with the photographers. Two came along when I went to Spain, and they had a great time."

"Then I'm happy for her. She seems like a terrific girl." Ellie cleared her throat. "Okay, so what have you got for me?"

Though back to wearing faded jeans and a plain and well-worn blue sweater, Patti still looked good enough to grace the cover of *Vogue.* "I used my notebook to make a list of the people I thought were most suspicious, just like you suggested."

Ellie cocked her head. "Did anyone actually act as if they were hiding something when you spoke to them?"

"Not exactly, but I zeroed in on the ones who hung around the table or were always in the area, even though they didn't work on our project."

"Great idea," said Ellie. "Let's compare notes. That way we won't do double work."

Patti straightened in her chair, looking totally composed. "First off, let me begin by saying this detective business is hard work. It took me a while, but I found out that I'd learn much more by listening than I would by asking questions. Though after a while even that grew old."

"I tried to tell you it would be tough, but you insisted—"

"I know, I know, and I'm okay with it." She cleared her throat. "Let's begin with Dominique and Claire and the flap they got into over a man. Dominique was supposed to model for Lilah, but she hated her so much after that, she refused to accept this job. But Jeffery understood her misgiving and moved her over to Fiona Ray."

"Do you think she's devious enough to doctor a page in Lilah's perfume book, then return it to her swag bag?"

"I'm not sure, but I do know she received the same scent in her gift basket as Lilah had in hers. That means she wouldn't have had to bring Lilah's perfume pad out.

She could have added peanut oil to her own and dropped it in Lilah's bag when no one was paying attention."

"Hmm. Then Lilah's swag bag would have had two perfume packets in it. Too bad the cops have yet to find Lilah's basket, because that might be a clue."

"Are they still looking for clues?"

"I saw Detective Vaughn asking a couple of people questions this morning, but I don't know why he was speaking with them." He'd nodded to her from across the way, but hadn't acted as if they had anything to talk about, so she figured he was finished with her. Ellie flipped to Dominique's page and made a notation. "Who's next on your list?"

"Do you know Lawan?"

"She's Daisy's mom, right? Tall, black, and beautiful?"

"Yep, and she had a beef against Lilah, too. It seems that when Lilah worked for Donna Karan last year, she was in charge of shoes and accessories.

"The way Julie hopes to be someday?"

"Exactly. And because Lilah was in her usual rush, she let Lawan take her walk down the runway wearing the wrong pair of shoes and the incorrect handbag. The audience noticed and started to comment. Next day, there was a photo of Lawan wearing the mismatched accessories in the trade papers with a very unflattering comment above the picture." Patti frowned. "Lilah played innocent and accused Lawan of screwing things up, but Lawan swore it was Lilah's doing. Claims she lost jobs over the bad run, but there was no way it could be verified."

Ellie jotted down Lawan's name as Patti continued.

"Karen Hood got caught up in that disaster, as well. She was the hairstylist on the job, but Lilah claimed she was lax. She should have caught the error before Lawan left the changing area. Karen was furious, told Lilah to do a better job, and words got ugly."

Ellie added Karen Hood to her notebook. The list was growing longer by the minute.

"And you know about Clark Fettel, right?"

Well, crap. Rudy was right. She should have asked the surly man about his relationship to Lilah while he was here. "Sort of. Do you know the whole story?"

"Lilah poked fun at him whenever she could. Laughed at his clothes, his hair, his, um, pudgy physique, and he called her on it. It seems she had a bee in her bonnet about weight, as do most of the people in this industry, so everyone laughed. It made Clark furious." Patti sifted her fingers through her long dark hair. "And speaking of weight, you and Marcus seem tight. Did he tell you about his youngest sister?"

Ellie reached back in her memory bank. Was Patti talking about the nasty comment Lilah had made about her full-sized figure in front of Marcus? And what did his sister have to do with anything? "He mentioned having siblings a time or two, but he never said exactly what was up with them. Why?"

"It was tragic, said Patti, "but I was in Europe when it happened, so you should ask someone else—"

Before she finished, Rudy bounded over with Nola and Morgan in pursuit. Racing to Ellie's chair, he plopped down in front of her and put his paws on her knee.

"Look who I found," he yipped, as if bringing her one of his squeaky toys.

"Look who we found," said Nola, almost at the same time. Dressed in a black silk sheath with red trim, a red belt, and sling-back Manolo pumps, she grinned. "Your boy was entertaining a group of models with his tricks." When she took the chair next to Patti, Rudy sprang onto Ellie's lap. "He's just the most clever little man."

"Finally, someone who knows how important I am."

Ellie shook her head. "He's clever all right, sometimes too clever for his own good."

Patti closed her notebook and Ellie followed suit. It was probably best that the supermodel's involvement in this venture remain a secret. That way, people might be more inclined to talk about their difficulties with Lilah in front of her.

"Rudy is a sweetie," said Patti, standing. "And on that happy note, Cheech and I are off to take care of another matter." She gave Ellie a nod. "We'll be back as soon as we can. I'm hopeful we'll have everything you asked for."

Morgan waited for Patti to saunter away, then pulled a chair from the row and formed a more private triangle. "Sorry it's so late, but we were in meetings most of the day. I don't know if Kitty told you, but Jeffery was arraigned this afternoon." He loosened his navy-and-red-striped tie, a perfect match to his navy suit. "The attorney you recommended, Keller Williams, made arrangements, and he's out on bail."

Relieved to hear that Rob's lawyer had helped Jeffery, Ellie gave a sigh of relief. At lease she'd been of some assistance with his dire situation. If Patti was successful in her quest, they'd be on track to take care of his problem.

"Kitty dropped by this morning and mentioned her brother had a bail hearing, but she didn't return, so I wasn't sure what happened. I just assumed she was playing catch-up with the other designers, and she didn't think to tell me what occurred with him. I take it things went well, and Jeffery is no worse for wear."

"Bail was set at half a million, half of what the district attorney wanted, mostly because Nola and I vouched for him and put up the bond."

"That was kind of you. You must think very highly of

him," she said, though she imagined the fifty thousand in cash he and Nola had outlaid was chump change to people with their kind of money. "Does that mean you'll let him return to work?"

Nola fanned a well-manicured hand in front of her face, as if trying to brush away a rush of tears. "Heavens, no. It's bad enough we have to listen to the industry gossip. We don't want him where people might say uncharitable things. He'll be with us tomorrow to watch the grand finale—other than that, he can spend time with that clever Mr. Williams and work on his defense while he keeps a low profile in the office."

Collecting herself, Nola sat primly in the chair. "We're hoping Kitty's wonderful creations will carry through to the next round. We'd love to announce her as the winner of the contest, but only if she truly deserves it. That should be a load off Jeffery's mind and hers."

Though fairly certain she knew the answer to her next question, Ellie had to ask, "What did you want to see me about?"

Nola squeezed her partner's hand and Morgan took control. "It's about that favor we asked of you yesterday. Have you made a decision? Are you going to help clear Jeffery's name?"

"I thought we were already doin' that," said Rudy, shoving his nose into Ellie's chest.

"I've given it a lot of thought—" she began.

"And?" Nola asked.

"And?" Rudy echoed.

"If you really want me to look into things, then yes, I will. I only have one concern—"

"We said we'd pay you. Just name your price," Morgan said, jumping on the statement with more than a touch of vehemence in his voice.

"Now, darling." Nola continued to clutch his hand.

"Ellie already said she wouldn't accept our money. Don't push her into doing something she won't be happy doing."

Still wearing a look of reproach, he arched a brow. "I don't like being held for ransom, Ms. Engleman. We've offered you carte blanche to clear Jeffery's name. If it's not some type of payment that worries you, then tell us what you want."

Ellie blew out a breath, hoping to get the discussion on a more professional level. "I'm not trying to make things difficult for you, or Jeffery and his sister. It's just that I don't want to get your hopes up. We—I—can't promise that things will work out the way you expect them."

She caught Rudy's eye and signaled him to stay quiet. "As I said yesterday, I'm not a professional detective. I've simply had good luck in rooting out the truth. The police don't have to listen to me, so they could ignore whatever evidence I might find. Worse, I might be arrested for obstructing an ongoing investigation."

Laying her free hand over her heart, Nola blinked. "Oh, my. Has that ever happened?"

Ellie had lost count of the number of times Sam and Vince or some other detective warned her about sticking her nose where it didn't belong. "Not yet, but I've been threatened by a few officers, including my boyfriend. They keep reminding me that the guilty don't approve of strangers digging into their past or their personal relationships. They don't like the fact that I've ferreted out the truth when they thought they were home free. Suspects can't avoid the cops, but they certainly don't have to talk to me."

"You tell 'em, Triple E. They need to know you're takin' our life into the danger zone."

Ellie gave a mental ten count. Talking about the hows

and whys of getting involved in murder always set her off. "Just like the police figured, Jeffery had a personal gripe against Lilah Perry. What they don't understand, or didn't look into, is the fact that about a dozen other people had reason to want Lilah dead. It sounds as if she irritated just about everyone she dealt with in her climb to the top of the design ladder. And the real killer won't be happy if they find out I'm looking into things that could clear Jeffery and implicate them."

Nola curled the hand resting over her heart into a fist. "What are you saying? Are you afraid they'll come after you? That your life will be in danger?"

"It's been known to happen," Rudy muttered.

Her boy was right, but only Rudy, Sam, and Viv knew the particulars of her run-ins with killers. "I believe this person was fixated on Lilah alone, but there's no way to ensure they won't try to stop me if I get too close to the truth."

"You're losing me with all this blather. I just need to know one thing. Will you or won't you help Jeffery?" Morgan's sour tone made it clear he was tired of the discussion. "And what do you want in return?"

She'd been given a lot of thank-yous from the people she'd helped out of trouble over the past year, but she never asked a for a fee or even a favor, and she wouldn't start now.

Nola leaned back in her chair and crossed her legs. "I have an idea. How would you like one of our designs?" She gave Ellie a cool once-over. "You look like a size twelve to me, and we have several beautiful new designs at our fingertips."

"You're talking about the ones that were shown here, these past few days?" asked Ellie, crossing mental fingers.

"Absolutely. Since this is our contest, we own every

design, whether or not the designer wins the grand prize. Did you see anything you like?"

Before Ellie could answer, Nola snapped her fingers. "I know. What about that wonderful jumpsuit with the ginger-colored suede edging Kitty made for casual day?"

"Oh, no, I couldn't," Ellie said, so happy she found it hard to express her true feelings.

"Take what she's offerin', Triple E. That's the outfit you said you'd buy, isn't it?"

"Then choose another. Anything. Just name it and it's yours," said Nola.

"Uh, well, if you're truly offering the jumpsuit . . ."

"Then the original is yours. If it doesn't quite fit, it can be altered." Nola's perfectly outlined lips rose into a smile. "In fact, you can have any of our designs free for the next ten years if you'll see to it Jeffery is exonerated." She looked to her partner. "I think that's a fair trade. Don't you agree, darling?"

"I think it's more than fair," said Morgan, finally sounding more rational. After standing, he helped Nola to her feet, then held out his hand to Ellie. "So we have a deal, Ms. Engleman?"

She accepted his offer of a handshake.

"Now don't let us keep you. I'm sure you have a lot to do," said Nola as her partner led her away.

Hugging Rudy to her chest, Ellie waited until they were out of earshot before saying, "Things got a little hairy there for a minute. Do you think they actually understood what I told them could happen? That we might not be successful?"

"Beats me. Sometimes humans say one thing but mean somethin' else." He snorted out a sneeze. *"I will tell you one thing, that Prince guy is more like a court grump, and that Nola woman borders on sickly sweet."*

"You're right. Morgan Prince is a handful, though I

don't mind Nola's cloying personality." She shrugged. "At least I'll be getting that jumpsuit out of the deal."

He gave a snarky grin. *"Hmmph. If you ask me, it could'a went a whole lot better."*

Drawing back, she almost laughed out loud when she saw his frazzled expression. "Better how?"

"A free bag of Dingo bones a month for the next ten years would'a been just the ticket."

Holding three leashes in one hand and four in the other, Ellie crossed mental fingers. She was supposed to meet Patti near the rear entrance to the conference hall, where she hoped the supermodel would have what they needed.

She glanced at the dogs as she led them outside, noting that most of the little guys were hungry, needed a nap, and didn't care who was taking them home, which worked to her advantage. She wanted to give a rousing high five when she saw Patti standing a few feet away, holding up her large shoulder tote like a prize.

"I know you won't believe it, but I have everything you asked for right inside my bag."

Ellie gave an over-the-top bow to show Patti an exaggerated sign of respect. "I figured you were an amazing talker when you convinced NMD I could handle this job. I had complete faith you'd be able to cajole six models into giving up their addresses and apartment keys. Someday, you'll have to tell me how you did it."

"It wasn't that big a deal, really." Patti's complexion flushed pink. "When I reminded them that their babies were probably tired and hungry, and wouldn't want to be stuck at a boring party, they practically jumped at my offer. I knew they'd all be excited to attend a celebration given by the world-renowned Isaac Mizrahi without worrying about their dogs." She set Cheech down and continued to talk while he watered the lawn. "You want to hear the best part?"

"Sure," said Ellie, though she was fairly certain Patti's ability to make a group of supermodels see things her way was a big deal by itself.

"Not a single one of them asked me why you and I were being so thoughtful instead of going to the party. Talk about self-centered."

"See, see, what I told you? If a human as important as Patti agrees with me, it has to be true."

"They reminded me of the cool girls in high school," she went on. "You know, the trendsetters who wore the latest clothes and knew how to put on makeup without looking like a clown. The ones who made the cheerleading squad and dated the jocks."

"Oh, boy, do I know," said Ellie. "But I find it hard to believe you were like me—studying all the time, hoping to get into a good college, going single to the big dances, or just not going at all."

They began walking north toward Broadway. "Ha! At five eleven and one hundred twenty pounds, it was a given. Add my braces and flat chest, and I bet I win the prize in this pity party."

"Yeah, well, I had braces, too, and my hair was out of control, never mind my potato-sack figure." Traipsing side by side, they let the dogs sniff and explore until they arrived at Madison Square Park, where they sat on a bench to regroup.

"I'm hungry. How about you?" Ellie asked. "And don't try to placate me by saying yes, then eating crackers and a salad the size of a tapas plate. I'm buying, and I expect you to eat."

"Now you're starting to sound like my baby sister," Patti groused. Scanning the surrounding area, she spotted a deli. "There's a sandwich place across the street and they still have outdoor tables up. I'll sit with the dogs and you can treat me to a turkey on rye, mustard, lettuce and tomato, with a Diet Coke, provided you let me bring half of it home."

"Better yet, how about we share?" asked Ellie, leading the way to the sandwich shop. "Even though I haven't walked my usual fifty miles this week, I still have to eat."

Once they settled at a table, she handed Patti the leashes. "I'll be back in a couple of minutes. Sit tight." Inside, she placed the order and organized her thoughts while waiting. The Mizrahi party was scheduled to last until midnight, so she and Patti had a couple of hours to organize their schedule. They'd hit the places that were closest first, dropping off dogs as they walked.

Eventually, they should be able to find a taxi driver or two kind enough—or crazy enough—to pick up women with more than a few dogs, and finish their delivery. Then they could share a cab home and call it a night.

She carried a tray to the table, divided the sandwich, and opened their drinks. Then she explained their next step.

"Here you go." Patti passed over her notebook. "I think Dominique is nearby. So is Lawan."

Ellie gave the addresses a good going over and copied down the buildings in visit order, hoping she had a handle on the relative proximity of the addresses. After sharing a bite of turkey with the dogs, they finished their food, tossed the trash, then headed toward Gramercy Park, which seemed to be the closest area in which a model lived. And since Sam had once lived there, she had some idea of where she was going.

They led the pack east on Twenty-third, turned right on Second Avenue, and found Dominique's building, a brick six-story with an outside foyer and elevator.

"This is where I live," said Kiki, Dominique's dog. *"And I'm glad to be home."*

"Not to worry, little girl. You'll have your dinner and be in bed soon," said Ellie, hoping to reassure the bitty canine. Then she saw Patti's grin. "Uh, I'm just trying to keep her calm and relaxed."

"Sure you are," said the supermodel. After using the key to open the door, she held it wide. "Dominique said we'd find Kiki's food in the fridge. I'll drop the leashes and we can fix her dinner." Her smile stretched across her face. "Unless you want to get down on the floor and talk to her instead."

Too embarrassed to speak, Ellie just laughed as if she got the joke. It was one thing for Patti and her sister to hear her say sweet things to Cheech and Chong, but another to have them listen to her chatting with a strange dog as if she were actually holding a conversation. She had to watch her mouth on this foray and keep her fingers crossed that Rudy was monitoring the pack and keying in on their thoughts. Not her.

Heaving a breath, she glanced around the kitchen and found that the entire pack had disappeared. "Hey, nobody said you had free run of the place," she shouted. "Get back here, all of you. Rudy, Cheech, come!"

"You're doing it again," teased Patti, digging in the fridge for Kiki's canned food. She found what she was looking for and turned, her gaze scanning the room. With not one canine in sight, she laughed out loud. "And look how obedient those pooches are."

Ellie headed down the hallway. Rudy had told her to snoop, but she just didn't feel right about nosing in people's private space, even if she was looking for clues to a murder. She'd done it a few times in the past, and Sam always seemed to know about it, which caused trouble between them. Yes, the models had given Patti their keys, and they knew she would accompany Patti in bringing their dogs home, but did that give her the right to snoop through their apartments?

Hunting for the dogs, she found two in the bathroom sniffing around the wastebasket. "Hey, you two aren't allowed in here," she told Muffin and Daisy.

Muffin gave a loud sniff. *"But it smells so good. There's perfume and makeup, all the things that make Dominique beautiful."*

Ellie put hands on her hips. "That stuff makes a lot of women beautiful, and you already have the identical scents at home. Now, where's Rudy?"

"Beats me," said Daisy. *"But he asked Kiki if Dominique had an office, so you'll probably find him there."*

"Fine. You guys go to the kitchen and see what Patti is up to. I'll be there in a minute." She gazed at the bathroom counter and decided to take a quick look around. Opening the medicine cabinet, she found the usual array of drugs and health paraphernalia: aspirin, Midol, dental floss, a kit to whiten teeth, toothpaste, a box of condoms, a variety of off-the-shelf sleeping aids, and a few prescriptions.

When she opened the drawer to her left she found a mass of makeup in liquid and powder forms, and everything in between. The right drawer was just as crowded with a variety of beauty products: two dozen tubes of lipstick, a couple of brands of eyeliner, shadows in every shade imaginable, several wands of mascara, and enough hair brushes to paint the apartment.

Squatting, she opened the cupboard below and took stock of the toilet paper, tissues, blow dryers, curling irons, and crimpers. Hoping to find an EpiPen, she—

"Hey, look what I got."

Jumping in place, Ellie whacked her head on the

doorframe. "Yee-ouch!" She gave Rudy a frown. "What are you doing here? I told you to stay in the kitchen and talk to the dogs."

Rudy dropped a chunk of newspaper on the tile floor. *"Yeah, but they scattered, so what was I supposed to do?"* He shrugged doggie shoulders. *"Besides, I found something you should see."* He picked up the paper and waved it at her. *"Take a gander at dis,"* he said through clenched teeth.

Ellie grabbed the folded sheets and stood.

"Now who are you talking to?" asked Patti, walking to the bathroom door.

"Um, myself," Ellie lied, startled. "Whenever I try to get a handle on what I'm looking for, I make a mental list and go over it out loud."

"Sure you do," answered Patti, still wearing a silly grin. "So what's that in your hand?"

"Uh, I don't know. Rudy found it and brought it over."

"Sure. Blame me for everything, even if it's something important."

"Are you going to keep it a secret?" Patti asked. "Or will you let me in on whatever that is?"

"I don't know what it is yet. Now, why are you here?" said Ellie, hoping to get her off topic. "I thought you were feeding Kiki and settling her in for the night."

"I'm finished, and she's eaten. I took the liberty of checking the pantry for peanuts and oil while I was getting her dry food out, but all I found was olive oil. Maybe there's a copy of Lilah's perfume pad in here, or an EpiPen."

"Uh, not that I could see." She tucked the paper under her arm. Then she looked at Rudy. "I have to find out where he got this from and put it back or Dominique will know we snooped."

"*I think it was her office. The room had a desk and a computer, and lots of bookshelves.*"

"I passed by an office on the way here. It would make sense it came from there," Patti unknowingly added.

They walked up the hall, and Ellie thought aloud. "I'm not sure we should be doing this. We should probably be on our way once I put this back."

"I don't think there's anything wrong with looking around while we're here," Patti assured her. "We'll scan the office and put whatever it is Rudy found in a logical place in the room."

They stopped at the room in question. "Okay, we're here," said Ellie. They crossed the threshold. "You check the carpet to make sure none of the dogs had an accident in here while I take a better look at this paper."

"Fine, give me the dirty work," said Patti, her voice upbeat. "But you have to let me in on whatever you have in your hand."

Ellie knew they had to inspect the paper, because Rudy said it was important, so she sat in the desk chair, and opened the sheet. A moment later she gasped.

Chapter 11

"What? What is it?" asked Patti, rushing to the desk.

Ellie straightened the sheets on the desk blotter. "Oh, boy. This isn't good."

"Told ya it looked interesting," said Rudy, climbing up her leg.

She stared at the publicity photo of Lilah situated next to her obituary in the *New York Post*. Adorned with a mustache, beard, and devil horns, along with a crude replica of a smoking gun pointed at Lilah's head, it showcased Dominique's innermost feelings about the designer. Some might consider it amusing, but not if the person doing the artwork was known to have had a personal disagreement with the deceased.

"If nothing else, it's certainly proof that Dominique didn't care much for Lilah, and wouldn't have minded if she were dead," said Patti.

It was obvious that Dominique had also added her own commentary, writing "liar," "ha-ha," and several f-you remarks next to certain passages.

Rudy climbed into her lap. A moment later, he said, *"But why the gun? Lilah wasn't shot. She was allergized, or whatever you call bein' killed by somethin' she was allergic to."*

"You think she was allergized?" Ellie repeated, as if Patti weren't there.

"That's an odd way of explaining how Lilah died," the model answered. "Though I must admit, the word sort of makes sense."

"You bet it does," Rudy agreed, jumping to the floor.

Ellie sighed. She was sunk. There was no way they could stop now. She opened a bottom drawer. "Maybe she squirreled something away in here."

"Squirrel? There's a squirrel in there?" Rudy pawed at the desk. *"Let me at 'im. I'll get that little rodent and toss him out on his fuzzy—"*

"Rudy, stop. He hears the word 'squirrel' and he goes nuts," she told Patti.

"Doesn't it just figure. Another human saying that doesn't make sense." He stuck his nose in the drawer. *"And what else do you think is in there?"*

Patti had already inspected and closed the drawers on the opposite side. "I guess that's how Dominique took out her anger on Lilah," she said, gazing at Ellie. "Can something like this be used as evidence?"

Folding the paper, Ellie matched the creases. "Maybe, but how do you suggest I explain the way we got hold of this to the cops?"

"Just tell them your dog found it. Cheech is always pulling stuff out from under the sofa or one of the trash cans. He's little, but he knows how to knock the darned things over like a pro. Chong, too. That sounds simple enough to me. Then they can get a search warrant or—"

"Sorry to tell you this, but according to Sam, an officer of the court needs to have a solid reason for obtaining a search warrant." Ellie ran fingers through her hair. "I'd first have to confess to Detective Vaughn that I found this in Dominique's home while I was here to deliver Kiki. Do you actually believe he'd buy the story of Rudy finding this? It's as bad as the dog ate my homework."

Patti hung her head. "Oh."

"Oh is right," she answered, the guilt causing her stomach to turn. If Sam found out . . . "But now that it's done, it can't be undone, so we just have to put it behind us and follow our plan of delivering the dogs. We won't snoop, but if something's out in plan sight it could give us an important clue. We have the keys and the models' permission to go into their apartments."

"But wouldn't a drawing like that show contempt or—or— something?" Patti continued her campaign.

"Contempt of Lilah? Sure, but a dozen other people hated her, too. Dominique just happened to put her dislike on paper and turn Lilah into a female version of Satan."

"Well, it has to point to something more devious." The supermodel *tsk*ed. "Finding stuff like this always seems to lead to an arrest on *CSI* or one of those television police dramas."

"That's the reason Sam hates those shows. He says they get things all wrong and it hurts the entire department." She recalled the evening she'd asked him to watch an episode of one of the most popular dramas on TV. "I tried to get him to take a look at *Castle* because the hero is a writer and the story goes into character interaction, not the crime, and he took all the fun out of it. Kept pointing out every place where the female detective's language was phony, and how they would never allow Castle to do the things he did in each episode."

"You really need to get Sam to lighten up," Patti said. Then she heaved a sigh. "So where are you going to put that newspaper? If Rudy brought it to you, you can't know where he found it. But he is your dog, and the way you talk to him all the time, I say you can just ask him to show you."

Rudy gave a full body shake, then sidled over to the trash basket next to the desk and moved it with his nose.

Ellie glanced at Patti. "I think that might be his answer, don't you?"

Rudy snorted out a sneeze. *"This is draggin' on waaaaay too long. I found the newspaper here. Just stick it back inside so we can go."*

Making a decision, Ellie pulled out her notebook.

"What are you doing?"

She flipped to Dominique's page. "Taking notes on our discovery, in case something else falls into place that we can attribute to Dominique." She stuffed the notebook back in her tote, stood, and pushed in the desk chair. Then she slid the evidence into the trash can.

Hoisting her tote bag over her shoulder, Ellie headed into the hall with Patti beside her. In the kitchen, they found the dogs relaxing on various spots on the tile floor. "Are you sure you left things the way you found them?" she asked Patti.

"I did." She bent to retrieve more leashes. "I still say whoever killed Lilah was devious. I didn't care much for her, but geez, what a way to die."

"I know, and I wouldn't wish it on my worst enemy." Smiling at Kiki, she gave her a pat on the head. "You're walked and fed, and your mom will be home soon. Have a good sleep, little girl."

At the door, she caught Patti's grin. "I know, I know, but I can't help it. To me, dogs are next to human. I know they have feelings and thoughts that coincide with ours. Kiki won't settle happily until Dominique is home, and

I thought to offer a bit of comfort to help her calm down."

Hands on hips, Patti's expression softened. "I'm just teasing. The way you care for our dogs, for all of those you walk, is why Janice and I love you. If you ever went out of business, I don't know what we'd do."

"That's very sweet of you to say, and I appreciate it." They led the dogs out of the apartment. "Where did Dominique tell you to leave her key?"

"Where else?" said Patti. Squatting, she slid the key under the mat and straightened it. "Dominique said the tenants in this building keep an eye on everything. She claims she has her own personal bodyguard living right across the hall."

Raising her gaze to the mentioned apartment, Ellie started when the door snapped closed. It showed that at least one thing from those television police dramas was true: The typical New York apartment building had its share of busybodies.

They took the elevator down to the foyer and left the building. "Where to next?" asked Patti.

Three hours later, bedraggled and ready to call it a night, Ellie and Rudy entered their apartment. She dropped the mail on the kitchen table and walked back to the front hall, where she unhooked Rudy and hung up her coat. When she returned to the kitchen, her boy was sitting next to his placemat, his eyebrows raised in doggie exclamation points.

"I guess you want your dinner," she said, removing his food bowl from the dish strainer. She measured a quarter cup of kibble from the pantry, added a spoonful of Grammy's Pot Pie from the fridge, and dropped in his chopped carrots and green beans, mixing everything together. "I don't know about you, but I'm beat, and I still have a ton of stuff to study up on before tomorrow."

"Food first. Then I can think."

He pattered a four-foot happy dance when she set his dish on the mat. By the time she finished microwaving a cup of relaxing chamomile tea, he was through eating and ready for more. "You suck your food the way a vacuum cleaner does the carpets. Did you even taste the expensive kibble and veggies in your dish?"

"Sure I did, but the taste don't matter that much, as long as it fills my belly." He gave a doggie belch. *"And it did, but I'm still hungry."*

"You're always hungry." She returned to the cupboard, found the special airtight jar that guaranteed to keep dry treats fresh, and removed an apple-and-carrot cookie. "How about a biscuit from Sara Studebaker's canine bakeshop? That always tops you off. Makes you less cranky, too."

"Cranky? Who you callin' cranky?" he asked, right before catching his biscuit in the air.

"Cranky is the way you're bossing me around about what we uncovered. It's not my fault I can't do anything with the stuff we found. You know what a pain the cops are when I stick my nose where it doesn't belong." Sitting at the table, she took a long swallow of tea, then pulled the notebook from her bag. "And I'm certain that's what Vaughn would say if I tried to explain all this nonsense."

"Nonsense? What's so nonsense about it? Patti had the keys, and the models knew we'd be in their apartments." Planting his bottom, he used a rear leg to scratch a spot on his neck. *"And after going through those apartments, Dominique isn't the only one we have a reason to suspect."*

"I agree. Unfortunately, you can't have an opinion in

this matter, at least not one the police would care to hear." She rubbed her nose as she flipped past the page on Dominique and moved on to Lawan. "And they aren't going to believe me any more than they'd believe you, even though I'm human."

"Then I guess we have to think it out ourselves." He circled his mat a couple of times, then plopped down and curled into a ball. *"So take it away. Let's go over what we got again."*

Ellie heaved a sigh. "Okay, after we went to Kiki's apartment we went to Daisy's, which is also Lawan's. She's the one who had the identical newspaper picture of Lilah tacked to a dartboard and hung on the back of her kitchen door. And we didn't have to snoop to find it."

"Oh, yeah. Daisy said Lawan was breathin' fire when Lilah accused her of messin' up that runway walk on her own. Daisy said Lawan was gonna see to it Lilah never reached her dream of being a fashion designer."

"And she won't. But where does that put Lawan on the list? Threats alone won't convince anyone she was the killer, especially the threats a Chihuahua overheard. And I doubt her using the photo for a dartboard would go over any better."

"So let's make her a maybe. Who's next?"

"Kate and Baby. That was some apartment, wasn't it? Almost as terrific as Patti and Janice's."

"Isn't she one of them famous plus-sized humans?"

"That she is, as if you couldn't tell by all the magazine articles and pictures she had framed on her walls. The apartment was like her own personal walk of fame. Who knew being a size twelve could be such a ticket to the high life."

He gave a doggie snort. *"I bet you could be one of 'em, if you wanted."*

Ellie couldn't help but smile. Leave it to her boy to

see only the best in his mistress. "You are too sweet. I could never be like Kate. First of all, parading around in my underwear in front of a crowd of reporters, photographers, and fashionistas isn't exactly my idea of a good time."

"You could get used to it."

"And all that fussy makeup and humongous hair?"

"You'd get used to that, too."

"Never, plus I don't take that great a photo."

"But Marcus said he wanted you for his model."

"Marcus David was blowing smoke, trying to earn points because for some reason he wants to get into my—my—well, you know what I mean."

"Sure he does. The testosterone leaks offa him whenever he gets near you. It's almost as bad as the pheromones Detective Demento reeks. And all I can say is ee-uuuw!"

"I don't need any more of your commentary on testosterone, no matter who's involved. And Kate didn't have a thing in her apartment that would make me think she cared a fig about Lilah Perry."

"Neither did that Crystal babe. Probably 'cause they're both too big to need Lilah for anything. That's why she never bothered Patti, either."

"Patti is smart. She avoided Lilah at all costs, and made sure they never got into any type of disagreement."

"But she's really diggin' her heels in on this one. Goin' all out to help get Jeffery off the hook."

"I know, and I find that amazing. In the two years we've walked her dog, I never once heard her go loopy over a guy. I just hope Mr. King appreciates it."

"So we went through all the keys we had, but there's more suspects."

"Clark Fettel, for one." She moved to the next page. "And Karen Hood, and Anton Rouch. And Yasmine didn't go to the party, so we couldn't get her key. I wasn't aware she had a beef against Lilah, but the way things are going there was probably some kind of bad blood between them."

"Don't forget that testosterone guy, Marcus."

"Marcus? Really?"

"Just because he has the hots for you don't mean he can't be a killer. And remember what Patti said about his sister."

Ellie did remember, because Marcus mentioned it, too. But what would his dead sister have to do with Lilah? "I realize that. I just don't know how to go about getting the skinny on him, or Clark, or Yasmine."

"You'll have to figure Fiddle-faddle and Yasmine out on your own, but I'm sure we could get into Marcus's place." He gave a doggie grin. *"If you were available next time he asked you out."*

"You are incorrigible. People have a name for a woman who leads a man on, and it isn't very nice."

"So who cares? It'd just be for one night. You wouldn't even have to swap spit. Just drop by and say you were in the neighborhood. Get him to ask you in, tell him you need to pee, and bingo, you're in position to check out his bathroom, find an EpiPen or peanut oil."

"And when do you propose I do this bit of skullduggery?"

"Whoa, now there's a word. Skull-whatery?"

"I think it means the kind of activity one does on the side when they want to get information. Sort of sneaky."

"Good call, because you'd definitely need to be sneaky. Didn't he say there'd be lots of pictures and magazine stuff goin' on tomorrow night, when they announce the contest winner? Why couldn't you hang around and see what that's all about? Then get him to invite you to his place . . . or somethin'."

"Hmm. There is supposed to be a celebration for the winner, and the losers are supposed to hang around for photos, too."

"And you could offer to lend a hand watchin' the dogs while the models are gettin' their pictures taken."

"I guess maybe I could. It does seem reasonable."

"It might even help you get on Fiddle-faddle's good side. He thinks you got paid too much for the job you're doin', so you'd be makin' up for it by offerin' a freebie dog-sit."

She finished her tea while she thought about Rudy's suggestion. No doubt about it, her boy could probably sell igloos to Eskimos if the need ever arose. "Okay, you've convinced me."

"So find out now. Call Patti. I bet she can give you an opinion. Or maybe Kitty would let you know. You could say you're callin' about her brother, then bring up the big win party and ask if anyone would mind."

"The only people whose opinions count would be Clark, or Nola and Morgan. It's their party, but I don't have any of their numbers."

"Patti might."

She checked the time on her microwave. "I guess I could give her a call." She shrugged, then took her phone from her tote bag and dialed her number. "Hey, Patti, it's me," she said, trying to sound perky instead of ready for bed. "Do you have a minute?"

"For you, anything."

After going over her thoughts on the party, she asked Patti for the phone numbers, but had no success. "I'm just an NMD contract worker, so I don't have their numbers, but I do have Jeffery's."

"You do?"

"Sure. It's on my contract as the contact. The office

number is printed, but he wrote what he said was his 'private' line under it. Do you want that?"

"Do you think he could give me approval for staying at the party?"

"I don't see why not. He's still an NMD employee and he was the chief contact until he was arrested. He also knows you're working to set him free."

"Okay, then, give me the number and I'll make the call."

"Don't forget, you should probably check and make sure Julie got the ex-terminator her tickets."

After taking Jeffery's number from Patti, she disconnected and frowned. "Oh, great. You're right. I should check. But if I'm lucky I'll get the judge."

"And Amber. Did you call and ask her how the gang was doin'?"

"With all the snooping, I forgot."

"And Detective Doofus. 'Cause I wanna know if I can sleep in our bed, or is he comin' home to kick me out?"

Ellie heaved a sigh. At this rate, she'd never get to sleep, but she made every call.

The next morning, the sound of Ellie's cell phone buzzing on its nightstand charger woke her. Groaning, she rolled to the right and checked the number. It was her mother, of course. Who else would be up at the crack of dawn and pestering her?

"Good morning, Mother."

"Thank goodness you answered," said Georgette, her tone desperate. "I need to ask you—no, no—first I have to thank you for the tickets. The judge gave them to me this morning, and I'm speechless."

If you're speechless, why are you calling me? was Ellie's first response, and the one she kept to herself. "Your birthday is tomorrow, and it was something I could do. You aren't the easiest person to buy for, you know."

"Oh, pooh. You say that all the time, yet you still manage to surprise me with delightful gifts."

Ellie swung her legs over the side of the mattress and sat up. From the sound of it, this was not going to be a quick discussion. "So what's your question?"

"Well, first off, I need a bit of guidance. What should I wear today?"

"Wear? Today?" Georgette had to be kidding. She had a closet as big as Ellie's guest bedroom and it was filled with clothes. "Mom, you do realize this is me, your daughter, right? The girl who buys off-the-rack."

"I know it's you, darling. And you've been at Fashion Week for the past four days. Surely you've had a chance to scope things out and take note of what the audience members are wearing."

"You know I don't pay attention to that kind of thing. Clothes are clothes. They should be clean and comfortable and bear a close resemblance to what's what in the twenty-first century. Tan and gray don't go together, and neither do brown and black. After that, anything goes."

"But what about the designers? Who's most popular right now?"

"Isaac Mizrahi had his showing yesterday, along with a big party and he—"

"You went to a party given by Isaac Mizrahi?"

Ellie imagined her mother sitting with her hand over her heart, as if she was having palpitations. "I didn't go, Mom, but you could call Patti Fallgrave. She's my supermodel client, and she wasn't there either, but she can tell you what to wear."

"I know her name. She was on last month's cover of *Vogue*. You walk her dog."

"That's her, and here's her number." She repeated it slowly twice. "And don't nag her, just do what she says."

"I have a list of what I own by whom, and I'll let her tell me which designer to wear. How does that sound?"

After yawning, Ellie said, "Sounds great. Now I have to run and get ready."

"Will we see you today? Stanley and I were so hoping we would."

"I'm on canine patrol, but I'll be peeking out from behind the wings during the Nola Morgan contest. If you see me, wave, and I'll wave back."

She set the phone in its cradle and it buzzed again. Heaving another sigh, she answered. "Hello."

"Hey, when are you leaving? Can T and I share a cab with you? It'll be my treat as a thank-you for giving me the ticket," said Viv.

"I don't think you should bring Mr. T." Ellie glanced at her boy, curled on his pillow next to her head. "There are too many dogs onsite as it is."

"Well, crap." Viv breathed a sigh of her own. "Okay, I'll walk him, and maybe Amber can do him at noon. Will that be okay?"

"Fine by me. I have to call her anyway, so I'll remind her. Oh, and do me a favor, please."

"Sure, anything."

"Call the ex—I mean Georgette—and tell her you're willing to give her some help choosing an outfit for today." Patti and Janice were late risers, and she knew Patti didn't have an assignment until the middle of the morning. If she didn't answer Georgette's call, Ellie would be back to sparring with her mother, and she had no time for more mother-wrangling this morning. "She'll appreciate it, and so will I."

"You want me to talk to the ex-terminator?"

Thanks to Georgette's four divorces, Viv never could call her mother by her real name. "Yes, phone Georgette. She'll be agreeable, believe me."

Ellie again set her phone in the charger. Then she concentrated on Rudy, sitting on his pillow like a sultan on his throne. That meant Sam hadn't come home. Which wasn't that odd, though he usually let her know he was working. If only he'd returned her call from last night.

"Are you ready to start your day?"

"This early?" He stretched his legs out in front of him, then flopped to his back and wriggled. Flipping around, he shook from head to tail, then jumped to the floor. "Okay, I'm all set. I just need a breakfast nibble to get started."

"Give me a minute. I have to find something that's comfortable for today but won't make me look like an outcast at the party."

She opened her closet door and focused. She had black wool slacks and a white silk blouse. If she wore that with a pale yellow cashmere pullover sweater, she might be able to get by.

She pulled everything out and, holding the sweater and slacks up to her front, turned. "Will this do?"

Rudy gave her his Buddhalike stare.

"Make sure you put on a little bling. Use that necklace with the single diamond that the defective detective gave you for Christmas."

"Got it, and I think I'll actually wear a little makeup. That ought to do the trick."

"Don't forget the hair. Put that gel stuff in it that makes the curls shiny."

"Okay, that too. I'll give you your morning nibble, then shower and dress. Half an hour and we're out of here."

Chapter 12

Ellie, Rudy, and Vivian climbed out of the cab and headed for their usual entrance, the rear door of the Fashion Center.

"You could go in through the front, you know," Ellie said to her best human friend. Viv wore an elegant long-sleeved wool dress the color of paprika. Smart and sexy, it showed off her mile-long legs and black, strappy Beverly Feldman shoes. "You have a ticket, so you're legal. And you certainly look like you belong inside."

"Thanks for the compliment, but it's just eight thirty. Are they open to the public yet?"

"Hmm. I'm not sure but you might be right." Ellie led the way, let Rudy water the small patch of lawn next to the walkway, and opened the door. Inside, chaos reigned. The caterers had added an extra table to the original they'd been using for the snack service and were piling it high with more substantial goodies. The dog pen was stationed closer in, so people had a broader walkway on the far side of the area, and the setup crew had squeezed two more chairs into the normal row.

Gofers and assistants raced past, dodging each other as if they were equipped with built-in sonar. People pushing or carrying piles of shoe boxes, racks of clothes, armfuls of fabric, hats, wigs, just about everything a body could wear, flew by at warp speed.

A tall, skeletal assistant with a cigarette hanging from her puffy pink lips slowed the parade when she spotted Rudy, who was sitting out of the line of traffic. "Is this dog yours?" she asked, blowing smoke from the side of her mouth.

"I'm my own man," Rudy snarled.

"Yes, he's mine," said Ellie, a sinking feeling in her heart. What had her boy done now? "Why?"

The woman shifted the garments she was carrying to one arm, removed the cigarette, and tossed it on the floor. "He was over at Elie Saab's station yesterday and he got underfoot. I tried to catch him but he darted through the crowd and tripped two models."

"That wasn't me."

"He almost ruined the Givenchy show, too, and Riccardo Tisci was furious. Told me if I found the owner I should—"

"No, he should take a hike. His so-called designs are yesterday's news."

"I'm so sorry," said Ellie, ignoring her boy's commentary. Just as in all city establishments, smoking was banned in the Fashion Center because of the damage a match or dropped cigarette could do to the designer creations. Thanks to the woman's careless attitude, she decided there was no reason to listen to her rant about Rudy. "I try to keep him here with me, but he's like Houdini. He manages to escape no matter how I pen him in."

"You're a terrible liar, Triple E. And she's stinkin' up the place with those minitorches. I say we report her."

"I'm just warning you to be more careful with him, that's all. Next time, security will toss him out." Leaving the butt on the floor, the girl stalked away, her thick black hair bobbing from the untidy bun on top of her head.

"They'd have to catch me first, and I move like a snake. I'd be gone before they saw me leave."

Oblivious of Rudy's snarky remarks, Viv turned up her nose. "And the ex-terminator was worried about what *she* planned to wear? Did you see what that woman had on? Ratty jeans, a striped tunic that looked about ten years old, and bald sneakers—no laces. And she's a smoker. Someone should tell her she's going to get wrinkles."

"She's not a model or a designer. Assistants aren't in the spotlight, so they can wear whatever they want. And I say let her wrinkle. It's what she deserves for being such a slob. But I do hope someone reads her the riot act for smoking on the premises."

Ellie walked to the still-glowing cigarette, stepped on it, and carried the crushed butt to the trash bin. "I expect the models any minute now. You can sit here and watch, or you can take off on your own and find a designer ready to show. The choice is yours."

Viv threaded her long fingers through her mink-brown, shoulder-length hair. "Maybe I'll find that guy named Eduardo, the one who takes care of the cover models, and see if he'll give me a couple of makeup tips."

Ellie raised a brow, taking in her friend's flawless complexion, perfectly outlined green eyes, and lightly stained lips. "You don't need makeup tips. You look like you're ready to walk the runway."

"Thanks, but I'd rather hear it from a professional."

She took Ellie in from head to toe. "I must admit, you look good today. Not designer A, but a solid B in regular wear. You're even sporting a full complement of war paint." She gave a sly grin. "I can't wait to meet Marcus David in person."

"Hang on a second." Ellie raised a hand. She was used to Viv critiquing her choice of clothes, but accusing her of dressing or wearing cosmetics for a man was an insult. "Do you think I did this to impress a guy?"

Viv's expression segued to one of innocence. "Who, me? Nuh-uh. I know you'd never let a man influence what you wear or how you do your face. Still . . ."

"Still what?" Ellie asked in a loud whisper.

"You've talked about him quite a bit lately. That's all."

"Well, I didn't dress like this for Marcus David. I did it for the big shindig they're holding after the NMD winner is announced. Since I agreed to help Jeffery King get the charges dropped, I have more work to do than take care of the canines."

Viv's eyes opened wide. "You didn't tell me. When did you make the final decision to help him? And does Sam know?"

"Sam and I have had different schedules for the past few days, so he isn't aware of what I'm doing. And I plan to keep it that way."

"The big dick wouldn't understand."

After straightening the dog pen, she pulled Rudy's travel bed from her tote, placed him in the pen, and pointed a finger. "You are to stay here today. No visiting other shows or sticking your fuzzy snout where it doesn't belong."

"But stickin' our fuzzy snouts into things is the reason we're here!"

"I don't want anyone to toss you out. No more messing around."

He circled his bed and dropped to a sit. *"Yeah, yeah, yeah. I live to obey."*

"I still can't get over the way he pays attention when you talk to him," said Viv, studying Rudy through narrowed eyes. "It makes me believe what you told me at my sister's house. You and Rudy really do communicate and understand exactly what the other is saying."

Inside, Ellie cringed. She'd almost blown her big secret this past summer when she, Vivian, and their dogs had gone to the Hamptons. "You read Twink, don't you? It's the same with Rudy and me. We're just a little more ... emotional."

She closed the dangerous conversation by scouting out the area, hoping to find Julie. A moment later, her new assistant, bright orange hair piled high on her head, trotted over leading Baby and Kiki.

"Look who I picked up. And while I was on rounds I ran into Marcus. He's a little panicked because Claire is out and he has a new model, Beatriz Alfonso."

"What happened to Claire?"

"He says she's sick, and NMD was told by the CFDA to use this Beatriz person to replace her."

"CFDA?" asked Ellie. She'd heard the initials, but couldn't remember what they stood for.

"The Council of Fashion Design of America," said Julie. "I talked to a few of the big names, and they said they'd never heard of her, but the council rules. And she looks good, fits a twelve, and owns a mini Schnauzer. Anyway, Marcus told me to ask you if you'd made up your mind."

"About what?" Ellie and Viv asked at the same time.

Shrugging, Julie hustled the dogs into the pen. "Beats me. He acted like you'd know."

Ellie raised a shoulder in Viv's direction. "I have no idea what she's talking about."

"Uh-huh, sure."

"I bet it's tomorrow night's big to-do at the NMD penthouse," her boy reminded her.

She shook her head, giving Rudy a silent signal to keep quiet. "Really, I don't. He did invite me to a party Saturday night, but since I'm invited, too, it wouldn't be a date-date. He said we could go as friends but—"

"You're not going?" Viv frowned. "Don't be a dope. It can't hurt to rub noses with this crowd. Imagine walking Calvin Klein's dog, or Donna Karan's. You could become a dog walker to the stars."

Ellie jutted her chin toward Baby, a Yorkie with attitude, wearing a big yellow bow in her hair and a sable-colored fur pull-on coat. "No thanks. That little girl's jacket probably cost six hundred dollars. I'd be the first to damage it." She waved her hand to encompass all the dogs, including two who had just arrived with their models and were being passed over to Julie.

"My guess is those five canines are wearing duds from The Dog Store, Edward Alava's luxury shop over on East Sixty-first, or maybe Lorilee Echternach's fancy fashions. I'm such a klutz I'd ruin the clothes, and I can't afford to replace them."

"You don't have to dress the dogs; you just have to walk them." Viv sniffed. "And you'd make more money if you stuck to the going rate instead of giving your clients a break."

Money might be Viv's main line of business, but it was always a problem between Ellie and Sam. It irked him that she wouldn't let him pay more than half the mortgage, but as far as she was concerned, the case was closed. Money just wasn't that important to her.

Julie grabbed one of the models by the arm and pulled her over. "This is Beatriz, Ellie. Her dog is in the pen."

Beatriz, a pretty woman who looked a bit older than

the other models, smiled and held out her hand. "It's nice to meet you, and I know you'll be fine with Lucy. My girl loves everyone."

Ellie watched Beatriz walk away, noting her normal stride, which was very unmodel-like, and her larger-than-model-sized rear. "Interesting," she muttered. "I just don't see her as someone who fits in with such a big-scale event. They put such an emphasis on the perfect appearance around here."

"That's what I was thinking," said Julie. "But you and I don't do the choosing. Maybe she knows someone, who knows someone, and so on. Either way, I have an errand to run. I'll be back soon."

Yasmine tottered toward them in six-inch platform heels, Jojo and Klingon in tow. When Ellie saw that the model couldn't handle getting them into the pen without throwing herself off balance, she ran to help.

"Here, let me do that." She grabbed the leashes. "I've been meaning to ask, how is Klingon doing?"

The model shook her head and her coal black curls danced. "Not very well."

"Is that the reason you missed the Mizrahi party?"

Her dark brown eyes filled with tears. "I couldn't let him go home without me. He's not sleeping or eating, which tells me he misses Lilah. Since he's probably the only one on the planet who does, I don't know how to help him."

Ellie had yet to talk about the murdered designer with Yasmine, and she sensed this wasn't the time. "Does he have any symptoms other than the eating and sleeping problems?"

Yasmine shrugged. "He just doesn't warm up to me. Won't let me cuddle him or give him an ear rub—you know, the things animal lovers do to make their pets feel secure."

Her explanation brought tears to Ellie's eyes. Rudy had told her the agony he'd gone through when he thought he would lose her. Klingon had to be miserable without his forever mom, even if she had been a not-so-likable designer. "Maybe I can help you come up with something."

"That sounds great. I know you have a handle on what dogs are feeling, and I'd really like a read on the little guy." She crossed her arms. "One more sad thing: I can't keep him. My building allows just one animal per unit. I managed to convince the super he'd only be with me for couple of days, but when the show is over, he has to go."

After that, Yasmine walked off, her dark orange suede skirt trailing, and Ellie glanced in the pen. Lucy, Jojo and Klingon were mini Schnauzers, identical salt-and-pepper dogs with big attitudes. It was probably time she asked Vaughn if Lilah had family, and if so, were they willing to take Klingon into their home.

Sighing, she turned to have another chat with Vivian, and someone called her name. The voice made her wish she could shrink to Lilliputian size, but it was too late. She was caught.

She put on her game face and smiled.

"Mother, what are you doing here?" Ellie asked, vowing to keep her cool. "I thought I told you the ticket-holders weren't allowed backstage."

"You did, but I met a very nice man who said it was fine after I told him we were related. He was such a tease. He thought I was your older sister."

Ellie gave an internal eye roll. Thanks to chemical peels, Botox, Juvéderm, five-hundred-dollar cut and color hair appointments, and her diminutive size-four figure, Georgette Engleman blah-blah-blah-blah Frye could easily pass for forty, not the fifty-nine she would be tomorrow. How lucky for her.

"But where's the judge? I can't believe you left him alone in that crowd of fashion junkies."

"Stanley and his electric scooter are fine. He's checking out the shows we plan to see, finding each of their start times, that sort of thing." Georgette clasped both hands to her heart. "I cannot thank you enough for those tickets."

"Mom, it was no trouble, really." Her mother smiled at someone standing behind her and Ellie felt a hand on her back.

"Why, Vivian, how nice to see you," said Georgette, her tone sugary sweet.

"Mrs. Frye, it's good to see you, too. I'm so happy you took my suggestion to heart. It's wonderful to see you in Chanel, and I love the shoes."

Ellie followed Vivian's quick once-over and noted that her mother wore a light gray suit with a standup collar and pearl buttons, and a pencil skirt that ended at the top of her knees. Her shoes, matching suede pumps with pearl buttons across the top, were Louboutin.

Georgette preened under Viv's first-rate observation. "Ellie is so lucky to have a friend like you. When do you think you can convince her to go shopping for a new winter wardrobe?"

Viv poked a finger in Ellie's back, her way of saying "Go ahead and shoot her." Instead, Ellie stepped back and did a three-sixty turn. "Come on, Mother. I did good for today. Wool, silk, cashmere, and the colors complement my hair and fair complexion. Viv said I look great."

Viv continued before Georgette could comment. "I have an idea, Mrs. Frye. Why don't you and I find the judge and see what he's learned about today's shows? I hear he's giving you one original for your birthday, and

I'd love to help you pick it out." She gave Ellie a side-long glance, as if to say you owe me big-time and steered Georgette away. "I can't wait to see what's on the schedule."

Ellie had yet to catch her breath when Clark Fettel, parting a group of models, bustled over. The line of six women, each wrapped in a black plastic cloak, each crowned with huge pink rollers, marched behind a determined-looking woman with a short brown bob.

"Ms. Engleman, we need to talk," he said, ignoring the women he'd passed so rudely.

Ellie watched the models file by. "Who's that hairstylist leading the conga line?"

"That's Karen Hood." He raised an eyebrow when Ellie did a double take. "You mean you haven't met her? She's famous, does all the big heads, if you get my meaning. Between her and Eduardo, they probably take care of a dozen covers a month." He narrowed his reptilian eyes. "You should make an appointment. Her precision cuts are worth every penny. I'm sure she could do something with that mop you call hair."

Clark's nasty comment didn't faze her. When she tamed the frizz and kept it trimmed, her russet hair was one of her best features, and she'd taken extra time today. Sam loved her hair, and Viv said the same. Perhaps Clark, with a left-to-right comb-over that did nothing to hide the top of his skull, was jealous.

Steeling herself, she decided he was having a bad day, which she would use to her advantage. "I'm curious, Clark. Where were you when Lilah had her attack?"

"That's the spirit, Triple E. Catch him off guard and make him sweat."

His eyes grew round, the gray irises darkening to pewter. "I don't believe that's any of your business. Now, I have a question—"

"You do understand that I'm asking for our employers, Nola and Morgan, don't you?"

He inhaled a gasp. "You think I had something to do with that—that—bitch's murder?"

"I don't know, which is why I'm asking. Nola and Morgan are positive Jeffery is innocent, and I promised to help him out of the jam. Right now, I'm simply speaking with anyone that I heard had a problem with Lilah, and I've been told you were one of those people."

Hands on his hips, he huffed out a breath. "That's ridiculous. People have disagreements every day. So what if I got into it with Ms. Perry once in a while?"

Ellie pulled her notebook from the pocket of her slacks and found Clark's page. "I was told she poked fun at you behind your back, embarrassed you in front of your superiors, made you the butt of sarcastic jokes and—"

He made a grab for the notepad, but she jerked it from his reach.

"Atta girl. Make him work for it."

"Who told you those hurtful things? Yasmine? I saw you talking to her a moment ago, and I knew she was out to get me. Or was it Eduardo?"

"Yasmine has never mentioned you, and I have yet to talk to Eduardo, but maybe I should."

"About Lilah Perry? Of course you should. He and Lilah had a dustup three months ago, when she was dressing Phillipa Bloom and she took it upon herself to add another color to the girl's eye shadow. When Eduardo saw what she did he blew a gasket." Clark shuddered. "Those Latin men have vicious tempers."

"You still haven't answered my question. Where were you when Lilah was onstage breathing her last?"

Clark's lower lip thrust out in a pout. "Standing behind the curtain on the opposite side of the stage. I saw what happened, and I wasn't upset, or angry, or—or—anything. The bitch was dead."

"I don't like the way he's tossin' that word around. It's an insult to all female canines."

Ellie refused to smile. Rudy was correct, but she doubted Clark would appreciate the comment. "And before that, earlier in the day, when Jeffery King brought over the swag bags?"

"I helped him put them together at the office; then I stayed there while he and the assistants carted them off." His expression hardened. "Why?"

"I guess you don't read the papers. The coroner's report said that Lilah died from coming in contact with peanut—"

"Peanut oil." He *tsk*ed. "Everyone knows that."

"But did you know they determined the oil came from one of her perfume strips? And they think someone who had contact with the gift bags was able to get hold of the scented strips and doctor them?"

When Clark's face folded into a question mark, she decided to ask the big question. "You and Jeffery were in line for the same job, weren't you? So with him out of the way . . ."

His confused expression shifted to anger so quickly Ellie had to blink. "You think it was me! That I framed Jeffery King for the murder?" His voice jumped a hundred decibels. He took a step back. "That's—that's crazy."

"You're the one who's crazy, Fiddle-faddle. Tell him I said so."

When she jotted a notation in her notebook, he gasped.

"What are you writing about me? Are you saying I should be brought to trial like a—a—common felon?"

"I take notes on all my conversations when I'm on a case." This was the first time she'd ever truly "grilled" someone and she was beginning to enjoy it. "All you have to be is truthful, and I won't have any reason to mention your name to the cops."

He clenched his hands into fists and she swallowed. Was Clark Fettel a violent man? If she continued to prod, would he take a swing at her? She'd gone to a lot of trouble with her makeup and wasn't about to let this nutcase mess it up.

"I think we've discussed everything we need to, don't you?"

His eyes narrowed to slits, then strayed to something over her shoulder and opened wide. "Yes, I think so," he said, backing away. "At least, for now." He took a few stumbling steps before running away.

Ellie took a deep breath before turning around. People in this place knew how to sneak up on a person like nobody's business, and she couldn't imagine who Clark Fettel would be fearful of.

"Ms. Engleman?"

She spun on her heels and almost bumped into the new arrival. "Oh, Mr. Prince," she sputtered. "I didn't see you there."

An imposing man with a thick shock of white hair, her employer wore a pale gray Armani suit with an open-collared bright orange shirt. It would have looked ridiculous on someone like Clark Fettel, but on Morgan Prince, well, it actually looked . . . princely.

"Apparently Clark did. What was that all about?"

"I was going over some questions that needed answers and he wasn't willing to cooperate. Why would he run like that when he saw you?"

Morgan shrugged, his broad shoulders bunching the fabric of the suit. "Clark and I don't exactly get along. Nola seems to think he has potential, but I'm not so sure." His generous lips tightened. "Was he bothering you?"

Ellie shook her head. "He's a bit pushy, but I can handle him. Were you aware he didn't get along with Lilah?"

"I knew it. But then, she had so many enemies it wasn't a surprise. You spoke with her, so you must realize she had what some might call an acerbic personality." He cocked his head. "How are you coming along with the investigation?"

"I'm still in the questioning stage with a few people, but there are a couple I consider possible suspects. Unfortunately, I don't have anything concrete to report."

She walked to the chairs and he followed. When she took a seat, he did too, leaving a chair between them. "Sorry if that isn't what you wanted to hear. It's just that there are so many suspects I can see why the cops simply zeroed in on the first person that made sense." She crossed her legs and wrapped her hands around her knee. "You and Nola have told me you believe Jeffery King is innocent, but what makes you so certain?"

Morgan got comfortable and rested an arm along the chair back. "Jeffery's worked for us since he graduated college, and his efforts have been impeccable. I pride myself on being able to read people, and so I knew he had a good work ethic and a creative mind."

He pursed his lips. "When he came to us with his suspicions of Lilah and what she'd done with Kitty's designs, he explained them logically and never lost his temper. It was unfortunate he had no proof to support his accusations, and when we told him so he let the matter drop. We simply didn't get the impression he'd resort to violence.

"Once he told Lilah what he thought of her he never mentioned the incident again. That's why Nola and I are sure someone else did her in." He thinned his lips. "Someone like Marcus David."

Marcus David? Before Ellie could answer, the three mini Schnauzers wandered over with Rudy beside them. *"Uh, Ellie, think you could give Klingon a cuddle when you're done talkin'? He's really down in the dumper."*

"I, um, I'll look into it," she told Morgan, wondering if Rudy was right about the designer.

"Klingon, Triple E. He needs a little lovin'."

She gave the dogs a slow once-over, hoping to do as her boy asked. But she couldn't tell which was Jojo, which was Klingon, and which was Lucy.

Morgan saw her inspecting the dogs and said, "I understand Yasmine's been watching Lilah's little pal."

"Yes, and the poor boy seems to be depressed. She told me he's not eating and he doesn't sleep. Yasmine says he really misses his mother."

Morgan stood and picked up one of the mini Schnauzers. Taking his seat, he held the pooch on his lap and ran a hand over his ears and down his back.

"Are you sure you have the right dog? Is that Klingon?" asked Ellie.

He flipped the metal ID tag and took a look. "That's the name on his tag."

Klingon licked Morgan's hand, then nestled into his thighs, his actions completely different from what Yasmine had reported.

"He seems to like you. He'll be needing a home, you know. Yasmine told me she won't be able to keep him after the show is over, and I have yet to hear from Detective Vaughn. He's supposed to be checking with Lilah's family to see if any of them will take the little boy."

"I'll talk to Nola. Maybe she'll agree to a new dog in the house."

"That would be a nice gesture. Especially since he looks so happy to get your attention."

Morgan stood and passed her Klingon, then nodded. "We'll see. Now, if you'll excuse me, we have a long day ahead of us. We'll talk later."

She scratched the underside of Klingon's chin and the dog heaved a sigh. "You seemed to like that man. Is he someone you could live with?"

The dog rested his body against her chest. *"I guess, if my mom is gone."*

She'd never heard Klingon's voice before, so his answer was encouraging. "He seemed to like you. Maybe you could get along with him and another woman."

"But I want Lilah." The dog shuddered in her arms. *"Why can't I have Lilah?"*

"No one can get her for you, baby boy. Your mom is at rest, waiting for you in a better place."

The words brought a tear to her eye. She was sorry it was the best she could say.

Chapter 13

"There's another nose job, and it's a bad one."

Ellie sighed.

"And the girl wearing that long red dress is chin implant number two. She'd probably look like a turkey without it." Viv's voice was just above a whisper. "Any idea where they found a plastic surgeon who does such mediocre work?"

Ellie put her hands to her temples and rested her elbows on her knees. It was close to noon, break time for the big shows, so many of the models had dropped by to munch a carrot stick or three. Vivian had the perfect seat to conduct her blatant commentary on the facial sculpting in which so many of the models had taken part.

"Viv, really—"

Vivian jabbed her in the ribs. "I'm serious. Take a look at the cheek implants on that girl with the bare midriff. The one sifting through the fruit salad. Talk about razor sharp, they're like a knife edge, or a—oops—cheek implant number three just joined her."

"Not every model has had work done, you know. Just ask Patti Fallgrave."

"Cheech's mom? I thought she gave you a list of repairs she had done."

"Dental work, which anyone with an overbite would take care of, and some hair stuff, but that was it."

"Okay, fine. Some of the big-name women were born beautiful, but a lot of them weren't. It gives a normal girl hope. Get a new nose or chin and you too can be a supermodel."

"What about the photogenic part? You have to look great in the eyes of a camera, and don't forget being six feet tall and thin as a stick."

Viv shrugged. "All right, I'll give in to the height issue, but it's still fun to see who's had what done."

Ellie hissed another sigh. "Don't you have somewhere else to be? What happened to escorting my mother and Stanley?"

"You expected me to have lunch with the exterminator?" Viv shivered. "You've got to be kidding. Your mother is a royal pain in the you-know-what. I don't see how that sweet old judge can love her, let alone put up with her."

"Oh, come on. Georgette's not that bad," Ellie said, thinking hard to find one of her mother's better qualities. "She's honest. That's a plus."

"Honest? Her honesty cuts like a Wüsthof knife." Viv inhaled a gasp. "And speaking of knives—there's a fourth cheek implant." She gave Ellie another elbow jab. "Really. Take a look."

Ellie raised her gaze as a model wearing a sheer dressing gown walked by. "I'm still confused. How can you tell?"

"Trust me, none of those women were born with

those rapier-like bones," Viv answered, her tone as sharp as the cheeks she'd just inspected. "If they had been, they would have sliced their mother going through the birth canal."

"Oh, Lord, you are so bad," said Ellie, finally cracking a grin. "It's no one's business what a model does to get work. The sad thing is the way the fashion industry dictates their body size. So many young girls are bulimic or anorexic because they think they won't get ahead unless they're skinny as a rail."

"I'm well aware of that. Lucky for me I can eat like a dockworker and not gain an ounce."

"What you can do doesn't matter. It's what they have to do, or think they have to do, that counts." Ellie settled back in her chair. "At least my job keeps my weight under control."

"Don't remind me. You look great now, but I remember when the dickhead expected you to wear a size six. Talk about cheekbones. You were absolutely gaunt."

"And starving most of the time. I'm lucky Sam likes his women with curves."

"Sam is a great guy, who loves you for you, not for your size. And I apologize for what I said earlier about dressing for that designer guy."

"You already did that."

"Well, now I'm serious. After you were married to Larry Lipschitz for ten ugly years, I can understand why you'd never let a man influence your fashion sense again. Being true to yourself is one of the things I love about you." Viv matched her grin. "I can always trust you to tell me the truth. I guess that's something you share with Georgette, only without the Wüsthof knife."

"Thank you—I think."

They continued observing the hairdressers, makeup

artists, gofers, and models converging around the goodie table. The new model, Beatriz, was there, wearing a regular dressing gown instead of a see-through type, and she seemed to be deep in conversation with Dominique. Again, Ellie sensed that something about her was different, but she couldn't put her finger on what it might be.

A minute later, Viv gazed out into the crowd. "Here comes your new assistant. She's sort of sweet. How's she doing?"

"Just fine, now that she's gotten the hang of things, though I think she'd rather be styling supermodels than handling canine care. But the dogs seem to like her, and she's a friend of Kitty's, so she's on Jeffery's side." Ellie folded her arms. "She even agreed to keep her ears open and report back if she heard anything interesting about Lilah Perry's death."

"That's a plus, right. She knows the crowd, so she knows who talks a good game and who doesn't." Viv checked her watch and stood. "Oops, I have to go. It's time to meet my hot date. I'll see you later."

Hot date? Ellie blinked. Viv was devoted to Dr. David Crane, veterinarian to the pets of the rich and famous on the Upper East Side. "You have a date? With who?"

"Oh, don't look so disapproving. With Eduardo. I found him while I was making rounds with your mother and he gave me a consult appointment so we could go over my makeup questions." She heaved a sigh. "Georgette wanted a consult, too, but he said he only had time for one. He gave her his card and told her to call him."

Poor Eduardo, thought Ellie. Georgette could be difficult, even with a professional. "Do you think he knows what he's getting himself into?"

"He handled her okay when she tried to talk him into an appointment, so I got the feeling he's used to dealing with bitchy women." Viv frowned. "Sorry, but you know that's how Georgette can be."

"I know, but a lot of it's for show. Did he say how much he charges?"

"I have no idea." Viv hiked her Chanel bag over her shoulder. "But I don't care. Today is my day to rub elbows with the true fashionistas of the world. I'll pay whatever he asks for his expert advice." She waggled her fingers and headed out into the crowd, passing Julie on the way.

"Hey," Julie said after grabbing a bottle of water from the table and taking a seat next to Ellie. "How are things going? Do you or the dogs need me?"

"The canines have to be taken for a midday walk in a half hour or so. What have you been up to?" She decided to keep the next question casual. "Did you get any new information from the crowd?"

"Not the kind of information you're looking for, though I did try. These people love to chatter, so I usually hear all kinds of gossip when I listen to the designers talk about the look they're trying to create. By the way, Marcus asked about you again."

A rush of heat rose from Ellie's chest, a sure sign she was blushing. Marcus appeared to be the kind of man who didn't take no for an answer. He might make a good friend, but there could never be anything personal between them. "I'll talk to him later, when he comes by to get his dogs for the big show."

"It's nice to see he's interested in someone. He's pretty much kept to himself since he lost his sister." Julie crossed her legs and let her thong sandal dangle off her toes. "You know about what happened to Sylvie, right?"

The question set off a warning bell in Ellie's brain. Marcus had dropped a comment or two about his siblings while they talked, but he'd never given her the details of his sister's death. "I heard something about her, but I didn't know her name."

"He had three sisters, and Sylvie was the baby of the family. She wanted to be a model in the worst way, but she was a big girl, so she was always on a diet. She hung around here whenever a call went out for open tryouts, but she never seemed to make the cut."

"Open tryouts?" Ellie sat up straight. "What's that?"

"It's an industry thing. Every so many weeks the student designers have to show what they've created and they need girls to model the outfit. We usually get a bunch of high school kids in, each one hoping to break into the business. Sylvie was here all the time, but Marcus was the only one who ever chose her as his model."

Ellie shrugged. "It's what I'd want a brother to do for me—if I had one."

Julie nodded. "Me, too. Trouble is, everyone thought that she was on the runway only because he was her brother, so no one else asked her to dress for them. After a while, she began to diet big-time, starving herself really, which was not a good thing for her to do."

"It's not a good thing for anyone to do," said Ellie. "Viv and I were just talking about it, and we decided it was the number one problem with this business."

"I agree, but Sylvie had a bad heart as well, and the yo-yoing weight issue was making it worse."

"How old was she?"

"Only seventeen, and like a typical teen she was headstrong, wouldn't listen, kept dieting, ragging other designers to let her model, and stressing herself over it."

"Don't keep me in suspense. What happened to her?"

"She came in one day and targeted Lilah Perry with her begging. Unfortunately Lilah told her, in her typical crude Lilah manner, that she was too heavy and would never make it on the runway. Sylvie started to cry and ran out of the building."

"Where was Marcus?"

"On his way in. When he saw Sylvie sobbing he blew up. Even dived on Lilah and tried to choke her, but a couple of folks pulled him off before he did any damage." Julie swallowed another gulp of water. "Lilah, of course, made herself look completely innocent, so Marcus ran after his sister, but it was too late. When she bolted from the building she headed straight for the street."

"Oh, no. Please don't tell me—"

"Yep. A yellow cab ran her down. It was so sad. Marcus got there right after it happened. Sylvie died in his arms."

Ellie reared back in her chair. "Sylvie David ran out of the building and was hit by a taxi. She died in her brother's arms, and he blamed it on Lilah Perry?"

"A lot of folks did. Lilah even threatened to file charges against Marcus, but when she realized that wouldn't be tolerated and she might be blackballed, she pretended the incident never happened. And she wasn't blackballed for the way she'd treated Sylvie, either."

"Because—"

"Apparently someone at the top thought she had talent and allowed her to continue working at the center. It blew over after a couple of months, and she and Marcus kept their distance."

Tears sprang to Ellie's eyes and she swallowed to regain her composure. "How awful." She swiped the droplets away and took a deep breath. "No wonder Marcus doesn't want to talk about it."

"He seems to be crazy about you. I'm sure he would have told you eventually."

"I've tried to dissuade him. Told him I have a serious

boyfriend, but he doesn't want to listen. And I've been so busy trying to untangle the Jeffery King thing that I haven't said much more."

"It's been almost a year now that Sylvie's been gone. Like I said, Marcus is a good guy. It's nice to know he's interested in something, or someone, besides work. Do you think he has a chance of winning the NMD contest?"

Ellie blew her nose and cleared her throat. "I have no idea. His work is good, but I'm no judge. What's the word in the changing rooms?"

"Everyone is saying it's between him and Kitty. There's even a betting pool."

"A betting pool? Like they do for football games and other sports?"

"Yep."

"Who's in charge?"

"One of the security guards, I think. I don't get involved, but I do listen to who's saying what." Julie stood. "I'm going to the restroom, but I'll be back to do the dog run."

She left and Ellie blew out a breath. Then she locked eyes with Rudy, who'd been sitting in the pen and listening.

"You okay?"

She nodded. "I take it you heard Julie's story? The one about Marcus's sister?"

"Sure did, and it was sad."

"I think so, too."

"I get why you're upset, but I don't like to see you cry."

He rose up on his hind legs and she hoisted him from the pen. "Did any of the dogs talk about Lilah and why their owners hated her? Has Klingon said anything about his mistress?"

"He's not talkin'." Rudy cocked his head and pointed his nose toward the mini Schnauzer, curled on a dog bed

at the far end of the enclosure. *"This morning, when that Prince guy showed, was the only time he made a comment on anything. Apparently, he knew the guy because of Lilah."*

"Because of Lilah Perry?" She had sensed something was fishy when the little guy got so comfortable with Morgan Prince, but what? Right then, she decided to give her boy a job that would keep him occupied and out from underfoot at the same time. "How about if I give you a new assignment?"

Rudy rested a paw on her shoulder. *"I'm ready, madam general. Fire away."*

She kissed his nose and he sneezed. "Okay, pay attention. Your job is to get Klingon to explain how well he knows Morgan Prince. What kind of relationship do they have? And why does he trust the guy? That kind of thing. But be subtle. I don't want to frighten him."

"I got it. Be sneaky, but subtle. Now, you want to know what I think about your *next assignment?"*

"My next—" She realized they'd been talking for a while and scanned the area. Good thing just about everyone had cleared out. "I guess it's all right if we continue the conversation. So give me your orders."

"I think it's time you found a way into Marcus David's apartment. If what Julie said is true, he's a prime suspect in Lilah's death."

Ellie closed her eyes, unable to agree, even though she had to admit Rudy might be right. But Marcus was a sweet man, and he'd lost someone he loved. Would he kill for his sister? "I understand your reasoning, though I can't see it. Marcus doesn't seem the type to commit murder."

"You know as well as me there is no 'type' for a murderer. If he thinks it was Lilah Perry's fault his sister died, he could have decided it was time to get rid of her, and the

contest was the perfect place to do it." Rudy gave her cheek a sloppy lick. *"You got to check him out."*

"You watched the swag bags that afternoon. Could he have unloaded Lilah's EpiPen and doctored her perfume strips?"

"Sure he could have, but so could about a thousand other people who walked by and peeked inside. I only remember Marcus, because he kept saying his bag had better be rigged for a man, no froufrou stuff."

"I wonder why he didn't want froufrou stuff. He has a mother and two sisters he could share with."

"That's what I've been sayin'. It shouldn't be too hard for you to find a way inside his private space. Just bat your baby blues and his testosterone level will go through the ceiling. You can handle that, no sweat."

Before she could answer, Julie returned leading Lucy, Daisy and Muffin.

"I met a few of the models and they told me to bring their pals here. Said they'd be in final fittings for the big show for the rest of the afternoon, and the dogs were your job."

Ellie nodded. "You might as well take them and the mini Schnauzers for a walk, then bring them back and hook up the rest. I imagine the designers will be here soon." She took stock of the pen. "Cheech is due in, and so is Kiki. While you're here, I'm going to the designers' stations. I need a timeline for pickup. Once the dogs are dressed we have to keep them looking groomed and ready to go."

Ellie scanned Anton Rouch's work space, but found no sign of the man. Curious, she took note of his sketchbook, set neatly in a corner of the table, with a one-inch margin on a side and bottom of the tablet. After flipping open the pages, she saw his designs arranged in order with short dresses to long, short skirts to long, short sleeves to long, and an exactness of spacing on all sides of the drawings.

His pins were stuck exactly a hair's width apart in four cushions, which were color-coded according to pin size. His scissors were lined up in size order, too, smallest to largest, and tucked in a leather carrying case.

Neatly folded cloth was stacked under his table, arranged by fabric and color order. Alongside stood two three-tiered thread holders, one for small spools and one for larger, and they were color-coded, too. Then came a lineup of finishing tapes, tissue paper, ribbon, and all manner of trim, also arranged by size and color order.

The exactness of the space made her head ache. How could anyone work in such an orderly manner? Would the world fall apart if a single pin was one-sixteenth of an inch closer to another? Or the pink fabric was mixed with the fuchsia, or the silk with the satin? Worsted wool with tweed? Wide-wale corduroy mixed with narrow?

It was obvious the man was a neat freak, most likely suffering from obsessive-compulsive disorder, though she'd never met anyone with the condition. Years back there'd been a movie with Jack Nicholson and Helen somebody, where Jack had collected bars of soap, stacked them in his medicine cabinet, and thrown them out after one use. If she recalled correctly, the movie also had an adorable small dog in the cast, another plus in its favor.

She walked to the rolling garment rack centered on his single wall and read what looked to be his schedule. He had the entire day planned out, including his time to pick up Daisy and Baby.

Ellie wrote down the time in her notebook and

moved to find Fiona Ray's station. When she got there she stood still for a moment—in shock. Head down, Fiona was wielding a huge pair of scissors, tearing into a bright orange fabric as if it was tissue paper. Her black hair, bunched on top of her head in a total rat's nest, held about a dozen pencils. She wore an apron over her pants and T-shirt, and every pocket held a different set of objects.

One was filled with scissors, another with a ruler and a couple of pens, a third appeared overfilled with spools of thread. Pinned into the top of the apron was an assortment of sewing needles, paper clips, even a small knife.

Out of the blue, the designer raised her head and glared at Ellie. "Something I can do for you?"

"Fiona, hi. I apologize if I'm interrupting you."

"Why the hell not? Just about every other person involved in this fucking contest has traipsed through here today. Now the dog lady is here." She fisted the hand holding the scissors on her slim hip. "What do you want?"

Surprised to hear Fiona speaking so rudely, she tried for a friendly smile. "I just need to know your scheduled time to pick up and dress your dogs. No one's told me in which order the designers will show their work, but I imagine the dogs will be dressed and paraded down the catwalk in the same order."

Head down again, Fiona began to cut. "Talk to the NMD folks. No one's told me a fucking thing. I imagine we'll all find out five minutes before showtime."

"Ooo-kay," said Ellie. There was no reason she had to stay and listen to nasty language and put up with her snotty attitude. But Fiona had never acted this way before. She hadn't gushed or made like a friend either, but she'd been cordial. What had happened to turn her into a—a—a Lilah Perry?

Swallowing, she tried to get hold of the situation. "Fiona? Has something happened? Are you all right?"

The girl's head jerked upward and she heaved a huge sigh. Then she looked at Ellie. "Tell me, dog lady, how much do you know about this business?"

"Not a lot, but I've been paying attention. I learned quite a bit by listening, too." She hadn't questioned Fiona on Lilah Perry's death, but maybe she should have. "I don't know if you've heard, but I'm trying to get Jeffery King off the hook for Lilah's murder. Nola and Morgan asked for my help and I said yes."

"Did you now?" Fiona narrowed her dark brown eyes. "What are you, some kind of dog-walking detective?" She giggled a laugh. "Sounds like a setup for a television show."

"I doubt anyone would be interested. Dog walking is pretty boring, but I love it. And I've helped a few friends when the police have arrested the wrong person."

"So in all your investigating did you find out anything that could help Jeffery?"

"A bit. Do you have anything to offer? Do you know if someone had a grudge against Lilah?"

Fiona raised her eyebrows. "Marcus David, of course. He thinks Lilah's the reason his sister is dead."

"I heard, and I'm looking into it. Anything else?"

"Good luck trying to get these people to talk about Lilah. They're too self-serving to care."

"I don't know about that. I've met some really nice people while working here."

"Then you really haven't heard about what goes on behind the scenes. The gossip and backbiting; the odds for a favorite and a not-so-favorite. That kind of thing."

"If you're talking about the betting on the outcome of this contest, Julie just told me."

"So how would you feel to know the odds are against you? To learn that everything you've worked for is going up in smoke because some a-hole is taking bets on your talent over someone else's? And the odds that you'll win are a hundred to one?"

Wearing her most compassionate smile, Ellie walked to face her across the table. "I'm so sorry to hear that's what's going on. But do you really think Nola and Morgan will let some betting business sway their decision?"

The designer closed her eyes for a long moment, then shrugged. "I don't know. I'd like to think they're going to decide on creativity. They're supposed to be looking for outfits that are simple yet classy and in tune with today's modern woman. The clothes aren't supposed to be right for the high-end trade, just things that a working mother can wear to her job, to take care of the kids, to shop in, and go out on the town.

"I made the cut, but I'm not that kind of designer." She raised a hand and pointed to her rack of finished outfits. "They're edgy and unique, not for taking the kids to soccer after working all day. I never should have entered the contest, but I did. And I gave it my all, but I don't think I can continue designing that type of clothing." Fiona set the scissors on the table and crossed her arms. "I tried to take Lilah's advice, which gave me an in, but now I'm wondering . . ."

"Wondering what?" asked Ellie after a few seconds went by.

Fiona shook her head and her rat's nest of hair jiggled. "Nothing. Just . . . it's nothing."

"Can I get you anything? A bottled water or a plate of fruit?" How else could she lend Fiona a hand? "Maybe you need to go outside for a few minutes."

The girl heaved another sigh. "Nah. I'm fine." Her smile trembled. "Thanks for the offer, but I have to take care of myself. And you can bring the dogs over anytime. Their outfits are cut. I just have to do a final fitting."

Focusing on the table, she lowered her head and went back to work, cutting her fabric in a calmer manner. Her dismissal was clear, so Ellie walked on with fingers crossed. This was taking longer than it should and she had to get the schedule of two more people. She only hoped Julie could handle the dogs.

Chapter 14

Ellie arrived at Kitty's design station, happy to see that things there appeared more normal. Stacks of fabric sat on the table, but not in any particular color order. Spools of thread were piled next to the fabric, as were needles, pins, measuring tapes, trim, tissue paper, and scissors.

The petite designer was so intent on finishing the outfit she'd stretched over a toy canine, she didn't realize she had an audience. The lovely, soft green costume she'd created had columns of interesting chain work circling the neckline and four vinyl booties tied like Christmas packages on the stuffed canine's paws.

She waited until Kitty finished pinning another row of chain on the backline of the coat before clearing her throat to announce her presence. A moment later, the girl raised her head and they locked gazes.

"Hi," said Kitty, her smile thin. "I didn't see you there."

"I know. And you were so busy working, I didn't want to disturb you. I guess that outfit is for one of the mini

Schnauzers. It looks like you ended up with Jojo and Klingon."

"Sizewise, I think it'll be okay, but I won't know for sure until the final fit." She set down her scissors. "I was so hoping Jeffery would be here today, but he has yet to make an appearance."

It figured Kitty's older brother would be on her mind. Ellie could only imagine how difficult it would be to compete in a life-changing event when your only sibling had been accused of murder. "Have he and Mr. Williams come up with a defense?"

Kitty rubbed her nose, her eyes filling with tears. "I think they're going to use reasonable doubt, but I'm not quite sure what that means. Do you know?"

"It means Mr. Williams will try to prove that anyone could have doctored the perfume strips, or unloaded the EpiPen into that orange," Ellie counseled. "Lilah had a lot of enemies, and from what I've heard, quite a few of them hung around the table while the swag bags were on display." She folded her arms. "It's the same with the tote bag that held her EpiPen. It sat underneath the food table for hours, while you and I ran around with the dogs. Anyone could have taken care of it, if they were sneaky enough."

"Then Mr. Williams needs to emphasize that being sneaky isn't Jeffery's way," Kitty said, her expression determined. "In fact, he's almost too honest. He never lies, just tells it like it is. That's the reason he had it out with Lilah as soon as he realized she stole my designs."

"I believe it when you say your brother is honest. If there was any doubt, Nola and Morgan wouldn't be defending him with such conviction. Unfortunately, Jeffery is also the most obvious suspect. He had motive and opportunity, which is all the cops needed for the arrest." She rested a hip against the cutting table. "I don't want to get your hopes up, but I already have several people I believe had motive and opportunity, too. And that's good for us."

Kitty's smile turned tremulous. "Really? Do you think you can get the police to work with what you discovered?"

"Sad to say, that's the hardest part." She didn't want to depress Kitty by playing up the negatives, but she had to be truthful. "I need a really compelling reason to convince Detective Vaughn to take a look at what I collected."

Kitty's eyes, a lovely bluish green, shined with gratitude. "And you'll find one, right?"

"I'll give it my best shot." Ellie straightened her shoulders. "I know your head is wrapped up in the contest, but I need to ask you a couple of things."

"If it has to do with helping free Jeffery, I'll put the contest aside. Winning won't mean anything to me if my big brother is in jail."

"Okay, think hard. I know we've discussed this before, but you were in and out with me the day Lilah died. Who did you see hanging around the table?"

Kitty raised her gaze to the ceiling. "The models, of course. They were all so excited about getting the expensive gift bags."

"Did you see any of them standing around a bit too long? Or inspecting bags that weren't their own?"

"I have no idea. The only way they could find out which bag belonged to who was if they read the tag, and that was tied to the handle."

"Right, I remember," said Ellie, recalling the delicate calligraphy that had spelled out her name. "And you say you saw every model sneaking a peek?"

"I don't think any of the big-name ones did. Just the second-tier girls."

"Second-tier girls?"

"You know, like Claire and Lawan. Crystal, Kate, and Patti are famous; the others all hope to achieve their level of success someday. As for the designers, I doubt Anton Rouch paid attention to anything other than his designs. He's an odd duck when it comes to following the rules. I can't imagine him caring about the contents of a goodie bag, even if it was full of costly gifts."

"I stopped at his station a little while ago. His area was, um, extremely neat."

Kitty raised an eyebrow. "He gets furious if he hears people talk about it, but he has OCD. Lilah knew it, and she used to bug him about it, which drove him nuts." She rested her backside against the table. "Do you think he might be the killer?"

"Not unless he had a chance to doctor those bags. Now, how about Fiona?"

"Fiona is odd, too, but in a different way. If she had trouble with Lilah, she'd have gotten right to it, not let it fester until she wanted to commit murder."

"Hmm." Ellie waited a beat, hoping Kitty wouldn't read anything into her next question. "And Marcus?"

"Marcus David is a very nice guy." Kitty cocked her head. "You do know that he wants to hook up with you, right?"

Heat again inched up Ellie's chest. "I got that impression, but there's nothing I can do about it. I heard he lost his sister a while back, and Lilah had a hand in that, too. What do you know about it?"

"Not much. I was out the day it happened, but Sylvie was always here. Lilah used to talk about her when Marcus wasn't around because she knew he'd call her on it. The morning of the accident, Marcus was late, but Sylvie came in on time. She just picked on the wrong designer."

"The story I heard was really sad. I don't blame Marcus for being angry or upset."

"He was more than upset," said Kitty. "No one could talk to him for days, months even. And he avoided Lilah like the plague. Everyone kept waiting for the big blowup between them, but aside from him trying to strangle her before the taxi accident, he never went near her."

"Do you think he's clever enough to have bided his time, waited things out until the perfect moment, then found a way to do her in and implicate Jeffery?"

"I hate to think he could do that, but I guess anything is possible." Kitty shrugged. "He and Jeffery weren't pals, but they were civil. In fact, my brother was pleased to hear the committee had chosen Marcus to be in this contest. He said Marcus had a good chance of winning the prize." She gave a tentative smile. "That was before I was added, of course."

"Okay, let's move on to other people. Who else was hanging around that day?"

"Hmm. Well, I saw Morgan Prince staking out the action right after Jeffery and his crew delivered the bags. There were a few of the hairdressers peeking in the baskets, too. Karen Hood, Eduardo, you know, the usual suspects."

"And all of them had a gripe against Lilah."

"Just about. She was a real piece of work. I still don't know why she wasn't blackballed after her altercation with Sylvie. Word was, someone high up in the business vouched for her, and she was allowed to keep her place."

"And no one knows who that was?"

"Not me, but maybe Jeffery does. Have you talked to him?"

"No, but I want to. I was hoping to find him here, cheering you on."

"If he shows up, I can send him to you. Would that help?"

"Yes, absolutely. Now, I've got to find Marcus, then get back to helping Julie with the dogs. What time are you planning to pick yours up for their final fitting?"

"No one's told me anything, so I assume we'll be in the same order we were earlier. I should dress them by five thirty, because the first catwalk goes on at six, the second at six thirty, and the grand finale at seven. Then the entire cast takes a break while the judges do their thing. The girls stay in the last design and we wait for the big announcement."

"How tough will that be for you?"

"To wait? Not as difficult as waiting to hear some good news about my brother."

"Then I guess I'd better get going, huh?"

Kitty grasped Ellie's hand and squeezed. "I know you'll give it your best effort. I'm counting on you."

With her mind churning on how to give Vaughn the information she'd amassed, Ellie headed for Marcus's workstation. His table was a good distance from Kitty's, which made perfect sense. If the contestants were separated, there'd be less complaints of plagiarizing a design. She'd paid attention to the fashion gossip, and knew that even fabric and color played a part in a designer's art. If someone took the same "look" as another artist, they were written off as untrustworthy and unprofessional.

She spotted Marcus from a distance, bent over his table, and was again impressed by his lanky-yet-muscular build. Today's apparel consisted of bright white high-tops, worn jeans that hugged his class-A butt, and a pale yellow shirt with the sleeves rolled up his forearms. He looked, as usual, like a man comfortable in his own skin.

Nearing the table, she saw that his area was laid out exactly like Kitty's, only a bit more disorderly. And he too was working on a canine creation, a dapper, bright red coat that was strapped under and around the belly of Lucy, the new model's dog.

Not wanting to surprise him, she stepped to his side and placed her hands on the tabletop, silently announcing her presence.

Marcus finished a last knot on the design and turned to face her, his expression confident. "Are you here to wish me good luck?"

"Of course."

He arched an eyebrow. "But you want Kitty to win."

"How can I not? She was my first assistant, and I grew to think of her as a friend." Ellie raised a shoulder. "Now that her brother has been wrongly accused of murder, I can't help but be on her side."

"It sounds to me as if you're positive Jeffery King is innocent," he said, cocking a hip against the table.

Unsure of how much to reveal to a would-be suspect, she waited a moment before answering. "Let's just say I've uncovered enough evidence against a few others to give his attorney a decent line of defense."

"Good for Jeffery, then." He grinned. "I never asked, but I've been wondering, what do you think of my designs?"

Ellie gazed at Lucy. "Hmm, I'm not sure I'd look good in that much red."

Marcus crossed his arms and nodded toward two designs on dummy models propped along the back wall of his station. Black coats with stand-up collars and red toggle buttons were draped over what appeared to be red and black checked dresses in a figure-skimming style.

"That's the people-wear, and red is only an accent. I thought I'd work the canine coats in the opposite direction, red topside with an accent of black toggles."

"Very clever," said Ellie, and she meant it. "Your human coat is practical, yet stylish. I'd wear it."

"That's good to know. I just hope the NMD people agree with you." He began disrobing Lucy. "This little girl is all set, so, if you like, you can bring her back to the pen for me. Unless you're on some kind of scouting mission?"

"I'm visiting all the designers," she told him, which was true. She hated being so secretive, but how much could she tell him? "I haven't had much experience watching creative geniuses at work."

"Creative geniuses?" His grin broadened. "Thanks for the compliment. It's important, coming from you."

Inhaling fresh air in hope of preventing a blush, she said, "Just remember, I'm a nobody in this contest. No one has asked for my vote, let alone my opinion."

"But if they did?"

"I'd have to think about it."

"Now there's a decisive answer."

"Ru-Rudy?" she sputtered, jumping when she heard his voice. She reached down and rubbed his ears. What was the little stinker doing here?

"Who else were you expectin'?"

"I noticed your little guy right away," said Marcus when she stood. "I thought you knew he was tagging along."

"I guess I sort of forgot about him," Ellie lied. Last she knew, her boy was in the pen back at the food tables. And she hadn't given him permission to leave Julie's care. "He's quiet that way."

"Home base got boring. I figured you had to be doin' somethin' more interesting."

She gave a mental ten count, careful to keep her thoughts to herself. "He likes being where the action is."

"I can tell from the twinkle in his eyes," said Marcus. *"See that. I twinkle."*

"That twinkle sometimes means trouble," she explained to the human in the three-way conversation. "He likes sticking his snout where it doesn't belong."

"I like stickin' my snout where it doesn't belong?" he asked with innocence. *"What about you?"*

"Sometimes he's such a pain, I forget what I'm doing." She gave her pal a pointed look, determined to get back on track with Marcus. "Julie told me something earlier, something personal about you, and I wanted to get the story straight from the source. It's about your—"

"My baby sister, Sylvie."

"I'm sorry, but yes. Is it too painful for you to talk about?"

His lips thinned. "What do you think?"

"I know how bad it can be to lose a loved one. I was fifteen when my dad died, and I don't think I'll ever forget it. In a way, that moment shaped the rest of my life."

Her father had loved dogs, even though her mother didn't. He'd encouraged her to get a fuzzy four-legged pal when she was out of the house and on her own. Then he promised to visit her, so the three of them could take long walks together.

"My dad was crazy about dogs, but my mom wasn't, and she ruled the roost, er, the kennel. It was one of the few things my parents didn't agree on, so my father caved and Georgette, that's my mother, got her way."

His eyes closed for a long moment. "My two middle sisters, Samantha and Sydney, always did their own thing, but Sylvie looked to me for advice and guidance. I was her big brother, her protector, her rock. There was only one thing we didn't see eye to eye on, and that was her dream to become a fashion model."

"I know there are quite a few rules for being a hit in

this industry: height, weight, lots of good hair, classic bone structure, and the ability to work with the camera. Did she have those traits?"

"She was tall enough and her hair was fine. Bone structure, too, but she never got thin enough to look good in front of the camera. She could have had a career as a plus-sized runway model, but she wanted more, and for some reason she thought I could get it for her. The other designers trusted me to make her understand . . . all of them but Lilah, that is."

Ellie hoped that, if she didn't push, Marcus would reveal something insightful. "And she gave your sister a hard time?"

He clenched his jaw and his fingers followed suit. "A hard time is putting it mildly. With Lilah, it was always over the top. If she found someone's weak spot, she used it to make them squirm. Just ask Clark Fettel or Anton Rouch."

"Did she tease you about Sylvie?"

"Me? Never. But she did get on Sylvie's case, and she did it on purpose." He relaxed his fingers. "The poor kid had a heart problem, but she begged me not to tell anyone. She didn't want pity, she wanted to make it on her own."

"Do you think if Lilah knew about the heart thing she might have gone easier on your sister?"

Marcus shrugged. "Beats me. Besides, it's useless to talk about it now." He pressed the heels of his hands into his eyes and released a sigh. "It's all useless. Lilah got what she deserved, and if I knew for certain who killed her I'd send them a dozen roses as a thank-you."

"He doesn't sound like a murderer to me, Triple E."

Ellie squatted and pretended to adjust her boy's collar. "I know, but we have to keep our emotions out of it," she whispered. "Just because he doesn't *sound* like a killer doesn't mean he isn't one, er, is one, er, well, you know what I mean. Now please be quiet and let me do my job."

"Talking to your dog again?" Marcus asked when she stood. "You do know that's one of the things I like about you?"

"You might think it's a good trait, but not everyone agrees. Clark Fettel thinks I'm a nutcase whenever he sees me do it, and so does Fiona Ray. And I bet there are a whole lot more folks who think I'm a flake."

"But not Nola or Morgan, and they're the people who count. If they thought you were a flake, they never would have asked you to prove Jeffery King innocent. I'd say that's a plus in this business."

"I guess," Ellie said. "And I'm grateful for their support. I just hope I can do what they expect."

"So how is the investigation coming along? Do you actually have proof that someone besides Jeffery could have killed Lilah?"

"I do. The difficult thing will be getting Detective Vaughn to listen to me."

"I thought you lived with a homicide detective."

"But he's not working this case. In this city, the cops don't step on each other's toes." She'd heard the rules from Sam often enough to remember them. "They only help with a case if they're asked or if they find something they think will benefit another cop. And my guy's been working on something that's kept him out of the house for most of the week."

"So you have yet to ask him about accompanying you to the big celebration party at Nola and Morgan's tomorrow night?"

Fancy parties were the last thing Sam wanted to attend. He was so antisocial, she had to work for weeks to get him to agree to show his face at one of Georgette's

Sunday brunches. She had no intention of asking him to the NMD celebration. "With all the time he's putting in, I don't think he'll be able to come with me."

"That's not what I meant and you know it," said Marcus, giving her a sly grin.

Another rush of warmth crept up her neck again, and she cursed herself for being a redhead. "Oh, you mean the date thing . . . with you."

Still smiling, he nodded. "Yes, with me. So how about it?"

"How about going to the party with you?"

He took a step toward her, closing the distance. "Stop playing coy. Yes, with me."

"I'm not—I mean I don't know how to play coy."

"That's for sure."

"Then say yes. We can go as friends, remember."

Tired of battling him, she heaved a sigh. "Okay, fine. As friends."

He took a second step and she caught the scent of his cologne, woodsy and fresh as the great outdoors. "Then you'll be my date for the party?"

"I'll be your *platonic* date for the party."

"Great. I'll need your address."

"My address?"

"So I can pick you up."

"Pick me up?"

"Oy!"

"My mother raised me to be a gentleman. If I make a date with a woman, I pick her up and I bring her home."

"Sounds like you'll have to confess to the defective detective that you're cheatin' on him."

"I would never cheat on Sam," she ground out.

"If this date is platonic, you won't be cheating. Now how about giving me your address?"

"Okay. I'll write it on the back of a business card and

you can pick it up when you retrieve Lucy and Cheech. How does that sound?"

"Like a plan."

He took another step forward and she ducked back, but before she could speak, Patti appeared behind him. "Patti, hello."

"Hey, you two." Patti's hazel eyes sparked with interest. "I hope I'm not interrupting anything."

"Not at all," said Marcus, his handsome face fixed in a smile. "And you'll be the first to know. Ms. Engleman just said yes. She's going to the big party with me tomorrow night."

"Is she now? That's great."

"Glad you think so," said Ellie. She held out her arms and Lucy jumped into them. "I'm going to bring this little girl back to my pen, er, space," she stuttered. "I need some time to think." She tossed Marcus a wave. "See you later?"

"How about if I walk with you?" asked the supermodel. "There's something we need to discuss."

Ellie only hoped it wasn't a discussion over Marcus. She couldn't remember the last time she'd been this flustered about a simple get-together with a man. She threaded her way through the crowd with Lucy in her arms, Patti by her side, and Rudy at her feet. "Don't you have someplace special to be?"

"My place is with you," her boy said.

"Who, me?" asked Patti. "Nope. Except for the big finale this afternoon, I'm through for the week."

"I'm through, too."

Ellie rolled her eyes. She was getting tired of stumbling through these three-way conversations. "Do you want to help Julie and me with the dogs for a short while?"

"I might, as long as the work isn't too complicated. I'm not a groomer, and since Cheech is almost hairless—"

"And brainless," Rudy gruffed.

"I don't really have much to do in the way of neatening him up."

"I'm not a groomer, either—"

"You can say that again."

Ellie tapped Rudy with the toe of her shoe. "But I do think we should brush them and make sure they're neat."

"I can manage that," said Patti. "But I would like your advice, if you have a minute."

They plowed past Fiona Ray's station, and it was then the supermodel put her hand on Ellie's forearm, causing her to slow down until they arrived at Anton Rouch's area. The designer was so involved in fitting his newest creation on Lawan, he didn't even acknowledge their presence.

"Take it easy," Patti whispered when they ducked behind his screen. "You're giving me a workout."

"Sorry," said Ellie, keeping her voice low. "It's just that I'm trying to process all the info I learned today, and it's a lot to swallow."

"Does any of it have to do with Anton or Fiona?"

"Not really. Why?"

"Just asking because we're here, and I don't want Anton to think we're talking about him." Patti blew out a breath. "He's a bit sensitive when it comes to his work."

"I heard about his OCD and Lilah's nasty habit of torturing him, but he isn't at the top of my list of suspects. Now that we've stopped, what did you want to tell me?"

"I just wanted you to know that Janice is going to sing

her first release while the judges are deliberating this afternoon. They're bringing in a piano, and she's ready to go."

"Wow. That's a great break for her."

"I agree, and I'm thrilled."

"But how is Janice taking it? Is she nervous or worried?"

"She says she'll be fine. She's used to singing live at a few of the clubs, so for her it'll be just another gig."

"Janice is a brave girl, putting herself out there for public opinion. If I were her, I'd be terrified," Ellie confided.

"We know," Rudy ruffed.

She ignored her boy and his constant commentary. "But you said you wanted my advice, and it can't be about your sister."

"No, it's about Jeffery."

"Jeffery?"

"Yes. I was wondering—well—if he shows up today, do you think I should talk to him?"

Ellie inched out from behind Anton's stall and Patti followed. "Let's talk about this at my station."

Chapter 15

After they arrived at the break station, Ellie placed Lucy in the pen with the other dogs while Patti took a seat. A moment later, she handed Patti a bottle of water. "Here, take a drink and catch your breath. I'm going to talk to Julie for a few minutes. I'll be right back."

She ducked under the food table, found her tote bag, and pulled out the grooming tools she'd brought from home to make certain her charges looked good on the runway. Then she carried the scissors, nail clippers, and two brushes to the other side of the pen.

"Sorry I was gone so long," she said to Julie, who was standing with Daisy in her arms.

"We're fine now, but Anton Rouch came by about an hour ago, and he upset Daisy. I've been trying to calm her down for a while now."

"He's not a nice human," Daisy said, snuggling into Julie's chest. *"I should have bit him."*

Ellie ran a loving hand over Daisy's soft head. "I'm

glad you were here to take care of this little girl. Anton has a problem and we just have to live with it, I guess."

"That problem is what he and Lilah used to argue about. But just because she's gone doesn't give him the right to take out his anger on a tiny pooch."

"You and I are in charge of the dogs until this competition is over, so we can't allow him or anyone else to upset our charges or do anything nasty when it comes to picking them up," said Ellie. Thinking about it, she then made a decision. "In fact, I'll send him a note, and the other designers too. You bring the outfits here, and they'll have to trust that we can dress their canines. That way, Anton and the rest of them don't need to dirty their hands, and the little guys won't be upset. I'll write the note. You can deliver it and come back to tell me what Anton and the rest of them said."

Julie set the white Chihuahua in the circular pen and walked with Ellie to her tote bag, where Ellie penned a message and handed it to her. Julie took off, and Ellie dumped her tools on the table, blinking when she saw that Patti had taken the trouble to clear the space, and used the cartons of water to close off an area where the dogs could be dressed.

"Wow, you've been busy," she told the supermodel.

"Do you think it will work? I was worried it was too close to the food."

"Oh, pooh. People know this is the canine area, so they enter and eat at their own risk. We keep the table-top clean, and these dogs are professionally cared for, so they're probably more sanitary than some of the furniture in their apartment. Plus none of them shed, so I don't see a problem."

"I agree, but there are folks like Anton who complain about everything," said Patti.

"Well, too bad. I'll handle it if they don't like it." Ellie stopped her tirade and took a good look at Patti, noting that her hair, done in a simple upsweep, was classy and unpretentious, just like Marcus's clothes. "You look great, and I'm guessing that new model, Beatriz, does too. Who gave orders for the low-key approach?"

"The designer, of course. Each of them has a hand in deciding how their models should be presented, and that includes their makeup and hair. Eduardo wanted to do more, but Marcus said no."

"Good for him. So when Julie gets back, how about the two of you spruce up Cheech and Lucy? Since you're ready to go, Julie will follow you when it's your turn to dress, and bring back the dogs' outfits. I decided we should do the canines here. The designers will just have to trust us to put their dogs in grade-A condition; then, as the models pass here for their last run, we hand them their pals."

"Sounds good to me." Patti gazed at the pen. "I only wish we knew if Marcus will still be first in the lineup. Should we assume the competitive order will be the same for the finale as it's been for the past few days?"

"You know, I've asked that question about a dozen times today, and no one seems to have the answer."

Patti's picture-perfect face flushed pink, and she broke out in a grin as she focused over Ellie's shoulder.

"Maybe I can help," said someone from behind. "What was the question?"

Recognizing the speaker's voice, Ellie turned and stepped back to include Patti in the conversation. "Jeffery, hello. It's good to see you here."

"There's no place I'd rather be right now. Kitty said you wanted to talk to me just before I had the chance to tell her I wanted to talk to you." He held out his hand. "I owe you quite a bit. How am I ever going to thank you?"

"Thank me? I haven't done anything yet. And I'm

only helping to investigate as a friend." She smiled, accepting his offer of a handshake. "No thank-yous are necessary."

He glanced at Patti, then again focused on Ellie. "But I only met you once or twice before the debacle broke. Was that all it took for you to know I didn't kill Lilah?"

Crossing her arms, Ellie cocked her head. "First off, I believe in your sister. Kitty is so positive you're innocent, I had no choice but to see things her way. Then there's Nola and Morgan. They believe strongly in you, and they're professionals with a head for business. I couldn't believe they'd take a chance backing a—a—"

"An accused killer?" His expression grew grim. "I know. And I'll never be able to repay their kindness."

"You have a lot more friends than Nola and Morgan." She nodded in Patti's direction. "Some of them have helped me in ways too difficult to mention."

"Ellie loves to joke about her investigative skill, but she's a special person and she knows what she's doing," said the supermodel, finally joining the conversation. "She's walked our dogs for a couple of years now, and Janice and I believe in her completely. She's solved enough crimes to know when she meets a killer, and I think she sees that isn't you."

"So you've vouched for me, too?"

When Patti continued to smile, he shook his head, as if finding it hard to pull out the words. "I can't—I don't know what to say." His eyes shined with unshed tears. "I'd better get down to business, then, so we can stop worrying about the competition and get to the heart of the matter." As if marshaling his thoughts, Jeffery straightened his shoulders. "Kitty said you had questions, and I figure they're pretty much the same as what the cops asked."

"Unfortunately, I don't think this is the right time to go over things. The finale should be starting soon, and it's going to get crazy around here." She read Patti's lovelorn expression and decided to do a bit of match-making. "Why don't you talk to Patti while I get the first pair of dogs spruced up? I imagine they'll be calling out the contestants soon, and her designer is Marcus David. He's been first up each time, so I don't think they'll change the order."

"You're right. According to Clark Fettel, who's sub-bing for me, the order is the same." A crooked grin lightened Jeffery's dour face. "I was hoping I'd have a little time to talk to Patti but I—are you sure this is okay?"

Julie took that moment to reappear on the scene. "Hey, Jeffery, it's nice to see you." She gave Ellie a salute. "Your assistant, madam, reporting for duty."

"Are things sane with the cantankerous Mr. Rouch?" asked Ellie.

"Sure. He stomped around his station a time or two, but when he realized he wasn't going to have to be in any further contact with the dogs, he shut up."

"That's what I hoped would happen. Why don't you gather all the dogs and give them a final trip outside before it's time for their grand entrance?"

Patti and Jeffery sat in the chairs, while Julie collected the first four dogs. Giving the pair a sidelong glance, she said, "Looks like those two have a lot to talk about."

Ellie read the complete focus on Jeffery mirrored in Patti's eyes.

"I'd do anything for true love, too." Grinning, Julie headed toward the back door, while Ellie gathered the last four dogs and her boy.

"What do you think he's telling her?" Rudy asked, gazing at the supermodel and Jeffery.

"Does it matter? Whatever it is, they'll work it out."

"Yeah, but it could be something important, like a confession, or a clue."

"That's no way for us to be thinking about our client. As far as we're concerned, Jeffery is innocent and he isn't hiding any clues."

"Sure, but—"

A bell sounded and he clamped his muzzle shut. A moment later, Julie returned the first group of canines and Ellie gave her boy a stern nod as she set him down to join the remainder of the crew for their trip outside.

Then Marcus showed up. "I'm here to collect Patti. Beatriz is already at my station. Here are the outfits for the dogs. I understand you and Julie are dressing them, and that's fine with me. Just do your best."

Patti hurried to follow Marcus as Ellie grabbed the canine creations. Then she carried the Chihuahua and the mini Schnauzer to the dressing table. "How are you two doing? Ready to trot out and wow the crowd?"

An announcement sounded, calling for the start of the last showing of fabulous Fashion Week. Cheech, the ever-silent Chihuahua, trembled, and she tried to console him. "Hey, it'll be fine. You'll be fine. There's no need to worry."

"He's a mess," Lucy confided. *"But I'll calm him down."*

"You mean he's actually talked to you?"

"Sure. He's chattered away since the moment I met him."

"And he speaks in—in English?"

"I guess. It's canine-speak. Why?"

She eyed her boy, the little stinker, now being returned to the pen by Julie. According to Rudy, neither Cheech nor Chong ever spoke a word. How could he lie to her like that?

"No reason. I was just wondering. So ..." She held up

the brush. "We'll let Julie take care of Cheech while I make you beautiful. You ready?"

"Just don't trim too much off my ears. And please don't button the top thingy on that coat. It's too tight. Fits me like a choke collar."

"I see you're talking to them again." Julie sidled next to Ellie after dropping the last group of canines into the pen. "Learn anything interesting?"

"They're nervous, so we need to stay calm, cool, and collected. That'll help."

"Got it." Julie began brushing the Chihuahua. "He looks good, don't you think? Should I put on his coat?"

Ellie finished trimming Lucy's muzzle, then passed Julie Cheech's outfit. A tingling sensation ran up her spine and she closed her eyes. The afternoon had been quiet. Too quiet. The dreaded tingle could mean only one thing.

"Hello, my darling girl," said Georgette, breaking into her thoughts. "What have you been up to?"

"Mother, what are you doing here?" Ellie glanced at Julie and rolled her eyes, then focused on Georgette. How had her mother managed to sneak back here now, when security was supposed to be heightened? "Where are Vivian and Stanley?"

"Out front, saving me a seat, of course. We've been here forever. Viv insisted we take our places early, and she was correct. You should see the mob out there."

A knot formed in Ellie's throat. "Then maybe you ought to claim your chair. With that many people, a security guard could confiscate your seat for someone truly important."

"But we have tickets. That would never happen," said Georgette, her sculpted nose raised in the air. "I just wanted you to know we were here with you." She inspected Lucy's red coat with the black toggles, then gave Cheech a once-over. "When will you be bringing the little creatures out?"

Creatures? "They're dogs, Mother, or canines, and I won't be bringing them anywhere. We're getting them ready for their fashion debut, but their owners will be in charge of taking them down the runway. Didn't you see their posters on the walls out there?"

"I did, but I still can't believe what I saw."

Ellie had an idea of what her mother was going to say, but she let Georgette have her way. "And what was that?"

Her mother scanned the canine ring, stopping her perusal when she laid eyes on Rudy. "Was that your boy in the photos, mingling with all the purebreds?"

Ellie gave an internal *tsk*. "Of course it was. In fact, he was almost a model until they decided to use another mini Schnauzer. Rudy is very photogenic."

"Wouldn't he be happier spending time at one of those doggie day spas that seem to be all the rage? I hear there's a wonderful shop on East Eighty-fifth, Canine Concierge or something, that does dog sitting."

She took a step toward the pen and Rudy stood up straight, causing Ellie to cringe inside. There was no love lost between her self-absorbed mother and her snarky four-legged friend. With the tension mounting, she had no idea what might happen between them.

"What's the ex-terminator doin' here? She belongs in a padded cell," Rudy announced.

The statement, so loud and accusing, had all the dogs eyeing her mother with interest.

Georgette continued her appraisal. "Spas are supposed to be the newest thing for canines. Your dog might enjoy it there instead of . . . here."

"Yer kiddin'. She wants to take me to a spa?" Plopping

his bottom on the floor, Rudy scratched his side with a rear leg. *"Hmm. Maybe that's not such a bad idea. It might be a nice change bein' pampered for a while."*

Ignoring her boy, Ellie set the dressed mini Schnauzer inside the pen and Julie did the same with Cheech. "And why is it you think Rudy shouldn't be here?"

"He is a mixed breed. Perhaps he doesn't belong with all this canine excellence."

Rudy jumped to four legs. *"Say what!"* When a few of the other dogs yipped encouragement, he gave a loud bark.

Ellie pointed a finger and raised her voice. "Quiet, all of you." Then she scooped up the next dog, and nodded for Julie to get Dominique's girl. Hoping her mother would take the hint, she announced, "Okay, guys, we're on a roll now. Everyone just keep it down. We have work to do."

Georgette spun around, took one look at Fiona Ray's purple and orange dog creation Ellie held in her hand, and stuck out her lower lip. "What in the world is that supposed to be?"

"A designer's idea of dog-wear that will match whatever she's come up with for her third creation." Ellie was not a fan of Fiona's work, and had to agree with her mother that this outfit was too over-the-top, but Georgette's comments weren't helping to win over the dogs.

"Why do we gotta wear that cat poop?" asked Spike, Crystal's French bulldog.

"Yeah, why? That thing is worse than the bunny ears and cotton tail I had to wear for Easter," Kiki added.

Ellie raised the garment up, and Julie lifted an eyebrow. "Your mother is right. I'm not even sure how to put the darned thing on."

"All we can do is our best," said Ellie, nodding at

Spike. "Sit still," she said to Kiki. Then she gazed at Georgette. "Mother, you need to get out of here. You're upsetting the dogs, and we have a lot of work to do. There's no more time to chat."

Georgette huffed out her displeasure. "Then I guess I'll be going. Viv's trying to get us invited to some big hosting spectacular that will take place when this entire event is over. I'll see you there."

Ellie steeled her spine as her mother flounced from the area. She was going to smack Viv if she'd managed to get her mother invited to tonight's big NMD celebration.

"Don't let her get to you," advised Julie, sensing Ellie's annoyance. "My mom would be just like yours, if she was here. Lucky for me, she's still back in Wisconsin, probably watching this entire thing on television."

"This is being televised?" Ellie asked, swallowing another knot of anxiety.

"You didn't know?" Julie grinned. "Why do you think I'm all dolled up?"

Ellie gazed at her assistant, assessing her mountain of red corkscrew curls, her clean purple jeans, and her fitted black bodice, laced with sparkly jet beading. Then she held the orange and purple doggie-wear high. "I don't mean to offend you, but you kind of match this creation of Fiona's."

"Golly, no," Julie said with a shudder. She rotated the dog wear up, down, and sideways. "I'm still trying to figure out where this fifth leg is supposed to—" She bit her lower lip. "Oh, no. Really? Do you think—Good Lord, does she actually want us to slip this on over his—"

Ellie quickly slid the outfit on Spike, including the fifth leg Julie was referring to. She couldn't imagine the practicality of taking your male dog for a walk while he wore this coat. Dogs dribbled when they did their business, and sometimes did worse. The coat would need a washing after every trip outside. It was obvious Fiona had no experience with canines.

Music sounded from the staging area and Kurt Jager welcomed the crowd. Gofers and assistants scattered as Patti and Beatriz came charging through the backstage mob, which seemed to part as if the models were holding magic wands.

"Where do you think Marcus is?" asked Ellie. In both of the earlier showings, the designers had gone out with their models.

"He knows his girls are pros," said Julie. "Or at least Patti is, and she'll guide that new girl. I'm sure he's concentrating on the next creation, so he'll be ready when they get back. It's a rat race from here until the end, with everyone aiming for the last design and its wow factor. Of course, having a four-legged friend that will ham things up could only help the designers' chances."

Ellie banged the heel of her right hand into her forehead. "That last design has to be flawless, and so do the dogs. Their personality has to shine through and sell the clothing, just like a model is supposed to do." She gazed at Rudy. "Why haven't I told them that?"

"Beats me," he answered with a yip. *"But maybe you should get Daisy and Baby ready, or that Rouch guy will throw a fit. And we sure don't want that to happen."* He jumped over the fence in one quick leap. *"Maybe I should be on the lookout for him."*

Ellie ran her fingers through her disheveled curls and squatted to face him. "Only if you promise to stay out from underfoot and don't leave this area. And whatever you do, don't go onstage. Think you can do that?" she asked in a whisper.

When he answered with a sneeze, she picked up the next two dogs, Baby and Daisy, and passed Baby to Julie. "Okay, we went out of order. Pair three is finished, and this is pair two. Do you have their duds?"

Ringing applause sounded from the runway, showing the crowd's approval of Marcus David's day wear designs. Kurt Jager continued his running commentary while Patti and Beatriz dashed back in and raced to change into the second creation.

As far as Ellie was concerned, the entire parade was a test of endurance, strategy, and focus, for both the designers and the models. Another round of applause accompanied Lawan and Kate as they snaked out and returned to go around the pen, giving Dominique and Crystal room to make their entrance in Fiona's first design.

In between watching the models strut to the stage, she and Julie continued to groom and dress the dogs. By the time the first round of creations went through the catwalk, all the dogs were finished in style.

"If it's okay with you, I'm taking a quick potty break," said Julie, racing past the snack table to the restrooms.

Ellie had just managed to catch her breath when the sound of Kurt Jager's voice broke out. "And now, Nola Morgan Design presents the second round in the competition. In this round, our talented designers give us, for your viewing pleasure, evening wear."

Just then, a woman slipped in through the rear entrance Julie and Ellie normally used to take the dogs out. Rushing past the crowd watching Anton's models, the girl ran to the dog area and dropped on a chair.

"Janice?" Ellie blinked. She'd completely forgotten that Patti's younger sister was supposed to be the entertainment.

"Am I on time?" Janice croaked. Then she cleared her throat. "I cannot believe this. I think I'm coming down with something."

"Something?" asked Ellie. "Something like what?"

Janice covered her mouth and coughed. "I don't know. A cold maybe or a throat thing. I woke up like this, but Patti had already left, so I couldn't tell her." Standing, she pulled off her hip-length jacket and tossed it on a chair. Then she brushed her black suede skirt and straightened her skintight black turtleneck sweater. "How do I look?"

Assessing the fall outfit of fitted suede and cashmere, with an eye-catching Yves Saint Laurent scarf tied perfectly around the singer's delicate neck, Ellie grinned. "You look great, just like a rising blues singer should. I have bottled water. Will that help?"

Applause filled the air and Janice turned to the catwalk entrance in time to see her sister glide back through the curtain. When she and Patti locked gazes, they sprinted toward each other and met halfway between the dog pen and the walkway.

"I was so worried. But you're here," said Patti.

"I know. I tried calling, but you must have turned off your cell," said Janice at the same time.

Ellie stood, preparing to take over and keep everyone calm. "All right, you two have said your hellos. Patti, it's time for you to get back to your station and dress for the big round."

"Oh, God, yes, you're right," said the supermodel. She gazed at her sister. "Are you sure you're okay? You sound a little ... funny. And not ha-ha funny. Kind of—of croaky."

"She's fine, she's fine," said Ellie. Turning Patti around, she shoved her in the direction of the station.

"She doesn't need to know about your possible 'something,'" she told Janice when her sister was gone. Then she did the same with Beatriz, who looked a bit confused. "Beatriz, just follow Patti. She's the pro, so she knows what to do. You got that?"

Beatriz nodded, but her manner was a bit too rough and tough. "I'll give it my best, but I'm new here, remember?"

"I know, and so does Patti." She looked at Janice. "We have a little time. How about if I fix you a cup of hot tea with honey and lemon?"

"Honey and lemon?" Janice whispered in a rattled voice. "You have that here?"

"We have everything," said Ellie, leading her back to the row of chairs. "Julie, there's someone you need to meet. This is Janice Fallgrave, Patti's younger sister, and she's here to sing. In fact, she'll be on in—" Ellie saw Lawan and Kate leaving the catwalk and gave her best guess, "About thirty minutes. She needs hot tea with lemon and honey, so do your magic and make it happen, please."

Julie went to work at the far end of the setup area. The catering company had arranged a professional drink bar that held tea bags, creamers, real and fake sugar, bottles of honey, cut lemons, canned whipping cream, and chocolate and cinnamon sprinkles to go with the heated pots of French roast and decaf that were brewed fresh each hour.

She sat next to Janice and patted her hand. "Have you checked anything out? Is your pianist here? Do you know where you're singing on stage? Have you met Kurt Jager?"

Janice heaved a sigh. "My pianist is on the other side of the stage, doing his thing. We've worked together before, so he knows my key and the songs I'm singing. No one told me anything else, so I'm—"

Another warning tingle tripped up Ellie's spine when Janice stopped midsentence and gazed over her head.

"Ms. Engleman," said Clark Fettel, his voice demanding, "I should have known you'd be the one to waylay our entertainment and upset the running of the show."

Chapter 16

Clark Fettel trundled off with a confused-looking Janice, and Ellie heaved a breath. Then she took a seat on one of the chairs, in search of a calming moment. The second round, evening wear, was almost finished. That meant the first models of the third round, Patti and Beatriz, would be there at any moment. Dressed in Marcus's final creation, they would pick up their clothed and groomed dogs, and make their big runway entrance.

Each group of models would then strut onto the catwalk with their dogs, receiving, she imagined, a volley of oohs and aahs because the little darlings were so adorable. After each trio did their thing, the designers would be called out to join their models, which meant eight models, eight dogs, four designers, and Kurt Jager all clustered on stage for a final round of applause.

When that was over, everyone would file backstage while Janice sang to entertain the crowd. Nola and Morgan would use the time to decide which designer received the big prize and, when Janice bowed to her last number, Kurt would call everyone back and announce the winner.

To Ellie, the entire scenario was mind-boggling.

"You gonna be okay?" Rudy asked, sitting on the chair next to her.

"I'll get through it, but it's really important that you stay out of the way. Think you can sit here and MYOB?"

"Uhh, yeah, but I'm not gonna like it."

"I know, and I appreciate your honesty, but please—"

Before she could finish, she spotted Patti and Beatriz, wearing their black toggled coats and dresses, marching toward her with Marcus following. She jumped to her feet and raced to the pen, where Julie was waiting. She picked up Cheech and passed him to Patti, while Julie retrieved Lucy, untangled her leash, and passed her to the new girl.

Ellie watched Beatriz stride behind Patti, her movements a bit awkward, her steps hesitant.

"Do you see the way she's carrying herself? I can't believe I got stuck with a novice," Marcus whispered from behind her. "I begged for a more seasoned model, but Morgan wouldn't budge. Maybe she's his latest conquest, but she doesn't seem the type."

His latest conquest? There was no time to ask questions. Lawan and Kate were already in front of her, waiting for their babies, with Anton Rouch standing behind, his face grim, his mouth a thin line.

"The mutts need to wear these. I don't care how you get them on. Just do it," he grumbled, passing Ellie two small, round sections of cloth.

She gazed at Lawan and Kate, who wore smart-looking hats set at a jaunty angle on their head. Groaning internally, she passed a tam to Julie.

"What in the hell are we supposed to do with these?" her assistant muttered, turning the bit of cloth in her hand.

The grumpy designer continued to stare as Ellie removed Baby and Daisy from the pen and passed Baby to Julie.

"Put that on your dog and keep your fingers crossed," she told the girl. "And be thankful you have some hair to work with."

Unfortunately, Daisy was almost hairless, so Ellie had to anchor the hat to the Chihuahua's ear. It was a totally impractical idea for a dog owner, especially one whose pet was near bald, and it only showed how little Anton cared about dressing a canine.

"Be good," Ellie told Daisy, once the clip was set. "That's all I can do. It'll only pinch for a bit; then we'll take it off."

Daisy gave a full-body shake and her tam dropped to hang off her ear. Ellie bent to refasten it and the Chihuahua yipped.

"Hey, watch it with that clip. It's pulling my ear out."

She gave another shake and the hat went flying. Anton rushed to rescue it, but it was too late. Beatriz stepped on the hat as she made her way off the stage, slipped on the tam, and fell on her backside.

Anton grabbed the hat and passed it to Lawan while Ellie and Marcus helped Beatriz stand. It was then Ellie spotted something strapped to the model's thigh.

She narrowed her eyes, focusing on the woman's leg as she stood and straightened the skirt. No, it couldn't be.

She blinked when Anton snapped his fingers. "Ms. Engleman, we're running behind. Get that hat on."

She swung around to help Lawan with the clip. Then
she scuttled alongside as the model walked to the curtain, still reeling over what she thought she saw.

"I got it," said Lawan, right before she strode onto
stage.

Spinning in place, Ellie searched for Beatriz and
found her with Marcus, standing out of the way while he
helped rearrange her coat and dress. Patti stood alongside, holding both dogs in a sit.

Was Beatriz truly wearing a gun?

The new model raised her gaze and their eyes connected. When she winked, a flush of warning crept from
Ellie's stomach to her chest.

Yes, she'd seen a gun, and Beatriz knew it.

"Hey, Ellie, how about a hand!" Julie said in a loud
whisper.

The question shook Ellie from her disastrous day-
dream and she turned. Dominique and Crystal were
waiting, and Julie was wrestling with their dogs. Spike
had stuck his back leg through the fifth sleeve and was
hopping like a lame rabbit.

"Oh, crap!" Ellie bent to undo the damage. Lawan
and Kate returned from the catwalk, and she stood.
Dominique and Crystal were off in a flash, their dogs
prancing at their side.

One minute later, Anton's models marched in to line
up behind Marcus and his crew, but Lawan held Daisy's
hat in her hand.

Ellie rushed over. "What happened?"

"The little stinker won't let me clip it," the model answered, her voice a moan. "It dropped on the runway
and I had to pick it up."

Anton clasped Ellie's arm. "Do something, dog lady,
or I'll—"

"What? Have her sew it on?" snapped Marcus, who looked ready for a fight.

Ellie wrenched her arm away and laid a hand on Marcus. "Don't start anything. I'll be back."

Rushing to Julie and Kitty, she helped with Yasmine and Cassandra's mini Schnauzers, making sure their jackets and chains were straight and their booties were tied tight.

Down in a squat, she smiled at both pooches. "You two look great. Remember to sell yourself for Kitty. She wants to win this thing, and you'll be stars."

Kitty grinned when Ellie stood. She followed her models to the edge of the curtain with Ellie by her side, and they watched Yasmine, in her pale green jacket and skirt, and Cassandra, in her identical jacket and fitted slacks, strut the catwalk with the dogs.

Lights flashed and the crowd oohed and aahed, just as they had for the other designs, but she again wished there was an applause meter at work. Because she was certain, if they had a meter in place, it would show that Kitty had won the audience vote.

She scanned the stage just as Yasmine and Cassandra returned to the waiting area. Kurt Jager thanked them and announced the models' and dogs' final return. Lined up in the order in which they appeared, everyone, including the designers, strode back to the stage.

Edging through the cluster of gofers and stylists trying to see around the curtain, Ellie craned her neck and searched the mob. All the movers and shakers were in place: Anna Wintour, Grace Coddington, the big guy from *W,* Stefano Tonchi, and the *Harper's* rep, Glenda Bailey. And directly behind them sat Vivian, Georgette, and Stanley.

Viv spotted her and waved, and Ellie raised her hand

high. She had no idea how Viv had gotten them such prime seats, but she owed her best friend a favor. Today was a day her mother would never forget, and she'd been a part of it.

She concentrated on the models, amazed at the way they managed to control their steps when so many were on the catwalk. Patti and Beatriz did a sort of glide and stride, though Beatriz appeared to be uncomfortable with the steps, and Ellie understood her awkwardness. She imagined she'd walk like a duck if she had a gun strapped to her thigh.

Lawan and Kate's footwork seemed sultry and sleek, which matched Anton Rouch's dresses, while Dominique and Crystal's walk was springy and fun, more camp than glamour, the way they decided it should be when they wore the outlandish creations of Fiona Ray.

Kitty's models, Yasmine and Cassandra were last, and they did a combination bump and slide that did perfect justice to their stylish outfits.

Each dog was on target, too, trotting beside its mistress as if it loved to dress in high fashion. Even Daisy, who refused to wear her hat, carried the tam in her mouth, which was a real scene stealer with the audience.

The room sparkled with light, from both the viewers' and photographers' cameras. The press crammed the edge of the stage, hoping to catch a quote from a model or designer, and some people even reached up to pet a dog.

After thanking everyone for participating, Kurt asked the group to leave the area, and they filed off in order. Backstage, the models raced for bottled water or juice. Eduardo stormed in with his makeup palette and began dusting faces with powder. The designers waited until he was through, then rushed to straighten the collars, cuffs, and hemlines of their creations.

"Phew! I'm glad that's over," mumbled Julie, propped against the far table with a juice bottle in her hand. "The pressure in here is so much more intense than on a regular shoot."

"The size of this prize is enough to make anyone serious," said Ellie. "The contract will bolster the designer's career. Can you imagine your clothes hanging alongside those of the Olsen twins? Or finding out the dress Michelle Obama wore to visit a school or cut a ribbon was yours?"

"I guess, because I sure would like to accessorize for the Row or one of the big houses." Julie swallowed a gulp of juice, then cocked her head. "Hey, listen to that voice. Patti's sister is good."

Noting the hush of the crowd as Janice began to sing, Ellie smiled. "Julie, can you do me a favor? Start down the line and make sure the little guys look okay, their clothes are on straight, that sort of thing. I have to talk to someone."

She scanned the models and found Patti standing with her eyes closed, her face a wash of color as she listened to her sister. Edging through the throng, she inched past Marcus and sidled up to big sis. When the first number finished to thunderous applause, Patti opened her tear-filled hazel eyes.

Ellie grabbed her hand and squeezed. "She's fabulous. Congratulations."

"I was so worried a while ago, when I heard her talk, but I guess that lemon and tea drink Julie fixed did the trick. I just hope Mom and Dad have the TV on. I reminded them, but sometimes they forget."

"Want me to call and give them another reminder?"

"Gee, would you?" Patti swiped a tear from her cheek and gave the number while Ellie punched it in. "If I don't stop crying Eduardo's gonna kill me." She sniffed, watching Ellie listen to the ring. "Thanks so much. I really appreciate it."

Minutes passed while Ellie spoke to the elder Fallgraves, who assured her the show was taping on their television screen and they were watching both their daughters. Grinning, she gave Patti the message and stepped back, bumping into Beatriz.

"Oh, gosh, excuse me. I didn't see you there."

"No problem," said the model. She arched a brow. "So you're the dog walker."

"I am in real life, but I'm a lot more here. Dog walker, dog watcher, dog groomer, dog dresser—anything they need done is my job—and my assistant's."

Janice began her second number and Ellie knew she didn't have much time to get to the big question, if she got to it at all. "So, you're a model?"

"Uh, yeah," said Beatriz, her expression blank.

"But you're new. I asked around and no one here has ever seen your work."

"I know. Marcus grilled me, but I couldn't give him many credentials either."

"So where have you worked?"

"LA runways, mostly."

"This is a prime job, you know. The way I understand it, girls were lined up for blocks when this contest was announced and the call went out that Nola Morgan Design needed models."

"So I've been told."

Beatriz's simple sentences ticked Ellie off. What wasn't the woman saying?

"So your agent must have told you about this job."

"Nope. Don't have an agent."

Song two finished to another round of applause, and

Janice immediately segued into her third number. There had to be a way to figure out the real reason the girl was here, Ellie decided. Pandemonium would break as soon as the winner was announced, and she might not get Beatriz alone again.

"Then how were you able to sub for Claire, if you don't mind my asking?"

Beatriz's features stayed cast in stone, her dark eyes unblinking, her lush mouth compressed. "I just happened to walk in looking for work when Mr. Prince found out the other model called in sick."

"That was a lucky break for you. I gather it's dangerous living in LA, with you wearing that gun and all."

The model's expression didn't change. "I'm sure you'll agree, a woman alone has to be careful in any big city."

Another roar of applause broke out and Marcus laid his hand on Ellie's shoulder. "Time to let us go. Wish me luck."

Just before she stepped back, he leaned down and kissed her on the cheek, his lips lingering. The models, designers, and dogs moved to the stage.

"Did I just see what I think I saw?"

Ellie turned to find Julie, her mouth creased in a smile, staring. "I thought you were checking on the dogs."

"I was, I mean I did, but Janice stopped singing and Kurt broke the applause to call the gang back out. When I looked up, there you were, and there was Marcus, kissing you and grinning like a fool."

"It was nothing. He wanted me to wish him luck." Intent on shutting Julie up, she shrugged. "No biggie."

"Okay, if you say so." It was obvious her assistant

didn't believe the statement. "And you're going to to-morrow night's party as his date."

"His platonic date," Ellie clarified. "I made that clear when I agreed to go."

Julie heaved a sigh. "I'd take a date with him, platonic or not. You are one lucky girl."

Ellie moved closer to the stage, and Julie followed. The cluster of assistants and stylists had grown, causing Julie, at no more than five-one, to jumped up and down. Ellie gave silent thanks for having a bit of extra height as she peered over several of the heads.

"What's happening? I can't see," whined her assistant.

"Then scootch in. I'm sure they'll let you through." Ellie nodded to the crowd hovering in front of them. As if on cue the throng parted and Julie was able to gain a few extra feet in her quest for the curtain.

Kurt Jager centered himself between the group of models, designers, and dogs, giving a megawatt smile. Then he announced the arrival of Nola and Morgan, the owners of Nola Morgan Design. Blinding lights contin-ued to flash while the piano player plunked out a jingle of excitement.

"Thanks to all of you for celebrating with us," Mor-gan Prince began. "As many of you know, this is our third year in business, and we're ready to take the next step in our career. We appreciate you all for being here to share in our good fortune."

Cheers sounded, along with applause.

"So, the moment is at hand," said Nola, her face flushed. "The winner of our grand prize, one hundred thousand dollars, and their line of clothing to be fea-tured in our fall 2012 collection is . . ."

The crowd held their breath, as if they were a single

entity. Ellie had no idea a break in the announcement could create such suspense.

"Kitty King."

Nola rushed to embrace Kitty, who already had tears in her eyes. Everyone was focused on the girl and her models, who were squealing with joy, but Ellie found herself drawn to the dogs, as they were always her first priority.

Amid all the racket, lights, and music filling the arena, Klingon had jumped into Morgan Prince's arms.

She did a double take, unsure of which dog he held, but Yasmine had gathered a mini Schnauzer to her chest, and that could only be her own Jojo.

"Pick me up, will ya. I can't see a thing through all these human legs."

She squatted in place and lifted her boy. "Did you hear? Our Kitty won. Isn't that great?"

"Sure, but why do you look like you swallowed squirrel poop?"

"I do not," Ellie huffed out. "Now be quiet and I'll let you see what's going on."

Rudy stretched his neck and scanned the stage. Ellie imagined chaos, but that was only a guess. There was so much noise, such loud music, so much applause and cheering.

She let him down slowly, and nestled him against her. "Seen enough?"

"There's more crazy goin' on out there than a Super Bowl win. I say we sit back and let things settle. I could use a biscuit, and I bet the other guys could, too."

"That's a great idea. Let me see if I can find Julie." The backstage crowd thinned as people seeped onto the stage. She guessed the press had given the high sign. They would let things stall for a couple of minutes, then take more formal pictures of Nola and Morgan with the winner and each of the other designers.

She set Rudy in the pen. "Hang tight while I look for her."

Ellie spotted a cluster of orange curls and made a beeline for her assistant. "I suggest you collect the dogs before they get hurt. With all those stilettos stomping around someone is bound to get stepped on, and there's a good chance a delicate bone might break."

"You got it, boss."

Julie left to do her thing and Ellie returned to her usual spot on the chairs next to the snack table, which had been expanded to hold a bevy of goodies. Upon arrival, she tried to hold back her surprise as she took a seat next to Jeffery King. She hadn't noticed earlier, but he wore the clothes of an ordinary gofer: plain khaki slacks, a worn dress shirt with the sleeves rolled up, and sneakers.

"You're not going to join in your sister's celebration?"

He raised a shoulder. "It's Kitty's time to shine, and I don't want to tarnish it for her. It won't look good in the papers if she's standing next to an accused murderer."

The words, said so strongly, hit Ellie in the heart. "I don't think she'd mind."

"She wouldn't, but the press would have a field day, and I don't want to take anything away from her big moment." He folded his arms and leaned back in the chair. "I love her too much to let suspicion cloud her dream."

"So you weren't there when Nola and Morgan were discussing the winner?"

"Nope. In fact, I was against a far wall at the rear of the auditorium listening to Patti's sister sing. The press saw me, and Detective Vaughn did, too."

"Detective Vaughn is here?"

"He has been for a while."

"But I never saw him backstage."

"Maybe he just wanted to keep an eye on me. Who knows?"

"Want me to find out?" It was time she spoke to Vaughn about what she'd learned, and quizzing him about his watching Jeffery would be a good lead in. "I have to talk to him anyway."

"So you're going to tell him what you discovered last night?"

"There are a few things he should know, and I can drop the question about you into the conversation, just to see what he says."

Movement from the crowd caught her attention and she raised her gaze to see Julie struggling with a group of canines. "Oops, I'd better help my assistant first, or there's going to be trouble."

"Can I do anything?"

Ellie counted the dogs and saw that four were missing, and one of them was Cheech. "You'd have to go on-stage."

"Don't worry. I can play invisible when I have to."

"Okay, then. Collect Patti's Chihuahua and any other dogs you see. I doubt the models will need them for a while."

Standing, Jeffery edged through the thinning crowd. The noise level had lowered, and things were calming down. She walked to the pen and helped Julie with her charges. Spike had again stuck a foot through the obnoxious fifth leg of his coat, and she bent to straighten it. Daisy had no tam, and Ellie could only imagine where it was. Lucy appeared calm and collected as if used to crowds, and so did Jojo.

"How are things out there?" she asked her assistant.

"Almost under control. The security guards are leading people offstage. I hear they're checking tickets. It appears about a hundred were marked with a purple X on the back."

"Ahh, who got those?"

"The ones given to the models and the bigwigs. I guess they figured the models would only give their extras to the 'in' crowd or family, and those folks are okay."

Ellie groaned internally. Great. She'd given Viv, Stanley, and Georgette Patti's tickets, so they had the ones with the X. Her mother would be at this party with bells on.

They turned at the rattle of bottles. The caterers were back, and they were pushing a cart stacked with cases of champagne. A three-tiered cart followed behind, that one filled with appetizers, and another followed with napkins, glasses, and all manner of serving supplies.

"This place is fast becoming a zoo. Where do you suggest we take the dogs?"

Julie scoped out the area, then smiled. "How about if we just move things back about twenty feet and set ourselves up a couple of chairs, sort of like a line of sitting guards? Think that will work?"

Jeffery came up behind them and joined in. "Sure. You two pull the pen out while I collect the chairs. We'll take our seats and stay in place, spell each other if we need the restroom or something to eat. No one gets close to these little guys without going through us."

Impressed, the girls followed his suggestion. In ten minutes the dogs were protected and munching on Sara Studebaker's gourmet biscuits, while Julie poured bottled water into their bowls. Some had even settled into their dog beds and were already asleep.

Now that she had a break, it was time for Ellie to do one of her favorite things: people-watch. First, she'd found the comment Marcus made about Morgan Prince fascinating. With all the gossip going around, why hadn't she heard this story before? She spotted him standing, hovering really, over Nola as if he were a papa bird. Was Marcus correct? Was the big man a phony? Did he really have secret affairs while pretending to be madly in love with his business partner?

She found Beatriz standing alone and noted there was no action between her and her employer. With her blank expression, was it possible she was one of those people who were good actors? Many folks had learned how to cover their tracks, even though they were involved in illicit activity. A few even thought cheating was a game, and enjoyed seeing how much they could get away with.

"Who are you staring at?" asked Julie.

"Morgan Prince," Ellie answered. Her assistant seemed to know everything about everyone. Now that they were relaxed, the mere mention of his name could be enough to trigger a reaction.

"Oh." Julie sipped her champagne. "Any particular reason why?"

"He's a nice-looking man, and he's been good to me. I understand he hired Beatriz, the new girl, with little to no references, and I wondered if he treated all women that way."

"So you've heard the rumors."

"Just one, from someone who doesn't gossip. It was a surprise, since he and Nola seem like such a loving couple."

Julie grinned "Do you remember the television show from a couple of years back? *Ugly Betty?*"

"I loved that show, hated when it went off the air. It was great fun." She raised a brow. "Are you saying what happened in that series was true? It was a good portrayal of the fashion industry?"

"In an exaggerated way, yes. You've been with us a week now, so you know there's plenty of talk about a woman's size, and the backbiting isn't quite so outrageous. But the sleeping around part? That was true."

"So you're saying our Mr. Prince isn't as well-behaved as he appears."

"He has a penis and he wields power, doesn't he?"

"And that means he takes advantage of his position? Then why hasn't anyone talked about it?"

Julie shrugged. "This is just a guess on my part, but up till now he's been running the show. It's not smart to gossip about someone who can have you dropped in a single sentence."

"Ah, I see. And now that his reign of power is over?"

"People will talk again, until the next time." She took another gulp of her drink. "So, who said what about him?"

"It doesn't matter. It was just a comment involving him with Beatriz, the new girl." Ellie waited a beat. "Do you know much about her?"

"No one seems to have any info, and that's odd, but if she comes from LA, well, they do things differently out there." She leaned back in her chair. "As for her and Morgan, who knows?"

"Then you don't think it's true?"

"Anything is possible, but . . ."

"If not her, who was he seeing?"

"The gossips threw a lot of names around, but no one

in particular. Once this contest got under way, his personal life was put on hold. All folks talked about was which designers would be chosen, and who would win the big prize."

"And Nola?"

"Is pretty much the way she appears. Far as I can tell, she's straight with Morgan and the people she deals with." She finished her drink and held out her glass. "I'm starving. I'd like to get a refill and some food. I can bring back one for you, too, if you want."

"That would be great," said Ellie, happy to get a little thinking time. She had a lot to mull over.

"More humans to add to the list," came a voice from behind her once Julie set out. *"Got any ideas?"*

She scanned the crowd before answering. She was tired of people asking why she spoke to the dogs. Clark Fettel grazed at the canapé table; Marcus was flirting with Kate and Claire, and no one seemed to be paying her or the canines any attention. She slid her bottom to the side and gazed at her boy. "How many more did you come up with?"

"Three, of course."

"Three? But Marcus is already on the list, so Morgan is my next choice. It's odd the way Klingon takes to him so easily—something's fishy there. And Prince is a cheater, which automatically makes him untrustworthy. Who else is there?"

"Use yer brain, Triple E. If that Prince guy is dishonest, who'd be after him?"

"About a dozen angry boyfriends?"

He snorted. *"Try that Nola lady. She'd be upset with anyone her guy was doing the human hula with. If he was friendly with Lilah Perry—"*

"Lilah Perry? Who said anything about him messing around with the dead designer?"

"I'm just asking because of Klingon. There has to be some reason why he trusts the prince-man, and it could be because the guy was seein' Lilah."

The idea had filtered through her brain, but it seemed too outlandish to be true. "So if he was?"

"It could'a made Nola so mad, she decided to do somethin' about it. Somethin' bad."

Chapter 17

"Sitting all alone, Ms. Engleman? I'm surprised." Detective Vaughn stared down at her, his mouth drawn in a frown, his gray suit wrinkled. "I hear you've been doing a bit of sleuthing. I'm sure you realize you could be held for interfering in an ongoing investigation if you continue to snoop."

Ellie heaved out a breath. She'd allowed Julie to peruse the food table and told Jeffery to spend some time with Patti. She had hoped to speak to Detective Vaughn, but not when he put her on the hot seat at the start of their conversation. And who had told him about what she'd been doing? Surely not the same people who had begged her to prove Jeffery King innocent.

"I've looked into a few things, but I did so only because Nola and Morgan believe Jeffery's been wrongly accused, and they asked for my help."

Leaving a chair between them, he took a seat and crossed his legs. "Just because a couple of people want your so-called expertise doesn't mean you won't be arrested."

Ellie twisted toward him in her seat. "Has someone complained about me stepping on their toes? Because I don't believe I've gotten in anyone's way. And I do have things to report that I think you'll find interesting."

He pulled the usual notebook from his inside jacket pocket. "Were these 'things' legal or did you find them out while breaking and entering?"

"I—what—what do you mean by that?"

"You must be aware of what breaking and entering means. I heard you and that dog of yours have done it plenty of times before."

Ellie inhaled a gasp. "Instead of digging to find out how I spend my time, you should pay better attention to this case. You might find out the same things I have, and that could send you in another direction in this investigation."

As if on traffic duty, he held up a hand. "Take it down a notch, Nancy Drew. Just because I arrested Jeffery King doesn't mean I've stopped looking into things."

Ignoring his Nancy Drew remark, she gazed across the room and spotted Jeffery still talking with Patti, Dominique speaking with Claire and Clark Fettel, and her mother and Viv deep in conversation with Marcus.

"Then you know there are a slew of people who had a beef with Lilah Perry, and they also had the opportunity to carry out the identical plan you've accused Mr. King of running."

He continued to frown as he skimmed through his notebook. "Let's compare information, shall we? There's Clark Fettel, for one. He and Ms. Perry battled frequently, he was up for the same job as Jeffery King, which he lost, and he was close enough to those gift bags to doctor them, correct?"

"Yes, and he's got a mean streak. I wouldn't put it past him to try such a thing."

He flipped a page. "And that model—Dominique? Everyone agrees she hated the deceased, but did she have the opportunity to depress that EpiPen and put the peanut oil on those perfume strips without anyone knowing? Managing all that took a fairly clever and calculating mind, plus some time. And the way I heard it, none of the models had a free minute on that first day."

Surprised that Vaughn was researching the same suspects she had gave Ellie pause. Maybe he wasn't quite the do-nothing cop she first thought. "Then you have your doubts about Jeffery?"

The detective arched an eyebrow. "I wouldn't say I have doubts, because I still think he's the one person who had motive and opportunity, but I do think Lilah Perry had a boatload of enemies who are happy she's gone."

"And if I knew for certain who killed her, I'd send them a dozen roses as a thank-you." Marcus's words rang in Ellie's brain. Should she mention that the designer had a special reason for wanting Lilah dead, or would that only get Marcus in hot water?

"Take Marcus David, for instance," continued Vaughn, as if reading her mind.

"What about him?"

"Word has it he thought Lilah Perry was responsible for his younger sister's death. Revenge is always a good motive for murder."

"I'm impressed. You have been looking into things."

"How nice to learn I have your approval. But, unlike you, I'm finding my info legally."

That was his second hint that he knew about her and Patti snooping in the models' apartments. But he also had to know they'd gotten the keys legally, which meant he'd have a hard time proving the case against them. Instead of worrying, she charged ahead. "Anyone else I should know about?"

His lips thinned. "You shouldn't know about any of them."

"You do realize that if someone complained about me, I might be getting close to the truth."

"Which means you should watch your back. People don't like strangers nosing into their private lives, and that's what you've been doing."

"Did you come here today to warn me, or are you here to keep tabs on Jeffery King?"

"A bit of both. I don't like cases that are a slam dunk. That usually means something's too convenient for comfort. And my case against Jeffery King is definitely a slam dunk."

"Then why arrest him? Why not let him go while you check out the other possibilities?"

"I'm checking them out in my own way, so I'll say it one more time. Stay out of my investigation." He stood. "Keep your nose clean, and let the NYPD do their job." He gave a curt nod. "Good day."

What a gasbag, came a voice from behind her.

She checked to see if anyone was watching, then turned to face her boy. "He's definitely a tough nut, but I kind of like him. He's not as crude or as lazy as Detective Gruning, and he's at least letting me know we have the same suspicions. That has to count for something."

Maybe so, but I don't like him gripin' because we're doin' a good job. Plus even if he's free now, our guy is still under arrest.

"But it sounds as if he'd be happy to release Jeffery if he came up with a better suspect. I think that's a big admission for a homicide detective."

"Doesn't seem like anything Detective Demento would ever do," Rudy groused.

"Leave Sam out of this. He'd listen if he thought I was on the right track. I just hope he's been so busy working his own cases that he hasn't had time to think about what's going on over here."

"It has been sorta nice with him outta the house this past week. I like havin' my bed back."

"Well, I miss him."

"You're in the minority."

Since when did her four-legged pal have a majority vote in their relationship? "Can we get back on track, please? I need to find a way to get closer to Marcus. I hate to say it, but I agree with Vaughn. Revenge is a great reason for murder, and Marcus is still mourning his sister. I just don't know how to do it without leading him on."

"I already told you, just bat your baby blues."

"That's the same as leading him on, you knucklehead. No thanks."

Rudy scratched his side with a back leg, then retreated to his favorite Buddha pose.

"What's that supposed to mean?" she asked him.

The shuffle of feet caught her attention and she spun in her seat. "Ellie, darling, I've just met the most adorable young man. And he has a respectable job that doesn't put him in danger or make him deal with the distasteful side of life."

Leave it to Georgette to describe an honorable profession like nabbing killers as distasteful. "I've met Marcus, Mother. He's a great guy."

"And single," her mother prodded, taking the chair next to Ellie.

"I know that, too."

"He told me he was escorting you to a party tomorrow evening, quite near our penthouse. Detective Ryder is a decent man, but his profession seems to draw you in, and you end up doing the same dangerous things he does." Georgette patted her daughter's knee. "I'm thrilled to see that you're coming to your senses."

Ellie gave an internal eye roll. "Sam is my guy of choice, Mother, no matter what his profession, and he does his best to keep me out of danger, so don't blame my brushes with murder on him." She crossed her arms. "As for Marcus David, he's well aware the date is platonic. The exciting thing is I'm going to need a new dress, something designer," she said, hoping to pull her mother off topic. "I've been told the party is private, with only the biggies in the fashion world on the guest list."

Georgette's complexion flushed pink. "Are you allowed to bring guests?"

"No. In fact, I think I'm a pity guest myself, just there because I was part of what Nola Morgan Design considered their team."

Georgette's expression deflated like a slowly leaking tire. "Oh, well, would you like some assistance finding the right dress?"

She was hoping to shop with Vivian, not her money-laden mother. But before she could answer, she spotted Nola McKay, without an entourage, headed in their direction.

"Ellie, I've been looking for you. I need a favor," said the designer maven.

"I'll be happy to lend a hand, but first let me introduce you to—"

"Your mother." Nola held out a hand and Georgette grasped it. "We've met."

"Nola, it was so nice talking with you earlier." Georgette placed her palm on Ellie's shoulder. "I know my girl will do whatever she can to assist you. She's such a clever young woman."

Ellie wanted to crawl under a chair to hide her embarrassment. Most mothers loved putting their daughter on the spot, and her mom was no exception. "Ms. McKay knows I'll help her in any way I can."

Nola grinned. "I hear you'll be at tomorrow night's party with Marcus David, and I so hoped you'd agree to wear the design we discussed at our first meeting. We did promise you Kitty's wheat-colored jumpsuit with the burnt orange trim, and I know it'll look great on you."

"Oh, gosh, I'd love to wear it." Ellie heaved a sigh of happiness. No dress-shopping tomorrow meant she could work on more important things. "Thanks so much for the offer."

"Wait." Georgette held up a hand, much like Detective Vaughn had. "You're asking my daughter to wear a designer original?"

"Why, yes. She's a perfect plus size, so the outfit won't need any alterations. We've asked all the models and their dogs to wear one of Kitty's wonderful creations, but since we already promised the jumpsuit to Ellie, well, it seemed only right that she be the one to have it for the party."

Before Georgette could comment, Stanley arrived on his scooter. "I thought I might find you here with our girl," he said, his voice hesitant. "I don't want to spoil the party, but I was hoping you'd agree to a trip home. This has been a long day, and I'm afraid it's worn me out."

Georgette practically jumped to her feet. "Of course we can go." She turned to her daughter and Nola. "I'm thrilled Ellie will have that outfit for the big party, Ms. McKay, and it's been a pleasure." She kissed Ellie's cheek. "Don't stay out too late tomorrow night, darling. Sunday is brunch."

"Georgette is charming, and so is Judge Frye," said Nola, watching Ellie's mother and stepfather leave. "Oh, and there's one more thing. Since the models will be bringing their dogs, we thought it only fair you bring your little man." She nodded at Rudy. "Now, let's get you that jumpsuit.

"Thanks so much for the help. I couldn't have done it without you," said Ellie, bidding Viv a good-bye at her door the next morning. "I'm even going to stop whining about the outrageous price I had to pay for the darned shoes."

"Hah! I'll believe that when I don't hear it," said Viv, juggling her packages so she could take the apartment keys from her bag. "Just promise me you'll forget about wearing a four-hundred-dollar pair of shoes and have fun. Marcus is an adorable guy, and he likes you. If Sam complains, tell him it was business. He'll understand." She opened her door. "I'm going to walk Twink. You want to meet me with Rudy?"

"I still have a lot to do to get ready, so he has to bide his time." She headed up the stairs. "And I have to phone Amber to make sure my charges had a good week."

She gave a final wave and climbed the steps to her floor. After unlocking the door, she slipped inside, hung up her jacket, and carried her tote bag and over-the-top shoes to the kitchen, where her boy sat waiting.

"Did you have a good nap?" She took a cup from the dish drainer and filled it with water. "I hope so, because you're going to have a busy night."

"Sleep is always good." He yawned. *"You sure I have to go to tonight's shindig?"*

Ellie put her cup in the microwave and went to the cupboard for a tea bag while she waited for the nuker to chime. "Yes, I'm sure. Remember, all our suspects will be there. We could find a clue or two that will break the case."

"I say you concentrate on that prince guy and his gal. Get into their private space and see what you can find."

"While you do what?" The microwave rang, and she removed the mug, dropped in the tea bag, and brought it to the table. "Talk to the other dogs?"

"I'm gonna concentrate on that mini Schnauzer. He's still not talkin' about the prince, but I got a feeling he knows stuff. Important stuff."

She used a spoon to remove the tea bag, then added a packet of sweetener and stirred. "Good. And remember to listen in on conversations. If people drink enough alcohol, they get to talking. Someone might say something we need to know."

"How about I check out the new girl, and try to see if she's still packin' her gun?"

"That's good, too. I would have asked Vaughn about her, but again, it would have sounded like I was spying, this time on a woman who wasn't even around when the murder was committed." She took a sip of her tea. "Hmm. Maybe Patti knows something. I'll have to ask her."

He put a paw on her knee. *"So what's in the bag? A new batch of Dingo bones, or maybe something from Sara Studebaker's place? I could use a treat right now."*

"No dog goodies, just shoes." Of course, some canines thought leather shoes were goodies, but not her boy. "Want to see them?"

"Sure, why not." He sat at attention.

"They're Jimmy Choos." She pulled the box from the bag, removed the top, and brought out the pumps. "What do you think?"

Rudy cocked his head. *"They're a little busy, dontcha think?"*

"I said the same thing to Viv, and she assured me they were perfect." She held up the pumps with a stacked heel. "I kind of like the straps and buckles, too. And they're not stilettos, so I'll be tall but not gigantic."

"With all those gigundo models around, that party's gonna look like a woman's basketball team celebration. You'll fit right in."

Ellie finished her tea, then carried her shoes to the bedroom. "I'm taking a shower and doing my hair and makeup; then I'll feed you and we can wait for Marcus. He's supposed to be here at eight."

"Okay, I'll chill. You do that beautifyin' thing human females do. But before you start, did you talk to Amber?"

She dropped the shoes on her bed and sat. "Oops. Thanks for reminding me." Since the dog walker hadn't phoned her, she assumed everything had gone well with her charges, but she still liked to check and make sure. She had Sara Studebaker's biscuits as a peace offering for Monday, and they should be enough to make her pack forgive her for being gone an entire week.

After several rings, she got Amber's voicemail and left a message. "That's all I can do," she said to her boy. "I'm sure she'd have called me if there was trouble."

"Probably so." Rudy jumped on the bed and curled on his pillow. *"I'll just catch another forty winks while you do your thing."*

Ellie went to the bathroom and started the shower. After getting in, she washed her hair and began the single-foot dance women did to shave their legs. Someday soon she was going to get her leg hair taken care of via one of the more daring processes done in a day spa. She'd heard sugaring was good. It took the pain and time out of a beauty routine.

Just as she finished, the bathroom door opened. Inhaling a gasp, she dropped her razor and spun around. Had she remembered to lock the front door? She peered through the frosted glass and heaved a breath.

"Sam?"

"No, it's a burglar." He slid the shower door open a few inches and began to strip. "How often do I have to tell you? Lock the door when you're home alone." Before she could answer, he was in the stall, his body ready for a bit of private time with his girl. "You're just lucky it's me, and not some mope on the hunt for a victim."

When he held out his arms, she stepped into them. "I have Rudy, remember?" She soaped a washcloth and began to lather him down. "He's my protector."

"Sure he is." Sam turned so she could do his backside. "That's why he wasn't at the door when I walked in. I still haven't seen him around."

"He has a sixth sense when people come in. He knew it was you." She ran the washcloth down his muscled bottom and across to his front, grinning when she found him ready for action. "Let's not argue about Rudy or the front door. I've missed you."

Sam faced her and moved his hands to her breasts. "And I've missed you. Sorry I didn't call, but I've been on watch duty and couldn't phone. Let's catch up on the good stuff, then maybe we can go out to dinner. I have the rest of the night off and tomorrow, too."

Ellie gave a mental groan. Didn't it just figure that he'd have free time and she wouldn't? But instead of giving him the bad news, she let the feel of his protective body draw her in, and lost herself in his seductive kiss. She'd tell him about Marcus later.

Hands fisted, Sam stood at the microwave and stared at the two diet meals spinning around in the machine. If he'd known he'd be eating alone, he would have called for takeout. And forget about going someplace fancy for dinner with his best girl. He was on his own, now that she told him she had plans.

Plans with another man.

He'd take part of the blame. He hadn't been around most of the week, and he hadn't called her. Unfortunately, stakeout duty made it tough to use the phone. He'd also had a court appearance and a mound of paperwork. Every time he'd been home to shower and change, Ellie had been gone.

He glanced down and locked gazes with her dog. Damned if the little stinker wasn't looking at him with a shit-eating grin. If he didn't know better, he'd guess the mutt was happy to be going somewhere with Ellie, and without him.

The microwave dinged and he opened the door. He'd checked the freezer and the only thing inside, besides her caramel ice cream, were those miniature "cuisine" meals that were so small they wouldn't fill a mouse. He'd need two just to take the edge off his hunger. He still couldn't believe he'd be home alone for the night, while Ellie had a date with a guy she'd met just this week.

He dumped both meals on the plate he'd taken down from the cupboard, pulled out a fork, and carried his dinner to the table. Digging in, he tried to figure a way to go to this party in some kind of official capacity. Maybe he'd call Vaughn and see if the detective planned on attending the celebration. If so, he could offer to be backup or a second hand.

But it was a dumb idea, so he set it aside.

He heard footsteps and raised his gaze to the kitchen door. Ellie walked in and he swallowed. Holy crap! She'd outdone herself. Her russet curls shined in the light from the overhead fixture. The one-piece suit she wore hugged her figure like a second skin accentuating her full bust, curvy butt, and long muscular legs. Hell, even her new shoes were sexy.

"Are you sure you're happy eating my Lean Cuisines?" she asked. She grabbed Rudy's dinner bowl from the dish drainer and walked to the pantry. "You could have called for takeout, or there's fresh turkey and Swiss cheese in the meat drawer, rolls, too. If you want, I'll make you a sandwich, dress it up with lettuce and tomato, mayo, the works."

"This is fine," he said, trying to keep his pissy attitude out of the conversation. "How late do you think you'll be?"

When she turned and smiled, he blinked. Damn, but she looked good. Her turquoise eyes and long lashes were outlined in something dark and mysterious, and her mouth wore a color that matched the shoes and made her lips full and lush.

"I have no idea, but I'm sure Marcus will bring me home when I ask." She began the prep work for making her dog's dinner. "I've never been to one of these high fashion celebrations before. I've been told there'll be great food, live music, and lots of champagne."

"Where are you going again?"

She pulled a container of chopped green beans and carrots from the fridge. "A penthouse over on Central Park West, somewhere near Mother's place. My date has the exact address."

"Your date?" He blew out a breath. "I thought you said this was a business arrangement."

She spun around on her shoes. "Oh, you know what I mean. Marcus is my escort for the evening." Her eyes sparkled when she talked. "Since I didn't know if you'd be available, he offered to pick me up, and I said yes."

"Sounds nice." He clamped his jaw shut. No need to crank out a lousy comment. "He's a lucky guy, having you as his date."

Ellie mixed her boy's food and set the bowl on the

mat. "Here you go, big man." Then she sat across from Sam and smiled. "You're okay with this, right?"

Hell, no. "Hey, business is business." He downed a forkful of chicken in some kind of plastic-tasting sauce. "Have you seen Detective Vaughn lately?"

"Yesterday. He's still nosing around, even though Jeffery's out on bail." She began pleating a paper napkin she'd taken from the holder. "I think he's having second thoughts about Jeffery King being the killer."

"Oh, and what makes you say that?"

"Just . . . things he mentioned."

"What sort of things?"

Her cheeks flushed with color, a sure sign she was keeping something from him. "It's not important. Stuff I already knew."

"And how exactly did you come to know this—stuff?"

She leaned into the table. "I did a little research, is all, and found out a couple of things I thought he should hear. We sort of compared notes at yesterday's party."

Sam stood and carried his plate to the sink, then turned and rested his backside against the bank of cabinets. "Are you telling me you've been running an investigation for this King guy?" He shoved his hands in his pockets. "And Vaughn knows about it?"

She stood and tried to reach for Rudy's bowl, but he snatched it up and set it in the sink. "Hold on. Let's talk for a minute."

She glanced at her watch, something pricey with a foreign-sounding name that her mother had given her when she graduated college. "I don't have time. Marcus will be here any minute and I have to—to—freshen my lipstick."

He stepped in front of her and held her hands. "Your lips are more than fine." Trying for pleasant, he made a point of checking her out from head to toe and back again. "All of you is fine. Now how about answering my question?"

"I—we—I've done a bit of sleuthing, but it was harmless. And only a few people knew about it."

Sam took a step closer. "Sorry, but that doesn't make much sense. Now what have you been up to?"

"Nothing illegal, if that's what you're asking." She heaved a breath. "At least I don't think it was. Let's talk about it tomorrow, on the way to Mother's brunch."

"Aw, hell, I forgot about that."

She smiled. "I figured you would, but you've already said you have the day off, so there's no way to get out of going."

"And if I don't complain, you'll answer my questions tomorrow?"

"Absolutely." The downstairs buzzer rang and Rudy raced to the door. She dodged around him and pressed the entry buzzer. "That's Marcus. Be good and I'll let you meet him."

I'll meet him, all right, Sam thought as he followed her into the hall. He planned to put the screws to the guy and let him know Ellie was his.

She opened the door and stepped back. "Marcus, hi. You're right on time."

He and the nondate appraised each other like sumo wrestlers. They were the same height, with an almost identical build and haircut. Only Marcus David was dark, where Sam was fair, with blue eyes instead of brown. And didn't it figure the jerk was wearing a tux, probably from some name designer, because the fit was perfect.

Ellie introduced them and he did his best not to break the guy's knuckles when they shook hands.

"Just give me a minute to hook up Rudy, and we can go," she told the guy.

She retrieved the leash from the closet, and Sam took it from her, snapping it onto Rudy's collar as if it was his idea. When she passed Marcus the lead, the guy grinned, taking her in from head to toe.

Sam followed the man's eyes and knew immediately what he was thinking. "Easy there, sport," he blurted. Too bad he wasn't wearing his gun. "Just remember, Ms. Engleman is spoken for."

"Sam!"

"It's okay, Ellie. I know what he's saying." Marcus took her elbow and began leading her out the door. "I'll have her back by midnight, Pop. Don't worry about a thing."

Sam grasped her other elbow and pulled Ellie near. "Watch yourself." Bending forward, he wrapped his free arm around her back and kissed her. "And be good."

Her lashes fluttered and she swayed, then she smiled and caressed his cheek. "I'll try. And I'll miss you."

Inside, he grew a foot. It was just the reaction he was hoping for. The door slammed in his face and Sam heaved another breath. Then he went to the kitchen and grabbed his cell phone. It was time to call Vaughn and get the skinny on what Ellie had gotten herself into.

He had a gut feeling tonight was going to be important, in more ways than one.

Chapter 18

Ellie stood in the humongous foyer of Nola and Morgan's penthouse apartment, admiring all she saw. Besides the fact that everything in the entryway—floor, walls, artwork—was either black or white and polished to perfection, a three-piece combo played sultry jazz in one corner while a professional bar stood in another.

Marcus had brought her and Rudy here by cab, and he'd been polite and amusing on the ride over, but he hadn't said word one about meeting Sam. Was he going to pretend she wasn't involved so he could continue to plead his case?

Now that they were at the party, she planned to soak up all the high-end air she could breathe, while at the same time working to find clues that would help prove Jeffery King innocent. With her date at the bar ordering drinks, she got the chance to check out the guests, but recognized only a handful. Most of the men wore tuxedos, while the women dressed in full-length gowns or, like she did, wore a cutting-edge design.

Stefano Tonchi, the head man from *W*, stood near the bar chatting with Morgan Prince and two tall and beautiful women she assumed were models. Along with photographers, designers, and fashion editors, many of the people who had paraded through the backstage area during the contest walked by, some smiling at her and a couple bending to pet Rudy.

Curious about her boy's take on things, she squatted and pretended to fix his collar. "What do you think? Has anything come through to you? Does anybody give off a vibe?"

"Who's had time to channel vibes? Will you look at the size of this place? I thought Lulu's house was big, and Georgette's too, but this joint is like a museum."

She glanced ahead into the living area and spotted about a hundred guests clustered in groups, waiters passing trays of appetizers, and small table and chair setups scattered around the twenty-by-forty-foot space, a space that was decorated like a Fine Living dream home.

When she locked gazes with Nola McKay, the design maven said something to Kitty, who was standing next to her and, their smiles broad, both women waved. Taking a second go around the room, she saw Patti Fallgrave seated at a table with Jeffery, and figured she would connect with them later. She even spotted Clark Fettel schmoozing with Grace Coddington and Michael Kors, and imagined he was in hog heaven rubbing noses with people who ruled the fashion industry.

"It is bigger than what I expected," she told her boy. "I just thought you might have caught a clue from someone walking past."

"I think we'd have better luck if we split up. I can spy on the humans, but the other dogs are my real connection. They're the ones I wanna scope out."

She heaved a sigh. Rudy was correct, as usual. She

knew from personal experience that dogs were aware of a whole lot more than folks gave them credit for, mostly because they saw things from a completely different angle. And canines could be the world's best snoops. No one held their tongue when a dog was near. People had no idea that, beyond the usual sit, stay, and down commands, their pets understood what they were saying.

"Okay, here goes." She unsnapped his leash and tucked it in her bag. "Just don't get underfoot. And come find me as soon as you learn anything useful."

Standing, she watched him trot off in full yorkiepoo mode, cute and cuddly and heading straight for Nola and Kitty. Well aware that he was adorable, her boy knew how to work a crowd. If he wanted to get on a human's good side, he could manipulate like the best puppeteer.

A glass of champagne came into view and she turned to find Marcus grinning as he held up her drink, and next to him was someone she'd kept an eye on all week.

"Uh, hi," said Ellie to Karen Hood.

The woman, dressed in an elegant red gown dotted with sparkling crystals, grinned. "I hear you've been asking about my work, so I thought it was time we met."

"I've been admiring your creations. Some of them were so wonderful they actually made me want to look at the model's hair instead of her dress."

"Wow, that's some compliment," she said, and took a sip of champagne. "Marcus told me about your hair and he's right, it's quite lovely. Do you mind . . ." She raised a hand and fingered Ellie's. "Good texture. Is the color yours?"

"With a bit of help to cover the gray," Ellie said, frowning. "Sometimes the curl is more than I can handle."

"Tell you what, since you're such a fan, how about

you phone my appointment desk and ask for a spot. Tell them I told you to call."

Ellie blinked. "Oh, no, I could never—"

"Sure you could," Marcus interjected. "Let her do what she does best. It'll be worth the price."

"It's not the cost, but I could never take up the slot she might need for someone important."

"Don't worry. I decide who I'll take care of, not people who think they're important," Karen said, lifting her glass. "Now if you'll excuse me, I have to talk to someone else before I leave."

"Well," said Ellie, watching her head into the living room. "That was a nice surprise. Thank you."

"No problem. I knew you admired her work, and she was in line for a drink, so . . ." Marcus grinned. "By the way, did I really see you talking to your dog again when we headed over?"

"Talking to my dog?" She took another sip of her champagne, savoring the bubbly wine's flavor. Thanks to Georgette and Flora Steinman, she was adept at identifying quality champagne, and this was some of the best. "Okay, you caught me again. But you must know by now that Rudy and I have a special connection. He knows—I mean he seems to know—exactly what I say or want him to do, and I use it to my advantage."

His lips rose up at one corner. "Your advantage?"

Ellie gave herself a mental head-slap. She really did need to come up with some pat descriptions of the bond she and her pal shared without spilling the beans on their special ability. "I guess it's the emotional advantage I'm talking about. He comforts me when I'm upset, listens to my ideas and never says they're stupid, supports me when I want to try something weird, that sort of thing."

"So if I listen when you're upset, never say you're

dumb, and cheer you on if you want to climb the Empire State Building I'll rise a notch on your love ladder?"

She inhaled a breath, hoping to will away the blush. Would Marcus ever stop flirting or trying to get on her good side? "I just drop the so-called friends who think I'm stupid. That way, everyone close to my heart listens when I complain or ask questions that some might consider to be a bit . . . below average."

"Even the guy you live with?"

Ah, finally, a question about Sam. "Of course he does. If he didn't, I could never love him." She arched an eyebrow. "You've met Sam. Surely you understand the type of relationship we're in. How we trust each other and allow each other to do what we think is right."

He straightened his shoulders, aligning his Armani tux as if preparing for a *GQ* photo shoot. "All I know is I met a macho guy who seemed to be an expert at subtle intimidation. His handshake was just short of a vise, his eyes warned me off his turf, and his body language said if I touched you the way I wanted to I was toast."

"He's a cop. Being assertive is cemented in his DNA." She took another swallow of champagne, ignoring the touch remark. "Now if you don't mind, I'm starving. I'm going to check out the food situation."

"You do that. I'd like to find Kitty. I didn't have time to congratulate her properly, and I should."

Ellie aimed for the dining room, where she found another thirty or so people either sitting at tables and enjoying the food, or talking while they wandered the length of the two buffet setups ringing the room.

Straight out of a photo in *Food & Wine* magazine, the beginning of the table was piled high with cold dishes. Huge shrimp, caviar on creamy white cheese, lobster salad, oysters on the half shell, and a dozen other top-of-the-line items graced one side while further down skewers of filet mignon, a whole carved turkey, a round of beef being sliced by a waiter, and a variety of other warm dishes sat waiting.

The second table, piled high with sweets, held trays of chocolate truffles, miniature fruit tarts, plates holding bite-sized creampuffs, and small bowls of lemon mousse. A huge cake, iced in white, filled the center of the table with the words NOLA MORGAN DESIGN CONGRATULATES KITTY KING written in bold red script.

While making her choices at the dinner table, something brushed her shoe and she held back a squeak. Glancing down, she spotted the two mini Schnauzers sitting upright, paws out, in the typical beg position, waiting for her to answer their request for a treat.

Squatting, she grinned. It was the first time she'd seen Klingon act like a real canine in all the time she'd known him, which boded well. Maybe the little guy was getting over the loss of his mistress. Locating an empty table, she waggled a finger, asking them to join her.

"You two should be ashamed of yourselves," she teased, taking a seat and setting her plate down. "You're both so adorable no human can resist you. How many goodies have you finagled so far?"

"Not as many as you think. Yasmine dropped us off only a couple of minutes ago and told us to be good, and we're givin' it our best shot."

She realized Jojo was the one talking and took stock of his outfit. The dogs were dressed in their identical designer creations, but he wore all four booties, which meant that Klingon was the mini Schnauzer that was bootie-free. "How are you doing, Klingon?" she asked him, her expression one of understanding. "Are you still missing Lilah?"

The dog shook from head to tail, ruffling his salt and pepper hair. *"I miss her, but Yasmine's been nice. She said she'd find me another home, but there's only one I want."*

Ellie opened and closed her mouth. "You already know where you want to live?"

"With the prince, of course. I know he likes me."

"Oh, well then," she muttered, trying to get hold of exactly what he was saying. What was it about Morgan Prince that made Klingon trust him? She finished her champagne and set the empty glass on the table. "Are you saying then Mr. Prince and Lilah were good friends, and that's how you know him?"

"Yep."

Before she could ask him more, Klingon did a little dance of excitement. "Ms. Engleman," said a voice she recognized. "I'm so happy you decided to join our party." Morgan Prince gave a lazy grin as he looked her over. "I saw you when you first came in, but I couldn't break free from my guests. That jumpsuit is perfect for a woman of your stature."

He took a seat and held up a hand, a signal for Ellie to hold back a comment. "Don't get me wrong. Just because I live in the fashion world doesn't mean I agree with those in this business who think thin is the only look a woman can have to be desirable. I find your ample dimensions to be quite pleasing."

Blindsided by his compliment, she drew in a surprised breath. "Oh, well, ah, thank you."

Klingon jumped into his lap, and Morgan ran a hand over the dog's head. "Our Ms. Engleman is an attractive woman, don't you think?" he asked the well-dressed dog.

The conversation was too off-the-wall for Ellie to handle. She'd been talking, really talking, to the mini Schnauzer, and now a man who was starting to stack up as a suspect was conversing with the dog, too.

And doing it while he made a pass at her!

The whole goofy scenario gave her brain pain.

"Don't look so surprised, Ms. Engleman. I've heard several designers comment on you tonight already. They've noticed the excellent way you carry yourself, and the way you look in that outfit. I think you could have a future in this business, if you wanted. What do you think?"

She felt another mental head slap coming. She'd been going over things in her mind while he'd been talking. Everything started falling into place. The gift bags had been put together in Morgan Prince's office. He'd been wandering the snack area during the morning of that first showing. And Klingon just admitted that Prince and his mistress knew each other well.

Lilah was caustic, brash, and had no care for anyone but herself. Did she and Prince have a personal relationship? One so intimate that she could demand he give her the win in the NMD contest? And when he said no, did she threaten to go to Nola McKay and tell her that she and Nola's trusted business partner were having an affair?

Her logic slammed to a stop. Then why would they hire her to prove Jeffery King innocent?

When she realized he was waiting for an answer, she collected herself. "I appreciate the kind words, but I could never put myself out there the way professional models do."

The answer popped into her head. Nola had been the one to insist they try to save Jeffery. Morgan probably went along with the idea because he thought it impossible for a dog walker to uncover anything of importance. Jeffery had an excellent lawyer. There were so many people who hated Lilah that cops would never be able to pin her killer down.

"There are lessons in deportment, body carriage, that sort of thing, available, you know," Prince continued. "Just consider it. We can talk later." Setting Klingon down, he smiled. "Now, if you'll excuse me, I believe we'll be lauding Kitty and cutting the cake in a short while. Wait here and you can enjoy the festivities."

Ellie leaned back in her chair, closed her eyes, and did as he suggested, but instead of thinking about becoming a model, which was ridiculous, she thought about the words he'd used to seduce her to his side. How dare he believe she would swallow his idiotic compliments and take him up on becoming a fashion model?

And how stupid of him to think she didn't have enough brains to prove he was Lilah Perry's killer.

Close to fuming, she saw Claire's gun-toting, so-so replacement, Beatriz Alfonso, filling a plate on the other side of the room. Dressed in Marcus's first creation, wide black slacks and a fitted red jacket, she turned and Ellie thought she saw an unflattering bump in the woman's back. Odder still, she wore a small black flower high on her left shoulder that looked out of place, especially since it wasn't a part of Marcus's original design.

She scanned the dining room, looking for her boy. Too bad Rudy hadn't heard Morgan Prince's words. He would have gotten an exact read on the man and his remarks. And where was Marcus?

She took a bite of her lobster salad as she again checked the room. Beatriz had walked off with her food, Morgan had disappeared, and the few people left were speaking privately at their tables. When a waiter came through the kitchen door, she decided the time was right. Standing, she strode through the archway.

The restaurant-sized kitchen buzzed with excitement. A pair of chefs dressed in white aprons and puffed hats puttered at the double sinks. After cleaning trays, they passed them across the island to hovering waiters who would use them to go into the apartment and clear the rooms. Some raised their heads and took her in, then went back to work straightening the area. No one asked if they could help her or questioned why she was there.

Spotting a cupboard that appeared the right size for a storage pantry, she edged over and peeked inside. Things were set up in an orderly manner with olive oils, both plain and flavored, vegetable oil, and peanut oil clustered together in a corner of one shelf. Next to the oils were teriyaki and oyster sauce, tomato paste, and expensive jars of bottled pasta toppings. The display made perfect sense, especially when paired with the boxes of penne, rigatoni, linguini, and various rice containers. No one would think the peanut oil strange, even the police if they happened to run a search.

"Are you looking for something special?" a dark-haired woman wearing an outfit identical to the other caterers' finally asked. "I'm the person responsible for the success of this party," she said in take-charge manner. "If you need something in particular, let me know, but the kitchen is closing. I believe they'll be cutting the cake and toasting the contest winner in the next thirty minutes."

"Oh, gee, I apologize," Ellie responded. "I was just, uh, looking for the nearest restroom."

The woman eyed Ellie as if she had two heads. "But this is a kitchen."

"Yeah, I see that now," she answered, feeling like a class-A dope.

The woman raised an eyebrow. "There's a half bath off the entry hall, another bathroom in the back hall through the living room, and another farther down between two guest bedrooms." Taking her by the arm, she guided Ellie to the door. "The only one that's off limits is Nola and Morgan's, in their living space behind the dining room."

Ellie nodded and took off, following a waiter carrying an empty tray. While she'd been gone, the dining room had filled with more guests, gathered there, she imagined, for the ceremony. With so many people in the room, she was certain no one would notice her.

Inhaling a breath, she entered the hallway to Nola and Morgan's private quarters.

Ellie shook her head the second she arrived in the room. What in the heck should she look for? What would be positive proof that Morgan Prince, not Jeffery King, had murdered Lilah Perry? She really needed Rudy. He'd have a handle on things, and he'd know exactly what they needed to prove Morgan guilty.

Raising her eyes, she gazed in awe at her surroundings. The room was enormous, with a canopied king-sized bed, nightstands, a chest of drawers, a mirrored dresser, and books crowding a wall of shelves that also held a large flat-screen TV.

She checked her watch. Marcus might be looking for her, but with the mob in the dining room he probably figured she was stuck behind a gaggle of models. She'd be out of here soon.

She walked through the first door on her left and took stock. The closet, filled with dresses, skirts, feminine suits and slacks on hangers, shoes and sweaters in a stand of plastic boxes, and handbags on a wall of shelves, was packed. The floor under the clothing was littered with shopping bags and more shoe boxes. All this stuff had to be Nola's, and from what Ellie could see, she wasn't very neat.

Peering into the next doorway, she studied the bathroom with its single sink, walk-in shower, huge Jacuzzi tub, and commode area. The counter around the sink held makeup, perfume, hairspray, brushes, and all manner of feminine products, telling her this room, too, was Nola's.

But she didn't want to snoop in the diva designer's things. She was looking for Morgan Prince's private space. There had to be a second bathroom and dressing area that belonged to him.

She darted into the bedroom and scanned the walls, searching for a door that might lead to another dressing area. And there it was, in the back corner, out of the way and unassuming. Crossing the luxurious deep purple carpet, she opened the door and gave herself a mental high five. She'd found what she was looking for.

The closet was smaller than Nola's, but it was still large enough to be considered a room, and definitely more organized. Men's suits, shirts, slacks, and jackets hung in an orderly and color-coordinated fashion, so all Morgan had to do was reach for a jacket and the slacks hanging above and he was perfectly matched. A dozen pairs of shoes sat in racks lined up under the clothing, while sweaters were stored in plastic boxes and ties were aligned on a walled hanger.

"You found anything yet?"

Hand on her heart, Ellie jumped a foot and spun around. "You scared the heck out of me. Why didn't you give me some kind of warning, a yip maybe, to tell me you were here?"

Rudy gave a doggie shrug. *"I thought I did when I asked the question."* He looked at the shoes, each pair costing hundreds of dollars, then eyed the suits, all designer and costing thousands more. *"The guy is some fancy dresser. Have you nosed around?"*

"I just got here and I'm doing the bathroom first. I'm trying to find a pad of those Forever perfume sheets in Lilah's scent, or maybe the entire swag bag. Someone took it out from under the snack table. If it's here, there's a good chance Detective Vaughn will bring Morgan Prince in for questioning."

"I'll check out the bottom part of the closet," he muttered. *"And investigate those fancy shoes. If that swag thingy is here, my sniffer will find it."*

Ellie ducked into the bathroom, which was smaller than Nola's, but still well-appointed in marble and mirrors. After rifling through the drawers and cabinets, she looked at her watch. She'd been in the bedroom for about fifteen minutes.

"Any luck?" she whispered to her boy as she returned to the closet. But Rudy was nowhere to be seen. She needed to get the two of them out of there. Surely Marcus or Patti, or someone at the party was looking for her. The last place she wanted to be caught was Nola and Morgan's private area.

There'd be questions. Questions she couldn't answer.

She raced back into the bedroom, but when she entered the room she skidded to a stop. "What are you doing?" she asked Rudy, who was dragging a bag out from Nola's closet

"Giving you the evidence you was lookin' for," he muttered. *"At least I think this is it."*

"What? No! Nola didn't take the swag bag. Prince did."

"Uh, I don't think so."

"What's that supposed to mean?" She put her hands on her hips. "Put that back where you found it, right now."

"I'm tellin' ya, the nose knows." Still dragging the bag, he backed into her foot. *"This is what you want."*

"That can't be the right bag. Nola wouldn't have taken Lilah's gifts."

He sat up, then nudged the opening. *"How about readin' the tag? That might help."*

Ellie dropped to one knee, grabbed the name tag attached to the handle, and read aloud. "Well, I'm embarassed. This has Lilah's name on it."

"Uh, Ellie?"

The hairs on the back of her neck tingled, telling her they weren't alone. But Rudy's warning had come too late.

Chapter 19

"Oh, dear," Nola said, *tsk*ing. "I knew I should have gotten that bag into Marcus's apartment sooner. He was the one who should have been arrested. But it was such a busy week."

She planned to frame Marcus? With Lilah's bag?

Ellie slowly stood and turned, her temper beginning to boil.

The design maven *tsk*ed again. "It's just too bad you had to find it before we could take care of it."

"Hey, I'm the one who found it. Give me a little credit, will ya?"

Nola shook her head and her ultraexpensive hairstyle swayed delicately, then dropped back into place. "The question is, what are we going to do with you?"

"W—we?" Ellie sputtered, rushing to come up with a plan. If she kept Nola talking, Marcus would be sure to come looking for her. "You mean Morgan knows what you did to Lilah?"

Nola's nasty laugh emphasized her sneer. "Of course

he knows. Once I thought it up, he was happy to do his part." Her eyes narrowed. "We were in this pickle because of him, so it was only fair he lend a hand."

Pickle? Nola McKay thought killing someone was a pickle?

"Let me guess. Lilah wanted to win the NMD contest and threatened to reveal her affair with Morgan if you didn't agree."

Frowning, Nola took a step back and reached into the right-side pocket of her wide-legged, red silk slacks. "Reveal their affair?" Her hand left the pocket holding a tiny gun, possibly a .22, with a pinkish cast to the metal. "Hah! If that were the only problem, I would have let her tell the world."

Hoping for a smattering of pity, Ellie heaved a loud sigh. "Do you mind if I sit down? I'd like to hear the entire story, and because of these new shoes, my feet are killing me."

Nola used the gun to gesture toward a wingback chair covered in a lovely flowered silk fabric. When Ellie took a seat Rudy jumped into her lap and gave her face a sloppy lick.

"I gotta plan, Triple E. It'll only take a minute. I'll find the right person and bring 'em back here."

She ran her fingers through his hair. Now was not the time to hold a conversation with her four-legged pal. "Okay, I'm ready," she said, smiling at her jailer. She didn't know a lot about guns, but the one in Nola's hand looked too small to do much damage. And Nola wouldn't dare shoot it, not with so many people in the apartment who might hear the noise. "I really do want to connect the dots on this story."

Nola took a seat on the bed, close enough to hit her with a bullet, but not close enough for Ellie to jump the woman without warning. "Don't think I'm blinded by your ploys, young lady. Patti Fallgrave was correct; you really do have a good head on your shoulders. You got much further in your investigation than Morgan and I gave you credit for."

Ellie sneaked a peek at her watch. Where in the heck was Marcus? "A ploy? I'm afraid I don't understand."

"Oh, but of course you do. You're hoping to keep me talking long enough for Marcus to rescue you." She shrugged. "Sorry, but that's not going to happen."

"Okay, I'll bite," Ellie answered, her stomach taking a dive. "Why not?"

"Because when I found him looking for you, I told him you'd left. I made up an excuse—something you ate didn't agree with you or some such nonsense—and you asked me to give him the news, then you took a taxi home. The poor boy left here before we cut the cake. I saw him walk out the door myself."

Did Marcus really believe she'd leave without telling him? "And Patti? Or Kitty and the other designers?"

"Why, no one's mentioned your name. That's what happens when you get involved in an industry where it's all about *you*." Nola grinned. "Everyone is so worried about how they look, what they're wearing, and who they can impress, they don't dare think about the worker bees."

"And Morgan? Where is he?"

"Saying good-bye to the last of our guests, I hope. I pleaded a headache—too much excitement—and even Kitty understood. Jeffery took her home right after the cake cutting and congratulatory toast."

"This dame's a whack-job, Triple E. Let me outta here so I can get the cavalry."

Ellie fingered Rudy's muzzle, hoping to shut him up. She couldn't think when he was jabbering.

He jerked back his head. *"All righty then!"* Diving off her lap, he headed for the door.

"Rudy, no!"

Still grinning, Nola watched him leave. "Not to worry, Morgan will catch him. Or one of the caterers, if any are still here. We arranged it so they'd return tomorrow to take care of the cleaning chores, so I imagine everyone is gone by now."

Did Morgan have a gun, too? If everyone was gone, would he use it on her boy? Rudy was a little dog, but if hit in the right spot, even a bullet from a small gun would kill him.

Morgan took that moment to walk, or maybe skulk was a better description, into the room. "I see you have everything under control, my dear." His smile was more of a leer. "Just as I figured."

"I'm getting tired of mopping up your messes, Morgan. Don't you think it's about time you started taking care of your own dirty work?" Nola's tone was sharp, and much nastier than that of a loving partner. "Now what do you propose we do with Ms. Engleman and her dog? And make it fast. We don't have all night."

"Stop blaming me for our problems." He continued with his cheeky grin. "You had a hand in this one, too."

"I'm still confused. What are you two talking about?" Ellie asked, trying to make sense of their conversation.

"Never mind," Nola bit out. "There's no need for you to stick your nose in our private business."

"But—"

Morgan pulled a gun from his tuxedo jacket, this one on the small side, too. "Shut up, and do as you're told." He walked to the window and drew back the beige satin curtain. "It's dark enough. I think we'll be able to leave in a matter of minutes."

Nola waved her weapon toward the door. "Check and make sure every guest is gone. And find that dog. We'll have to dump him, too."

The idea of being tossed out like a sack of trash sent Ellie reeling. "This won't work. People will be looking for me. I live with a cop. He'll put out an APB. They'll scan the tapes from your building's entry and see that I never left."

"Hah!" Morgan said with a snort. "Last time I checked, this building wasn't equipped with a security tape. And by the time you're reported missing, we'll already have you where we want you. In New Jersey, my old stomping ground. Remember that union boss, Jimmy somebody or other, who disappeared a while back? There are so many seedy places to drop a body in that state, you might never be found."

"I think you need to come up with a better plan," Ellie continued, hoping to waste more time. "There's DNA evidence, fingerprinting, search and rescue dogs, all kinds of forensic technology in use today."

"*Blah, blah, blah,*" Nola mocked. "We discussed this, but I never believed we'd have to go to these lengths. Especially on our big night." She glared at Morgan. "Get out there and make a final run. We have to move this along."

His expression froze into one of contempt. "Yes, Your Majesty. I'll happily do your bidding."

He left the room and Ellie searched for the words to keep the woman talking. "Instead of killing me, I think it would be wiser to plead out. Tell the police you didn't realize how serious Lilah's allergies were. You just wanted to get her out of the competition. I'm sure, with the right attorney, you could—"

"Oh, puh-leeze! Lilah never shut up about how serious her allergies were. Everyone in this industry knew about them." Nola again raised her gun. "Besides, once you've committed a first murder, what's one more? Just accept the inevitable and do as you're told."

"You have a doorman. Won't he wonder what's going on when you're practically dragging me out of the building?"

"First of all, you won't ever go past the doorman because we're taking an elevator straight to the parking garage. And I doubt you'll make a sound, once you realize your dog is at risk. I'm warning you, Ms. Engleman, give us one moment's grief and he'll be the first to get a bullet in the brain."

Ellie swallowed. Then Rudy trotted into the room with an empty-handed Morgan right behind him. *"Look who I found,"* he shouted, his doggie lips turned up in a smile.

Beatriz followed them both, her gun held high.

"I still can't believe you're here," Ellie said to Sam, who was sitting next to her on the white leather sofa of Nola and Morgan's penthouse suite. The apartment was crawling with cops, a forensic team, police photographers, and a bevy of other officers doing whatever it was they did to wrap a case.

"Thank that designer guy who brought you here," said Sam, his expression filled with annoyance. "I didn't like the way he kept sizing you up, so I decided to protect what was mine. I figured Vaughn would show just to make sure he had all the suspects sorted out, so when I called and offered to lend a hand, he was more than happy to say yes. He figured he'd need someone to ride roughshod over you."

She didn't mind that Sam talked about her as if he owned her, not really. What irritated her more was the fact that Vaughn didn't think she was capable of amassing the correct evidence. "But how did Detective Vaughn know I'd be in danger?"

Sam gave an evil-sounding chuckle. "You're kidding, right?"

"No, I'm not. I've—"

"We've—" Rudy, who was curled up next to her on the sofa, muttered.

"I've been in dicier situations than this, and I've—"

"We've," he again reminded her.

She rested a hand on her boy's head. He was the one who had saved the day, and Beatriz Alfonso might agree, though Sam and Vaughn would never acknowledge it. "I owe the rescue to Rudy. If he hadn't found Detective Alfonso hiding in that back bathroom and convinced her to follow him—"

"She'd already called Vaughn on her radio and told him she was ready to move on the arrest when your dog showed up." The undercover officer had used that out-of-place black flower she wore on her jacket to hide the two-way radio. "Your boy was just wandering the apartment, nosing around, as usual."

"Hey, hey, hey," Rudy said with a snarl. *"I resent that. I knew where I was headed, and I figured out she was undercover the minute I saw her wearin' that thirty-eight special a day ago."*

It was impossible to argue with Sam and her yorkiepoo at the same time. Truth is, it would have been nice if Rudy had clued her on his suspicions of Beatriz yesterday, but the stinker had kept the information to himself. When they were alone, they were going to have a long talk about sharing everything they knew about the people they dealt with.

"You should give him more credit. He was definitely looking for a way out for both of us."

"You can say whatever you want, but I'm right about this."

"You're dead wrong, Detective Doofus."

Sam raised his head and connected with Vaughn, who was signaling him from the entryway. "Sit here and don't move. I'm being summoned."

Ellie watched him walk into the foyer, then locked gazes with her boy. "I know you're not happy with Sam's take on things, but please stop interrupting. It's hard enough following his comments without trying to listen to yours. And how did you know the caliber of gun Detective Alfonso was wearing?"

"That thirty-eight? It's a Ladysmith six-forty-two. It's got a five-round shot, and it's double action. Won't do a ton of damage, but it had enough to stop the designer and her prince." He sneezed. *"Good thing those two dopes realized it."*

"You still haven't said where you learned so much about guns. Where did you go to pick up all that—" She stopped midsentence when tuxedo clad legs stopped to stand in front of her.

"I hate to belabor the point, but are you holding another conversation with your dog?" Marcus David asked her. "Then again, what else would you be doing?"

Ellie gazed up at her disappearing date. "Oh, ah, hello. How long have you been here?"

"In the building? I never left. I've been downstairs chatting with the doorman since I pretended to do what Nola suggested." He nodded at the empty cushion beside her. "Mind if I sit?"

"No, of course not." She heaved a sigh. "I'm sorry you had to be put out. I kept hoping you'd be the one to find me, but I guess Nola told you a good story."

"She tried, but I didn't believe her. I left because I

didn't want to ruin Kitty's big moment, and came downstairs to ask the doorman if he'd called a cab for a beautiful redhead and her dog. When he said no, I knew you were still upstairs and I phoned Vaughn. I figured something hinky was going on."

"But you didn't know what?"

"I had a suspicion it was something big. I knew you were looking into Jeffery King's case, and he worked for Nola and Morgan. We were in their apartment, as were all the suspects, and Nola had just lied to me, so it was inevitable something would happen." He put an arm behind her on the sofa back. "When I saw your guy and Detective Vaughn march through the downstairs foyer shortly after that, I hung around to watch."

"I take it someone's filled you in on your substitute model, and told you she's a cop."

"Yeah. Detective Vaughn thought the NMD people knew more than they were saying, so he went to the Fashion Council and had them intervene. An undercover model was the best they could come up with."

Ellie grinned. "Considering her real profession, I think Beatriz Alfonso did a pretty remarkable job on the runway, don't you?"

"Yep, and I already told her so, too. She's a nice woman."

"And attractive."

A flush of red crossed the designer's face. "Very."

"Homicide detectives have lousy hours, and they're always on duty, but they are dependable," she encouraged. Marcus needed someone in his life, and he and Beatriz might make a good match. "But that's something you should find out for yourself."

"One thing at a time," he said with a laugh. Then his arm dropped to her shoulder.

"I hate to be the one to tell you this," said Ellie, "but

I gathered from my conversation with Nola and Morgan that you were the one they wanted framed for the murder. Nola was going to find a way to plant Lilah's swag bag in your apartment, though I have no idea how they planned to get the cops to search for it there." She looked in his eyes. "Why did they choose you?"

He blew out a breath. "Probably because of the bad blood between me and Lilah. What's important is that you thought I was innocent."

"I must admit, the story of what happened to your sister put a bug in my ear, but something inside told me you were too nice a guy to kill anyone."

"And I guess you haven't been lying. You and Detective Ryder are truly in a good relationship, huh?"

"The best," said Ellie, taking his free hand in hers. "You're a great guy, Marcus, and I was so sorry to hear about your sister, but the past is over and done. It's time you moved on with your life."

"It took me a while, but I figured that out. I was just sort of hoping I could move on with you." He placed his lips on her temple. "But I realized that wasn't going to work the moment I saw the way Sam looked at you."

"He's a little possessive, and I like him that way, but he'd never stop me from helping someone who's wrongly accused unless he felt I'd be in danger. That's the reason he snared a spot on this raid." She scanned the room, noting many of the forensic team had left. "It looks like things are winding down and they're about ready to close up here."

Marcus moved his arm and set his hands on his knees. "Then I guess I should be leaving."

"I'm sure I'll see you in the near future, and think about giving Beatriz a chance. You might like a woman who wears a gun." Ellie kissed his cheek. "Take care of yourself."

Marcus stood. "You do the same. And keep talking to your dog. The way I see it, that's when you get your best ideas." He tipped his head. "Be good."

"He got that last part right," said Rudy. *"I am the giver of all good ideas."*

"I might be able to come up with a few of my own if you shared your information with me," she chided. Then she shut up. Detective Vaughn and Sam were headed their way.

"Ms. Engleman. I'm sending you home in the protective custody of Detective Ryder."

She stood and Sam locked their arms together.

"We have your statement, plus the confession of both Nola McKay and Morgan Prince, though I probably don't have to tell you they sang two very different renditions of the same old song."

"I imagine they would. They didn't seem like lovers or even agreeable roommates when they confronted me." She crossed mental fingers. "I don't suppose you could tell me why they did it."

"Ellie," warned Sam.

Vaughn canted his head, the barest glimmer of a smile on his lips. "It's fine, Ryder. She has a right to know," he conceded. "Depending on who you believe, Nola McKay and Lilah Perry were lovers. When Morgan Prince found out Nola betrayed him, he seduced Ms. Perry himself. The McKay woman said he'd cheated on her numerous times over the years, so she was just getting back at him. After sleeping with both of them, Ms. Perry saw an opportunity for blackmail and she took it. McKay and Prince knew the dirty information would not only cast a pall on their big contest, but ruin their introduction into the ready-to-wear market, as well."

"Hang on. They were both sleeping with Lilah?"

"Apparently. And when they received the blackmail demand, in person by Ms. Perry, McKay came up with the idea to get rid of the girl for good." He raised an eyebrow. "Hard to imagine, isn't it?"

"I'll say," Ellie agreed. "So they just pretended to be loving partners—"

"Their business thrived on it."

"But they slept with different people."

"Seems that way. My guess is once the story gets out there will be at least a dozen models, designers, and stylists who claim they slept with one or both of them, too." He shrugged. "This is one crazy industry."

"Geez, I'll say. Do you think they'll go to trial?"

"They'll do time, but the length will depend on the DA and the lawyers. Now, if there's anything else I can do for you before we call it a night?"

"How about a reward? A coupl'a bags of Dingo bones would be nice right about now."

"I do have a question," said Ellie, ignoring Rudy's suggestion. "I never did hear if Lilah had relatives, because I wonder about Klingon."

"Klingon?" Vaughn's face was blank. "Like in *Star Trek?*"

"Klingon, as in Lilah Perry's mini Schnauzer. He's been living with Yasmine, but she can't keep him any longer. Has anyone in the Perry family been contacted about taking him?"

"I'm not sure. I'll have to check and see. Knowing how you feel about dogs, I'll let you know." He shook Sam's hand, then Ellie's. "You'll be hearing from me about anything else we need via Detective Ryder. Have a good night."

Ellie rested her head on Sam's shoulder. "I'm sorry you had to spend your one night off babysitting me, but

I told you I'd be fine. It sounds like Vaughn and Detective Alfonso had everything under control."

He shrugged. "Maybe, but they didn't while you were being held at gunpoint. Between then and the time Vaughn arrived anything might have happened."

"Rudy was here. He would have—"

"Stop, already. I think you'd better come up with a new story, because that one's getting really old." He took her by the hand. "Let's get out of here. I'm beat and I'm sure you are, too, but we can sleep late tomorrow morning and—"

"Go to Mother's for brunch." Ellie pulled Rudy's lead from her handbag and snapped it on his collar. "Remember, you promised me."

Sam stood still for a long moment, then took the leash and walked her and Rudy out of the apartment. When he hadn't said a word by the time they got to the elevator, Ellie continued. "Okay, I'll understand if you don't want to go, but I have to show my face. The judge will want to hear about tonight, and Mother will give me hell if I pass on another brunch, especially since it's her birthday weekend."

He stepped aside and let her enter the elevator first. "So you'll go with or without me?"

"Both Rudy and I. I don't have much of a choice."

"Are you sayin' this is one time I'm willing to stay home with the defective detective, and you won't let me?"

She gave herself a mental head slap. Leave it to both the men in her life to join forces against Georgette.

Sam pressed the lobby floor, then wrapped an arm around her. "Don't be silly. If you go, I go. I gave you my word, and I'm not about to renege."

"Great. The big idiot has to disagree with me even when I'm willin' to see things his way. What a putz."

She put a hand on Sam's cheek and turned his head. "Thanks. I know Stanley is looking forward to seeing you. You're the best."

He kissed her, deep and slow, all the way down until the elevator door slid open.

"Come on. It's time to go home," he said, ushering her toward the front of the building. "Once we get there, I plan to do one more important thing before we call it a night."

Ellie caught the meaning in his smile and her heart skipped a beat. "That's fine by me."

"Ya know, I think I'd rather spend the night with the ex-terminator than be with you two when you get mushy."

Sam hailed a cab and, when one showed, she entered and slid across the seat as she whispered to her boy. "You'd be even more miserable if we were like Nola and Morgan, always bickering and sniping at each other."

"Those two were a piece of work," said Sam, though he'd only heard the last half of her sentence. "I don't want to think about us ever letting things go that far."

"How about if you just left us alone? That would work."

"You don't have a thing to say about it," Ellie answered, before she realized she'd spoken out loud. "I mean you don't have anything to worry about," she added when Sam gave her a look.

When they arrived at their apartment he paid the fare and held the door while Rudy jumped out, and she followed. "I suppose he has to take a walk."

"The man is a genius," her boy said, yipping.

"Just to the corner. We'll be back in a minute." They didn't go far before her yorkiepoo raised a rear leg and took his time watering a hydrant. "Sorry, I should have thought about this sooner."

"It was close, but I would'a spoke up if I wasn't gonna make it. Just give me another minute or two."

Ellie did as requested, then returned to her front porch, smiling when she saw Sam waiting. "I could have finished up alone out here. Rudy was with me."

In answer, Sam ran a hand through his hair, unlocked the entry, did the same to the interior door, and took her elbow as they climbed the stairs. She knew by his silence that he didn't agree, but he wasn't going to talk about it.

Inside, she took care of Rudy's leash while he locked up. "Do you want a cup of tea or something to help you sleep?"

"I'm ready to drop. You?"

"Same here. Use the bathroom first while I change, okay?"

He disappeared and she went to the bedroom, where she walked to the bed and grabbed Rudy's pillow, brought it to the guest room, and dropped it on the mattress. "There, you're all set. And you're going to cut us a break in the morning, and let us sleep a little later, correct?"

"You're not gonna need me to wake you. If I know the ex-terminator, she'll be on the line bright and early, reminding you about her grub and gossip party."

"Probably." She sat next to him after he jumped up. "We're good, right?"

"We're always good. It's me and the dastardly dick that—"

Hugging him close, Ellie kissed the top of his head. "I just want to say thank you again for finding Detective Alfonso and coming to my rescue."

"You're my girl, Triple E. I'll always be there to rescue you. I like to think you don't belong to anybody, animal or human, but me."

He curled on the pillow and she bent to give him another smooch. "It's you and me forever, no matter what happens between me and Sam."

"That's a promise, right?" Rudy asked, licking her cheek.

"Yes, a promise."

"Good, because I can't imagine it bein' any other way."

Epilogue

A week later, Ellie led an old college pal into the nearest Joe to Go, hoping to surprise Joe Cantiglia. "We'll have two Caramel Blisses and two blueberry muffins," Ellie ordered, after walking to the counter.

She grinned when Joe took a look at her companion and did a double take. "Karen? Karen Coleman? What are you doing here?"

"I'm helping Ellie," said the petite blonde. "When she called and said she needed a hand, I just had to say yes."

"A hand? From you?"

"You bet. I run Miniature Schnauzer Rescue of Houston."

"She was the first person I thought of when Detective Vaughn gave me the okay to help Klingon find a new home. You remember, he's the dog that belonged to Lilah Perry, the designer that was killed last week," said Ellie.

He gave his barista their order, then turned back to Karen. "That was nice of you."

"Not a problem. I'll do whatever's needed to give minis and Ellie a hand." She nodded at the dog on the end of her leash. "I couldn't say no when she told me about him, and he really is a sweetheart."

"I had no idea you were into dogs, like Ellie is. "

"I love these little guys as much as Ellie loves the dogs she walks." She jumped at the sound of breaking glass.

"Enough, Izzie," Joe said to his barista. "Sorry. I have to take care of this. I'll come find you in a couple of minutes."

"Not a problem," said Ellie. "It's a beautiful fall day, and we've already stopped at Sara's and bought the boys her special biscuits. We'll be outside if you want to talk."

She and Karen settled at a table, and both of them did the same thing: broke off pieces of Sara Studebaker's deluxe canine cookies and gave them to their dogs.

"I take it mini Schnauzer rescue has a lot of canines that need placement," said Ellie after she sipped her coffee.

"Dozens," said Karen. "But we're making strides. If you ever get the chance, fly down to Houston at the end of October. There's a big dog festival that gets thousands of folks who are looking to adopt. You and Rudy could sit and help work our table."

Ellie dropped her gaze to the cement. "Did you hear that, big guy? We've been invited to Houston. Would you want to take a trip south?"

Rudy crunched the last of his cookie. *"Only if we fly first class."*

Ellie had no problem telling Karen about the conversation. Anyone who loved their dog would understand completely. "Rudy said he's up for a trip to Houston, so I guess it's a go."

"I love the way you talk to your boy. You know, the more I look at him, the more I think he's part mini Schnauzer."

Ellie sighed. "There's no way to tell, unless I do that doggie DNA thing that's so popular right now. But it's so expensive, and I really don't care about his lineage."

"Oh, no. You're not gonna poke me with a needle just to find out what kind of nuts are hanging off my family tree."

"He's my boy and I love him no matter what his pedigree."

"Ah, that's more like it. I'm yours and you're mine. Who cares where we came from? We're together and that's all that matters."

Ellie took another sip of her Caramel Bliss while Karen talked about her rescue service. The dog lovers in Houston were a huge bunch, and they went all out to help their canine friends. From Karen's excitement as she explained about the big adoption event, Ellie determined she and Rudy really should consider taking a trip down to see her when the cold got to be too much in Manhattan.

But she'd never move out of the city. It was here she had good friends, an enjoyable job, a wonderful man, and on top of that, she had a fuzzy and faithful forever companion.

Her world was perfect.

"I'm going to get a coffee refill," said Karen. "Be back in a minute."

Ellie nodded, then relaxed in her chair. "Have I ever told you that I live in a perfect world?" she asked her little buddy.

Standing on his hind legs, he put his paws on her thigh. *"That's good to hear, but just so you know, I live in a perfect world, too."*

She ran her fingers over his ears, then down to the underside of his muzzle, his best scratching place. "Good for you, but what makes it that way?"

"I got Viv, Mr. T, and the buds we walk, and I get top-of-the-line food and Dingo bones whenever I ask. But that's nothin' compared to the best of the best."

She hauled him up on her lap and he gave her cheek a lick. "Oh, and what might that be?"

"It's you, of course. I got you."

Joe, Ellie, and Rudy walked into Sara's gourmet canine bakery and were instantly enveloped in the yummy aromas of the spices, vegetables, and fruits used in the Spoiled Hound's biscuits. The store made the best of the best in canine treats—so good, in fact, that Ellie knew several people who stopped there and bought the cookies to eat themselves.

The display case, now blocked by a crowd, held four different sizes of biscuits in the shape of bones, sneakers, and, for laughs, cats, as well as bags of heart-shaped dry kibble. As of the first of December, Sara had even started selling biscuits shaped like snowmen, Christmas trees, and Santa. One look at the offerings and a dog person knew love was the main ingredient in the items for sale.

Ellie locked eyes with Rudy, who was standing with his front paws on the case. "What are you up to?"

Just checkin' things out. Lulu loves the carrot cookies—the ones shaped like cats. Make sure you get plenty of those.

Rudy's best four-legged girl, a prize-winning Haven-ese named Lulu, loved to make demands on both Ellie and her dog. Still, buying a few extra of the requested treat wasn't a problem. "Okay, I'll get a double bag along with my regular order. Now, what do you plan to do?"

"I wanna go explore with my buds." He dropped down and scanned the store. *"They're runnin' free. How about me?"*

The customers and friends invited to this blow-out had been told to bring their dogs, which were now roaming freely throughout the shop. "Fine, but don't leave the store," she said, unhooking her yorkiepoo's lead. "And you know the rules: no begging, no pilfering food, and no fighting with anyone." She ran a loving hand along his back. "Understand?"

"Jeesh, puttin' it that way takes all the fun out of it."

"Just be good."

Not worried about talking to Rudy in front of Joe, she stood. He didn't know she had a special gift, but he was well aware that she spoke to canines as if they were people. He probably thought it was just one more crazy habit she had.

Stretched to his full height of six feet, Joe peered out into the crowd. Wearing butt-hugging Ralph Lauren jeans and a dark green sweater over a yellow, long-sleeved shirt only amped up his sex appeal. Ellie couldn't understand how any single woman was able to resist the man, with his Italian good looks and warm personality.

"See anyone interesting?" she asked him.

"I'll never find Sara in this mob," he grumbled.

"I thought you wanted to meet her mom and dad."

"You bet I want to meet the senior Studebakers. When I'm done romancing them, they're gonna beg me to marry their daughter. I'll convince them that I'm the perfect husband for her before they fly back to Jamaica."

Joe had fallen hard for Sara the moment he met her a few months ago. Unfortunately for him, the biscuit baker had yet to return his feelings. "Hmm," Ellie said, grinning. "How about you try romancing Sara first, instead of her parents?" She waved at one of her dog-walking customers as she continued talking. "You do want to win *her* hand, not her mom and dad's, correct?"

Joe blew out a breath. "That would be easy if I could ever get her out of this shop. So far she's refused every offer I've made—politely of course—but still, always *no, thank you.*" He crossed his arms. "Since she's been avoiding my direct offers, I thought maybe I'd get to her from the long way around."

"Then I guess you should go find her mom and dad and do your best. Meanwhile, I'll get a glass of champagne and take care of myself."

Wearing a determined expression, he ambled away, and Ellie found a free chair. She purchased all her dog treats here, but she also enjoyed seeing Sara and her two West Highland white terriers, Pooh and Tigger. As her gaze swept the store, she took in what she could see through the crowd of humans and canines.

Stainless-steel bowls filled with water were arranged on place mats in the far corners of the room. Old-fashioned, brightly painted sideboards rimmed in holiday lights held doggie toys and chews from companies that used only natural ingredients of the highest quality. And in between the sideboards were racks holding an array of dog magazines, including the bimonthly *Best Friends*, published by one of Ellie's favorite charities.

One front window housed a live tree decorated with the Christmas biscuits, twinkle lights, and red ribbon. Spaced around the center of the store were tables and chairs used by both two- and four-legged customers. Since Sara didn't sell people food, the Board of Health had no say in who she allowed in her shop. On many of her visits Ellie had seen folks carry in their coffee from next door, then buy a biscuit for their furry pal, and both would enjoy their goodies in the store.

The tables were now decorated with trays filled with an assortment of finger foods. A waiter passed by and she snagged a plastic flute of champagne. He continued on, clearing napkins and empty glasses as he edged his way through the crowd. Rudy reappeared and jumped into her lap.

"Sara's in back talkin' to the senior Suzukis, just like you thought," said her boy.

Ellie rolled her eyes. So far Rudy had come up with dozens of automobile company names to trade with Sara's last name, Studebaker. So many, in fact, that she just ignored him. "Who's supposed to be up here taking care of customers?"

"Beats me, but I don't think Sara's sellin' anything. And the Westies are sound asleep on their puffs in the kitchen."

"Sound asleep? They must have had a busy day." She caressed his ears. "Go have fun, okay?"

It was then that a tall, heavyset man pushed through the crowd and headed her way. Searching her brain, she tried to place him. Was he one of the customers she rarely saw when she picked up his dog? He wore a winning smile on his bulldoglike face, so she smiled in return, still not sure of his name.

"Hello. I'm Uncle Dom," he said, stretching out his left arm. "Sara told me to find you, and since you're the only curly-haired redhead out here, I figure you're Ellie."

She shook his hand and nodded. "That's me. It's nice to meet a member of Sara's family."

Middle-aged, five-foot-ten, with a receding hairline and florid complexion, he appeared the same as many of the well-to-do businessmen who wore two-thousand-dollar Armani suits while they walked the streets of Manhattan. He glanced around the crowded room. "This is some business she's built for herself. I'm as proud of her as if she were my own daughter."

"She's done a great job. My charges demand, er, insist—" Ellie sucked in a breath. "I mean they like her biscuits best."

"And you're another young woman who's got herself a successful business."

"I think I do, so thank you for the compliment."

He propped his bulky body against the bakery case and Ellie winced when the glass front creaked. "I hear dog walking is one of the most competitive businesses in Manhattan. Some of you dog walkers even pull in six figures."

"I didn't go into the work for the money." Her boy appeared and put his paws on her thigh. "I do it because I love dogs. This is my guy, by the way. His name is Rudy."

"Who's the big bopper? Is he botherin' you?"

"Say hello to Sara's uncle Dom," she told him. "He's part of her extended family."

"Really?" Rudy dropped to all fours and sniffed the man's Testoni loafers. *"If he's one of the nuts hangin' on her family tree, I say she drops him. He smells like a rotten cashew."*

"Cute little guy," said Uncle Dom, but he didn't pat Rudy's head. "Me, I'm a cat person. Canines make me jittery."

"That's because we smell the feline on you, you dumb bum."

Before Ellie could corral Rudy, Sara sidled through the throng and stopped in front of her. "Ellie, hi. Where's Sam?"

"At work for another hour or so, but he'll be here soon. The place is packed. You must be thrilled with the turnout."

Dressed in a red sweater with a small flashing green Christmas tree above her left breast, she was definitely in the holiday spirit. "Yep, and so are Mom and Dad."

"And me," said Uncle Dom. "I owe you one, by the way. Thanks for giving Brady that job. The boy needs the responsibility. You two stay and gab. I'll go back and find Phil. Nice meeting you, Ellie. I'm sure I'll see you again."

"He seems like a nice man," said Ellie, giving Rudy a nudge with her foot. "And it sounds as if he's on your side in this bakery venture."

Sara pulled a chair over and took a seat. "He is. That's why I hired one of his grandsons to work in the store. I figured it was about time I took some of Joe's advice."

"Joe? You asked Joe for advice?"

"Well, sure. We're sort of in the same field, and he has a good head on his shoulders. You went to college together. You must know that about him."

"Joe Cantiglia is a very smart guy. It's just that—" *He's head over heels in love with you?* "He, um, he's a man. And they're, you know, kind of, um . . ."

"Dense? Sure, I see that. When I first started asking his opinion, he always wore a dopey expression, but I gave him a chance, like you suggested, and now we're pals."

Pals? The word would definitely annoy Joe. "He's a trusted friend, and very good-looking. You notice that, right?"

"Oh, yeah, but you know how I feel about fancy wrapping. It's what's inside the box that counts. Give me a man with a brain first, then a sense of humor. Good looks fade as the years pass, but the rest of it hangs around forever. I want a man who knows what he's doing, makes me laugh, and promises to stick with me until death do us part."

"I do think Joe is that kind of guy," Ellie said.

"He might be, but I've seen him in the store, reacting to the women who come in and flirt with him. I bet he has a different date every night."

"Uh, no," Ellie answered, sticking up for Joe. "He's turned over a new leaf. He's looking for a woman he can count on. He wants kids, and a life with friends and family. The same thing you're looking for."

"Well, I hope he finds it. In the meantime, I'm happy he's given me a hand with a few business decisions, and convinced me to hire more help for the store."

Ellie bit back a laugh. It had been a long while since she'd met two people who saw things so differently. She was going to have to come up with a plan that would make Sara see Joe was the perfect man for her.

"Have you seen Joe, by the way? We came in together and then I lost him."

"I left him with my mom and dad. Funny how they seemed to hit it off after just a few minutes. That's when I decided to come find you."

"Are your parents staying long?"

"Until the first of the year, though I don't know if Mom will make it. All she keeps saying is they live in an island paradise, and here they are in Manhattan for the winter. She's dressed to avoid germs, so it's a good thing it's been mild or she'd be out of here like a shot."

"I take it you have a lot to do to keep them occupied."

"Dad wants to dabble in the kitchen, for sure. He said it's been too long since he puttered with a recipe, like he did with Grandma Millie's. He's dying to try the mix he brought me for a new cookie. Pooh and Tigger will be his taste testers, so please bring your four-legged clients in whenever you can to take their place. Otherwise the girls will gain weight and I'll never get them back to a healthy size."

A dog barked and Sara stood. "That sounds like Pooh or Tigger. I'd better see what's up. How about taking a walk with me? I want you to meet the rest of the family, including my new hire."

Ellie walked into her apartment, hung up her coat, and removed Rudy's leash. Sam had been a no-show at the party, which worried her, but she was smart enough to know that if the situation was urgent, he'd find a way to get a message to her.

Her detective took his job seriously, and he'd always been honest with her about the hours he put in. Ellie had made up her mind long ago that she wanted Sam in her life, flaws and all. Now if only he and Rudy could—

"So the dappy dick let you down again, huh?" came her boy's voice from below.

"Sam never let's me down. He probably got tied up—"

"Maybe on the tracks of a subway train."

"That's very unkind," she said, marching down the hall. "He'd forgive me if I got involved with my job. In fact, he's done so on several occasions, including that time you were kidnapped. He saved us both, if you'll remember."

"Sure, sure, but he'd still dump me first chance he got."

"I do not believe that for a second. Now, stop being difficult. It was a great party, don't you think?"

"Great food and even greater dogs. Who could ask for more?"

She stood and slipped out of her slacks. After removing her underthings, she drew a sleep shirt over her head and went to the bathroom to finish her nightly routine. When she returned to the bedroom, she found her boy curled up on his favorite pillow.

"I have no idea where Sam is or when he'll get home, so I'm going to relax for a while." She got under the covers and took the romance novel she'd been reading off the nightstand.

A short while later, Ellie closed her book and tried to doze, but sleep evaded her. She thought about Joe and Sara. Would they ever find each other, the way she and Sam had? What had happened to Sam tonight? Why hadn't she heard from him? And how funny was it that her dog and her man had so much in common, yet they would never realize it?

She finally fell asleep, but it didn't seem like long before she heard Rudy growl. The closet light turned on and she blinked, watching Sam's silhouette fill the doorway.

"Hey, you're home."

After toeing off his shoes and socks, he stripped off his slacks and hung them up, then dropped his shirt in the hamper. "Yeah, and I'm sorry I didn't call, but something came up. I ended up trading weekends with a guy whose son was in a car accident." Sam walked to her side of the bed. "Sorry, babe, but I'll probably pull duty this weekend."

She tried not to sigh. "I understand. Besides, there's always next weekend, right?" She entwined her fingers in his hand. "Just promise me you won't give up Christmas Eve or Christmas Day, no matter who needs a sub."

"I'll remember." He bent forward and they shared a warm kiss.

"Maybe we can snuggle for a while and I can fall back to sleep. I'm willing to give it a try if you are."

She wriggled into the curve of his body and was soon asleep. But when the phone rang, her eyes snapped open.

She checked the time. Who in the world would bother reaching her at six a.m. on a Saturday morning?

"If that's your mother, I'm gonna arrest her for disturbing the peace," Sam muttered, yawning.

She grabbed her cell phone from the charger and gave a muffled, "'lo?"

"Ellie, it's Joe."

Joe? "Uh, hi. What's up?"

"I need to see you. Now." His voice choked. "There's been a murder."

Judi McCoy

Hounding the Pavement

A Dog Walker Mystery

MEET ELLIE ENGLEMAN, PSYCHIC DOG WALKER

The newest dog-walker on Manhattan's Upper East Side can hear her canine clients' thoughts. So when a dog's owner turns up dead, Ellie must bone up on her sleuthing— and perk up her ears to find a killer.

Available wherever books are sold or at
penguin.com

Also Available from
Judi McCoy

Heir of the Dog
A Dog Walker Mystery

Professional dog walker Ellie Engleman is
more than just a pal to her pooches—she
can also read their minds. When Ellie and
her terrier mix Rudy find the corpse of a
troubled-but-harmless park-dweller in
Central Park, the dog walker becomes a
prime suspect for murder.

When it turns out Rudy is the sole
beneficiary of the victim's inheritance, Ellie,
Rudy, and Detective Sam Ryder follow the
trail of clues to a key to a safety deposit
box that just might point to the motive and
help them sniff out the real killer.

**Available wherever books are sold or at
penguin.com**

OM0019